RACHEL ABBOTT was born and raised in Manchester. She trained as a systems analyst before launching her own interactive media company in the early 1980s. After selling her company in 2000, she moved to the Le Marche region of Italy.

When six-foot snowdrifts prevented her from leaving the house for a couple of weeks, she started writing and found she couldn't stop. Since then her debut thriller, *Only the Innocent*, has become an international bestseller, reaching number one in the Amazon charts both in the UK and US. This was followed by the number-one bestselling novels *The Back Road, Sleep Tight, Stranger Child, Kill Me Again, The Sixth Window, Come a Little Closer, The Shape of Lies, Right Behind You,* plus a novella, *Nowhere Child,* which was top of the Kindle Singles chart in the UK for over two years. She has now sold over four million books in the English language, and her books have been translated into over twenty languages.

In 2015 Amazon celebrated the first five years of the Kindle in the UK and announced that Rachel was its number-one bestselling independent author over this period. She was also placed fourteenth in the chart of all authors.

In 2018, *And So It Begins,* the first title in a new series featuring Sergeant Stephanie King, was published in hardback by Wildfire Books – a Headline company. It was named by *The Times* as one of the best crime novels of 2018 and was top of the Amazon weekly chart for two weeks. The second book in the series, *The Murder Game* (*The Invitation* in the US), was released in April 2020.

Rachel Abbott now lives in Alderney and writes full time.

ALSO BY RACHEL ABBOTT

CLOSE YOUR EYES

Rachel Abbott

black dot
publishing

Close Your Eyes

Published in 2021 by Black Dot Publishing Ltd.
Copyright © Rachel Abbott 2021.

ISBN 978-1-9999437-4-5

Find out more about the author and her other books at
http://www.rachel-abbott.com/

PROLOGUE

I'm a bad person. I'm flawed. I'm guilty of greed and envy. I'm selfish, lazy. Try as I might, I don't seem able to improve, and my attempts to atone for my sins are ridiculed.

Any moment now, I will be summoned. I will stand alone, clenching and unclenching my fists, listening as my defects are exposed in all their glory. I feel weak, shaky, maybe because I haven't eaten today; nor did I sleep last night. I was instructed to rehearse my testimony, to be ready to confess to my shortcomings. But sleep is difficult. To sleep is to dream – and I can't bear that.

I walk to my bedroom window and look out over the garden. It's been hot for days, and it's a relief to see the first splats of thick, heavy rain hit the glass. I grasp the catch and pull the window open as the squall intensifies, relishing the feel of the cool water on my hot skin. A slow, steady drip from a faulty gutter splashes onto the terrace below, getting faster as the storm escalates, its pace keeping time with my racing heart.

I tell myself I shouldn't panic. It's not the first time I've suffered such humiliation, and I doubt it will be the last. It's all part of making me a better person, someone who is worth loving.

In truth I don't deserve anyone's love, and although my every weakness is about to be exposed, dissected, my true sins of betrayal, treachery and disloyalty will not be mentioned. No one will shout 'Traitor!' or 'Judas!' because only two people know what I did. And they will say nothing.

They don't need to. I know what I am.

TUESDAY

1

Tom groaned and turned over, trying to ignore the steady buzz that was breaking through his dreams. He'd been up twice with a teething Harry, and it seemed only moments since he'd drifted back to sleep. Exciting as their son's first tooth was it was also exhausting, so Tom had offered to take care of Harry overnight to give Louisa a good night's rest. Being woken by his vibrating mobile at 3.45 a.m. was the last thing he needed, but he couldn't ignore it.

He pushed himself upright, swung his legs out of bed and took the phone into the bathroom.

'Becky. What can I do for you?' he asked, stifling a yawn as he ran a hand through his short, dark blond hair.

'We've got a body, Tom. Sorry to wake you, but you need to come and take a look.'

He resisted the urge to sigh. It wasn't Becky's fault, and he didn't suppose she wanted to be up in the middle of the night any more than he did.

'You sound like you're outside. Where am I going?'

'We're not far from Roe Green, down a narrow alley. Head on the motorway towards Worsley. I'll text you the location. Jumbo's here with a team, but we won't move anything until you arrive.'

'Okay, I'll be with you in about forty-five minutes.'

He took a deep breath and switched on the shower. At least Jumbo, or Dr Jumoke Osoba to give him his full title, was the appointed crime-scene manager. He had more experience than anyone Tom had ever worked with, and he wasn't afraid to add his own hypotheses to his professional assessment either.

Tom switched the shower to cold for the last minute, hoping it would liven him up. He breathed in sharply as the chilly water drenched his body and dropped his head to watch the rivulets run down his legs and splash onto the tiled floor. Drying himself quickly, he returned to the bedroom and crouched down beside Louisa to kiss her gently on the lips. Her mouth turned up in a smile, even though her eyes remained closed.

'That's a lovely way to wake up,' she murmured.

'It would be even better if I could get back in there with you,' he answered. 'But I can't. I'm sorry, darling – I've got to go out. Harry's been awake twice, but he's asleep now. I thought I should warn you so you're mentally on baby alert.'

'Never off it, Tom.'

That was true. Even when he got up to see to Harry, Tom knew Louisa always stirred at their baby's cries.

He resisted the temptation to look in on his son, worried that any sound might wake him. Instead, he satisfied himself that he was sleeping by checking the video on the monitor. He kissed Louisa again and headed for the door.

As he walked along the landing, he glanced at Lucy's bedroom door, standing slightly ajar. The bed was empty, as he knew it would be. He missed his daughter more with every passing day.

He ran downstairs, picked up his keys, phone, wallet, identification – everything exactly where he had left it the night before in case he was called out – pulled the door closed as quietly as possible and headed for his car, stifling another yawn.

The dark clouds that had been hanging over the north-west of England all day had disappeared, and the roads were mercifully empty. The sky would begin to lighten soon, and at least it was warm and had finally stopped raining. Tom had spent too many nights of his career standing around in the cold and dark – often in freezing rain – chilled to the bone as he waited for the Home Office pathologist to arrive.

As he headed through Worsley, he thought how much he had always liked this part of Manchester, or Salford as it technically was, with its mature trees and well-kept houses. Sadly that hadn't prevented it from being the scene of a murder, and not the first he'd attended in this neighbourhood. Thoughts of the last time, of the young girl they had found in the woods nearby, made him shiver. It was a case that still haunted him, as did every case involving children.

Turning into a side street, he could see patrol cars and unmarked vehicles blocking the road ahead and he pulled up behind them. All the activity seemed to be taking place down a narrow passageway that ran from the road past a couple of attractive cottages. Tom gave his name to the police officer guarding the top of the alley and set off, following the approach path laid down by the CSI team.

Breathing in the musty smell of wet earth, he headed towards his colleagues as the first tweet of a lone bird announced the start of a new day. It was a little too late in the summer for a full-blown dawn chorus, and Tom was relieved: there was something eerie about listening to a symphony of sweet birdsong while staring at a bloodied corpse.

At the sound of his footsteps, Becky turned from where she was talking to a man with a shaved head who was bouncing on the balls of his feet: DS Rob Cumba. The young detective had only been with the team for six months, and he seemed to find it impossible to keep still, even at this ungodly hour.

'Morning Becky, Rob.'

'Morning, boss,' they answered in unison.

'What have we got, Becky?'

Becky nodded to where Tom could see a dark object on the ground – a body, curved into a foetal position as if protecting itself, lying in the remains of a puddle left behind after the earlier rain. From where he was standing Tom had no idea of the age, sex or ethnicity of the victim, but knew that, just hours earlier, this had been a living, breathing person. He took a long slow breath and turned to Becky.

'A woman, early thirties,' she said. 'We believe her to be Genevieve Strachan – lived at the last cottage you passed.'

'How did she die?'

'Blow to the back of the head,' Becky said. 'Then stabbed twice in the upper abdomen.'

'Who found her?'

'Her husband, Niall Strachan. He's about to be moved from the house so we can let Jumbo's team in. His clothes have been bagged. They're covered in blood – the victim's, as far as we know. He says he tried to revive her when he found her, but we'll see what the evidence tells us.'

Tom knew what Becky was suggesting. It wasn't unusual for the person finding the body to turn out to be the killer, but the pattern of blood on his clothing should tell them more. If Niall Strachan had tried to revive his wife, the blood would be smeared. If he'd killed her, or been there when she was killed, they would expect to see blood spatter.

As Tom was brought up to speed, the activity carried on around the body a few metres away. Men and women in white Tyvek suits were marking any spots of evidence, oblivious to the conversation between the detectives.

'Do we have any idea what time this happened?'

'According to the husband, it has to have been between eleven p.m., when he was last in contact with the victim, and just after one a.m., when he arrived home,' Becky said. 'He'd been at an investors' meeting in central Manchester and when he got back his wife wasn't in the living room, although the TV was on. It was a while before he realised she wasn't in the house – I presume he thought she'd gone to bed. He tried to phone her but got no answer. That's when he decided to run a check to see where her phone was.'

Tom raised his eyebrows. 'He was tracking her mobile? I'd love to hear what Louisa would say if I suggested tracking hers.'

Becky grinned. 'The same as me, I expect. Good way to keep an eye on your kids, though. Anyway, in this case I think it's all to do with Strachan's business. He kept saying he wasn't spying on her, but she was testing his app. I've no idea what he was talking about, but I thought that kind of detail could wait.'

Tom nodded. 'So that's how he found her down here. It's not the first place you'd think to look, is it? It's not a path that's likely to be used much at night – if at all – so if he hadn't tracked her, she could have been here a while. Does it lead anywhere?'

'Only to the Tyldesley Loopline.'

'The what?'

Rob answered. 'It's a walking and cycling track, boss, on what was the old railway line. It's an offshoot of the Roe Green Loopline, which runs from Monton to the outskirts of Bolton.'

'Okay, so no cars, I presume. But it's a potential access point for the killer – on foot or even on a bike. Possibly even a motorbike at this time of night. Rob, we'll need a map showing all the entrances to the Loopline – where it starts, ends, where people might park cars, et cetera. And when we do the house-to-house, we should ask if anyone heard a motorbike. Of course, whoever killed her may have walked straight down this path from the road or been hiding in one of the gardens further up the lane, so we'd better not get too hung up on the Loopline as the killer's route, even though it seems a good option. Has the house been burgled?'

'No signs of anything and no forced entry that we could see, but the CSIs will tell us more,' Rob said. 'The victim's house keys were in her pocket. I guess she could have heard someone in the lane and come out to investigate.'

'You'd have to be insane to come out here to check out a noise,' Becky said. 'I'm a copper and I'm used to putting myself in danger, but I'm not sure I'd venture onto this track on my own without letting someone know what I was about to do. It would have been pitch black. There was no moon last night after about nine thirty.'

'Fair point,' Tom said. 'So why leave the house?'

'Maybe she heard a scream or something. Either that, or someone lured her from the house.'

'It's all hypothetical for now, but if she arranged to meet someone, they could have made plans by text or a call. We need to get into her phone. Thanks for the update, both of you. I suppose I'd better take a look at the body.'

Tom turned to where he could see Jumbo squatting down up ahead, fully suited and booted. The big man looked up and got to his feet at the sound of footsteps. For someone so large, he was surprisingly agile.

'Tom,' he said with a nod. 'Sorry you got dragged out. The pathologist will be with us as soon as she can but she warned me she might be a while, so there's a bit of hanging around to do, I'm afraid. The good news is that it's Amelia Sanders.'

Tom liked Amelia, or Amy as she preferred to be called, and appreciated her empathy for the victims and her brisk, professional attitude. A pain that she was delayed, though.

'Until she gets here, any thoughts on time of death?' he asked Jumbo.

'Nothing that I would commit to, obviously. And don't tell Amy that I've suggested anything – you know how well that would go down! But based on my not insignificant experience of corpses, I can tell you that she's still slightly warm but has already started to stiffen a little. Not yet full rigor mortis. I'll let you draw your own conclusions. Also bear in mind that she was smartly dressed and all her make-up's still on – so it's unlikely she'd gone to bed and then got up again. We've rescued her phone. It was lying on the ground next to her. Her keys were in the pocket of what was once a white linen jacket. She was wearing heels too, so she'd not come out for a late-night stroll.'

'It sounds like something brought her out – or she came out to meet someone.'

'They don't have a dog. I checked before I sent the team in. I didn't want them attacked.' Jumbo grinned. 'I thought that if she'd come out with a dog before going to bed, then it might have been a random attack – maybe someone down here doing something they shouldn't, and she caught them at it.'

'Just wanted some fresh air?' Tom said without conviction.

Jumbo shook his head. 'They have a lovely garden over that wall.' He pointed to a brick wall about six feet high, which only Jumbo – and at a push, Tom – could look over on tiptoe. 'There's no gate in it to access this path, so she must have come out of the front door and walked down here.'

'In high heels. I get your point, Jumbo. It doesn't entirely make sense. What about footprints?'

Jumbo puffed out a long breath through pursed lips. 'Nothing that's any use. It seems the husband paced up and down while he called 999 and has been on his hands and knees in the mud around her body. Plus it rained earlier, and walkers might have come down here after it stopped.'

A perfect single footprint could have made life easier, but things were rarely that simple. 'Is her phone switched on?'

'It is, but it's password-protected. Probably uses facial recognition, but it's not going to recognise hers now, I'm afraid. Becky asked the husband if he knew the pass code, but apparently not. It's on its way to the digital forensics team as we speak, but you know how bloody difficult manufacturers make it to get into smartphones these days.'

Tom grunted. It was always a battle, but the phone might have something to tell them.

He edged as close to the body as he could without compromising the scene and crouched down. In the light of the arc lamps he saw a young woman lying on her side, one arm stretched out as if she had tried to protect herself when she fell, not knowing that it was too late. Her eyes were open, staring at a puddle, red with blood, just in front of her face. One false eyelash had become detached and sat on her cheek like a dead spider, and dark red lipstick was smudged across her cheek.

What had persuaded her to walk down here in the middle of the night? Had she driven home and seen something as she put her car in the garage? Perhaps she had never even gone into the house. Maybe it was simply a case of wrong place, wrong time.

It sounded like they'd have plenty of time to come up with hypotheses while they waited for the pathologist, and Tom hoped some bright spark would rustle up a cup of coffee from somewhere. He needed a caffeine hit badly.

2

MARTHA

I'm five minutes later than usual getting to work, and I realise the minute I walk through the door to the main office that something is wrong. There's a buzz in the air, and a look of blank shock on a few faces. Elise – the office gossip – is fit to burst with excitement. She turns as I open the door, tucks a strand of her white-blonde hair behind one ear and gives me what looks like a sly grin. I stare right back at her. She won't get any response out of me.

With a quiet 'Good morning' I walk straight through the room and into my own private sanctuary.

I hear her shout, 'Martha, you'll never believe what's happened,' but before she can tell me more, I close the door softly.

I couldn't bear to sit out there in the general office all day, listening to Elise disgorging her vitriol. I know some of the others are uncomfortable with her gossiping, but they don't want to become a target for her acid tongue so they go along with her.

Elise doesn't like me, and that makes the others wary around me too. It seems they have to conform to her code of behaviour. There's nothing I can do about it – nothing I *want* to do. They know nothing about me, and that's fine. Maybe I'm a tough person to like, and try as I might it's sometimes hard to ignore the voice in my head that takes me back to my teenage years and beyond: *You need to look at your failings, girl. You need to understand your faults; be a better person.*

I give my head a quick shake to shut out the voice. I know who I am. I know all the bad bits.

I drop my bag by the desk and pull out my chair, but it only takes seconds for Elise to barrel her way through the door. I can tell that my lack of interest in the latest rumour has irritated her.

'Don't you want to know what we're all talking about?' she demands.

I don't answer. I just raise my eyes and look straight into hers. She thinks it's spooky the way I never avert my gaze – she's told me so – and I see her mouth harden as her eyes drift beyond me to the window so she doesn't have to stare me down.

'It's Genevieve,' she says.

Niall's wife. I feel a shiver run up my spine, but still I don't rise to her bait. Instead, I reach down into my bag, remove my mobile phone, switch it off, pop it into the drawer, slam it shut and twiddle the mouse on my desk to bring my computer to life.

'Jesus, you're a cold bitch,' she says, her curling lip betraying her dislike for me. 'She's *dead*, Martha! I know you don't give a fuck about anyone, but Niall's our boss – the person responsible for paying our wages – and his wife is *dead!*'

The word echoes around my head, and I lift my eyes back to hers. But I ask no questions. I don't know what to ask, what to say. And anyway, I know she's going to tell me.

'The police are bound to be here soon. Let's see how cool you're feeling then.'

Against my better judgement, one word bursts from my lips. 'Police?'

This time she positively gloats. 'Yes, police. Of course they'll come here – we all knew her, and they'll definitely want to talk to you, won't they? Everyone knows how you feel about Niall and how uncomfortable you've made him. You thought it was a secret, but we knew. *And* we heard you arguing with Genevieve last week. What happened, Martha? Was there a showdown between the two of you?'

She knows nothing. She's just fishing.

'My conversation with Genevieve is nothing to do with you – or the police.'

'Well, let's see if they think the same. They're going to want to know everything – every little detail about anyone who might have had a grudge against her. Don't stand there looking at me as if you don't know what I'm talking about. Spence will be in soon, and he'll want to talk to us. He's already phoned me. He says Niall called him at five thirty this morning to break the news, and Spence said he was practically incoherent – it took him ages to get out of Niall what had happened. But he eventually managed to choke out the words. It turns out she's not just dead, Martha. She's been *murdered!*'

I hold myself firm, willing my body not to shake, but there are icicles running down my back. For the first time ever, I am grateful to Elise for being unable to hold her vicious tongue. Had she not been relishing the drama of it all, I might never have considered that the police would want to interview Niall's staff. Why would they? Genevieve didn't work here. She only ever came when she wanted something from Niall. I'm sure it will just be routine. Surely they have nothing to tie anyone here to her murder?

But there's one thing I know for sure: I can't be here when they arrive.

3

At last Tom was free to leave the crime scene after what had seemed an interminable wait for Amy Sanders. But as the pathologist had pointed out in a slightly acerbic tone when she finally arrived, Tom's corpse wasn't the only one in town. Amy or one of her Home Office colleagues had to attend every suspicious death, whether murder or not, and she was looking unusually frazzled. It seemed it had been a busy night.

As soon as her initial examination had been completed and the body dispatched to the mortuary, she'd turned to Tom.

'I'll be conducting the post-mortem later today, Tom. You'll be there, I assume?' she asked, her tone weary.

'I will.' He'd resisted the impulse to add 'unfortunately'. He hated post-mortems and had attended far too many. He didn't envy Amy, as it seemed likely she would have to conduct more than one that day after little or no sleep. At least all Tom had to do was observe and ask questions.

Rob had left the scene nearly two hours earlier to head back to the incident room so he could brief DI Sims, but Becky had stayed with Tom while they waited for Amy to appear, and they'd used the time to don protective clothing and have a look round the Strachans' home, now a crime scene crawling with CSIs.

It was a red-brick cottage, probably Victorian, and much bigger than it looked from the road. It had probably been lovely, Tom thought, but at some point all the character had been stripped from the inside. Either the Strachans or a previous owner had clearly had an obsession with downlights, which shone brightly in every room, making the still bleary-eyed Tom blink in their glare.

The study was the only room that didn't look as if it had come straight out of an interiors magazine. Three walls were lined with workstations, each with a keyboard and two monitors. Wires looped behind the furniture, linking every computer to a big black box which Tom assumed was some kind of server. Whatever it was, it seemed to be busy, with constantly flashing lights showing signs of activity. This was way beyond the average home computer system, and Tom didn't pretend for a minute to know what it was all doing. But he did know that it would have to be examined. Some of the force's tech guys would be in their element.

'What's your thinking, Becky?' he asked as they looked around.

'There's no immediate evidence that the perpetrator set foot over the doorstep, and no obvious signs of violence on the premises. But there's always a chance that the killer was waiting inside for Genevieve when she got home, and then took her out into the lane to kill her.'

'There's also the chance that her husband wasn't where he said he was. He remains a suspect until proved otherwise. You spoke to him. What did you make of him?'

'Struggling to process what's happened, as you might imagine,' Becky said. 'He kept staring at his hands as if he couldn't quite believe what he was seeing. There was a lot of blood, and he'd obviously been in very close contact with the victim. I explained that his home had to be treated as a crime scene and offered him the choice of going to a friend's house or even to a neighbour. But when I mentioned that we could take him to the police station in Swinton, he seemed relieved to have the decision taken out of his hands.'

Tom could understand why the man wasn't keen to go to a friend's house. Although his clothes had been seized, in theory to deal with any issues of cross-contamination but in reality to check for evidence, he would still be covered in his wife's blood, unable to shower in his own home until the CSIs had completed the forensic examination. At least he'd have a chance to clean up at the station.

Now that the body had gone and Jumbo's team was busy searching the path, the Loopline and any adjoining gardens, Tom decided it was time to leave. He needed to talk to Mr Strachan, who was their best bet for understanding why anyone might have wanted to kill his wife. 'Jumbo, we're off,' he called.

Jumbo raised his head from where he was peering over the shoulder of one of his team, who was gently moving blades of grass in search of evidence. 'I'll catch up with you later,' he mumbled, returning his concentration to the grass.

As they reached their respective cars, Tom turned to Becky.

'You've got the details of the lawyers' office where Mr Strachan's meeting was held, and someone should be there to take your call by now, so let's get his alibi checked.'

'Will do,' she said, before slamming her car door and setting off at a pace Tom wasn't even going to try to compete with.

As he drove towards the local sub-divisional headquarters in Swinton, he pictured the murder scene and tried to imagine what would have persuaded Genevieve Strachan to leave the safety of her home at some time around midnight to walk down an unlit passage in high heels.

Did she have a lover? Maybe her call to her husband had been to check that he wasn't going to be back for a while. But then why meet in the alley? Why not invite him into the house? Or maybe she was being blackmailed and was lured out to make a payment.

Or she'd gone out to buy drugs. The options seemed endless. One thing was certain, though. Tom was as sure as he could be that she hadn't gone outside to take in the night air.

4

Tom and Becky were shown into what was supposedly a 'soft interview room', where a pale Niall Strachan was sitting on a brown leather chair that looked anything but comfortable. He'd been given some clothes to change into and had washed any remaining blood from his skin.

Tom walked across to shake his hand. 'Mr Strachan, I'm Detective Chief Inspector Tom Douglas, and I believe you've met Detective Inspector Robinson. I'm sorry for your loss, sir, and I apologise that we need to question you at such a difficult time. We don't want to add to your distress, but I'm sure you realise that the sooner we can get information, the greater our chances of finding out who did this.'

'Ask me anything you want,' Niall said, his voice slightly unsteady.

Tom and Becky took seats opposite him.

'The thing we need to understand is why your wife would have gone out into the lane – which would have been pitch black – so late at night. We don't have a time of death yet, but maybe you can help by telling us anything you know about her movements last night.'

Niall dropped his head and stared down at his hands, clasped between his knees.

'She went to her sister's. Sara. She lives in Leigh. I've written down her details because someone has to tell her, and I don't think I can.' He pulled a piece of paper from his pocket and pushed it across the low table between them.

Tom glanced at it. 'That's okay, Mr Strachan. We'll talk to Mrs Osborne. What else can you tell us?'

'Genevieve got home at about eleven. I know because she called me to ask what time I was getting back. She wanted to know how the meeting had gone with the investors – that's where I was. In a stuffy meeting room in an office in central Manchester, with a load of lawyers.'

'And what time did you get home?'

'Just after one.'

'Late meeting, then?' Tom said.

'Have you ever been to an investors' meeting, particularly one that involves signing contracts? They argue about every bloody comma as the lawyers rack up their charges.'

'Do you think your wife might have seen someone in the lane as she arrived home? Or seen something she needed to check out, perhaps as she was pulling the car into the garage?'

Niall shook his head. 'No. When we spoke she was already in the house. I could hear the TV on in the background. It was still on when I got back, which is why it seemed odd that she wasn't there.'

Tom thought 'odd' was a bit of an understatement, but maybe Mrs Strachan had a habit of going out after midnight.

'I know DI Robinson has already asked you this, but have you by any chance remembered the pass code for your wife's phone? We'll be checking her records, and we're hoping to get the numbers of anyone who she spoke to or texted. Someone may be able to explain why she left the house.'

'I don't know her pass code. She probably told me, but I can't remember. She's unlikely to have used SMS or made a mobile call, in any case. She and her friends always used iMessage or FaceTime, so her service provider isn't going to have a clue who contacted her.'

Strachan was right, of course. Whether she'd used mobile data or WiFi, with iMessage the only record of who had contacted her – if, indeed, anyone had – would be on the phone itself.

'DI Robinson mentioned you found your wife on the lane because you were able to trace her phone, is that right?'

He lifted one shoulder nonchalantly. 'That's right. My company designs AI systems to integrate with mobile phones. The app on Genevieve's mobile could be triggered to send me her location – fairly standard stuff as I'm sure you know – but also to emit a beep if she didn't respond to my request for her whereabouts.'

'AI systems for mobiles?'

Niall sat forward in his seat, more animated than they had seen him until now. 'We're at the cutting edge. We're combining predictive behaviour with artificial intelligence. You don't need to program our apps to switch things on at certain times – you know, like lights, heating, et cetera – they learn your behaviours, predict what you're going to do and act independently. It's going to revolutionise people's lives.'

Tom had no idea what he meant, and after his brief burst of enthusiasm, Niall slumped back into the chair.

'So your wife's phone was beeping?' Tom said, steering the interview back to the relevant facts.

'It was. And emitting an intermittent flash. I could see the phone on the ground, but I didn't see Genevieve until I was almost on top of her because I was pointing my torch at the path to avoid the puddles. Suddenly, there she was. I thought she'd fallen.'

Niall suddenly gulped and jumped to his feet as if the tragedy had struck him all over again.

'I'll try to remember her pass code, but please excuse me. I'm sorry. I need a minute.' Head down, he hurried towards the door.

Tom gave him a sympathetic nod. 'Of course.'

It was frustrating to have to wait, but not only had the man just lost his wife, he'd also been the one who had discovered her.

'Becky, while he's out of the room, can you get on to Rob? Ask him to go and talk to the sister to check if the times tally. See if there's anything she can tell us about Genevieve's state of mind.'

'Sure. I'll call him from the hall in case Mr Strachan comes back.'

As she closed the door, Tom pulled out his own mobile and did a quick search on Niall's company. The screen was flooded with mentions of XO-Tech. He was still ploughing through the reports when Becky came back.

'All sorted,' she said. 'You're looking engrossed.'

He lifted his eyes from his phone for a moment. 'He wasn't joking about the powers of this app of his.'

'What makes you say that?'

'His company's just had a significant injection of venture capital so they can further explore this artificial intelligence he was telling us about. It gives an example here: listen to this. "If it's your normal practice to text your partner as you leave the office, the app will monitor your location, and if it's the right time of day, or thereabouts, and you're heading to the office car park, it will automatically trigger a text to say you're on your way. As you get closer to your car, it will unlock the door. Then as you approach home, your electric gates – if you have them – will open, and if your house is suitably equipped it will switch on the heating in anticipation of your arrival." Bloody hell,' he muttered.

'A bit of a bugger if you decide to pop in to see your lover on the way home, then,' Becky mumbled.

Tom laughed. He couldn't help thinking it was a pity the AI hadn't predicted that it was dangerous for Genevieve to leave the house in the middle of the night.

'When he comes back, we need to ask if any of that tech equipment belonged to Genevieve,' Becky said. 'A laptop or iPad, for example – she might have message-forwarding set up. Might be easier to get into.'

'I was about to ask that very question as he left the room.'

Before Tom could say more, the door opened again and Niall made his way back to his seat, looking if anything even paler than when he had left. His shoulders were hunched, and there was a thin sheen of sweat on his skin.

'Can we organise a cup of coffee, or maybe a sandwich for you?' Becky asked.

'No thanks. The thought of food makes me feel ill. I did think of one thing, though – about her phone.'

Tom and Becky both looked at him, waiting for him to continue.

'It's a company phone. All employees have them because from time to time we ask them to test the app as it's being developed. We gave one to Genevieve. They're all password-protected, but we set the codes and ask them not to change them, although they can set them up with facial recognition if they want to. A lot of the staff have their own personal phones too, but not Genevieve. She wasn't prepared to weigh her handbag down with two phones.'

One side of his mouth curled up in a half-smile as he spoke.

'Did she have a laptop or an iPad? Anything else that might have her messages on?'

'No. She didn't need one. I honestly don't think I've ever seen her use a computer.'

'How can we get hold of Genevieve's pass code?' Tom asked.

'You need to speak to Martha Porter. She's my office manager. She keeps the records.'

5

As Becky pulled into XO-Tech's car park to wait for Rob, she mulled over everything they had learned, which wasn't much. A phone call had been enough to provide an initial confirmation that Niall Strachan had been at the lawyers' office, as he had said, although statements from each attendee would need to be taken. It seemed he left between 12.30 and 12.45 a.m., which tied in with when he said he got home. At that time of the morning, it would have been a quick journey.

The post-mortem had yet to be carried out, but given Jumbo's assessment of the victim's body when he reached the scene, it seemed probable that she had been there for at least three hours.

Rob had gone to visit Genevieve's sister in Leigh and was on his way to join Becky. All he'd said in their brief call as he left Sara Osborne's house was that he would fill Becky in when he arrived at the XO-Tech offices, but he'd had an interesting chat.

Becky looked at her watch. She was wasting time. If Rob didn't arrive in two minutes, she was going in without him. Pushing open the car door, she got out and instantly regretted it. Yesterday's heat combined with the rain made the air feel heavy, and there were more storm clouds building.

With a final glance at her watch, she was about to head inside when Rob's dark blue Audi came flying into the car park. He skidded to a halt and leaped out of the car.

'Sorry, Becky!' he shouted. 'Bloody East Lancs Road was half blocked by a broken-down lorry.' He jogged across the tarmac.

'That was a hell of an entrance,' she said.

'From what I've heard, I've got nothing on you.'

'Have you been talking to the boss?' Becky asked, and Rob grinned.

Becky's driving was a bit of a talking point, but she could never understand why. She considered herself a good driver.

'Do you want to know about the sister first, or shall we go and get the pass code for the mobile?' Rob asked, changing the subject.

'Pass code first, then we can get into Genevieve's phone and see who she was in touch with. Keith Sims has been on to the network provider. No text messages or calls, which doesn't surprise me, and nothing on the landline. As her husband said, everything would have gone via WiFi or mobile data.' *Bloody smartphones*, she thought. She'd worked on no end of cases where they'd helped solve crimes, but the latest levels of security were a nightmare. 'While we're here, Rob, the boss also wants us to talk to the staff – see whether Genevieve was a regular visitor and try to get some sense of who she was. It'll be good to know what they think of Niall Strachan too, because however good his alibi, we'll have to look at him carefully.'

As they approached the entrance, Becky glanced up at the building, which looked as if it had been constructed in the 1930s. A portico stood slightly proud, with huge windows reaching upwards, double glass doors providing access to the reception area. Rob pulled open a door and Becky walked through, disappointed to find that there was no real sense of the history of the building inside. It had been refurbished in a stunning if inappropriate industrial style with bare brick walls and floors of oiled boards, although the tall windows made up for it, flooding the space with light.

The reception desk was deserted.

Becky walked across to see if there was a bell or some other means of communicating with the staff. She could see nothing and turned to Rob with a shrug.

'I guess we'd better show ourselves in, then,' she said.

'Absolutely.'

They looked around at the doors off the reception area, most of which stood open. They appeared to lead to meeting rooms, all empty. Rob opened a closed door. 'Kitchen,' he said, 'but I think I can hear voices from upstairs. Shall we check it out?'

Becky nodded, and they made their way further into the building, their footsteps sounding on the bare boards. No one seemed interested. They climbed a metal staircase to the first floor and Becky pushed open the door that Rob indicated.

Seven people were congregated around a man in his early forties, dressed in jeans and a bright red Glastonbury Festival T-shirt that, to Becky's eyes, made him look as if he was trying too hard.

He spun towards them. 'Who are you?' he asked, a nervous edge to his voice.

'Detective Inspector Becky Robinson from Greater Manchester Police. My colleague is Detective Sergeant Rob Cumba. We're looking for Martha Porter.'

A young woman with thin lips said, 'I told you they'd want to speak to Martha,' in a whisper that was undoubtedly meant to carry to Becky's ears. She ignored the remark but filed the thought for later.

'Can you tell me where I can find her, please?'

The man seemed to have pulled himself together a little. 'I'm sorry, Inspector. I'm Spencer Johansson, Niall Strachan's business partner. I'm afraid I was just giving the marketing team here the dreadful news. I've been trying to speak to Martha, but she won't open her door.'

Becky frowned. 'What do you mean?'

Spencer nodded his head towards a door at the far end of the room. 'Martha's office. It's the anteroom to Niall's office, but obviously he's not here. And Martha seems to have locked herself in. I imagine she's upset about Genevieve.'

A scoffing sound came from the woman with the thin lips. 'She won't care what's happened to Genevieve, Inspector. She didn't like her. I can tell you that.'

Spencer turned to the woman. 'Elise, I know you're not Martha's greatest fan – you make that perfectly clear. But please, don't start making trouble. Let the police do their job.'

'Well, you tell them about the party, then! That might make them think.'

Becky looked at Spencer Johansson and waited.

'Stop it, Elise. I'm sorry, officers. I'm happy to tell you anything you want to know, but we don't want to sidetrack you with gossip.'

Gossip was good, as far as Becky was concerned, but she wouldn't give this Elise the pleasure of knowing she might have scored a hit.

'Let's talk to Martha and then maybe we could have a chat with you in private, Mr Johansson.'

'Of course.'

He walked over to the door and knocked. In a voice edged with stress, he mumbled, 'The police are here, Martha. Can you open the door, please?'

Silence.

Becky glanced at Rob, who banged a little more forcefully. 'Miss Porter, can you please open the door? This is Detective Sergeant Cumba, and I need to talk to you.'

Still there was nothing.

'Do you have a spare key to this room, Mr Johansson?'

'I do. Give me a moment and I'll get it.'

He scurried off.

'Can we help while you wait?' Becky didn't need to turn to know who was speaking. The woman had stood up, revealing a short skirt and pink knees that appeared to have caught too much sun over the weekend. *Elise.*

'I'm sure you'll have some very useful information,' Becky said. 'But we need to speak to your colleague first as a matter of priority.'

'I bet you do,' came the half-whisper.

'Shut up, Elise,' a young man said. 'You're not helping anyone.'

Give that man a medal, thought Becky.

Two minutes later Spencer was back, and he began fumbling with the key in the lock. He wasn't making any progress, so Rob took over. 'Key's in on the inside,' he said to Becky as he twiddled and pushed.

Suddenly they heard a clatter as the key fell to the floor on the other side of the door, and Rob unlocked the office.

It was empty.

6

MARTHA

As I hurry along the street, away from the office, I glance at my watch. *Will the police be there by now? When will they realise I've gone?* I speed up, walking fast, not wanting to draw attention to myself by running, but if I could I'd sprint down the street. I can feel sweat trickling down my back as, paradoxically, goosebumps run up my arms.

Elise had proved difficult to get rid of. I thought she'd never go. She stood leaning against the door jamb, arms folded tightly, her bare legs crossed at the ankles, waiting for me to say something.

'I'm sorry to hear about Genevieve,' I said finally, knowing that some response was required.

It wasn't enough for Elise, and when she realised that I wasn't going to speculate, she tutted, spun on her heel, calling over her shoulder, 'You know you're not supposed to turn your mobile off,' and flounced off to where her colleagues were discussing theories about who could have killed the boss's wife.

I sagged with relief, but I had no time to think. I had things to do. But as I tried to focus on my plan – the one I had made the day

I started work at XO-Tech more than two years ago – memories flashed into my mind of Genevieve's visits to the office. She always pestered Niall to take her to lunch or go shopping with her, and while she waited for him she would throw her weight around, demanding that someone make her a drink or, better still, raid Niall's booze cupboard for something stronger. Given that Niall always pleaded poverty – he could only pay the lowest wages to his staff until the company saw success – Genevieve didn't seem to go short of much. She always found a way of flashing the red soles of her Louboutins and of making sure the exclusive label of whatever jacket or coat she was wearing was visible as she took it off to toss carelessly over a chair.

I've always known how much Niall draws from the company. It's my job to manage the finances, so I'm aware that the staff shouldn't have had to wait so long for the much-vaunted success of the business before being paid a decent salary. He knows it's information I would never consider sharing, because I need this job – or I did. Now it seems my time with XO-Tech is done and I feel a tinge of regret. Much as I find Elise evil, the others aren't unpleasant – just meek and amenable, which is why Niall employs them. I think his game plan has always been to search out people who are competent, then from among the pool of hopefuls he selects the most gullible.

There's nothing in his behaviour that surprises me. I've seen it all before and I know that being easily led has nothing to do with a lack of intelligence. It's to do with seeking something to have faith in, and Niall has gathered people around him who believe in him and the future of his company. Everyone from his second in command, Spencer – who Elise always calls Spence in an overly chummy way – to the receptionist; they are all primed to go the extra mile to win a smile from the boss.

I'm the exception, of course, and he has never known how to deal with me, although he's been particularly demonstrative in his antipathy towards me recently – especially when there are spectators. He seems to visibly recoil, and I don't know who he's trying to impress. It certainly has no impact on me.

Difficult as it had been to dislodge Elise from my office, as I watched the door close behind her my only thought had been escape. Mentally I ran through the steps I'd practised so many times, pushing the voice in my head – the one telling me that I was bound to make a mistake – into a black hole where I could no longer hear it.

The first step was to check there was nothing personal of mine in my desk. I doubted it, but had to be sure in case I'd become sloppy and made a mistake. I hadn't. I logged on to my computer and followed the procedure I'd rehearsed to remove all traces of myself. I didn't need to delete any personal searches from my browser history. I've never used my work computer or my work phone for anything that isn't directly related to the job. I grabbed the special wipes I'd bought online and cleaned all the surfaces I'd touched, until I knew for sure that there was nothing of me left in the room.

I moved across to my office door and silently locked it, certain that it would be a while before anyone tried to get in. My lack of response earlier would have made them wary of speaking to me. At least I hoped so. Eventually they would try the door but probably assume I was being difficult. As usual.

I picked up my bag and opened the door from my office into Niall's – empty, of course. I walked to the far end of the room and opened a door that everyone else in the company, with the possible exception of Spencer, believes leads to a store cupboard. It doesn't. It gives access to a small corridor with a private bathroom and a staircase down to a side door. The building used to be the offices of an engineering company, and the boss used this route to access the now non-existent workshops. These days it just leads to a quiet alley. Niall uses it when he wants to sneak out without anyone knowing. Anyone except me, that is.

Once out of the door, I had to force myself to walk, not run. I didn't know how much time I had, but no one at work knows where I live, and it should take the police a while to find me. Elise will no doubt relay exaggerated stories about me – everything from her version of the events of the disastrous office party to Niall's attitude to me. And she'll tell them about my argument with Genevieve.

Is any of that enough for them to suspect me of her murder? Maybe not – but they'll want to know more about me than I'm prepared to divulge, and the thought of what they might discover and the inevitable consequences have spurred me into action. I have no way of finding out how much they might already know about me.

Now, my body feels sticky – whether from the sultry weather or from fear, I can't say – and I force myself to stop worrying about what they will think, what they might discover, and go over the steps in my plan once again.

Mentally back on track, I reach into my bag for my personal mobile – the one XO-Tech doesn't know about – and grab the spare SIM from my purse. I could change it blindfolded. The screen displays my list – the vital notes I wrote in case panic forced me to make mistakes – and I press a link to call a taxi company, one of the three alternatives I'd stored just for this moment. I have three options for everything, always erring on the side of caution should my first choice prove impossible – a busy taxi company, a fully booked hotel. I believe I've thought of everything.

'Could I order a taxi to pick me up from outside Brooke's chemist in thirty minutes, please?'

'Where are you going, love?' asks the friendly man who answers.

'Salford Royal.'

'Can I have your name?'

'Of course. It's Cheryl.'

7

Becky thought Spencer Johansson was finding the day's events a bit much. He looked like a goldfish, his mouth opening and closing as if he didn't know what to say, and his skin looked waxy, although that could have been down to the clammy weather. He'd obviously had no idea that Martha wasn't in her office, hiding behind a locked door so no one would bother her, although why her disappearance should cause such consternation, Becky had no idea.

There was another door leading from Martha's room, and Spencer rushed towards it, throwing it open.

'Martha?' he shouted, but there was no response.

Through the opening, Becky saw a long board table and a smart, well organised desk. Niall's office, she assumed. But there was no sign of Martha.

'How could she have left without going through the main office?' Rob asked.

Spencer glanced over his shoulder at the staff, who were craning their necks to try to see into the room. He kicked the door closed with a thud.

'There's another staircase. The staff don't know about it. It gives

Niall the opportunity to bring investors in without the staff knowing what's going on, and lets him pop out for meetings without having to say where he's going. You know the sort of thing.'

Becky knew exactly the sort of thing. In her experience, if someone was sneaking out of their office without anyone knowing, it was unlikely to be business related. She could be wrong, but suspicion was her middle name.

'Martha knew about the private entrance, I presume?' she asked.

'It seems so. Martha kind of knows everything that's going on. She's not like the others.'

Becky looked at the man's anxious face. 'What does that mean?'

Spencer sighed. 'She keeps herself to herself. She doesn't make friends easily, and most of them don't get her. That's why she's so valuable. She manages all the day-to-day financial stuff: payroll, human resources, pensions – all the crap that Niall and I don't want to be bothered with but is an essential part of running a business.'

'And what was her relationship with Niall?' Becky asked.

For a moment, Spencer looked cagey. 'Well, it's hard to say.'

Neither Becky nor Rob spoke, knowing that an edgy Spencer would fill the silence. He didn't disappoint.

'They've always been fine, until recently. She's totally professional, but we could never tell who she really was, if that makes sense. She was so *controlled*. But she did her job. A few weeks ago we had a party to celebrate completion of the next phase of the app, and since then I've noticed a bit of distance between her and Niall – particularly on his part. He didn't seem to want to be in a room with her on his own. I asked him about it, but he said I was imagining things.'

Becky decided not to pursue this for now. It would be better to ask Niall if it was in any way relevant. And at the moment she wasn't sure it was.

'If she had a dentist's appointment or something like that, would she have gone out this way?'

'I doubt it. She's very upfront about stuff.' Spencer scratched his head. 'It's hard to explain Martha without knowing her. Not that any of us do, really. She never talks about family, friends – you know, the usual stuff. She's very much a loner, but at the same time she'd consider it dishonest to go to an appointment without telling us. Not that she'd have asked permission; she'd have stated it as fact – something not to be discussed, if that makes sense.'

'Well, whatever her normal behaviour, we've come here this morning because Mr Strachan told us she has the pass codes for all the company mobiles. We understand Mrs Strachan used one, and as part of our investigation we need to access it. Do you know where Martha might have kept that information?'

'On her computer, I imagine.'

Spencer walked round to the other side of Martha's desk and twiddled her mouse.

'Ah. It's password-protected.'

Of course it is, thought Becky.

'Can you access it? I presume as it's company property you have a procedure for this – in the event someone leaves without notice, for example?'

'I'll have to speak to the tech boys, but yes, I'm sure we can get into the computer. It might take a bit of time, though.'

Becky clenched her teeth with frustration. Where had this woman gone? Maybe it was a doctor's appointment, or she was going for an interview for another job and she didn't want anyone to know.

'Do you have a phone number for her?'

Johansson looked shocked, as if it was something he should have thought of.

'Yes! Sorry, of course we do. She has a company mobile, like we all do. The number will be on my phone.' As he spoke, he pulled his own mobile from the back pocket of his jeans, scrolled through a list and pressed the screen.

He pushed the phone to his ear and waited. After a few seconds he lifted his eyes to Becky's and shook his head. 'Martha, this is Spencer. We need to speak to you urgently. The police need access to some of your files and we can't get into your computer. Can you please call me back as soon as you get this? Thanks.' He ended the call. 'As you probably gathered, it went straight to voicemail. That's odd too. It's a company phone and she's supposed to keep it switched on and with her all the time, to test the app.'

Becky felt her irritation mounting. This should have been the easy bit. 'Okay, can you dig out her address, please? We'll have to assume she's gone home – at least we can start there. We'll get an officer to go round and ask her to call you with the password. In the meantime, please get someone to try to unlock her computer because we really need to get into Genevieve Strachan's phone.'

Spencer Johansson looked anxiously around the office. 'Her address will be in the personnel records, but I'm not sure where she kept them. Certainly on her computer, but maybe she had hard copies too.'

He walked over to a set of three filing cabinets and seemed to pull drawers out at random.

'I'm sorry. We seem a bit disorganised. But you see Martha has her finger on the pulse for us, so we don't need to worry about where stuff is.'

He riffled through the folders. Becky was itching to help; even from where she was standing she could see they were all clearly marked, and yet he seemed to be looking through folders marked AUDITORS and EXPENSE ANALYSIS. It was not until he reached the third drawer that he found a section labelled PERSONNEL.

'I think this must be it,' he said, lifting the entire section from the filing cabinet and bringing it to the desk.

The file was subdivided alphabetically by the surname of each member of staff, and he laboriously checked each page, licking his fingers every now and again, until finally he reached the P section. He looked up, his gaze roaming from Becky to Rob and back to Becky again.

'There's a record for Matthew Parsons, but the next one in the folder is for Stella Roberts.'

Becky knew what this meant. There was no file for Martha Porter.

8

MARTHA

To my relief, the man at the taxi company confirms that they are not too busy, and they'll be there to pick me up on time. I thank him and hang up, dashing up the front path to the childminder's, an excuse about a sick family member at the ready. Thank God it's the school holidays. At least the childminder doesn't ask too many questions as I scoop up my son, Alfie, to hurry home.

I clutch him tightly in my arms and kiss him.

'I want to walk, Mummy,' he says.

'I know, poppet, but we need to be quick, so I'll carry you for a while. Is that okay?'

I don't want to stress him, so I make up silly little rhymes about running as I trot along, but I can hear my voice shaking.

'Too tight, Mummy,' Alfie grumbles. He's right. Every muscle in my body is taut, and I'm squeezing the life out of him. I put him down, and suggest we have a race. His face lights up.

'I bet I can win you,' he says.

'I'm sure you can,' I agree as I take baby steps by his side, squeezing his hand in mine, wishing he could run faster.

Our flat is on a busy road, on the first floor above a chiropodist's surgery. The thought of living somewhere with a communal entrance, where people could get in as others leave the building, has always terrified me. Here we have our own front door at the side of the house, and I rarely have to come into contact with anyone. The chiropodist tried to be friendly at the outset, but gave up when I didn't reciprocate. I can't have friends. They would ask questions that I couldn't answer truthfully, so it's better to keep my distance.

'I've got a surprise for you,' I tell Alfie as I pretend to chase him up the stairs to our hall.

He stops at the top. 'What is it?' His eyes light up. He loves a surprise.

'We're going on a little holiday. Come on. Let's get ready. We need to be quick.'

He beams with delight and follows me into my bedroom, where I clamber onto a chair and lift down a leather backpack from the top of the wardrobe. I don't need to check its contents. I know everything is there.

'Can you take your shorts and T-shirt off, Alfie? We need to get changed,' I say as I strip out of my dark blue suit and pristine white blouse. I pull open a drawer to grab black jeans, striped T-shirt, red jacket and red trainers – the kind of clothes that no one here has ever seen me wear.

My hair, tied back fiercely into a tight bun, is released from its hold, and I tip my head upside down to shake the wild black curls free. I throw my glasses onto the bed and grab a bright red lipstick.

'Mummy, you look different,' Alfie says, staring up at me, his eyes wide.

That is exactly what I want to hear.

I quickly dress Alfie, pulling a sun hat on. His hair's as curly as mine and I want to cover as much of it as I can.

'Are we ready?'

Alfie looks down at his clothes and turns to the full-length mirror on the wardrobe door.

'Can I please wear a different T-shirt?' he asks. 'I look like a girl.'

I don't like to tell him, but that's the idea. It's pale pink with a little frill round the bottom.

'No time now, sweetheart – but you don't look like a girl. That colour's trendy now, you know. Jamie likes it. He told me to buy it for you.'

He looks a bit confused, as well he might because Jamie is his imaginary friend. Much as I want to rush my son, I don't want to upset him. None of this is his fault.

After a couple of seconds, he nods. 'Okay then,' he says, beaming.

'Good boy. Maybe I'll call you Jamie today, shall I? You can pretend you're him.' He grins. He loves to play pretend, and I encourage it because I never know when it will be useful. 'Off we go,' I say in my cheery voice. 'It's holiday time!' If only that were true.

As I hurry to the top of the stairs, I take a moment to look around. This has been our home for two years. I always knew it wouldn't be for ever, but I've tried my best to make it comfortable, even though little of what I see belongs to us. We can take nothing, and it hurts me to abandon Alfie's paintings, toys, books, and what few clothes we have. We've been happy here in our own little world, but now we must leave it behind.

For just a moment I'm tempted to hunker down and wait for the police to find me, as they inevitably will if I stay here. But I can't. It's not fair on Alfie. With one last glance over my shoulder, I walk down the stairs and out of the door, double-locking it behind me, knowing we can never come back.

It's a ten-minute walk to the pharmacy, but I can't risk asking the taxi driver to come to the house; minicab companies keep records.

He isn't there when we arrive, and for a moment I feel a rising tide of panic. I don't want to stand out on the street for long, even though I'm unrecognisable with my hair set free, no glasses and bright lipstick. I try to interest Alfie in the shop window, but there's a limit to the fascination of a chemist's display to a five-year-old. Just as he's starting to get fractious, I hear a car horn and turn to see a large man leaning across the front seat of a taxi to shout out of the open passenger window: 'Cheryl?'

I nod, ignoring Alfie's quizzical expression, grab his hand and head for the taxi.

'Sorry, love, I didn't know you had a little one. Give me a moment and I'll get the car seat out of the boot. You okay for time?'

I'll have to be, so I nod again and try not to gaze anxiously around while he heaves himself out of the car, gets the seat and attaches it. Every second seems too long, and I feel as if eyes are burning into my back.

'There you go. In you get, pet,' he says to Alfie, panting a little with the exertion. He smiles over his shoulder at me as he climbs into the front seat. 'Pretty little thing, isn't she? Salford Royal, is it? Hope it's nothing serious. Which entrance?'

'Main entrance, please. Oh, excuse me, my phone's vibrating.'

I reach into my bag and pull out my dead phone.

'Hi,' I say to the silence. 'Yes, of course. That makes sense. See you soon.'

I push my phone back into my bag.

'Sorry, can I make a slight change? We need to meet someone so we can go in together. Could you drop me at Stott Lane car park, please?'

'Course I can, love. Not a problem.'

The taxi driver tries to make conversation with me, and I do my best to respond. I don't want to stand out in his memory, so I need to strike the balance between being friendly and not overdoing it. I don't want to be interesting enough to be the subject of a conversation with his wife or his mates.

He drops us off, and I'm careful to give him an appropriate tip.

'Hope everything goes well for the little 'un,' he says, having gleaned from me that Alfie has an appointment for a minor procedure. Nothing too interesting or life-threatening. Routine. Everything has to seem routine. Fortunately, Alfie had no idea what we were talking about.

As the taxi disappears down the road, I crouch down.

'We've got a bit of a walk, sweetheart, then we're going on a tram! That'll be exciting, won't it?'

It's clear that Alfie's excitement quota has been used up. Our life is usually orderly, and he's been rushed around from pillar to post. I vow to make it up to him as soon as I can.

We walk down the lane, away from the hospital, towards the tram stop. I resist the temptation to keep looking over my shoulder.

We only have a few minutes to wait, and I play 'I Spy' with my son, but I can tell he's tired, and I hope he will fall asleep on the tram.

My wish is granted, and within seconds of getting on board, he's nodding off. I ease him away from my shoulder so I can remove my jacket. It won't look strange because it's a sweltering day. I take Alfie's hat off too. The tram isn't busy, but I wait until the lady in the seat across the aisle from us has reached her stop, and then, keeping the jacket low so no one can see, I slowly pull the arms through, turning it inside out. My red jacket has become bright blue. The same with Alfie's hat, which is now yellow. I pull a T-shirt for him from my bag. I'll wake him when we get close to St Peter's Square – our final tram stop – and whip his pink one off to replace it with the yellow striped one to match his hat.

I know I might be being overcautious, but I have no idea where all the CCTV cameras are in the city centre, and I'm not taking any risks.

Finally, we're off the tram and heading towards the hotel I booked online while we were travelling. I had three stored in the memory, but there was availability at the first one I tried, just three minutes' walk from the tram stop. Once we're in our room, I can give my complete attention to Alfie, who must be totally baffled by all that's going on.

I push open the door to the reception area of the hotel and bend down, my back to the receptionist, as if to tie the lace of my trainers. I surreptitiously lift the bottom of my T-shirt to where I can feel the thin body pocket strapped to my waist, quickly unzip it and pull out the debit card that is never separated from me for more than the time it takes for me to shower.

Having secured my shoelace again, I stand and force myself to smile at the receptionist.

'I have a reservation,' I tell her, 'in the name of Kalu.'

I don't know if it's a mistake to use that name, but it's the name on the card, and it's the only untraceable source of funds that I have.

'Yes, I have your booking here, Ms Kalu. And who's this little one?' She gives Alfie a smile.

'This is Jamie,' I say as I hand her the card, hoping and praying there won't be a problem.

Alfie giggles but says nothing as he leans against my leg.

The receptionist looks at the card. 'Oh, it's a debit card. I'm afraid we'll have to take payment in full now, Ms Kalu, and you'll need to pay for anything else you need throughout your stay – room service, restaurant and so on – at the time of purchase. Is that okay?'

I give her my most relaxed smile. 'Of course.'

I glance down at Alfie, wondering if he's suddenly going to ask who Ms Kalu is. But despite the momentary fun of being introduced as Jamie, the poor child is exhausted and confused. I need to cuddle up with him on the bed and tell him a story.

He doesn't know that we're running away. And I don't know what to tell him.

9

LAKESIDE

'We're not running away, DeeDee!' Mum said, glancing over her shoulder. Her mouth was a tight line, and I knew she was cross with me for being sulky, but I didn't understand why I had to be taken away from all my friends. 'Look, we'll be there soon, and you're going to love it. Anything has to be better than that awful flat.'

I saw her cast an anxious glance at Dad, knowing he believed we'd only been living in such a dreadful place because his factory job didn't bring in enough money for us to live in the kind of house that Mum was used to. Mum was doing office cleaning jobs to try to 'make ends meet', whatever that meant. And anyway, that 'awful flat' was the only home I had ever known, and I loved it there. At ten years old I didn't understand much about money. We didn't seem to have either more or less than any of my friends, and Mum and Dad had always been so happy.

The thing I loved most about our life was the nights when we danced. Even though we didn't go out much, Dad made the weekends fun, playing his favourite music and dragging Mum up from the sofa to dance with him, his hips swaying as he pulled her closer, his hands on her waist, singing in her ear. Then he'd pull me up too, and when I was smaller he used to dance with me in his arms. Even though he was born in south London, Dad said he must have inherited his moves from his Nigerian ancestors.

I caught sight of his eyes in the car mirror. 'Come on, DeeDee. We'll make lots of new friends, you know. Especially when you go to your new school. And there's an enormous garden so we can have parties too.'

I knew I was upsetting my parents, but they hadn't let me say goodbye to my friends. I didn't even know we were leaving until this morning when Dad told me to pack one small bag with my favourite things because we were moving to somewhere completely new. They said they hadn't told me before because they wanted it to be a surprise, but I don't think that's true. Things had been weird for a while. I even heard Kelsie from next door shouting at Mum when I came home from school one day. They stopped arguing when they saw me, but Mum wouldn't tell me what it was about, and Kelsie didn't say goodbye this morning. She saw us going but just turned her back.

We'd caught a bus at the end of the street and got off close to a car showroom. Dad went in while Mum and I waited outside. I'd asked her what was happening, but she just said, 'You'll see,' and gave me a shaky smile, glancing over her shoulder as if she thought someone was looking at us.

I watched through the showroom window as a man jumped to his feet at the sight of Dad and hurried across to shake him by the hand, as if he was expecting him. They chatted for a few minutes and then walked together out of the door, the man resting one hand on Dad's shoulder as if he was one of his mates. They strolled across to a long silver car, and to my surprise Dad got into the driver's seat. The man crouched down, and I could see he was pointing at things on the dashboard. Then he stood up, shook

Dad's hand again, gave us a jolly wave and went back into the showroom.

Dad beckoned us across.

'In you get,' he said with a grin.

'Whose car is this?' I whispered, scared that we were doing something we shouldn't.

'It's ours,' he said, patting the leather-covered steering wheel.

My eyes must have been popping out of my head. We'd never had a car, and this one was really fancy, but he turned and wiggled his eyebrows to make me smile, and I didn't ask anything else. I didn't know what to ask – everything that day seemed so strange.

Since that moment I'd barely spoken until I asked why we were running away. But whatever Mum said about that not being true, it's how it felt to me. Posh car or not, everything I had ever cared about, except for Mum and Dad, seemed to be receding into the distance behind me.

We had been driving for ages. 'Are we nearly there?' I asked.

Mum turned her head. 'Not long, DeeDee, I promise.'

'Don't call me DeeDee. I'm not a baby any more.'

I folded my arms defiantly and stared out of the window. There were more trees than I'd ever seen lining the sides of the road, their leaves shades of orange and red, fluttering in the breeze as they floated down to rest gently on the road. I didn't want everything to look so perfect, with the sun glinting between the branches; I wanted the sky to be thick with black cloud, because that's how I felt.

'Okay, okay,' Dad said, his voice sounding too chirpy. 'We won't call you DeeDee. Maybe we should call you Thingy. Will that do?'

I didn't answer. He was trying to make me laugh, but I didn't want to. I'd always been DeeDee because when I first started to talk I couldn't say my name. The closest I could get was DeeDee, and it stuck. Everyone – even my teachers at school – called me DeeDee. At the thought of school, my eyes filled up. *What had happened?*

Why were we running away? What about my friends? Would I ever see them again?

Mum must have heard me sniff, and she reached over to Dad's thigh and squeezed it gently. 'Pull over, Joel. I think we need to talk to her,' she said, her voice quiet and serious. I didn't like the sound of that.

We drove on for a few minutes until Dad saw a lay-by and pulled off the road. Mum jumped out from her side and got into the back with me, putting her arm round my shoulders and pulling me towards her. Dad twisted in his seat so he was facing us as best he could.

'Listen,' Mum said, and for a moment I wished I hadn't told her not to call me DeeDee. 'We're sorry we rushed you away from everything so quickly. We thought it was for the best, but now I realise it must have been a huge shock. We were trying to protect you. Children aren't always kind to each other, especially when they hear the things their parents say.'

'*What* things?' I asked, my voice rising. I was feeling more and more scared. I couldn't think of one single good thing that could make us run away like this.

Mum took a deep breath. 'You know Dad and I watch something called the National Lottery on the television?'

Of course I did – it was on a Saturday night, and sometimes I was allowed to stay up late enough to watch it with them.

'And you know people can win a lot of money if they get the right numbers?'

I nodded. Mum was squeezing me a bit too tight, so I pushed back to look at her.

'Well, Dad had some winning numbers a few weeks ago.'

I was still confused. *So what?* It seemed it had been enough for him to buy a car, but why did we have to move away from our flat, my friends, my school?

Dad took over the story. 'You see, DeeDee, when someone wins a lot of money – like we did – it can cause problems, so we thought it better not to tell anyone. You can choose to be anonymous. That means no one knows who's won. We chose that option, but then decided to share our good fortune with just a few special people – the friends and neighbours we thought we could help by giving them some money.'

I didn't really understand this, and Dad must have sensed my confusion.

'Sweetheart, people don't always appreciate help when it's offered. Some people thought we should have given them more, because they knew how much we'd won. They thought we were being mean. Others thought we were being patronising – that's a hard word to explain, but they thought we believed we were better than them now.'

'Is that why Mum and Kelsie were arguing?'

I looked at Mum's face, her eyes full of tears.

'Kelsie said we'd never really fitted in. Apparently I've always behaved as if I think I'm too good for where we lived, and now for sure I would be. That's not true, but the people we thought were our friends turned out not to be. We didn't want you to suffer, because when the kids at school got to know about it, you might have been bullied – you know, older kids asking you for money. We thought it best to leave before that happened. We've got a new home now – it's called Lakeside, and you'll love it. There's nothing left for us in London, sweetheart. But everything will be different now, DeeDee. You'll see.'

I still didn't understand. If the money was causing so many problems, why didn't we give it all away? I just wanted to go home, and whatever excuses they made, as far as I was concerned, we were running away.

10

Becky and Rob had commandeered Niall's office, with Spencer's reluctant agreement, while they waited until someone could get into Martha's computer.

'He doesn't like mess, I'm afraid,' Spencer had said, which was apparent both from Niall's orderly office and his pristine home.

'We're not in the habit of making a mess, Mr Johansson,' Rob said, rolling his shoulders as if the inactivity was making him twitchy.

With a frown, Spencer finally nodded. 'Well, I'm sure it will be fine, under the circumstances.'

'What can you tell us about Genevieve Strachan?' Becky asked, waving her hand towards a seat to invite him to sit down.

Spencer perched on the edge of a leather chair. 'I didn't know her that well.'

'But you work closely with Niall – his business partner, you said?' Rob asked.

'Well, sort of. I'm in charge of sales and marketing, and Niall has promised me a bigger role, once the funds are in. He's very keen to keep me, you know, and it's such an exciting opportunity.'

'So you're not a partner?' Rob persisted.

'Niall sees us all as partners in this enterprise,' he said, pursing his lips. 'He's quite a genius, you see, and we'll all gain when the app is finished and released to the wider world. And I'm prepared to put my money where my mouth is.'

Rob frowned. 'You'll have to explain that one to me.'

'Niall is seeking investment – essential for a company that's breaking new ground like we are. I'd be a fool not to back him.'

'I assume you mean financially?'

'Of course. The value of this company is about to go stratospheric!' Spencer raised his arms theatrically is if to suggest an explosion, and Becky resisted the temptation to look at Rob, who she knew would have to bite his lip. 'I need to get back to the team, but while you're waiting, can I ask someone to bring you a cup of coffee?'

Becky would normally have said no, but she'd already been working for seven hours, and at a guess had around another eight to go before she stood a chance of going home.

'That would be lovely. Black for me, please. No sugar.'

'Same, please,' said Rob.

'Can you ask around, see if any of the staff have an address for Martha, or even a vague idea of where she lives? In case we can't break the password.'

Spencer gave them a worried frown, but nodded and left them to it, leaving the door ajar. Rob walked over and gently closed it.

'What do you make of all this?' Rob asked.

'Well, Spencer isn't quite the business partner he claimed to be. His face when you challenged him on it was a picture. Other than that, not a clue. We only wanted the bloody password to Genevieve's phone, and now Martha Porter is adding a new and wholly unnecessary layer to the investigation.' Becky blew out a long, frustrated breath. 'I suppose I'd better give the boss a call. He won't be happy about the delay. The fact that there's no personnel record for Martha feels dodgy to me. Was it there and someone's removed it? Has Martha removed it? I think we should ask Keith to have a dig around – see what we can find out about her.'

'I'll call the ever-efficient DI Sims while you call the boss, then I should probably update you on my chat with the victim's sister, Sara Osborne.'

Becky nodded her agreement, and as Rob asked to be put through to Keith she broke the news to Tom that they hadn't been able to access Martha's computer and so didn't have the pass code to Genevieve's mobile.

Tom muttered something about them wasting too much time on this, and maybe the digital team would have more success breaking into the phone. Becky couldn't argue with that, but she had to wonder why there was so much mystery around Martha Porter.

'Keith's on the case,' Rob said as he ended his call. 'Low key for now – she's not a suspect, although it's odd that as soon as she heard about Genevieve she disappeared. The two things are probably entirely unrelated. I bet we find out she's gone to the post office for some stamps.'

Becky was about to ask Rob to tell her what Sara Osborne had had to say when the door opened and Spencer came in, balancing two mugs and what looked like a plate of expensive home-made biscuits.

'We get these in for the staff – fresh every day. These little treats mean a lot, we think.' He gave a self-satisfied smile as he put the plate down, but there was still a quiver at the corner of his mouth, and Becky could see they were making him nervous.

'Thank you, Mr Johansson. Any news about an address for Martha?'

Spencer shook his head. 'No one has ever been invited to her home. A couple of people have tried to be friendly and asked where she lives. She said she has a house in Winton but wasn't specific. She doesn't have a car, but no one has ever seen her at the bus stop, and we're a bit of a way from a tram route.'

'Do you think you could have a look in her desk? Would you be okay with that? She might have something in there with her address or phone number.'

Spencer nodded, a little more enthusiastically than the situation warranted.

'Of course. Do you want me to do it now?'

Becky looked longingly at the coffee and biscuits.

'Could you give us five minutes, please? And thanks for the biscuits.'

'*De nada,*' he said with a little wave of his hand. He backed towards the door as if he didn't dare take his eyes off them. Perhaps he thought they might put a coffee cup on the table, ignoring the coasters that he'd thoughtfully provided. But finally he was gone.

'*De nada?*' Rob said, grinning at Becky. 'I think Mr Johansson believes himself to be too cool for school. I'm surprised he didn't say "Ciao for now" when he went out.'

Becky chortled. 'Good biscuits, though,' she said, taking a bite. 'Tell me about the sister.'

'Well, she was upset – how could she not be? But I'd say she handled it pretty well. Shocked, but she was coherent at least. I got the impression that they weren't particularly close, but not because they'd fallen out. More because their lives and values were so different.'

'What do you mean?'

'Sara Osborne lives in a perfectly nice, ordinary house. It wasn't dirty, but unlike her sister's, you could tell people lived in it. She has three small boys, and her husband manages the home-decorating department of a DIY superstore. She said that she had never understood her sister's priorities. Apparently Sara wasn't allowed to visit what she called "Strachan Towers" with the children for fear they would make a mess.'

Was that down to Genevieve, or Niall? Becky wondered.

'Did she say her sister was worried about anything, or anyone?'

'I got the impression there *was* something, but when I pushed her she shook her head as if she thought it was her imagination. I said it didn't matter how off the wall it sounded, but she just said Genevieve sometimes got daft ideas in her head and didn't seem to understand that Niall was totally tied up in making the business work. He didn't have time to give her all the attention she craved – she'd *always* craved, were her exact words.'

'So the marriage wasn't rock solid?'

Rob pulled a pensive face. 'She didn't go that far, but she said that, according to Genevieve, Niall couldn't afford to piss her off.'

'That sounds interesting. What the hell does it mean?'

'She didn't know. I think when she's had a bit of time to process all this, I'll go back and talk to her again, see if I can dig a bit deeper. I could see from time to time a vacant look in her eyes, as if she was remembering Genevieve and not focusing on my questions.'

A knock on the door interrupted any further discussion. A young Chinese girl with purple hair and several facial piercings popped her head round. 'Spencer told me to come and find you,' she said. 'If you want me to access Martha's computer, I'll give it a go. Don't suppose it'll be difficult.'

Without waiting for their response, she turned and went back to the outer office.

Becky looked at Rob's raised eyebrows as he watched the girl leave.

'That's one of the "tech boys", is it?' he said. 'Sexism is alive and kicking at XO-Tech, it seems.'

Becky grinned. 'I guess we'd better follow her, then.'

11

MARTHA

Alfie has fallen asleep, cuddled up next to me on the bed in our hotel room. I don't know how I'll be able to explain to him what's happening, but for now he thinks we're having a little holiday.

'We'll be back in time for school, won't we? I like school,' he said, and I felt for him. I'd liked school too, and I don't want Alfie to suffer because of my shortcomings. I need him to have the best life he can. He only has one parent, and that's the way I want it to be. But this one parent has to give him everything he might need, which includes security, and right now I'm a danger to him.

If the police find me, not only will they question me about Genevieve's death, they might want to know more about me. They will discover the black hole that is the past life of Martha Porter, and I have no idea what might happen then. If I'm detained for questioning, arrested, charged, Alfie will have no one. Social services will take him. They will want to know about his father, but I won't tell them. For me there is only one thing worse than my son spending his childhood in care, and that's spending his life with his father. My throat tightens at the thought.

I slowly extricate myself from Alfie's grip, moving a pillow into my place so he has something to cling to, and cross to the TV, switching it on and turning the volume down low.

It's the lunchtime local news, and it's not long before I see streets that I recognise, a house that I know belongs to Niall and Genevieve. I perch on the end of the bed, holding my breath to hear what is being said.

'The body of a thirty-two-year-old woman was found in the early hours of this morning by her husband,' the newsreader says. 'The deceased is believed to be Genevieve Strachan, and her husband is Niall Strachan, owner of an up-and-coming software company, XO-Tech. Detective Chief Inspector Tom Douglas of the Greater Manchester Police was unable to give out any details at this time, but said that enquiries are progressing well. At the moment we have no more information about this shocking crime.'

My mouth floods with saliva and for a moment I think I'll be sick. I drop my head towards my knees until the feeling passes and I have calmed slightly. I need to know more.

I pull my mobile from my bag and log on to Facebook. I don't have an account in my name, and the one I've set up can't be tied to me. I've used someone else's photo – carefully chosen to fit in with the story I have woven about myself. I have made friends with a few people who seem careless about who they accept into their network, and created some random posts about clubs in and around Manchester that appear to be favoured by the C-list. I've neither seen nor visited any of them.

I was sure this fake persona would appeal to Elise, so I asked her to be my friend. She accepted, of course, believing this mythical person to be right at the heart of Manchester's nightlife scene.

Elise is not the only person I've targeted. I've identified gossips in all the narrow circles to which I'm loosely connected, including mothers of children at Alfie's school. I need to know what they're saying, particularly if it involves me or my son.

I go straight to Elise's timeline, knowing she would have had to share her 'inside knowledge' of Genevieve's death with her friends. I'm right.

> AWFUL news this morning. My boss's wife is dead. MURDERED, would you believe? I can't stop crying. I can't say anything else just yet – too upset – and I don't want to give away any crucial evidence. The police will want me to share everything I know with them first. I'll be back with more as soon as I can.

There were no signs of tears when I saw her, but I know her game. She wants people to beg her for details, and they do just that.

> 'How awful! What happened?'
> 'What was she like?'
> 'Are you okay, Elise?'
> 'Dish the dirt, Elise – come on! Don't keep us hanging on!'

What is wrong with people?
Elise must have decided to wait for a while – probably because she wanted to build up anticipation – and her next post offers a pathetic and transparent apology.

> I'm so sorry. I shouldn't have posted anything about this dreadful crime, and I only started because I wanted to share the devastating news. I had to stop. I was too upset to go on typing and I've had to take something to calm me down – something legal, of course :-)

Why is she posting smiley faces in the middle of news about a murder?

> Genevieve was a friend of mine on Facebook and I've been checking out what some of her other friends have to say. I

don't know this for sure, but I've heard she was knifed loads of times – sounds like a frenzy to me. And she was such a lovely person. I'm sorry – I'll have to stop again for a while.

I close my eyes and try to control my breathing. Elise couldn't stand Genevieve – said she was a stuck-up bitch, although she was sugary sweet to her face.

I know I'm focusing on this trivia to block other thoughts from my mind – those that haunt me every minute of the day. But it doesn't work. My head is full of images. I'm staring at a knife in my hand. I smell blood, I hear a voice whispering in my ear, 'You did what you had to do.'

How did it come to this? How did I become a woman who can't tell a soul who she is for fear of what might happen?

Who am I?

12

LAKESIDE

After Mum's little pep talk in the back seat of our new car, I tried to be less sulky. I wasn't happy, but something told me I was making things worse for them. It must have been instinct, because I'm sure at ten years old I wasn't wise enough to work that out for myself.

Mum told me that Dad had been to look at some houses – we were in Lincolnshire, apparently – and he thought Lakeside would be perfect for us.

'Where's Lincolnshire? Is it still in England?'

'Yes, of course it is. And it's got beaches too, so you'll love it.'

I'd never been to the seaside. Holidays hadn't been an option, and for a moment I felt a bit brighter. But it wouldn't be so much fun playing in the sand and the sea without my friends.

'Are there no nice houses in London?'

Dad couldn't turn round because he was driving his new car – very carefully. He called out his answer above the gentle hum of the engine. 'Houses in London are expensive. If we'd bought somewhere special, we wouldn't have had much left, so I came here, where we can get a lot more for our money. Wait until you see what we've bought, sweetheart. It's *huge*! And there's loads of money left to live on for the rest of our lives.'

I wanted to ask why we needed such a huge house when we didn't have any friends to invite, but I kept that thought to myself as we rounded a bend and saw a high wall in front of us, with a rusting gate hanging from one hinge.

'And here we are!' Dad's voice was crackling with excitement. 'We need to do some work on it to bring it up to how it should be, but I thought it would give us something to focus on, now we don't have to go out to work each day. What do you think?'

He steered the car through the gateway, and I was struck dumb. The house was enormous, with a winding drive covered in weeds leading up to the front door. On one side I could make out what looked like a lake, and I couldn't even see the other side of the garden for all the bushes. Later I discovered there was a river there.

Mum was quiet too, and I saw Dad cast an anxious glance in her direction.

'You okay?' he asked.

'It seems so much bigger than it did in the picture,' she whispered.

'I know, but look at it! The brickwork is beautiful, and we have steps up to the front door. It looks like a palace to me. But if you don't like it…'

Mum reached across and touched his arm. 'It's beautiful, Joel. I agreed with your choice, even though I only saw the photos, and if we don't like it we can always find somewhere else and sell it. Let's just enjoy it.' She stroked his arm and smiled.

'Okay.' I could tell Dad was worried that his wonderful plan had somehow failed.

'I think it's brilliant, Dad,' I said. 'I can't wait to explore.'

He grinned with delight that at least I seemed to be pleased, and I was glad because he was usually so cheerful, and I didn't want to spoil that.

He stopped the car in front of the door and pulled a bunch of keys from his pocket. 'Wait until you see inside,' he said, waving the keys in the air. He jumped out.

Mum turned and smiled at me before opening her door to follow him. 'Come on, DeeDee. Let's see what we make of our new home.'

Dad pushed open the huge front door. It gave a loud creak, and we stepped slowly inside, almost as if we were afraid to enter. Was this house really ours? It was vast. A palace. A space that even I could see was far too big for three people. I walked round with my mouth hanging open. Our voices echoed in the empty rooms, the ceilings so high that I wouldn't have been able to touch them even if I stood on Dad's shoulders. I wandered off down a dark corridor and stepped into a room with floor-to-ceiling windows that looked out over an untamed, overgrown garden, thick with what I was later told were brambles.

Suddenly I felt alone, isolated. I couldn't hear their voices any more, and I hurried back along the corridor, scared that I would be lost forever in this enormous house.

I was just about to panic when I heard Dad's voice. I followed the sound. He was talking to Mum, trying to convince her that it wasn't too big, making noises about a cinema room, a snooker room, a gym and a kitchen to die for. He liked to cook, as did Mum, although they had completely different styles. Dad laced his food with every spice he could afford to buy, while Mum's meals spoke of her family background of roast dinners and holidays in Italy. I understood why they might enjoy a big kitchen, but why did we need all those other rooms?

I couldn't help asking, and Dad crouched down by my side.

'Well, maybe we'll have to fill the house with more people. What do you say, DeeDee?'

I didn't know what he meant, but he turned and winked at Mum, who bent down so her face, pale with the stress of the day, was level with mine.

'We never had enough money for a sister or brother for you,

sweetheart. But now we can afford a whole tribe of children.' She squeezed me, and I saw a look pass between her and Dad. They shared a secret smile, and suddenly everything felt better. 'We've got plenty of time to fill the place.'

I knew what she meant about time. Mum had me when she was eighteen. She never hid the fact that her parents – whom I'd never met – had thrown her out when she decided to go ahead and have Dad's baby. Dad wasn't suitable father material, in their eyes, and I was never sure if it was because of the colour of his skin, which even at the tender age of ten I was aware could cause baffling hostility in some people, or because he had been brought up in care and had no real education.

A joke that Mum and Dad often shared when one of them said something the other didn't agree with was, 'What would they say at the golf club?' According to Mum, her parents had had to choose between supporting their daughter's choice of partner or being the butt of derisive remarks at their smart golf club. The golf club won. If she was having the baby, she had to leave.

But now, at just twenty-eight, Mum had lots of time for more children and plenty of money to look after them all.

'You'll see, DeeDee – the house will soon be full of people. You'll love it,' Dad said.

He was right about one thing. It took a while, but eventually the house *was* full of people. And I didn't love it one little bit.

13

Tom was standing in the middle of the incident room talking to Keith Sims when Becky and Rob returned. He glanced at Becky's face and sensed from her frown that things hadn't gone the way she'd expected at the offices of XO-Tech.

He nodded to Keith. 'Let's get the team together and pool our intel. Give Becky and Rob a chance to grab a coffee, then we'll chat about what we've got – or not got, which is probably more to the point. I'll be back in a few minutes.'

Keith nodded, and Tom moved to a quiet part of the room, pulling out his phone to call Louisa.

'Hi, darling. I just thought I'd check in with you, make sure you and Harry are okay. Sorry I left in the middle of the night, and I'm even sorrier to say that I don't know when I'll be back.'

'That's fine,' she said. He could hear the smile in her voice, and he was sure she was looking at Harry. There was a certain tone to her voice when she gazed at him. 'There's something you need to know, although I debated whether it would wait until you're home.'

Tom felt a flash of alarm at her tone. 'What?'

'Don't panic – it's not bad. Well, not bad for us. Lucy's on her way home, as is Kate.'

Kate was Tom's ex-wife, and Lucy their fourteen-year-old daughter. Kate had met a man when she was on a cruise, and promptly decided to marry him and move to Australia, taking a reluctant Lucy with her.

'What's happened?' Tom looked behind him to where the team were taking their seats. 'Actually, can we talk in a while? As long as no one's hurt and Lucy's okay, I guess it will wait.'

'She's fine, Tom. I would have called you if there had been a problem. Lucy's a bit cross with Kate. She FaceTimed on your home laptop this morning and I answered. I'll fill you in later. Get back to solving crimes, love. It can wait.'

Tom could only imagine how Lucy must feel. She'd been at a new school in an unfamiliar country for a matter of months, and now it was all change again. Against Tom's advice, Kate had sold her house, so it wasn't clear where she was planning to live. But he pushed all this to the back of his mind and walked over to the meeting table.

'Becky, Rob, any progress since you called?'

'Not a fat lot,' Becky said with a disgruntled sigh. 'We got into Martha Porter's computer – well, a girl with purple hair whose fingers whizzed over the keyboard faster than my eyes could follow got into the computer.'

'What did she find?'

'Almost nothing. Every folder was password-protected. Bao – the techie girl – said that breaking into individual folders was a step up from accessing the computer. We've asked Niall Strachan's business partner, Spencer Johansson, if he could look through the paper files in Martha's filing cabinet to see if there's a list of the mobile passwords.'

Tom thought it highly unlikely that a tech firm would hold extensive paper records, but they could live in hope.

'Given how crucial we believe the password to be, and given that we've got bugger all else to go on,' Becky continued, 'I explained that we needed to get our own digital forensics team to access the files on Martha's computer, and Johansson agreed. It's with them now.'

Tom nodded. It was the right decision.

'There was one interesting thing. We asked Spencer to look through Martha's desk, and in the top drawer he found her company mobile. She'd left it behind when she went out, which apparently she's not supposed to do. Switched off, of course, and no one knows the password.'

'Course they don't,' Tom said with a groan. 'That would be too bloody easy by far. Do we know if Martha Porter had any kind of relationship with Genevieve Strachan? Was she devastated, maybe, when she discovered she was dead?'

Becky shook her head. 'Not that we know of. I was starting to get concerned that we were wasting time chasing her for one scrap of information, but now I'm not sure. Why did she disappear, and why is there no record of her address, or anything else for that matter, in the files?'

Tom turned towards Keith. 'Have we got anywhere at all with tracking her down?'

'Absolutely nowhere, sir. As far as we've discovered, she has no driving licence or passport, not even a National Insurance number. We haven't committed a lot of resources to this so far – it didn't seem like a priority – but there are no obvious traces of her.'

'Christ, that's all we need. An invisible person. How the hell did they pay her wages without her NI number? Becky?'

'Johansson says she invoiced them as a contractor, so she was never on the payroll.'

'Marvellous! But I don't think we can justify going through her finances just because she's not in her office and we can't access her computer. Let's see what else we've got before we make a decision.'

Rob had been rocking back on his chair, but he now brought the front legs down with a crash. 'Apparently she knows everything there is to know about that company. What if there's some kind of corporate crime involved? Perhaps she'd been stealing information about the company, and knowing the police were bound to investigate because of Genevieve's death, she thought she'd better make a run for it. Or maybe someone's killed her too.'

The thought that she might be another victim had occurred to Tom, but from what he'd heard, that made little sense. Martha had come into the office that morning as usual, gone into her room and locked the door, before leaving via the private stairway. They had no reason to believe anything had happened to her. Rob's other suggestion – that she was involved in something illegal – seemed more plausible.

'We know she left her company mobile, so does that mean she has another one?'

'There's nothing registered in her name,' Keith said.

Somehow that came as no surprise, and Tom was worried they were wasting a lot of time on Martha Porter, who was more than likely irrelevant. She wasn't a suspect, but her disappearance had to be a concern. He parked the thought for now, keen not to get distracted.

'Let's make sure we're informed if she turns up. In the meantime, what – if anything – have we got from the scene-of-crime guys?'

'Dr Osoba is going to give his report later, sir,' Keith said. 'They haven't found much in the way of trace evidence on the victim's clothes yet. The blood on her husband's clothes is consistent with his claim that he tried to revive her. No spatter, just smears. They're still searching the vicinity for whatever she was hit over the head with and, hopefully, the knife. He said if there were any red flags, he'd call you straight away.'

'Okay, we'll have to wait and see what he has to say. Have they finished in the house yet?'

'Yes, sir. Mr Strachan is being escorted back there now from Swinton divisional offices.'

'Good. I'll go and see him again, have another chat now he's back on home territory. Rob, can you send me everything you have on the Tyldesley Loopline before I leave, please? We need to know all possible access points. Becky, you're with me. And wear something sensible on your feet. We're going for a walk.'

14

Tom had opted to let Becky drive. Over the years he had come to enjoy the faint sense of terror he experienced as she approached each corner at speed.

'I think we should have another look at the scene in full daylight and take a walk along the Loopline. It's closed to the public, and it would be good to get a feel for it and check out the access points before we speak to Mr Strachan.'

Becky pulled up on the main road just beyond the entrance to the Strachans' drive, and they set off down the path. It was a sticky day, but the passageway acted as a wind tunnel, and a warm breeze blew towards them.

'I bet it's wicked here in the winter,' Becky said.

Tom looked at the high walls of the adjoining gardens. There was nowhere for the air to go, so it was forced to howl along this narrow alley, which was still cordoned off by police tape. It felt slightly uncomfortable to be walking over a spot where only a few hours earlier a dead body had lain.

At the end of the passage were steep steps down to the Loopline. A police officer stood guard at the bottom; he stepped back to let Tom and Becky onto the wide tarmac path.

'Have you had many people trying to get access?' Tom asked.

'Quite a few, sir. They've all turned back without too much moaning, though. Mainly being nosey, I think.'

Tom nodded. The officer was no doubt right, although lots of people must use this path regularly. He turned to look up and down the Loopline, the route of the long-dismantled railway, and could understand why it attracted walkers and cyclists. Overhanging trees thick with glossy green leaves cast deep shadows on the ground, and birdsong softened the hum of traffic from the nearby East Lancashire Road. The steps leading down to the track had a narrow groove down one side, presumably to accommodate bicycle wheels.

Tom pointed to the steps on the opposite side of the path. 'What's up there?' he asked the officer.

'An unmade path through a field, sir. It's cordoned off too. Dr Osoba's team have already searched there – at least as far as the fence.'

Tom nodded his thanks to the officer, walked towards the steps and ran to the top. Ahead, almost obscured by the leaves of an old sycamore tree, was a wooden gate beyond which he could see post-and-wire fencing on either side of the path, presumably to prevent walkers from straying into the adjacent fields.

He walked back down the steps. 'We need to check access to that field, Becky. There are no houses up there. Based on Rob's hastily drawn map, the field backs onto the main road. We need to know if there's parking nearby, because our killer could have left a car there, jogged along the path that cuts through the field, down these steps and up the other side towards the Strachans' house. A matter of a couple of minutes, I'd have thought.'

He stood still for a moment longer, looking around, then nodded to Becky and set off along the leafy path. 'Come on. Let's go and find Jumbo.'

'Pretty along here, isn't it?' Becky said, a note of surprise in her voice.

'It is – at least, in daylight. But imagine it in the early hours of the morning. Even if there was a moon those trees would block out what little light was available and dampen any ambient sound. With the high banks on each side it would feel like a tomb. You'd have to be fearless to walk along here at night.'

'Or desperate.'

With that thought, they walked side by side in silence to where, up ahead, Tom could see the substantial figure of Jumbo talking to another white-suited member of the team. He turned at Tom's approach. 'We're starting with the area closest to the path, checking for bike tracks, footprints. We may even get lucky and find one of the weapons.'

Tom nodded. 'If it were me, I'd have taken them with me and disposed of them somewhere far away from here, but we know murderers are not always rational. The trouble is, the blunt-force trauma to her head could have been caused by a branch from one of these trees, and there are bound to be a few broken ones lying around.'

At that moment there was a jubilant shout from a CSI up ahead, standing over a culvert where a small stream crossed under the path.

Without a word, Jumbo spun on his heel and hurried towards the man, who was pointing at something with his gloved hand. As Tom and Becky caught up, Jumbo beamed at them.

'A knife! See, Tom? Not all murderers are smart!'

Without touching the railings, they looked over the side. Another CSI had already climbed down and was taking photos of the knife *in situ* just under the bridge, on a ledge.

'It's out of the water,' Jumbo said breathlessly and somewhat unnecessarily, but Tom knew why he was excited. With any luck that meant there would still be traces of blood so they could match it to the victim. And there was always the faint hope there might be fingerprints.

Despite rain the day before, there was little more than a trickle in the culvert and it seemed to Tom it wasn't the smartest place to chuck a murder weapon. If the killer had thrown it right under the bridge, into the dark recesses where the stream bed was full of pebbles, it would have been harder to spot.

'If it turns out it's the murder weapon, then it tells us he came this way. Whether on foot or on a bike we still don't know,' Tom said. About fifty metres ahead, a road passed over the path. 'I know this area. Do you remember the girl we found in the woods a few years ago?'

'Oh God, yes,' Becky said. 'That was awful. The poor kid.'

He lifted one hand to point. 'That road goes right past the woods where we found her. Maybe that's how Genevieve's killer got here.'

It would have been easy for him to park close to the entrance to the Loopline, then run down the steps and along the path to the end of the alley where the body was found. It was no more than a couple of hundred metres.

But why did she go out, and why did someone want to kill her?

He had no answers, and until they understood more about their victim, her relationships, her friends, her marriage, they didn't have a single line of enquiry to pursue.

15

MARTHA

I've been so absorbed in my thoughts about who I am and what I have become that I hadn't noticed Alfie has woken up, but suddenly I realise he's staring at me. Those beautiful eyes of his seem able to penetrate my thoughts, so I close my mind to what I have been thinking.

'You hungry, sweetheart?'

Alfie nods. 'Cos we're on holiday, can I have pizza please, Mummy?'

I don't know what we can have, because I'm not prepared to leave the room.

'It's going to be more exciting than that,' I say, trying to make him feel that room service is a delight to look forward to. 'We get to choose from a menu, and then someone will bring it to our room. How about that, Alfie?'

He's at that age when my tone of voice and fake excitement can still work magic, but I know the time is coming when he'll question me more than he has done up to now. The thought of what he might ask terrifies me. I don't want to lie to my child, but there's so much I can't tell him.

I know that one day he will want to know about his father, and maybe want to meet him. That's when I will have to lie, because it can never happen. I'm surprised he's not asked already, but the only time he's shown any interest he simply asked if he had a daddy. I'd answered, 'No, Alfie. There's just me,' and that had seemed enough for him. It won't be for long, though.

I push the thought aside as I show him the menu, and we talk through the options. Pizza is on the list, and while we wait for it to arrive, I guiltily settle him down in front of the TV and pull out my phone. I head straight for Elise's Facebook page.

It's all hotting up! There's a woman who works here who's fixated on Niall – our boss and Genevieve's husband! She tried it on with him at the office party, and he was horrified by the whole thing. Anyway, she arrived at work this morning, but when we said the police were coming to investigate – you'll never guess what? She did a runner! Guilty as sin, I'd say. What do you think?

I close my eyes. Now everyone will wonder what happened at the party. I can still see Niall's face, so close to mine; his hands on my hips, the expression in his eyes. Spencer had seen me run from the room, but I hadn't said a word. I'd been trying to control my panic. I didn't want to lose my job – I was managing my life to the best of my ability, and everything had been okay. I had been confident I could remain at XO-Tech with no questions asked for the foreseeable future. And then I'd messed up.

It was never mentioned again, but Niall made a show in front of everyone of asking to have the door left open if he was in a room with me, walking out of rooms if I came in. I could see what he was doing: he wanted people to think he was uncomfortable being alone with me.

There's a knock at the door, and my hand jerks, my mobile clattering to the floor. Then I hear a faint voice: 'Room service.'

Even though I've ordered food, I take care to look through the peephole, certain that this is a trick. But it's a young girl holding a tray, so I breathe again and open the door.

How long am I going to have to carry on living in fear? Will there ever be a time when I can walk down the street, smile at people, invite them to our home? Or will I forever be the woman who has to check the peephole in every door, change SIM cards in my phone so I can't be traced, and hide from the world?

16

LAKESIDE

Our first Christmas at Lakeside – a name which even I thought lacked imagination – was difficult. We'd been in our new home for over a month, and it still felt strange. I had a huge bedroom next to Mum and Dad's, and they'd told me I could decorate it any way I liked. I wanted every wall to be lilac, and it had been fun for a while as I helped Dad slap on some paint.

None of the plans for the downstairs rooms that Dad had talked about had come to much. He'd asked Mum to choose which one to decorate first, and I'd found her more than once sitting on a wooden kitchen chair in a cold empty room, a faraway look on her face. But she hadn't managed to come to a decision about any of them by the end of the year.

Mum and Dad both tried to make Christmas exciting for me with an enormous tree in the double-height hall, and they had hidden my Christmas presents. I think Dad was disappointed when I told him I didn't believe in Father Christmas any longer. I hadn't for a year or two, but until then it had been more fun to pretend he was real. The treasure hunt took ages, and we all scurried around the house following Dad's clues, then sat down to a delicious turkey dinner. We'd only been able to afford chicken in the past, but this time we had everything you could dream of for a traditional Christmas.

The strange thing was that Mum had bought everything ready-prepared from the supermarket, and that was so unlike her. She had always loved to cook, and looking back I realise now that this was the start of her problems. Even as a child of ten I could tell she was missing the friends and neighbours who would come knocking on the door bearing a bottle of cheap wine or a few cans, usually with some home-made mince pies to share. Or even a bag of crisps. We didn't care. Everyone was welcome. Who would have thought that our good fortune with the lottery would change all that?

In Lincolnshire there was no one. It was just us, and it was as if Mum didn't think it was worth the bother to cook everything from scratch. Dad had tried to persuade her to join in with a few activities in the village, to make new friends, but she said she didn't want people asking questions, knowing our business.

'What do I say when people ask what I do for a living – or what you do? If I don't have an answer, they'll guess, and then the trouble will start. It will be like it was in London.'

I had no friends either because I hadn't started a new school. As it was my final year at primary school, Mum said she would home-school me until the summer. Come September, I could go straight to secondary school.

It never happened.

Dad worked hard to get me and Mum excited about the year ahead, and on New Year's Eve he got us all to sit down and talk about what we were most hoping for in the next twelve months. I knew he wouldn't want the truth from me – that I wanted to go home – and I could see the concern in his eyes when he looked at Mum, so I did as he asked and pretended to be enthusiastic. Mum was harder to persuade, but he tried.

'Nic, let's start planning our new kitchen as soon as the

holiday's out of the way,' he said, grabbing a pen and paper. 'We'll make a list of all the things you've ever wanted in a kitchen, and then we can go and look at some showrooms. How does that sound?'

Mum tried to play along, but I could see she wasn't excited. Later, I heard her talking to Dad about her feelings and although I knew I shouldn't have been listening, I wanted to understand what was wrong.

'The house is great, Joel. A fantastic choice and I'm honestly thrilled with it all, but it's such a big change. I need a bit of time to adapt. I'm sorry, darling.'

'It's what you deserve, though. Before you met me, you never had to worry about where the next meal was coming from. You gave all that up – for me! Now it's my chance to put that right, and you never know – your family might even change their minds about us – about me.'

Mum laughed, but I could tell she didn't think it was funny.

'I don't want them back in my life. Not after the way they treated you. And they disowned their own daughter, Joel. Can you imagine me ever doing that to DeeDee? It just feels strange not to have to go to work or worry about whether we can afford to buy Christmas presents for our child.'

'I get that, but when we moved to London you adapted so well. You went from a kid going to private school to a mother working as a cleaner to help pay the bills. Now you can change again – have anything you want.'

Mum sighed. 'I didn't adapt, though – at least not at first. I fell apart. You know I did.'

'But you got there in the end, Nic.'

'Look, I know it's difficult for you to understand, but all my life I've had *rules*. Growing up, there was a code of conduct. We laugh about "What will they say at the golf club?" but I knew exactly what I was supposed to do, how each day would pan out. I did what was expected of me.'

'That sounds brutal.'

'Maybe, but once all of that structure was gone, it felt as if the rug had been pulled from under my feet. After we moved to London, I was in a daze for months – wondering what I was supposed to do, how I was expected to behave.' Mum's voice was rising as she spoke, getting more and more agitated. 'But I had a baby that needed me. If we wanted to eat, we both had to work, so I created my *own* rules, my *own* structure. Now I'm back to that lost feeling, as if I'm floating with nothing to anchor me. I no longer have a code of conduct that tells me what's expected. There is nothing I absolutely *have* to do each day.' There was a pause, and when she spoke again, her voice was quieter, but shaky. 'I'm so sorry, love. It's not your fault. I need some time to acclimatise, that's all. I'll get there, I promise.'

I heard Dad's deep voice, whispering all kinds of lovely things about how he adored her, and he would do whatever she wanted. And I knew he would, if only he knew what that was. She swore she didn't want to go back to our old life. She just needed to find some meaning in this new life of ours.

I had no idea what she meant.

The early part of the new year passed quietly, with Dad treading softly around Mum, who was doing her best to smile. She hadn't found whatever it was she was looking for, until one day she read an article in the local paper.

'Listen to this, Joel,' she said. 'There's a man coming to the area to give a talk. According to the write-up, he's inspirational. It says he's helped many people make the best of their lives.'

'Mmm. Sounds like a good line in sales talk, don't you think?'

'I don't know, but it might be worth going along to find out.'

'You've said you don't want to get to know people in the village. So why the change of heart?'

Mum scrunched up the paper and chucked it on the floor. 'Fine. I won't go then.'

Dad looked up from one of the DIY books he'd taken to reading, as if we couldn't afford to pay builders to do all the work.

'Sorry, Nic. I didn't mean to be dismissive.'

Mum bent down to pick up the paper again and flattened the pages.

'I know what I've said about the village. But he's not coming to *this* village. It's about twenty miles away, so no one would know me.'

Dad nodded. It was the most enthusiastic we'd seen Mum for a while, and I could see he was mustering his best smile. He put his book down. 'Tell me about it. What's he going to be talking about?'

'The title of the talk is "No one saves us but ourselves", and the subtitle is "Why no one is ever satisfied with who they are". It sounds just what I need, Joel. I know I'm lucky in so many ways – I have you and DeeDee, which should be enough for anyone. And we have this fabulous house and all that money. But yet I don't seem to be able to – I don't know – *find* myself, I suppose, if that doesn't sound too pretentious.'

'Of course it doesn't. If it's what you want, then go, by all means.'

And she did.

I didn't see her when she got back that night. It was late, and I was in bed. But the next morning I woke to the sound of her singing and the smell of bacon cooking. I ran downstairs without bothering to get dressed, and there was Mum in the kitchen, smiling, make-up on, looking like the Mum I had known for the first ten years of my life.

'Morning, DeeDee,' she almost sang. Dad looked up from where he was sitting and gave me a smile. But he looked slightly mystified.

'Put something nice on today,' she said. 'We're having a visitor!'

'Who?' I asked, and I remember how delighted I was that finally we might be getting back to the life I had always understood.

'The man who gave the talk last night. I had a long chat with him at the end of the evening. He was *brilliant*! Anyway, I asked if he might have some time to spare, and he said he was hoping to stay in the area for a few weeks, so I invited him to lunch.'

We spent the morning in a flurry of activity. We hadn't done much to the house, even though by that time we'd been there for several months. It was mainly due to Mum's lack of interest, but now she wanted everything to be perfect.

Finally, the moment came, and I heard a car draw up. I looked out of my bedroom window, expecting to see a car rivalling Dad's, but I was wrong. It was a minicab.

Out of the car stepped a man, and from where I was standing at the window, he looked ordinary. He was tall with closely cropped dark hair, and was perhaps a few years older than Dad. He picked up his bag from where the driver had put it by the steps that led to the front door, turned slightly and lifted his chin to reveal an equally close-cropped beard. He stood still for a moment and seemed to be listening. But then he slowly raised his head and looked straight at me. His pale grey eyes narrowed as they met mine. His lips tightened, and I got the distinct impression that he was angry. But I had done nothing.

Suddenly he turned away, towards the door, a smile on his face, and raised his hand in greeting. Mum had gone out to meet him. The spell was broken, and I felt drained, as if I'd been caught doing something I shouldn't. I knew I was supposed to go downstairs, but I didn't want to. I threw myself on the bed and buried my head under my pillow.

17

Becky raised her hand to knock on Niall Strachan's door, but before she made contact, the door was opened by a woman she recognised as a family liaison officer – FLO, as they were more commonly called.

'Hey, Charley – I wasn't expecting to see you here,' Becky said. Charley Hughes normally specialised in cases involving children, and she did a great job of putting them at their ease, so it was a surprise to see her at the home of a bereaved husband.

'I know. It's not my usual type of case, but I was available. Good afternoon, sir,' she said to Tom. 'Niall – as he's asked me to call him – is in the kitchen.'

Tom and Becky both looked at the pale carpet ahead of them, then at each other, and without a word slipped their shoes off. This place reminded Becky of a house she had visited once where there were clear plastic runners everywhere. She couldn't understand why you would want something so precious on the floor that you were scared to walk on it.

As they went into the kitchen, they could see that a built-in bean-to-cup coffee machine was working its magic. Niall was standing by it, pressing buttons. Becky hadn't fully appreciated how tall he was until now. He was well over six feet, and today he looked every bit the successful trendy tech company boss in a crisp white shirt, open at the throat and hanging loose over what had to be designer jeans. However, his thin face looked washed-out, and black brows over hooded eyes made it hard to read their expression.

He turned towards them. 'Coffee?'

'Not for me, thanks,' Tom said.

'I'm fine,' Becky said. 'I'm sure you're glad to be back in your own home, sir, and I'm sorry we had to ask you to leave for a while.'

Niall gave a slight shrug. 'I understand. It's all a bit hard to get my head round, though.' He picked up his coffee and walked over to the wide central island to perch on a stool. 'Please, take a seat.'

Becky hitched herself up onto another stool and glanced at Tom. He gave her a quick nod, clearly wanting her to ask the questions so he could focus on Niall's reactions and check for any hint of guilt in his behaviour.

'I know this will be difficult for you, Mr Strachan,' she began, but he held up a hand.

'Niall, please. It would make me more comfortable.'

Becky nodded and carried on. 'We need to understand why your wife would have left the house in the middle of the night to walk down a pitch-black lane. Maybe you could tell us if this kind of nocturnal rambling was a habit, or whether you think it's strange too.'

Niall closed his eyes and shook his head. 'She wouldn't have been going for a walk. Genevieve exercised hard, but only at the gym. For her, it was a social thing as much as anything. She and her cronies exercised like hell all morning, then cleared off to the nearest wine bar to eat some skinny salad or other, washed down with copious quantities of Chablis. She invariably took a taxi home, which says it all. But it made her happy.'

Becky couldn't decide if this had been said with a hint of bitterness or not. Genevieve hadn't worked – a fact they had already established – and they would need a list of these friends at some point. Maybe alcohol loosened her tongue and she had shared something with her friends that might point to her killer.

'We're still unable to get into her mobile. Have you spoken to Spencer Johansson in the last hour or so?' Becky asked.

'No. He rang, but I rejected the call. I'm not up to speaking to him right now. It's all I can do to speak to you.'

He was pale, that was true, and Becky hadn't missed the fact that his hands were shaking as he placed his coffee on the table. She had given up trying to assess the level of a person's grief; everyone behaved differently. Niall Strachan was in control, but barely.

'He was probably calling to tell you that we went to the office to speak to Martha Porter, as you suggested. But she wasn't there.'

Niall was gazing into his coffee, stirring mindlessly, but his head shot up at Becky's remark.

'Not there? I don't believe Martha has had a single day off since she started two years ago. What's up with her?'

Becky shook her head. 'We don't know. She apparently arrived as usual and then disappeared down the private staircase from your office. No one seems to know where she lives, or anything about her. Is there anything you can tell us?'

Niall looked genuinely shocked.

'I don't know what to say. She occasionally left the office to buy things we needed – stamps, coffee – but she always asked, or should I say *told* us what she was doing. Are you looking for her?'

Tom rested his forearms on the worktop. 'Not actively, no. She's not a key part of the investigation, but we asked Mr Johansson's permission to take her computer from your offices for our technical team to look at. We need to get access to your wife's phone, and the pass codes are on Martha's computer, apparently. In case you're worried, we won't be looking at anything else. I appreciate there may be confidential content relating to your business, so the remit is only to get the password file.'

Niall was looking down again, as if unable to meet either Tom or Becky's eyes.

'You won't have to go through her emails, then?'

'We have no reason to, no. Is there something on there that you're worried about?'

'Not worried, exactly, no. Look, if you don't need to access her emails, that's fine. Forget I asked.'

Niall's phone chose that moment to burst into life. 'It's Spencer again. I think I should take it this time, if you'll excuse me.'

With that, he walked out of the room. Becky turned to look at Tom and raised her eyebrows. No words were necessary.

18

When Niall returned to the kitchen, he looked slightly more pallid than before.

'Spencer says there's no sign of Martha, and she left her office mobile in her drawer. No one's supposed to do that; they're supposed to have it with them at all times. It's how we monitor whether the app is working.'

'I don't profess to understand these things too well,' Tom said, 'but if they're company phones and this new app of yours is on them, doesn't that mean you can extract data from them?'

Niall gave a ghost of a smile. 'We have to protect people's privacy. It's only when they're asked to test a certain function – a specific element of predictive behaviour – that we retain their information. The data is stored, encrypted, on their phones for the main part. It's only in testing phases that we can check up on where they are, what apps they're using, and so on. And they're always made aware of it.'

'But you were able to use your wife's phone to track where she was last night?'

'Yes, but that's only because I'd asked her to test a new feature with her safety in mind.' He pulled a face as he realised how ironic that sounded under the circumstances. 'I've fixed our garage door so it can sense the location of Genevieve's car as it approaches – assuming she has her mobile with her. It opens automatically without her having to stop and wait. I had her location data recorded online for testing.'

'So why wait so long between when you got home and when you checked where she was?' Becky asked.

Niall walked over to the coffee machine again, once more turning his back to Tom and Becky as he pressed a few buttons. The sound of beans grinding masked his words as the aroma of coffee filled the air. Tom was beginning to wish he'd accepted the previous offer.

'I'm sorry, I didn't quite catch that,' he said.

'I said I don't really know. My head was full of the meeting, I suppose. It was a success. The company can go on developing the app, and we've got the funding for the launch. I came home excited, and I just assumed Genevieve had decided not to wait up and had gone to bed. I was pissed off, to be honest. It was a big moment for me. So I poured a Scotch and sat down, mulling things over, wondering how long until we're ready to release the app to the world.' His coffee ready, Niall returned to the counter and sat down again. 'After a while I decided to wake her. I was sure she'd want to know, so went upstairs. She wasn't there. I was a bit cross that she'd gone out again.'

'Where did you think she could have gone at that time of night?'

He shrugged. 'I don't know. I spoke to her at eleven, and that's not that late, is it? I thought perhaps one of her mad friends had called to say they were at a fantastic party and she'd ordered a cab to pick her up. I tried to call her, but of course there was no answer.'

Tom was finding all of this a little far-fetched. But maybe he was out of touch. Maybe people *did* decide to go out on a whim after eleven on a Monday night. Maybe he was just getting old.

'Can I pick up on something you said earlier about your app?' Tom asked.

Niall nodded with a look of surprise.

'You said you had Genevieve's location recorded online – which is how you could check where she was. Does that mean you could also see where she'd been?'

'Yes, but it's not going to tell you anything. It's clear from the data that she was with her sister, then drove home, stayed here for about an hour and then walked down the lane. There's nothing more to know.'

'And how far back does the data go?'

'A couple of weeks, since I asked her to test the app. Why?'

'Because it might be useful for us to know where she'd been in the weeks leading up to her death. It could tell us if something about her movements was out of the ordinary. Could we have a copy, do you think?'

Tom was asking politely, but he would take the data whether Niall liked it or not. It could lead them to discover something she had been doing that involved her killer.

Niall hadn't put up any resistance to sharing his wife's movements and had left the room again, saying he would download the data onto a thumb drive. Charley, who had been sitting quietly in the background, went with him as they needed to be sure he didn't compromise the data, and Niall didn't seem to mind.

Tom had briefed Becky to restart the questioning, and she was happy to oblige. As Niall took his seat and handed the thumb drive to Tom, she opened with something that had been concerning her since that morning.

'I need to ask you a couple more questions about Martha, if that's okay.' Niall shrugged as if it wasn't important. 'When I arrived at the office this morning, a young woman suggested that someone should talk to me about a party – about something that happened that involved Martha.'

Niall tipped his head back with a 'Hah!' and his thin lips curved upwards in a slight smile.

Becky waited.

'The young woman who suggested this would, without a doubt, have been Elise Chapman – although I'm not sure how she knows anything about it.'

'About what, sir?'

'Look, it's a little embarrassing, but it seems Martha got slightly the wrong idea about my feelings towards her. It was unfortunate, but I think I handled it well.'

Becky wasn't sure if that meant Niall had acted inappropriately and Martha had overreacted, or it was the other way round. 'Can you be more specific, sir?'

He sighed as if he didn't want to tell this story, but there was a glint in his eye, as if he was secretly pleased to be sharing the events of that day.

'Just off Martha's office – directly opposite the door into my room – there's a small nook where we've put a few bits of kitchen equipment. We've got a fridge for wine, and Martha likes to be sure we have some slices of lemon and a bucket of ice for gin, especially if we have a meeting that's going on late into the evening. The thing is, this nook is hidden from the outer office even when the door to Martha's room is open.'

Becky was certain she knew where this was going and wished he would cut to the chase.

'We had an office party. Martha was in her cubbyhole, getting some ice, and I went in to tell her to leave it to someone else. She should come and join everyone, and relax. I put my hand on her shoulder – in a friendly way, you know – and she turned towards me, took a step right up to me and rested her hands on my chest. I thought for a moment that she had misunderstood my gesture and was going to push me away, but she wrapped her arms around me and lifted her face to mine. She thought I was going to kiss her.'

Niall stopped.

'And?' Becky asked.

'I explained that I was only being friendly. That I loved my wife and I wasn't interested in anyone else. She turned and ran out of the room – out of the building. Some people saw her go, but I didn't say anything to anyone apart from Spencer. He must have told bloody Elise.'

'And was that the end of it?'

'Not entirely, no. There were a few emails after that. I was worried they could still be on her computer, and your tech guys might find them when they start delving.'

Tom shook his head. 'They're not looking for emails. But perhaps we should take a look, if that would be okay with you? We'll need your permission.'

Niall closed his eyes and groaned softly. 'I wish you didn't have to. It's not important, and I was dealing with it. I tried to avoid being in the same room as her if the door was shut – that kind of thing.'

Becky could only imagine how that might work, given the fact that Martha was the office manager and sat in a room right next to his.

'One last thing, sir. We were also told that Martha had an argument with your wife recently. Do you know what that was about?'

His eyes opened wide. 'I didn't know about that. No one told me, and Genevieve didn't say a word. I'm sorry, I don't have a clue.' He shook his head rather more emphatically than was necessary.

Becky didn't need to look at Tom to know that he didn't believe Niall Strachan any more than she did.

19

MARTHA

My stomach is churning, and I can't blame the pizza. I didn't eat much of it, although Alfie seemed to enjoy it. It tasted like cardboard. I'm too scared to eat. I'm dismayed by Elise's poison, and certain the police will double their efforts to find me.

When I devised my escape plan, I thought the best option would be to stay in a hotel for a few days. I imagined the police scouring CCTV from train and bus stations, looking for me, so I decided it would be best to lie low. But now being in Manchester seems more dangerous than moving on. My chest feels tight with anxiety, and I don't know if it's fear or guilt. I can't wipe from my mind Genevieve's face as she shouted at me, her mouth wide open, her skin flushed with anger.

Surely they can't find me. I haven't used a credit card in the name of Martha Porter; I don't have a registered mobile phone; the taxi dropped me by the hospital rather than the tram stop, and I look nothing like the person who worked for XO-Tech. And yet each time I hear a police siren outside the window, I believe they are coming for me.

There's a part of me that wants to hand myself in, to tell them everything and let them do their worst. The heavy burden I'm carrying would be lifted from my shoulders. Then I look at Alfie's sweet, innocent face and I'm scared for him. In so many ways, I want to stop running, but he has to be my priority.

He is snuggled against me on the small sofa that faces the TV, my left arm holding him tight as he looks at one of his favourite books. Suddenly he makes a tiny moaning sound.

'Hey, baby, what's the matter?' I ask, pulling his hot little body closer.

And then I realise that his body really *is* hot. It's *too* hot. The air in the room is stifling, with ineffective air conditioning and a window that only opens about two inches, so I had assumed it was just the heat of the room.

'I feel funny,' he says.

'What kind of funny, sweetheart? Does your head hurt; do you feel sick?'

He gives a long, drawn-out, 'No.'

I rest my hand on his forehead. It's hot, so I pull away and crouch in front of him. His face is flushed. Maybe it was because I was holding him too tightly.

'Let's get you cooled down a bit.'

I open the door to the bathroom and grab a flannel to run under cold water and return to the room, wiping his hands and face.

'Does that feel better?'

'A bit, but I still feel funny.'

I know there is no point in asking him to be more specific. There have been many times in my life when I have felt not quite right and it hasn't been possible to point the finger at one cause, and he has slept more than usual today. I thought I'd just overstressed him.

'Come on. We'll give you a nice cool bath and see how you feel after that.'

He's listless and whingey, and that's not like Alfie. I bathe him in lukewarm water, but as I kneel on the bathroom floor to dry him, he starts to cry and rests his head on my shoulder. I know if we'd been at home, I would have thought nothing of this. I'd have given him a cold drink and waited to see if it passed. But we're not at home, so what happens if he's ill? *Really* ill?

The first thing is to get his temperature down. If I can do that, I'll know it was nothing much. I won't panic until then. But I'm not taking any risks either.

'I tell you what, Alfie. Let's get you dressed, and we'll go out into the fresh air for a little while. Shall we see if we can find you an ice lolly?'

We will actually go to the nearest chemist, but I don't think that's enough to entice him to leave the room.

'Can I go to bed, please, Mummy?'

I want to weep. I can't leave him here in the hotel room alone. He's five and perfectly capable of opening the door and wandering off. I might only be away for ten minutes, but that's too long.

'We'll get you a lolly, or maybe an ice cream if you like, and then straight back here to bed. How does that sound?'

He doesn't look convinced, but he's such a good boy he gives a sad little nod.

I quickly dress him, not prepared to push my luck with the girly clothes I made him wear earlier. But I put his sun hat on, fluff up my hair and apply some bright lipstick. I'm sure that even if I bumped into Elise on the street, she wouldn't recognise me.

I run a hand over my stomach, as I do so many times a day, to check that my body pocket is there and I can feel the hard plastic of the debit card inside, and I head for the door.

I'm relieved to see that the receptionist who checked us in isn't there. The thought of her seeing me twice makes me nervous.

Anonymity is the key. It always has been. I try to alternate the shops where I buy groceries, use different pharmacies on the occasions that we need them. It was trickier when Alfie was a baby, but as soon as we could, we moved on from where he was born. Now it's only at work – a situation I can't avoid – where I see the same people every day, but I have my own office and I keep my distance – the only defence open to me.

To start with they asked me questions – of course they did – and when they asked if I was married, in a relationship, had children, the answer was always no. Where did I come from? I chose Devon. It's where my mum was from.

The key to remaining anonymous is to do nothing which attracts attention, so as I leave the hotel, I resist the urge to put my head down and rush through the crowded lobby dragging a reluctant Alfie along. I keep my head up, my face wearing a neutral expression.

I walk calmly to the door and out into the muggy air. It's late afternoon, and people are spilling out of offices and straight into the bars that line the streets around here. No one looks at us; they're too intent on downing that first ice-cold drink or getting home to their families. But as we head towards the chemist, which according to my phone is an eight-minute walk, I get the sense that I'm being watched.

I spin round to check behind me, but no one's there. Then I glance to my left. There's a car, pulled up at the traffic lights, window down. The driver is watching me, staring at me. He's young, shaved head, Asian, and for one awful moment I think he's someone I once knew.

My heart thuds. Given all the people who have come into my life over the years, I've always been certain that at least one of them would turn up in Manchester. That's why I keep out of the town centre and remain in my little bubble in a pleasant but unremarkable suburb that is unlikely to appeal to the people I used to know – to the person I used to be.

The lights change, and the car begins to move. I try not to look his way again, but I can't help myself. His hand goes to his mouth, and with an extravagant wave out of the car window, he blows me a kiss. *Was he just flirting or does he know me?*

All I want to do now is get something for Alfie and hurry back to the hotel. I had forgotten how terrifying it is to be out in full view in the centre of a city – a place where someone from my past might find me.

20

LAKESIDE

On that fateful day a few months before my eleventh birthday – the day Mum invited a visitor to our house – she came upstairs to find me. My head was still buried beneath my pillow, where it had been since the moment I had seen the way the man looked at me.

'DeeDee, what's going on?' she asked, concerned that I hadn't come downstairs to greet our guest. She sat down on the bed and rubbed my back.

'Don't call me DeeDee,' I mumbled, my voice muffled by the pillow. 'Not any more, and not – definitely not – if you're going to introduce me to that man.' I pushed the pillow aside, rolled over on the bed and propped myself up on my elbows. 'Promise.'

There was a look of shock on her face. My reaction must have seemed extreme to her, but I couldn't help myself. Little did I know at that moment that she would never call me DeeDee again.

'Okay. I'll use your proper name, and I'll tell Dad. But I don't understand what's upset you.'

'Him. That man. Who is he, Mum, and why does he stare like that?'

She visibly relaxed. 'Oh baby, he's got incredible eyes, I know. When he looks at you, you want to melt, don't you?' She had an expression on her face I hadn't seen before and didn't like much. She reached out and grabbed my hands. 'He can see into people's souls. He understands the cause of everyone's unhappiness, and he works with people to make them feel better about themselves and about life. He's going to help me, sweetheart. You know I've been confused since we've been here, but he understood without me telling him anything.'

She pulled me towards her and wrapped her arms around me. I have to admit that she seemed more relaxed in that moment than she had in a while.

'Come and meet him – listen to what he has to say. Whatever you're feeling, he'll understand, and he won't judge. He says that's the problem with the human race – we've created so many constraints, set so many rules by which we're all supposed to live that it's no surprise we feel like failures all the time. We should relax. We should just *be!*'

I had no idea what she was talking about, but her happiness was rubbing off on me and I was beginning to think I'd overreacted.

I slid off the bed, and Mum stood up and held her hand out. It comforted me to cling to it as we made our way down the wide staircase – as yet still lacking carpet – and into the sparsely furnished living room.

The man had his back to me as I walked into the room, but Dad was facing me and jumped up.

'Ah, here she is! Come and say hello. Aram, meet our daughter—'

'India,' Mum said quickly, giving Dad a quick shake of the head. 'Say hello to Mr Forakis, India.'

The man got up from the sofa and turned towards me. 'Call me Aram, please. I wasn't aware there was a child in the house – but it's a pleasant surprise. It's good to meet you, India, and what a delightful name!'

His voice was deep and mellow, his words unhurried, and at least he didn't say it was a strange name for someone whose roots were obviously in an entirely different continent – a jibe I had heard more than once.

Nevertheless I struggled to lift my eyes to his, which I knew was rude. I could feel his gaze burning two holes in the top of my head, and eventually I looked up. I swallowed. I was expecting to see the same look as earlier, as if my very existence displeased him, but now he was smiling. I must have been wrong.

'Let's all sit down, shall we?' Mum said, her voice overly bright. Dad was looking slightly bemused by the entire thing, but if he had one rule, it was that whatever made Mum happy made him happy too.

'Joel, India, I've asked Aram here because I think he can help me, and perhaps both of you, to understand why I'm not finding this exciting chapter in our lives as fulfilling as I'd hoped. I've been feeling lost, as you know – lacking in purpose – and Aram thinks he might be able to help.' She looked hopefully at both of us. I didn't know what to say, and Dad didn't have the heart to burst her bubble. 'Aram, can tell us how you think you might guide me back to the happy life I had before?'

Aram looked from one to the other of the three people staring hopefully at him. He leaned forward, resting his forearms on his thighs, and smiled gently at Mum.

'I'd like to tell you it will be a quick fix, Nicola, but I'm afraid it won't. I don't have any angel dust I can sprinkle that will transform your lives in half an hour. We *will* find a way, but I'm afraid it will take work, time and a fair degree of patience from your loved ones.' He looked briefly at Dad, but his eyes settled on me. I felt he was asking me a question, and I nodded, not entirely sure what I was agreeing to, but certain it was expected.

Mum's face changed from expectation to alarm. 'I'm happy to

do the work, but I'm sure you'll need to move on from here soon. Will we be able to do what we need to before then?'

Aram dropped his head, his gaze focused on the carpet. Mum was obviously desperate to speak, to try to persuade him, but it was as if she didn't want to break his spell.

After what seemed like minutes but was probably only thirty seconds, Aram spoke.

'I have a number of engagements that I feel obliged to fulfil, but fortunately they're all within an hour's drive of here. I can feel your pain, Nicola, and I can see from your wonderful family that they love you and want you to be happy. You need my help, and whatever I can do for you will be good for Joel and India too. We all need to be in this together.' Once more he looked at Dad, then at me, then back to Mum. 'Can I think about how best we can make this work? I don't want to leave you as you are now – lost and lacking direction. If that means I need to make some sacrifices, then so be it.'

Relief was written all over Mum's face. 'Oh, thank you. Thank you so much. And we have an enormous house here, so if you need somewhere to stay, we can easily put you up, can't we, Joel?'

I looked at Dad, who beamed as if suddenly he could do something useful. 'Yes. Yes, of course. If it's going to make things easier for you, it's no problem. I hope you'll be able to show me what I can do to help Nicola too.'

'We – the human race, that is – have created so many false rules by which we live, and as a result some people find themselves in constant turmoil, wanting to do one thing, but forcing themselves to stick to a code of conduct that tears them apart.' Aram seemed to measure his words. He spoke slowly, as if he thought it would be difficult for Dad to understand. 'I'll need to work with each of you to find out what's constraining you, stopping you from being the real you. To do that, I'll have to strip you back to who you are underneath, explore your *true* values, not those you've been forced to accept.'

I didn't have the first idea what he was talking about, but I could feel a sense of relief in the room, as if Aram was the answer to all of our prayers, and it seemed suddenly that everything was going to be okay.

And then he mentioned me.

'As I said earlier, I hadn't realised there was a child in the house. Beautiful as she is, she'll make things more difficult.'

Mum looked horrified. 'India is a good girl, Aram. She won't cause any trouble.'

He didn't speak, just looked at me, and once again I felt as if he was asking me a question I didn't know the answer to. Was I going to be the one to ruin things for Mum?

'Why do you see a child as a problem?' Dad asked, and I sensed a tinge of irritation in his tone. Aram clearly picked up on it too.

'I'm sure she's a good girl, Joel, but as we go through the process, I need Nicola to be totally focused on her own renewal, not on the demands of a child.'

I was feeling sick. I was the problem. I looked at Dad, who clearly couldn't decide what to do. This man was offering to help Mum get over whatever was causing her unhappiness, but I could see he didn't like the way Aram was talking about me. Mum cast a pleading glance at Dad, then at me.

'I can keep out of the way. I won't bother you, Mum,' I said, my voice cracking with suppressed tears.

I expected her to say I wasn't a bother, but instead she looked at Aram, clearly hoping for his approval.

He stood up and to my surprise came and knelt in front of me, his eyes level with mine. When he spoke, it was as if we were the only two people in the room.

'It's not going to be easy, India. You'll have to respect the process your mother is going through and not make unnecessary demands on her time. Do you think you can do that? Shall we try, together?'

I had been trying not to let anyone see I was crying, but as I looked at Aram my tears dried. I could do this. We could *all* do this.

When Dad spoke, he broke the spell. 'I'll take care of India. It'll be great to spend more time with her. We'll be fine, won't we, sweetheart?' He gave me one of his big beams, and suddenly it felt as if everything was going to be okay.

Aram had accepted our offer of hospitality and cancelled some of his other engagements.

'I go where I'm most needed,' he said. 'And right now I think that place is here.'

There was no doubt that Mum was thrilled with his decision, and his presence in the house had certainly lifted her spirits. When he joined us for meals he talked about how well she was doing, how honest she was being, and praised us for our support. Nevertheless I was conscious of his concern that Mum would be too focused on me, so I tried to keep out of everyone's way. If I saw Aram I scurried off in the opposite direction, anxious not to be seen as a nuisance, so it came as a surprise when he stopped me one day in the hall.

'India, if I'm going to continue to help your mother, as both she and I believe I can, I need to know you better. I need to build the inner strength of those around her, which means you and your father. I've asked your parents if I can spend some time with you, and Joel has suggested maybe we could walk in the garden and talk there. How do you feel about that?'

I wasn't sure. I didn't know what he expected of me.

'It's to help your mother.'

How could I refuse?

For the first few days I noticed that Dad was always somewhere nearby, digging a flower bed or spraying weedkiller on the drive. I know he was watching to make sure I was comfortable, and I was.

Each day I skipped along by Aram's side as we strolled either to the lake or to the river. We were surrounded by water, and I loved being with him as he pointed out the beauty of the wild flowers and the birdsong. I remember him telling me not to be afraid of the water voles. They wanted to live their lives without fear like we all do, so I should let them be and try not to frighten them.

The time with him began to feel like the highlight of each day. My parents were distracted: Dad was anxious about Mum, and although she was much brighter, her thoughts seemed to be anywhere but with me. Meanwhile, Aram made me feel as if he had all the time in the world for me, until one day I thought I had ruined it all.

He was pointing out some wild flowers and asking me to think about their beauty.

'You know a lot about the flowers and birds,' I said. 'Were you brought up in the countryside?'

He stopped walking. 'Never ask anyone for personal information, India. It's impertinent. I thought you would understand that.'

'But I only asked—' I said, horrified that I had done something wrong.

'You asked me something that, had I wanted to, I would have volunteered. It's intrusive. Neither ask for, nor volunteer, information which is irrelevant.'

His tone was mild, but his rebuke stung. He carried on walking, leaving me standing forlornly in the meadow with no idea what I had done wrong.

21

Tom and Becky left Niall in the kitchen drinking yet more coffee, with Charley Hughes on hand should they need to update him or ask him for clarification on any points. They had been through all the usual questions regarding Genevieve's relationships with others, any problems, past partners who may have been giving her trouble. But nothing stood out as important.

Crucially, they had a list of her friends, although Niall had said he didn't see any of them as close confidantes.

'They're a group of women who appear to get together solely for the purpose of competing with each other. Who has the most successful husband? Who has the flashiest house? Who's going on the most exclusive holiday? I never hear talk of anything that's gone wrong in their lives. It's as if that would diminish them.'

Tom was disappointed. A good friend could have made all the difference, particularly if there were aspects of Genevieve's life that her husband knew nothing about. Nevertheless, someone would be tasked with following up on the women. He decided to let Becky drive back to headquarters. It would give him more time to think.

'Who do you think's the best person to talk to Genevieve's friends?' he asked.

Becky didn't hesitate. 'Rob. Definitely. He's charming; he's attractive – in a Lewis Hamilton kind of way – so if they're the kind of women that Niall is suggesting, he's the man for the job.'

Tom grinned. 'That's what I thought too. I'm sure I'd be a poor choice. I don't even understand my ex-wife, and I've known her forever.'

Becky glanced at him. 'What's Kate been up to? I'd have thought she was far enough away not to worry you any more.'

'She's on her way back. It's great news because Lucy is coming with her, of course, but God knows what Kate thought she was doing, buggering off to Australia. She only lasted five minutes with her new man.'

Becky grinned. 'Well, to be fair, she had a nasty scare with the cancer and perhaps thought life was about taking a few risks.'

'Fine – with her own life. But she's messing my daughter about too. *Watch out!*' he shouted as Becky nearly overshot a junction.

'Chill, Tom. I'm in control.'

They drove in silence for a few moments, and then Tom spoke again: 'When we get back, I'll have to go to the post-mortem. Can you chase the tech guys, find out why it's taking so bloody long to get the password from the computer? We need to get into that phone, because we've bugger-all else to go on. And brief Rob to go and chat up those women.'

'Rob thought there might be more to be gleaned from Genevieve's sister, so I might have a chat with her myself. I'll check out the thumb drive too – see where Genevieve's been going. Strachan didn't object to us looking at those emails from Martha, so I'll check those too.'

At that moment Tom's phone rang. He put it on speaker.

'It's DI Sims, sir. I've collated all the feedback from the people at the meeting with Mr Strachan last night. He was trying to raise additional funds for his business, and the original investors were meeting with the new ones to hammer out the details of the preference shares, earn-outs, et cetera.'

Tom glanced at Becky, who was pulling her 'What the hell is he talking about?' face. Tom didn't know much about corporate finance, other than the fact that investors did everything they could to protect their money and maximise their returns.

'At the moment I'm not too interested in the content of the meeting, Keith. What did they have to say about Niall Strachan's presence or otherwise?'

'It seems that at various stages in the evening suggestions were made about tweaks to the contract terms, and each group of lawyers would go off into private offices to discuss whether they were prepared to accept the amendments. The last break took place at about eleven thirty. Niall Strachan was with his lawyer for a while, but when the contracts came back for final checking, he excused himself. The lawyer has no idea how long he was out of the office; she was absorbed in her reading. But the legal executive said she saw him leave the building.'

'What time was this, Keith?'

'She thinks it was about eleven forty-five. The meeting was supposed to reconvene at twelve fifteen a.m. but was delayed because a few people were late back to the room – including Mr Strachan. But he was there to sign by twelve thirty and left for home at about twelve forty.'

'So technically he had time to go home, kill his wife and get back to the meeting. That's what you're saying, isn't it?'

'It is, sir, just about. But I understand from DS Cumba that there would have been a lot of blood.'

Keith was right, but Niall Strachan was a smart guy and perfectly capable of equipping himself with some slip-on coveralls to protect his clothes.

'We need to seize his car, Keith. Full DNA check, the lot. If he killed her, he wouldn't have had much time to dispose of whatever he was wearing. He could have dumped something on his way back into town, but not without leaving a trace in the boot or on the back seat. And start checking CCTV and ANPR on the A580. He didn't have a lot of time, so the East Lancs Road would be the obvious route.'

Tom hung up. Maybe there was nothing complex about this murder at all. Maybe it was just another case of uxoricide – the killing of a wife. An ugly word for a dreadful crime.

22

'Tom! Excellent timing,' Amy Sanders said as Tom appeared at the mortuary. She put her head on one side and looked at him. 'You don't like this, do you?'

'Not especially. I know it has to be done, but even after all these years I struggle to ignore the thought that less than twenty-four hours ago, the woman lying on your table was walking around, eating, drinking, laughing, crying. On the other hand, seeing her like this is what drives me to find out who killed her.'

'Why do you think I do this job? A post-mortem can tell you so much about what happened.'

She was right, but it didn't make him like it any better. 'I realise you've not started yet, but do you have anything you can tell me?'

'I can provide a reasonably accurate time of death, but I bet Jumbo's already given you his best guess, hasn't he? He likes to do everyone else's job,' Amy said with a grunt. 'He's bloody amazing at his own, so I grin and bear it.'

'Don't worry. His wisdom's not confined to your area of expertise. He'll be here soon, so let's see if he's right.'

At that moment the door opened and in walked the man

himself, along with a small Asian girl Tom knew to be the exhibits officer.

'Tom, Amy,' Jumbo said, his face serious. 'Let's get on with it, shall we?' He hated post-mortems as much as Tom did.

'I think you were about to talk to me about time of death, Amy?' Tom said.

The pathologist tried and failed to hide a smile, and Jumbo grinned, clearly guessing they had been talking about him.

'I arrived just after seven thirty a.m.,' Amy said, 'and based on the usual factors – body temperature in relation to air temperature, degree of rigor mortis and so on – I would say she died some time around midnight, maybe up to thirty minutes later. She was killed where she was found – the body hadn't been moved.'

Amy walked across to where Genevieve's body lay on the autopsy table.

'If you look here, you can see her hair is matted with blood. She was hit with a heavy object, which didn't kill her – or at least not immediately because she pumped out a lot of blood from the stabbings. But it was probably enough to slow her down, stop her fighting.'

'We haven't found whatever was used to knock her out, but we're going further into the fields on either side of the Loopline,' Jumbo said.

Amy pointed to the puncture wounds in her abdomen. 'Two deep, penetrating wounds. What I find interesting is that the knife went in, but instead of being pulled straight back out again, it appears to have been twisted. That maximises the damage caused, but I'm not sure how many people would know that. I've also tested the angle of the blade. Our victim was a tall woman, a fraction under six feet – 181 centimetres – and she was wearing high heels. I think whoever stabbed her was shorter. The blade was angled upwards, although that's to be expected if the hand was thrust up from waist height. But it seems a more acute angle.'

Jumbo spoke to the exhibits officer, who produced a plastic bag containing the knife they had found in the culvert.

'It's been checked and printed, so it's okay to touch.'

Tom looked at it again. It was a kitchen knife with a long thin blade. There was nothing special about it, as far as he could see, but given the blade he wasn't surprised it had been lethal. He knew from past post-mortems that a knife usually had to penetrate quite a long way to hit a vital organ or artery.

Tom listened as Amy talked through the visible injuries, and then she was ready to make the first incision. He focused on her words, rather on what was happening on the table in front of him.

Ten minutes into the examination, Tom's phone buzzed in his pocket.

'I'm sorry, I need to take this,' he said, seeing it was Becky. He stepped away from the table to speak to her.

'Tom, we've got the list of pass codes from Martha Porter's computer and managed to get into Genevieve's phone. She received a message at eleven fifty.'

Tom could feel his pulse speed up, and he could hear from Becky's tone that she was excited at the breakthrough.

'Saying?'

'The most important bit was asking Genevieve to come outside. I'll read it.'

'Save it. I'm coming back. Who was it from?'

'We don't know – at least, not yet. A name didn't come up on the screen – only a number – so not someone in her contacts list. But we're tracking it now. I assumed you'd want to be here. Keith's heading to the mortuary to deputise for you. Is that okay?'

It was more than okay, but Tom didn't want to say so.

'It's fine. As soon as he arrives, I'll head back. By then we should know who sent it.'

'Unless it was a burner,' Becky said.

'Let's hope not. I'll see you shortly.'

Tom hung up. Now they could really get cracking.

'Sorry, Amy, Jumbo – I'll have to leave you to it, I'm afraid. I'll stay until DI Sims gets here, and he can take over from me.'

Jumbo grinned. 'I bet you got Becky to call you on some fake emergency or other, didn't you?'

'As if,' Tom said, returning the smile but unable to hide his relief.

23

As Tom walked through the door of the incident room, he immediately felt the buzz. Everyone was moving with a sense of urgency, and an animated Becky was speaking to someone on the phone. She looked up as Tom walked in and lifted her hand, signalling him to come over to her desk.

'You're sure about this?' he heard her say. 'Sorry, yes, of course you're sure. DCI Douglas has just walked in. I'll brief him and we'll get back to you. Thanks, Ted – much appreciated.'

She hung up and raised wide eyes to Tom. 'You've only been gone about an hour, and so much has happened that I don't know where to start.'

'The phone?'

'Yes. Let's start there. The tech team accessed the folder on Martha Porter's computer with the list of phones and passwords, including Genevieve's. They opened the phone and checked for messages, and as we thought, she was contacted via iMessage by another iPhone. The message said' – Becky glanced at her computer screen – '"Last week you begged me to tell you what I know, and I refused. But I've changed my mind. I'll give you what you want if you give me what *I* want – and you know what that is. He's mine – not yours. I'm outside, down the path to the Loopline. If you want answers, come and find me.'"

Her eyes went back to Tom's.

'We need to dissect each of those phrases, but for now do we have any clue who left the message?' he asked.

'That's what Ted was telling me. The phone used to message her is registered to XO-Tech, but he's gone through the list on Martha's computer, and it's not allocated to anyone. It's a spare.'

'At least it's not a bloody burner, so we have somewhere to start. A bugger it wasn't assigned, though.'

'I know. I've asked Spencer Johansson if there's any way he can check who might have had access to it. They control the apps on those phones, Tom. If someone has it in their pocket, surely they'll be able to track it? This has to be our murderer.'

'We can justify cell siting, too. I'll speak to Philippa.'

Tom didn't relish the thought of a conversation with his boss, Detective Superintendent Philippa Stanley, until he had some more information. She was very results driven, as she had to be, but she had a tendency to expect the unachievable.

'Moving on,' Becky said, 'we've pulled the email messages from the thumb drive that Niall gave us, and Ted has married them up with an email account in Martha's name, but not her office email address. She had a Gmail account, but it was difficult to find on her computer. There was nothing in her browser history, and it was only by doing some serious rooting around that Ted found it.'

'And the content of the messages?'

'Basically, Martha was saying she could offer Niall much more than Genevieve, who she described as a sponger. She progressed from that to saying she knew everything about the business, and she was in an excellent position to help him, as his partner in every meaning of the word. Vague threats wrapped up to sound like she was offering him something special.'

Tom blew out a long, slow breath. 'Is it possible she saw Genevieve as the only thing standing between her and Niall?'

'Not from what he said. He told us he avoided being behind closed doors with her, so she must have known he wasn't keen.'

'Are people always logical about these things, though? Was there anything else of interest on Genevieve's phone?'

'Ted's going to print out the lot, so we can go through it. We'll check her movements too, from Niall's tracker. But this seemed a priority. Rob's on his way back from talking to some of Genevieve's friends, who had apparently already convened to discuss the demise of their friend. They were in a wine bar overlooking the canal and seemed to have been there a while. He'll fill us in when he gets back.'

'Give me a shout as soon as he gets here. In the meantime, I'll go and brave the lioness's den!'

'So that's where we're up to,' Tom said, having filled Philippa Stanley in on everything that had happened in the last thirteen hours. He leaned back in his chair and waited, knowing she would have something to say.

Despite his occasional flippant remarks about his boss, Tom had huge respect for her, and she had dug him out of a few holes in the past. Their relationship was always tinged with reminders of when she was his probationer many years ago, although since then she had leapfrogged him in rank. He was happy with that. He wouldn't have had her job if they had quadrupled his salary.

Philippa was tapping her pen on the clean blotter in front of her. There was never a thing out of place on her desk, and she looked as immaculate as ever in her smart dark suit and white blouse. Tom had sometimes wondered how Philippa's chin-length brunette bob always managed to look identical. It never seemed to be in need of a trim, but on the other hand, she never had that just-been-to-the-hairdresser look.

'I'm happy to authorise the cell siting,' she said finally. 'The evidence suggests that whoever has that phone is either the murderer or was the last person to see Genevieve Strachan alive. I take it the victim didn't reply to the message?'

'No. Nothing. Its content was apparently enough to persuade her to go out to meet her killer.' Tom referred to his phone, displaying a copy of the message that Becky had forwarded. '"Last week you begged me to tell you what I know." We don't know what that refers to, but we do know that Genevieve was seen arguing with Martha Porter last week. No one seems to know what it was about. She could have simply wanted Martha to tell her where Niall was, as I understand he was out at the time. It goes on to say, "He's mine – not yours." The easy conclusion to leap to is that this is somehow related to the emails from Martha Porter, trying to entice Niall away from Genevieve, but I don't think we should make that assumption.'

'Why not?' Philippa asked. Tom was certain she knew the answer as well as he did but was testing his logic.

'Martha apparently made a pass at Niall and then subsequently sent him some emails saying she was the right partner for him. She also suggested she knew things about him that made her valuable. But it's equally feasible that Niall had a lover – not just someone who fancied her chances, as Martha allegedly did. He had a private staircase from his office to the street, and Spencer Johansson made some remark about him using it when he didn't want people to know where he was going. He suggested this was to do with the business, but…'

'Okay. No assumptions. I agree. There are two priorities, as far as I can see. Find Martha Porter and either establish her as a credible suspect or eliminate her from the enquiry, and second, find out who has the phone that was used to message Genevieve. I can help with the latter by getting a trace on the phone. But what are you doing about Martha Porter?'

'DI Sims knows more about this, but he's not here at the moment. He took over from me at the PM this afternoon – it seemed more important that I got back.'

Philippa raised her eyebrows. She had known Tom a long time, but she said nothing and waited for him to continue.

'He's been trying to find some background on Porter, but until we saw those emails, we didn't consider her hugely important. She was just a member of staff who either left because she had somewhere else she needed to be, or she'd freaked out that someone she knew had been murdered. That was it. So other than seizing her computer to check for passwords, we didn't consider any other action was necessary.'

'And now?'

'She fancied the boss. Is that any reason to kill, do you think?'

'You tell me, Tom. A fair number of the females here – and possibly even the males – have gone into a flutter over you in the past. Have you ever felt that they would kill to get you?'

Tom laughed. 'I think you're exaggerating, Philippa. And thanks for mentioning "the past" as if I could no longer be of any possible interest. Seriously, though, we're doing what we can to find Porter, even though I would have thought there'd need to be a much deeper motive for murder. She'd have to be a bit of a psycho to believe a man who had just lost his wife would fall into her arms.'

Philippa gave him a look. 'She wouldn't be the first. And anyway, it might not be so simple. Did he ever respond to her emails?'

'Not as far as we know, but he has the technical savvy to obliterate any trace if he had. I know what you're thinking: did he really reject her, or are they lovers and was this a pact to get rid of the wife?'

'And?'

'Very possibly. We're heading back to XO-Tech soon, and I'll talk to the staff again – let's see what the gossips have to say.'

As Tom finished speaking, Philippa was already picking up her phone, clearly indicating the meeting was at an end. Tom stood up to leave. She was issuing instructions before he reached the door.

24

There's blood everywhere. It's on my T-shirt, on my hands, under my nails. The body is on the ground, one hand stretched out as if she's trying to grab my ankle, and I take a step back into the mud.

I stare at the knife in my hand as a voice whispers in my ear, 'You did the right thing.'

She isn't moving. Her eyes are open, staring. Not at me – they're staring at nothing.

How has it come to this? What have I done?

The voice comes again, still a whisper, but urgent, pressing. 'You need to go. Run!'

I pause for a moment longer, then I'm running along the deserted path. I can hear water and I realise I'm still holding the knife. I throw it as hard as I can, and hear it clatter on the stones. It didn't go very far, but I can't stop now. I run and run, sobs choking me.

All my life I've been forced to confront the worst of myself. But I never thought I was capable of this.

25

MARTHA

'Mummy?' The frightened voice of Alfie wakes me, and I roll towards him on the bed, for a moment unsure of where I am. 'You were shouting,' he says, his lip quivering.

I shake myself awake. 'I'm sorry, sweetheart. It was just a bad dream. How are you feeling now?'

I'd dosed Alfie with medicine as soon as we got back from the chemist to try to bring his temperature down and lain down with him. I must have drifted off.

'Not as horrid now, I don't think,' he says.

I reach out a hand to feel his skin, and although it's warm, it no longer feels feverish. I, on the other hand, have sweat running between my breasts, and my hair is sticking damply to the back of my neck. But this isn't a fever. It's the dream. I push it to the back of my mind.

I've decided that the strain of being here, so close to home, is too great for either of us, so we're going to move on tomorrow – a day earlier than my original plan. I feel too vulnerable here. I hadn't thought it would be like this; I thought I would feel safe. I don't.

The man in the car freaked me out. I'm sure he was only flirting, but it's the reason I've moved so many times, always scared that someone would recognise me. I know the word will have been spread far and wide that I'm missing, and I never know when I might be seen, my presence reported back. I set myself a rule that the maximum time in one place would be a year, but Alfie is so happy at school, and I feel guilty about repeatedly disrupting his life, so it's been two years this time. He's a trusting, sociable child, and I don't want to knock that out of him.

I wish I had a better idea of what was happening with the investigation into Genevieve's murder. All I have is Elise's exaggerated posts, guaranteed to put her in the spotlight. Nevertheless, I can't resist quickly checking on her Facebook page to see what else she's had to say.

She's posted a photo of herself with a shocked look, one hand to her mouth, eyes wide open.

And then I read her post.

'*No!*' The cry escapes me before I can prevent it. *This can't be happening.* But it is.

More than ever, I wish I had someone to turn to – a friend or a partner. But there's no one. I've lost the only friend I had, and now I'm on my own.

26

LAKESIDE

One of the first lessons I learned after Aram came to Lakeside was how to be alone. I still hadn't started secondary school and I had no friends. Mum spent most of her time with Aram, and Dad hovered uncertainly, wanting to keep busy but anxious to be close by in case Mum needed him.

Every morning, rain or shine, I would walk to the lake to sit and watch the birds. Dad bought me a book so I could identify the different species. I copied the words into my notebook, and I gave the moorhens and the ducks names. They became my friends, and I spoke to them. I fed them scraps of bread and worried when any of them didn't turn up to see me.

I wasn't unhappy. I was just a little lost.

The good news was that from Mum's very first session with Aram, there appeared to be an improvement. She seemed to have found a new joy in life, and she always came out of their private sessions with a serene smile on her face. She told us that she now had hope. Her time with Aram gave her days a focus, and she understood so much more about trust.

'I'm not supposed to talk about the process,' she said to us one day when Aram was on one of his rare trips away from Lakeside. 'The important thing is that he's helping me to understand why people hurt each other – why the people who we think love us can turn against us, like my family, our friends in London, people we trusted. He's giving me a depth of understanding that won't change what they did, but which exposes the source of their negativity.'

Dad looked totally baffled by this, but I don't think he cared about 'the process'. All that mattered was that Mum was happier, so even though I'm not sure there was ever an active decision to allow Aram to move in rather than just stay with us until Mum's 'treatment' was complete, when he showed no sign of moving on, no one objected.

None of us knew then that this was only the start of all that was to come.

The change came slowly, almost imperceptibly, for me at least. After he chided me for asking him a personal question, for a while I was terrified of making the same mistake, but he behaved as if nothing had happened, and I started to relax. But not for long. A pattern emerged. One day he would tell me I made the world a brighter place, and I glowed in his praise. The next day he would find fault, and a sense of desolation washed over me.

'Does the fact that you talk too much during meals, drawing attention to yourself, indicate self-obsession, or are you simply an arrogant, thoughtless child?' he asked the first time he chose to rip me apart without any provocation. 'I knew a child in the house would disrupt your mother's recovery, and I was right. Are you thoughtless?'

I looked back at him in horror. 'No, Aram. Really, I'm not like that. I'm sorry. I didn't mean to upset anyone.'

Tears sprang into my eyes, and his mouth tightened. 'And now you're being a self-indulgent baby. Think of others, India. Not of yourself. Crying is a symptom of a self-centred nature.'

He ignored me the next day, and I longed to win back his

approval. The day after, when I was once again the beautiful child who lifted his spirits, relief rushed through me. The thrill of being back in favour had me questioning my every action from that point on, terrified that I would anger him again, and I worked hard to be the person he wanted me to be. I didn't need anyone else. All I needed was Aram's affection.

27

Tom had just arrived back in the incident room when Rob came striding through the door, and he felt like groaning. Rob had been up at least two hours longer than he had, having arrived at the scene of the murder at the same time as Becky, and yet he looked as if he'd just got up. Maybe having a shaved head was the thing – not a hair out of place.

Keith was also due back at any moment, so Tom suggested they regroup as soon as he arrived. In the meantime, he wanted to read up on Niall Strachan and his company, so he pulled up a chair to Keith's desk. Every sheet of paper was neatly aligned. Tom smiled as he adjusted the position of the monitor. He knew the team would have researched Niall's company, its history and valuation, and they could discuss their findings at the meeting, but he wanted to know more about the man himself, so he typed his name into Google.

Once he'd weeded out all the other Niall Strachans, Tom found precious little about the man's personal life. Almost every entry related to XO-Tech. He didn't appear to be active on social media, although the company was, and Tom could find no reference to previous employers. Deciding that a search on Genevieve might be more fruitful, he tried her maiden name. The page flooded with mentions and photos, mostly from the years before she was married to Niall.

She showed all the hallmarks of having been a young woman having the time of her life. Long auburn hair, shiny with vitality, skimmed her shoulders, short skirts made the most of her slim tanned legs, and dark red lips framed a white smile. And yet to Tom there seemed to be a slightly manic quality to that smile, as if she was trying a little too hard.

Prior to her marriage, Genevieve had dated a well-known Manchester United footballer, and together they had been photographed at a plethora of openings – clubs, bars, restaurants – anything of note that happened in Manchester. But it seemed the star player went to one party too many, and after he caused a major fight and ended up in custody for assault, Genevieve told the press that she was done with him.

'He takes too many drugs and becomes aggressive when we're alone. He's too possessive and threatens to punch anyone who so much as looks at me. I can't take it any longer.'

Some of the more scandalous tabloid reports suggested that Genevieve had seen her boyfriend's career waning, and that didn't suit her at all, so she had moved on. Tom wondered whether the footballer – Eddie Carlson – should be considered a suspect. It might be several years since he and Genevieve were together, but if he was that possessive, they should take a look at him. He made a note to ask one of the team to follow it up.

A shadow fell across the desk, and Tom looked up. 'Keith, do have your desk back.'

'That's fine, sir.' Keith reached out a hand as he spoke and adjusted his monitor back to precisely the right angle.

'Right,' said Tom, feeling strangely chastised. 'Becky, let's get everyone together and see where we're up to. Keith – as always, you're our scribe.'

The team gathered round, pulling up chairs or sitting on desks.

'DI Sims has been to the post-mortem, and I've no doubt we'll be getting the detailed results in due course, but for now anything particular of note, Keith?'

'Nothing unexpected, sir.'

Keith repeated the information that Amy had shared about time of death, the murder weapon and the probability that the assailant was shorter than Genevieve. In theory, that ruled out her husband, who was taller than his wife even when she was wearing heels. Tom wasn't prepared to write him off yet, though.

'We haven't found whatever was used to hit her with yet, but Jumbo's on it,' Tom said. 'Does the twisting of the knife suggest anything to anyone?'

'We've all heard of twisting the knife, boss,' Rob said, 'but from what I can gather it's not a natural movement – more of a deliberate action. Sounds like something a person trained in armed combat might be likely to do.'

'Hmm, or was it Genevieve's bad luck that they'd read about the technique somewhere? Rob, you went to talk to her friends. What did you get?'

Rob sighed and scratched his head. 'They were happy to talk, but as a group they had little of interest to say. They were all half pissed, to be honest. They'd met for an early lunch when they heard the news – to commiserate, I suppose. Some were genuinely upset, horrified that this could have happened to Genevieve. A couple of the others shed a few tears, but not enough to smudge the mascara.'

'Nothing at all that we can glean from what they said?'

'I spoke to each of them privately, and I felt they were trotting out the line Genevieve had given them. A happy marriage, successful husband, even a wonderful sex life – not that I asked about that, but I was told anyway. One of them, Tansy Wakefield, said Genevieve didn't share much with the group, but privately she'd told her there'd be a few changes coming. They were all going to be surprised, and no one more than Niall.'

'What the hell did that mean?'

'She didn't know, but she said Genevieve looked pleased with herself. She'd wondered if maybe she was pregnant, having always said it was the last thing she wanted.'

Tom gave Keith a questioning look.

'Not pregnant, sir. Dr Sanders was specific about that. And no sign of recent sexual activity, in case we were wondering if she'd met up with a lover.'

Tom was quiet for a moment. 'Becky, you're going to speak to the sister, I believe. Let's see if she can give us any other clues about what was going on in Genevieve's mind.'

Tom looked around at the eager but jaded faces. He was going to have to let some of them go home soon, while a small team continued to go through what little evidence they had.

'We all know that our most significant piece of evidence is the message apparently asking Genevieve to go outside to get the answers she had been seeking from whoever this person was. We should get the data back soon about the current whereabouts of the phone, and then we'll have something tangible to work with. Until then, do we have any news on the ANPR on the A580, Becky?'

'Sorry, boss. No sign of Strachan's car.'

Tom tutted. 'I'd have been surprised if there was. If Strachan did it, I don't think he would have had time to go by any other route. We've got his car, though, haven't we?'

Becky nodded.

'Good. Have them check for any signs of adhesive on the number plates – he may have stuck black tape on to change the letters and fool the cameras – or anything that suggests he swapped plates altogether, although time again would be a factor. Do we know for sure he went to the meeting in his own car?'

'We checked the cameras on his route around the time he left. Looks like he was telling the truth.'

'Sir!' The shout came from one of the officers manning the phones. 'We've heard from the telephony team.'

Tom signalled him to come across.

'Initially they had nothing. The phone was either switched off, or the SIM had been taken out. But it's just started to show up. We've got a location.'

Tom stood up, grabbing his mobile from the table and pushing it into his pocket. 'Is it moving or stationary?'

'Stationary. And it's at the offices of XO-Tech.'

'Is it, indeed?' He headed for the door. 'Rob, you're with me. Becky, go back and see Sara Osborne. We'll let you know what we discover in case there's anything we need to run by her. Keith, phone the director at XO-Tech – what's his name, Rob?'

'Spencer Johansson.'

'Yep, him. Tell him that no one must leave the building. We'll be there in twenty minutes.'

28

'With a bit of luck we'll get this all sewn up today, boss,' Rob said as Tom drove through the late-afternoon traffic.

'I wouldn't bet on it. And then we'd have to settle down and start the interviews. I don't know about you, but I'm not sure I can keep going for another twelve hours.'

'Oh, I'm fine. No problem.'

Tom glanced at Rob and could see he was telling the truth. But Rob didn't have a teething baby at home, and when he got the chance to sleep, he probably managed an uninterrupted eight hours. Tom wondered when that would next happen to him – not that he minded. Harry was the best thing that had happened to him in a long time. A smile came to his face every time he thought about his baby giggle.

He pulled into the XO-Tech car park, and was pleased to see that it was still full of cars, even though he suspected the work day had officially ended.

'You've met this guy Johansson, Rob – what's he like?'

'Like a man who's trying to live up to his idea of what a director of a successful tech company *should* be like, rather than being himself. You know, vocabulary and clothes that he thinks are expected, but neither of which sat comfortably on his short, portly frame. Twitchy as hell too, but then his partner's wife has been murdered, and he's been left holding the baby – by which I mean the business – so I can hardly blame him.'

Tom opened the car door. 'Okay, let's see if we can find this phone. You've got the number, I assume.'

'I have. If it's switched on, someone's jacket or bag should burst into song.'

The two men walked into the offices and found a young woman waiting for them, her eyes round at the drama unfolding around her. She seemed nervous, but then no doubt everyone in the building was feeling unsettled.

'We're here to see Mr Johansson,' Tom said. 'Greater Manchester Police.'

'He's waiting in the meeting room. I'll show you the way.'

Tom and Rob followed her into the room and thanked her.

'Mr Johansson? I'm Detective Chief Inspector Tom Douglas. I believe you've met DS Cumba.'

'Yes.' His eyes dodged between Tom and Rob. 'What's this about? Another officer called and told me to keep all the staff here, but he wouldn't tell me why.'

'We've extracted the information from the folders on Martha Porter's computer and found the password for Genevieve Strachan's phone. When we looked at the contents, there was a message from another phone, one that's registered to XO-Tech. I believe you've already been made aware of this, and you said it was a spare. We put a trace on it. Initially it was switched off, but then it was switched on here, in this building, about half an hour ago.'

Spencer nodded. 'That's right, one of your detectives called me. I checked the list myself, and there was no name against that number, so I didn't know whose it was. Or at least, not then.'

'Then?'

Spencer's eyes went to the table, where a mobile phone was resting. 'I think it's this one. I worked it out, you see.'

'What do you mean?' Tom asked.

'I remembered there was a mobile in Martha Porter's desk drawer. We saw it there this morning, didn't we?' he said, nodding at Rob.

Rob turned to Tom. 'We had no reason to take it, boss. We were looking for Miss Porter to provide us with the password to Mrs Strachan's phone, nothing else.'

Rob was right, but that situation had changed.

'Why didn't she have a phone allocated to her?'

'She did. This one.' He pointed to the phone. 'It matches the number I've got stored for her in my contacts, so she must have deleted her name from the list stored on the network this morning before she left.'

Tom was liking the sound of this less and less. Why would she do that? 'We'll have to get a team in to go through Miss Porter's desk, her office and possibly other offices too. Has anyone other than you had access to this phone today?'

'No. I brought it straight in here.'

'Has anyone else touched it since you found it?'

Spencer shook his head. 'No. Only me.'

Tom pulled a pair of gloves from his pocket and put them on as Spencer pushed it across the desk to him with a pencil.

The digital team had already looked up the pass code in the file they'd retrieved from Martha's computer and sent it to Tom. He tapped the screen and opened Messages.

Nothing. Not a trace of any message from or to this phone, which suggested that if Martha Porter had sent a message to Genevieve, she must have deleted it. Or someone had, because it had definitely come from this number.

There were other possibilities to consider. The phone had been sitting in Martha's desk drawer, so no one could say for certain who had sent the message to Genevieve. Maybe she wasn't the only one who knew the pass code.

'Chief Inspector, there's something I've been wondering about mentioning. It didn't seem relevant until now, but with Martha missing and everything...'

'Is she missing? We don't know where she is, but it's not necessarily the same thing.' Tom had his concerns, but he wasn't about to share them with Spencer Johansson.

'Oh, I see what you mean.' Johansson looked flustered. 'It's just that I'm not sure who Martha really is.'

'Go on,' Tom said.

'Well, after she made rather a fool of herself with Niall, he decided to look at her a bit more closely. It's a difficult one, you know, because Martha knows everything about this company – where all the bodies are buried, if you like.'

Tom tried not to react to such an inappropriate turn of phrase. 'And?'

'Well, he was thinking of asking her to leave but was worried about how we could ensure her continued discretion, so he tried to find out a bit about her. He couldn't find her on social media, which is unusual for someone of her age, so he called one of the companies that had given her a testimonial. "Who's Martha Porter?" they asked. And it struck us then that we didn't actually know.'

29

MARTHA

I read Elise's post again, hoping that I'd misunderstood the first time, but I hadn't.

> OMG – the police are back. They've got a team coming in to search the building. Spence told Karen on reception that he thought they'd want to start with Martha's office. WTF? What HAS she done? And no one knows where she is! I'm going to find her company profile, grab her pic and post it. Maybe the police can't find her, but I bet Facebook can! I'll stick it on Instagram and Twitter too. Hang on, guys, I need you to share this.

She's going to post a picture!

I'd thought that if the police decided to issue my photo, the one XO-Tech have, it would only be published in the local press or news, but this will go nationwide, possibly worldwide. There's no knowing who might see it. We're not safe. We need to go – and go now. But go where? Is anywhere safe?

I've always tried to make sure my office look is severe, with scraped-back hair and heavy-rimmed glasses, but am I unrecognisable? Probably not. I thank God no one has a photo of Alfie; it would be much harder to disguise a child.

I want to cry at the hopelessness of it all, but I force myself to take a breath, to think. I won't relax until we're out of here, out of Manchester, so I switch off my phone, stick it in my pocket and head for the bathroom.

I never unpack when I'm on the move. Any clothes we're not wearing are already packed, so all I need to get is the small toilet bag, which contains nothing but toothbrushes, toothpaste and deodorant. I grab it, look round the bathroom to make sure I haven't left anything that can be used to trace me and rush back into the bedroom, shoving the toilet bag into my backpack.

'Alfie, listen, sweetheart – I've got an idea. We're going to move on to the next part of our holiday, and we're going now. You can sleep as we go, and when you wake up, you'll be all better, and we'll be somewhere really special.'

Alfie's eyes open wide. He's confused by all these changes and I think for a moment he might cry, so I crouch down. 'I wasn't planning to tell you this – it was supposed to be a surprise – but we're going to the seaside!'

His face instantly lights up. He has always wanted to play on a beach, see the sea, and I've never had the chance to take him, because Martha Porter can't drive. She has no licence.

But India Kalu does.

Two minutes later we are stepping out of the lift into an area to one side of reception. The girl who checked me in is back behind the desk, and I don't want her to see me. My bag isn't big, but it's the one I came in with, and she'll notice we're leaving.

To the left is the hotel's restaurant, open to the public, who can access it from the street, so I steer Alfie that way. There's a sign asking me to wait to be seated, but as a waitress ambles towards me in no rush to serve her customers, I hurry Alfie towards the main doors and out onto the street. My heart thumps so loud I can't believe Alfie doesn't hear it.

I can see a line of three black cabs and nobody queuing, so I open the door of the front taxi and bundle Alfie inside. He looks slightly stunned. He's never been in a black cab before, and I'm hoping he doesn't make too much of a deal out of it. We don't want to draw attention.

'Manchester Airport, please.'

'Terminal?' the bored-looking taxi driver asks. I expect he's hot, sitting here waiting until someone needs him, so I don't take offence at his tone.

'Terminal Three, arrivals.'

Alfie is still looking at me, and I can see the excitement in his eyes. He knows what an airport is, although he's never been to one, but he'll be disappointed when we get there.

'No questions, Alfie. It's a surprise,' I say, giving him a squeeze.

I would give anything for my son to have a normal life in a normal family and go to the airport to watch the planes – or even fly away in one for a holiday, perhaps with grandparents, something I always wanted as a child. But I'm all he's got, and to take him out of the country we would both need a passport. That's not going to happen. The guilt hits me again, stronger than ever.

When we arrive, I pay the driver, we get out of the taxi and I grab Alfie's hand to give it a squeeze. 'We're not going into the airport this time, sweetie. But we're doing something we've never done before. You'll see.'

I'm glad his brief fever has subsided, but his disappointment at being denied a look at the planes drains him a little. I need to be quick and get us on our way.

Outside the terminal we board the bus for the Car Hire Village. As usual, I press my hand against my stomach, checking my card is still in place. It is. I had to look hard for a hire firm that would rent a car on a debit card, rather than a credit card. But I took out the full insurance, so they're covered should I fail to return it.

It takes a little longer than I'd hoped in the office because I didn't have a chance to pre-book. I bite the inside of my cheek as the agent checks my card and driving licence. Will they have traced me? Do they know that Martha Porter and India Kalu are the same person? Has Elise posted my photo yet? Will she recognise me?

She scans my licence, and I wonder if some warning will pop up on her screen, but after a long moment she asks me to put my card in the machine. There's a pause as she looks at the screen again. What is she seeing there? Then she looks up, smiles, and tells me where I can find the car.

'Have a pleasant trip, Ms Kalu,' she says as she hands me the keys.

'Thank you.'

'Where are we going, Mummy?'

I smile at the agent and whisper to her, 'He's dying to know, but it's a surprise.'

I hurry Alfie out of the door, wondering if what I am about to do is another mistake, to add to the many I've made in my life.

30

LAKESIDE

It was perhaps six weeks after he first arrived that Aram told us, while we were eating breakfast one morning, that he would like to talk to me and Dad. It sounded serious, and I didn't know what to think. I glanced nervously at Dad, who reached out his hand to grab mine and squeezed it.

'I'll be there too,' he said.

With Mum's help, Aram had turned one room into a 'meditation space'. For weeks workmen had been coming and going, and I'd heard the sound of machinery; then there was a smell – something like furniture polish but much stronger.

'They're sorting out the floor,' Mum told me. 'We need it to be clean, don't we?'

Did we? I was still young enough to accept that she was right. It wasn't until our first session with Aram that I saw the transformation.

'Did you know it had changed so much?' I whispered to Dad.

'Mum showed me, yes. It looks great, doesn't it?'

I wasn't sure who he was trying to convince – me or himself.

The wide bay window now had two floor-to-ceiling glass doors leading out to a patch of the garden that had been newly planted with flowers in shades of purple, pink and blue. Huge cushions were scattered all over the gleaming wooden floor, and fat cream-coloured candles sat on tall glass tables.

Aram was sitting on the floor, his back to the window, the morning light cascading around him. He held a small glass sphere in his hands, which he was rotating slowly between his palms. His face was in shadow, and I shivered with apprehension, unsure whether to be excited to be there, or fearful that I had done something to displease him. I was increasingly uncertain how he felt about me, as he switched from apparent delight in my presence to disgust with my mistakes.

'Sit, please,' he said. It was strange being given permission by this man to sit in our own house, but I pulled a cushion close to Dad and we did as he said.

'Have you ever tried meditation?' he asked.

I had no idea what it was, so shook my head.

'I don't think it's for me,' Dad said. 'But I'm pleased if it's working for Nicola.'

'Why don't you think it's for you?' The voice and tone were mild, and yet there was a sense that Aram was disappointed by the answer.

Dad shuffled a bit on his cushion and mumbled, 'I've never been much of a one for introspection. It seems a bit self-indulgent.'

Aram's head tilted to one side. 'Interesting. Does it occur to you that your lack of willingness to reflect on your own shortcomings could be the cause of Nicola's distress?'

I felt Dad stiffen beside me. Before he had a chance to speak, Aram's head turned towards me. All I could see of his shadowed face was his eyes.

'And you, India. Do you think you bear any responsibility for Nicola's unhappiness?'

It was strange to have someone refer to Mum as Nicola when

talking to me, but I was soon to learn that, according to Aram, no one should be defined by a title. We are all individuals, and false titles give us more power than we deserve. All of that was still to come. For now, I was just horrified that maybe I was the cause of her earlier misery.

'I'm sorry, Aram,' Dad said, 'but please don't suggest that India had anything to do with it. She's a good kid.'

Aram nodded but said nothing for a minute. I didn't know if he was expecting something from me, but once again I felt like crying. *Was it my fault?*

'Do *you* think you're a good kid, India? Do you ever doubt it? Before we go any further, I want you to think back – try to remember something you might have done or said, knowing that your words or actions were upsetting Nicola.'

Now the tears were welling in my eyes and they started to spill down my cheeks. Sometimes I was difficult. I didn't always do as I was told, and I knew that on the way here all those months ago I'd been sulky. Had I made Mum like this?

'Stop, Aram. You're upsetting India.' Dad reached out an arm and pulled me close. 'Come on, poppet. We're going. I'm sure Mum wouldn't want you to feel like this.' He started to get to his feet.

'Thank you, Joel,' Aram said quietly. 'Your actions have told me so much about your relationships – not only with Nicola and India, but your relationship with yourself.'

Dad stopped and turned towards him. 'What do you mean?'

'You're scared of looking deep inside yourself, of discovering who you really are. You're carrying the burden of your birth, your childhood, your heritage and the damage done by prejudice. Even the prejudice of Nicola's parents, who I understand rejected their daughter because of her love for you. Through you, she lost everything in her life that was real, solid, reliable. Now I'm offering you a chance to look into your own soul, to let go of everything that's holding you tightly in its grip. For Nicola, and ultimately for India. Meditation will help.'

I saw Dad swallow. He didn't know what to do, and I could sense his indecision. Aram had struck a chord.

I squeezed Dad's hand. 'I'm okay,' I said. 'If it will help Mum, I'm okay to stay.'

I should have refused. I should have run out of the door screaming. Then Dad would have come after me. Instead, he stayed and listened as the first droplets of poison were dripped into his mind.

And neither of us recognised it for what it was.

31

Sara Osborne's eyes were puffy, and Becky hated having to intrude on her grief.

'I'm sure you'd rather not be bothered with questions at this time, Mrs Osborne, but the sooner we can understand more about your sister, the greater the chance of finding who killed her.'

The woman sniffed and pulled a tissue out of the pocket of her jeans, opening the door wide and indicating that Becky should come in. 'It's okay. But I thought you knew who it was.'

Becky stopped dead in her tracks. 'I'm sorry? What gives you that impression?'

'It's all over social media – first Facebook, now Instagram. I don't know about Twitter – I don't use it. Too many people thinking their opinions matter.'

Sara Osborne had a point, but what the hell...?

'You don't know what I'm talking about, do you? Oh God, I thought it was all going to be over. Come into the kitchen. I'll show you. Excuse the mess. I haven't managed to clean up; it was all I could do to feed the kids.'

Becky followed Sara, not at all put out by the dirty pots. She glanced sideways through an archway into what looked like a family room, where the backs of three small heads were silhouetted against a TV screen.

A laptop was sitting open on the kitchen table. 'Help yourself,' Sara said, pointing at it.

Becky stared at the profile image at the top of the page. Was that Elise Chapman? She looked vaguely like the woman Becky had met, but this was an over-the-top glamorous version. Then her eyes were drawn to the post below, which featured a picture of a mixed-race woman with long hair pulled back tightly from a slim face. Heavy black glasses almost hid her eyes, but there was no disguising the lovely shape of her pale mouth with its perfect cupid's bow and a full lower lip. A bright red arrow pointed at the face, with the words HAVE YOU SEEN THIS WOMAN? in a flashy font underneath.

Becky leaned forward to read the post.

This is her – the one I've been telling you about. No one knows where she is – so doesn't that say it all? For Niall and Genevieve's sake, we have to find her – so be on the lookout!

Bloody woman! What did she think she was doing?

Becky scrolled back to the previous post and a picture of a woman with her hand to her mouth. It was definitely Elise; she remembered her from that morning. She read the post and lifted her eyes to look at Sara.

'I need to call my boss, Sara. I'm sorry about this. It shouldn't be happening. Please don't believe any of this. Excuse me for a moment.'

Becky walked out into the hall and called Tom.

'I'm with Sara Osborne, Tom. She's seen some content that Elise Chapman – an XO-Tech employee – has been plastering all over social media. She's saying the killer is Martha Porter, and she's posted her photograph.'

'*Shit!* She must have heard something. The phone used to call

Genevieve last night was Martha's – Johansson found it in her desk drawer – but there's no evidence she's ever used it. There are no texts stored on it, and the telephony team have checked with the network provider. It's never been used to make a call. Not once. It doesn't make sense to me, but the last thing we want is some vigilante grabbing Martha in the street. It's not helped by the fact that Johansson is casting doubt on who Martha really is.'

'*What?* We don't know yet if she's a victim herself, and if someone on Facebook spots her, they'll tell Elise. She could have us running in circles following up fake leads.'

'Leave it with me, and thanks for alerting me. I'm still at XO-Tech, so I'll speak to the bloody woman. And apologise to Sara Osborne on our behalf.'

'Already done,' Becky said. She could hear the weariness in her own voice, and needed some strong coffee to keep her going.

'Becky, as soon as you've finished there, go home. Otherwise you'll be no good to anyone tomorrow, and there are others who can take over. We've got the search team here at XO-Tech; I'll talk to the staff – including sodding Elise – and then I'll send Rob packing and go home myself. I'll see you in the morning.'

Tom was right. She'd been on the go for about seventeen hours after no more than two hours' sleep. But she wasn't going anywhere until she'd spoken to Sara Osborne.

She hung up and returned to the kitchen.

'You look even more done in than I feel,' Sara said, giving Becky a weak smile. 'Come on – let's have a coffee, or tea if you prefer. Ask me your questions and I'll do what I can to help.'

As she switched on the kettle, there was a shout from the family room and a plaintive call of 'Mum, it's not fair!'

She sighed. 'It never is, is it? Excuse me. I'd better sort it before war breaks out. My husband's away on a course, but when I told him what's happened he cut his trip short and he's on his way back, but his train doesn't get in for another hour. I'll shut this lot up and then send them to bed. Help yourself to a biscuit.'

As Sara left the room, Becky sagged into a chair and stared into space. She should probably have been following things up or calling Keith for an update, but she needed a breather for a moment. She couldn't get Elise Chapman's Facebook post out of her mind. Why would she do that?

Becky knew the type – someone who wanted to be the centre of attention, and who got there either by behaving outrageously or being the person who knew everything and everyone. But the fact that she had posted a photo declaring Martha Porter to be a killer was monstrous.

She forced herself to stop thinking for a few moments to give her mind a break from the relentless questions. She focused instead on a vase of roses on the window ledge, on their apricot petals and the delicate perfume that she could just catch from where she was sitting, and gradually she felt her breathing relax a little.

The moment was short-lived as Sara returned from having a quiet word with her children, all of whom appeared to have gone upstairs to get ready for bed.

'They're probably fighting up there too, but at least we won't hear them, and I'm fairly confident they won't kill each other.' She smiled for a split second, and then a look of horror spread across her face. 'Oh crap. What a terrible thing to say!' She collapsed into a chair and burst into tears. 'I'm sorry,' she gulped. 'I've been trying so hard to keep it all under control in front of the kids. *Jesus!* Genevieve might sometimes have acted as if she was a cut above the rest of us, but she was my sister, and I loved her.'

Becky stood up and moved across to the kettle to finish the job that Sara had started. The coffee was already in the mugs, so she gave the woman a moment and then placed the hot drink on the table in front of her.

'I'm so sorry, but I have to ask you some more questions, Sara. I know DS Cumba talked to you this morning, but we thought you were perhaps in deep shock then, and even though I'm sure you can't feel much better now, I wondered if you'd had time to think, and if so, has anything occurred to you?'

Sara wiped her eyes with a tissue and lifted her head. 'I don't know. There's nothing in particular. I suppose it's normal to feel guilty when someone dies – to wonder if you could have done more, or if you should have been kinder, more understanding. She only wanted to be special, you know. It's not a sin, and I feel terrible.'

'I think it's only natural,' Becky answered. 'In my job I speak to a lot of people who've lost those they love, and honestly, everyone says the same thing. I'm sure your sister knew how much you loved her. Let's concentrate on finding who did this – that's the biggest help you can be to Genevieve right now.'

'And you don't think it's the woman whose face was posted on that Facebook page?'

Becky wanted to be honest with Sara, but needed to be careful about what she told her.

'We don't know. It's not helpful if she's found guilty by social media, though, and if she knows anything at all, she may well go into hiding.' *If she hasn't already.* 'Especially if she knows something about the killer – possibly even their identity. She could be at risk.'

'But she's missing?'

'We don't know where she is, although that's not necessarily the same as missing. No one seems to have an address for her, so she may well be at home, reading a book or cooking dinner. We have it in hand, and we're looking for her. In the meantime, was there anything in your sister's life, as far as you know, that could have put her in any danger?'

Sara rested her chin on her upturned palms and stared blindly across the room. Finally, she shook her head. 'Nothing that bad, no. She could be difficult. Money seemed to matter to her, more than I thought was healthy sometimes. She always seemed to feel she had to be in competition with everyone about everything, but I could never work out who she was trying to impress.'

'Can you give me some examples of times when she was "difficult", as you put it?'

Sara blew out a long breath through pursed lips. 'She was being a bit weird about Niall. I think she felt it was time he realised there was more to life than what she called his "bloody app". I told her the same bloody app was paying for their lifestyle, but she just smiled and said she was going to give him a bit of a reality check.'

'She didn't say what she meant?'

'No. I think she was hankering after the days when all she did was party. I suppose you're aware she went out with that footballer? He was a dick, and Gen knew it, but she liked the kudos, you know? We had a massive row about it. I told her that a relationship with a man who genuinely loved her would bring her far more happiness than going to fancy parties, pushing God knows what up her nose and thinking that getting hammered was fun. But she was livid – said I was tedious beyond belief, old before my time and several other choice phrases that I prefer to forget.' She paused. 'But that was a long time ago now. I hoped she'd settle down with Niall, but then he's flash in his own way too.'

'Before we get on to talking about Niall, we were wondering about the footballer – Eddie Carlson. Apparently he could get nasty when he was jealous. Do you know how things ended between them?'

Sara gave a short, sharp laugh. 'His jealousy had nothing to do with love. He just didn't want to be seen to be losing out to anyone else. And he was always pissed, so it was largely the booze talking. Gen told the world – and the press – that she dumped him because things were getting out of hand with his drinking and drug-taking, but he said *he* dumped *her* because she was always trying it on with his mates, and she showed him up. He put out a statement denying that she'd ditched him, but the press didn't bite. Someone as insignificant as Genevieve getting dumped by him was of no interest. Her ditching him, a famous footballer, was much more newsworthy.'

'So you don't think we should consider him a suspect?'

'Not really. He was furious with her for all she said, but I think he's playing for some second-rate Spanish club now. If he'd been going to react, it would have been sooner.'

Becky nodded and took a sip of her coffee. 'What about Niall? How were things there?'

Sara pushed her chair back from the table. 'Do you mind if I have a glass of wine? I think I need it, and you're welcome to join me. I must check on the kids in a moment too.'

'I'd love one, but I can't, I'm afraid. You carry on, though.'

Sara opened the door to the fridge and spoke without turning round. 'Niall is okay, but I really don't know him that well. I think I mentioned to your colleague that we're not invited there much because of the kids, and although we ask them here, it's not his idea of fun being surrounded by my noisy brood. Not Gen's either, if I'm honest.'

'Did she seem happy with him?'

Sara returned to her chair and took a long drink from her glass. 'She seemed happy with what he provided, if that doesn't sound too cynical. She had a lovely house, although it's not as fancy as Eddie's place, and she didn't need to work so she could hang around all day with her friends – go to the gym, have lunch and a gossip, a bit of shopping. What a life! Do you know, since finding out about Gen I've had friends call me and offer to take the kids; others have called round with food, offered to do the shopping or just volunteered a hug. I would put money on none of her friends getting in touch with Niall, or even really mourning her.'

Becky didn't want to tell her that, according to Rob, she was spot on.

'It was all a bit artificial. When I asked if she was happy with Niall – if she loved him – she said, "What's not to love? He's got plenty of money, he's good-looking, and he's not a bad lover." But having said all of that, I got the impression recently that she was worried about something. And it was something to do with Niall.'

Becky leaned forward. 'Do you have any idea what?'

Sara shook her head slowly. 'No. Strange as it sounds, I don't think she would have been that bothered if there was another woman, as long as no one else knew he was being unfaithful – loss of face, you know – and provided he wasn't going to leave her. If he did, she'd be left with nothing, you see. She's not had a job in years. But then they've been married a while, so I guess he'd have had to give her half of everything.'

Becky knew but didn't say that this was not necessarily the case. It was always the starting point, but other factors could be taken into consideration.

'They didn't have a pre-nup?' Becky asked.

'Not that I'm aware of. I'm fairly certain Gen wouldn't have married him if he'd asked her to sign away her rights.'

Becky didn't like what she was hearing. Sara seemed to have loved her sister, but Genevieve sounded shallow and self-centred. Becky's mind flashed back to Niall's disdainful tone when he talked about how his wife had spent her days, and she wondered what their marriage had really been like.

32

There wasn't much more that Tom could do at XO-Tech. A search team had arrived, and they were stripping Martha's office. Rob had volunteered to stay behind with them.

'It's not a problem. I'm not doing anything tonight,' he said.

Except maybe sleep, Tom thought, but kept the idea to himself.

He'd had a word with Elise Chapman, who had been very defensive.

'I liked Genevieve. She was a friend, and Martha wasn't friends with anyone here. She didn't give a damn about any of us. Anyway, I saw her arguing with Genevieve only last week. I heard her shouting – Genevieve, that is. The door wasn't closed properly, but I couldn't hear what they said.'

Tom noted the position of Elise's desk – at the far side of the room from Martha's office, where it was unlikely she would have heard a thing. 'Where were you when you heard the conversation between Martha Porter and Mrs Strachan?' he asked.

Elise had the grace to flush slightly. 'I was putting a notice up on the board.' She pointed to a cork board which held some official memos and a few party invitations. 'I couldn't help overhearing.

Well, not the words, but Genevieve was furious with Martha about something.'

'Did anyone else hear?'

'I think Caroline did, but she was further from the door so she wouldn't have been able to hear what they were saying either.'

'I understand you were the last person to speak to Martha this morning. Can you remember anything she said?'

Elise grunted. 'What *she* said? Bloody nothing, cold bitch. She carried on as if I wasn't there, faffing with her computer and her phone, ignoring me. But she acted a bit weird when I mentioned the police.'

'What did you see her do with her phone?'

'She took it out of her bag and put it in her drawer, then fiddled with her mouse as if I wasn't there.'

'You're sure she took the phone out of her bag?'

Elise's eyes narrowed. 'Yes. Why?'

'No reason. I'm trying to understand more of how your phones are used – with the app on them.'

Tom needed to distract Elise from the idea that the location of the phone was important, so he read her the riot act for posting accusations against Martha online. 'We don't know that she was involved in any way, and I'd like you to remove all posts relating to Ms Porter, please.'

She had looked rather disgruntled, but then a slight smile touched the corner of her mouth, and Tom knew she was going to make much more of this than she should. Her next post would place him in the role of villain and paint her as his victim. But he was too weary to worry about that now. As long as she took the posts down, that was all that mattered.

Tom drove home carefully, his window wide open to maximise the breeze, and finally pulled into his drive at 8.30, glad to be back. He needed food, a drink, some time with Louisa and – when Harry woke for his next feed – a cuddle with his baby. And then sleep.

Louisa was in the kitchen, and there was no sign of Harry. Perhaps that was for the best. Tom would enjoy him all the more when he'd had time to put the day's events behind him. He hated the thought of holding his son while images of the gruesome scene they had found that morning flashed through his mind.

'Hi, Tom,' Louisa said as she pulled a large bowl of salad from the fridge. 'Are you okay? White wine, as it's so hot and sticky?'

Tom was pleased to see that she looked less tired than she had the day before, and he hoped she'd had a chance to rest. He felt slightly guilty about the wine, as Louisa wasn't drinking while she was still breastfeeding Harry, but she swore she didn't mind.

'I'm fine, and white wine sounds perfect. Thank you. How are you feeling? And Harry?'

'It's been a good day. Harry has one rather pink cheek, but he seems to be over the worst for now. He's been a little sweetie today. You should have seen him rolling around on his rug after his nap! He made me laugh, and he was very chatty in his incomprehensible way. Lots of "bur bur" sounds.'

Tom smiled at the thought. Louisa was desperate for him to make any sound that she could interpret as 'Mummy', but Tom kept telling her not to wish the time away.

'Do you want to tell me about Lucy and Kate?' he asked as she passed him his wine.

'Of course. Do you mind if I speak with my back to you? I want to cook these fishcakes to go with the salad. Unless you'd rather wait?'

'No, it's fine. I'm starving.'

Louisa pulled a plate bearing the promised fishcakes from the fridge and switched on the hob.

'I gave you the basics on the phone. The new man turned out to be not quite what she expected. Lucy didn't give many details, and I didn't speak to Kate. All I could glean was that he'd given up his job on the ship and thought he'd take some time to have a look around to decide on his future direction.'

Tom sighed. 'Poor Kate. She's spent her life trying to find a man who will keep her in the style to which she would like to become accustomed, and then she ends up with someone who it seems has the same idea, but in reverse.'

'Are you gloating, Tom?' Louisa said, turning round to give him a fake-stern look.

She was right – he shouldn't make fun – but all those years ago Kate had hurt him badly when she left him for another man, taking Lucy with her. Then, when that relationship went sour, she decided a return to Tom was her best bet. Tom had turned her down, even though he missed Lucy.

'I tend to be a tad cynical where Kate's concerned. Too much history. More importantly, how's Lucy taking it?'

'Delighted to be coming home, missing Harry – and she belatedly remembered to say she missed us too, but I'm sure she does – as much as any teenage girl would. I think she's annoyed because she was starting to make some friends in Australia, and now she's coming back but not even to the same school. Kate told her she doesn't think they can afford to move back to that area. Since she sold the house, I think she must have spent a lot of the money. She told Lucy they may have to rent a small flat somewhere.'

Tom was pleased that Louisa had her back to him. He didn't want her to see his expression. He knew exactly what was going on here, but she didn't know Kate as well as he did, and despite some of his ex-wife's behaviour, Louisa made an effort to get on with her.

Kate was planting problems in Lucy's mind – a different school, a run-down flat, a different lifestyle. She knew Lucy would report all of this to her dad, and it was her way of preparing the ground for what was to come.

'You know what's coming next, don't you?' Tom asked as Louisa flicked the golden fishcakes onto a plate.

'Of course I do. And I know what you'll do. It's fine, Tom. You didn't think I'd object, did you?'

'No, but I wouldn't blame you if you did. Not everyone would accept their baby's father shelling out to put a roof over the head of his ex-wife. Why is it always about money with Kate?'

'That doesn't matter, because you're not doing it for her, are you? You normally won't touch Jack's money, but I'm assuming that's where it will come from.'

'There's nowhere else!'

'So it's fine. And I'm sure Jack wouldn't mind.'

Talk of Jack was always difficult for Tom. He missed his brother and longed for the evenings they used to spend together drinking whisky and arguing about music, politics or crime. Louisa was wrong about Jack, though. He wouldn't resent Tom spending the money on somewhere for Lucy, but he'd be bloody annoyed with Kate for taking the piss – which is exactly what he would think she was doing.

33

MARTHA

I was certain that once I started driving, Alfie would fall asleep in his seat, his head propped against the side rests. I was right. The day's activity and the brief episode with his temperature have taken their toll.

We travelled north from the airport, towards home initially. That made me nervous, but it was the fastest route, and I knew that the sooner we were on the motorway heading east, the happier I'd be. I've been driving for about forty-five minutes now, and I'm scared to stop, to have to get out of the car for fuel or when we reach our destination. Who knows how far Elise's post has spread?

I glance in the mirror and my momentary calm evaporates. A police car is coming up fast behind me, blue lights flashing, and I grip the steering wheel tightly, waiting for it to catch up with me. It pulls out to pass, and the officer in the passenger seat looks my way. I'm waiting, knowing they're going to signal me to pull over, and I keep my eyes on the road ahead, trying to convince myself that by ignoring them, they will go away. The siren wails, and a groan escapes my lips as the car sails by, speeding along the outside lane, other vehicles moving out of its way. Whoever they're after, it isn't me.

I put my foot down, keeping below the speed limit, but I want to reach my destination and get off the road as soon as I can. My intention has always been to go to Northumberland. I've researched the area well, and it sounds wonderful. I like the idea of moors, hills and beaches. We'll be happy there. At least, that's what I've always thought.

Now I think of what's ahead of me – finding a new home, a new job, maybe even new names for both of us, all the while praying that no one recognises me.

How long can I keep doing this to Alfie?

For over five years we've been in and around Manchester. It's a big city, so it was easy to move from one side to the other and think that it was a whole new part of the country, especially as we kept out of the centre. I thought I was keeping ahead of the game, but I'm not any longer. The police will investigate me, and hiding will become increasingly difficult. How long before Alfie starts looking for answers?

I look at him now in the mirror. His skin is paler than mine, but his hair is just as wild and curly. I know I should cut it shorter – even without the pink T-shirt he sometimes gets mistaken for a girl – but it's so glorious as it spreads around his cute little face like a black halo. It's impossible to believe that there was a time when I doubted he would ever be born.

I shudder at the thought, and Alfie stirs, pushing the memories from my mind.

'Mummy, I need a wee.'

I don't want to stop, to walk into a bustling service station, but I can't deny him a visit to the toilet.

'We'll stop soon, sweetheart. Can you hang on?'

I watch in the mirror as he frowns in concentration. 'I'll try.'

Five minutes later I spot a sign to the services.

'Nearly there, Alfie – just a couple of minutes.'

I pull into the car park and, keeping my head down, we walk through the double glass doors into the concourse. Alfie is looking around, his little face a picture of awe. He's never been anywhere like this before, but I hurry him along, towards the bathrooms.

It's as we are coming out that I glance up at a large television and I stop, my legs suddenly weak. The screen is filled with an image of Genevieve. A photo of Niall pops up in the left-hand corner and I swallow the lump in my throat. The audio would never be heard over the sound of so many people talking, laughing, shouting, so subtitles flash up every few seconds, and I struggle to read them before they disappear. I see POLICE and LINES OF ENQUIRY, and I know without a doubt that I will be one of them. Maybe I shouldn't have run. Maybe it would have been better to stay and pray they didn't look too closely at me, that they would confine their search to Martha Porter and never discover who I used to be. I've covered my tracks well, or at least I thought I had. Now I'm not so confident.

They can't have any evidence against me for Genevieve's murder, can they? An image flashes into my mind of a bag of blood-covered clothes. Do the police already have it? If they do, their hunt for me will intensify, but I don't know and I have no way of finding out.

I look at my son's sweet, innocent face and the future no longer seems clear. I want to flee – to get as far away as I can – but I can't keep running. It's not the right thing for Alfie. He needs a life that's normal, predictable, secure. He loves being with people. He needs friends and the chance to follow his dreams without being tied to a mother who's permanently looking over her shoulder.

It's as if Alfie senses that I'm worried, because he doesn't chatter as we walk, hand in hand, back to the car. He climbs into his seat without a word, and I get in the front. But I don't start the engine.

It's not just the police I need to worry about. They are not the only people looking for me. There are others: faceless people, nameless people. I wouldn't know them if they were standing right next to me, but I do know that if they find me, life for me and for Alfie will never be the same.

In the nearly six years I've been on my own, I've found my soul. I have my own values, and I need to take responsibility for my own actions. Alfie deserves better from me. It's time to stop hiding from my mistakes.

I make a decision. A pain so intense that it makes me moan out loud clutches at my heart. I start the engine and make my way back on to the motorway, knowing that when I reach the junction I won't turn left and head north to Northumberland; I will turn right and head south, to Lincolnshire. One way or another, this has to end.

34

LAKESIDE

After Aram's arrival at Lakeside, for a while things followed a predictable pattern. He would spend hours with Mum in his meditation room, and often she would come out laughing, happy again – the mother I had always known. Other times she would be in floods of tears. Dad and I didn't know what to expect, and we waited nervously when we knew she was about to emerge from his lair.

I remember when Aram made her cry for the first time.

Dad was horrified. 'Darling! What did he say to you?'

Silent convulsive sobs rendered her speechless.

'That's it, Nic. He's got to go,' Dad said, his hands resting on her shoulders. He pulled her towards him so he could hold her, and I jumped up from the table to rush over to join in. We all needed a family hug, something we had been doing less and less in the last few weeks.

Mum stopped sobbing and raised her tear-stained face to Dad. 'No! He can't go, Joel. I need him. He's the only thing that makes sense in my life.'

If Dad was hurt by that, he didn't show it. 'But Nic, he's tearing you apart!' He sounded as if he was about to cry too.

'You really don't understand, do you?' she said, pushing him away, her hands against his chest. Dad looked bewildered. 'This is what our sessions are all about, and it's not Aram who's hurting me. I'm crying because I'm beginning to understand all that's wrong with me – all the things I've messed up, the values that I thought meant something. He's making me face them all. I *have* to be torn apart, turned inside out, so I can rebuild myself as a better person.'

Dad tutted and threw his head back. 'That's fucking ridiculous, Nic. You're a lovely person.' He rarely swore in front of me, and I think they'd forgotten I was there, locked as they were in some battle that I didn't understand.

'I'm not a good person, Joel. *We're* not good people. We have this obsession with what's ours. Everyone wants to *own* stuff – we even think there are *people* we own. You think I'm yours, don't you?' Dad was speechless. 'We make ourselves sick with envy, greed, jealousy. And why, Joel? *Why?'*

He didn't have a clue how to answer. I could see how confused he was, but something snagged the corner of my eye and I turned my head slightly. The kitchen door was standing open, the corridor beyond dark, and someone was there. A glimmer of light reflected off pale grey eyes, and I could see the ghost of a smile around his mouth as Aram slowly moved away and out of my sight.

Aram's sessions with Mum only occupied part of the day. He regularly demanded to see both me and Dad, but rarely together now. Dad sometimes came out looking as if he'd been punched, other times he was smiling, his eyes slightly unfocused as if he was thinking of something wonderful. I never knew what took place, but despite his earlier qualms, it seemed Dad had agreed to try Aram's form of meditation.

I had such a strange feeling about my own sessions. I trembled for hours before it was my turn to go to the meditation room in a kind of frenzied anticipation. I was half longing to be there, half terrified of how Aram might make me feel. Sometimes he would tell me stories, sitting facing me on the floor, rolling the glass sphere in his hands. It sparkled with iridescence, the light catching its polished surface, flashing bright colours as it whirled between his palms. And I listened.

He made the tales so exciting, so colourful, and I was mesmerised. He would give me one of his potions to drink, made with herbs that he grew in the walled garden at the back of the house. Some were sweet and tasted of flowers. Others were bitter, and I wanted to spit them out. But I never did.

He didn't always smile. There were times when his face would be harsh, his tone cold, and he would talk to me about the demands I made on my mother for her attention, telling me I was selfish and self-centred.

'Nicola needs your acceptance for who she is and the journey she's on. I'm helping her to develop a roadmap that will give meaning to her life, and everyone's individual journey has to be taken alone. If you hang on like a limpet, you'll slow her down – you'll be nothing more than a burden that she must drag along behind her.'

'But she's my mum!' I whinged one day.

'And how might that be relevant?' he asked, leaning forward, his thick eyebrows forming a deep V.

I didn't know the answer.

'I'll tell you, shall I? Giving birth is an act of nature. As a baby, you need your mother to provide you with food. But you're not a baby any more, India, and Nicola is free of the obligation to nurture you. Your reliance on her is restricting both her growth and your own – you're a deadweight that's too heavy for her to bear. That's why I've decided you should sleep in another part of the house.'

My heart was hammering in my chest. Were they not my parents any longer? Didn't they love me any more? I hoped Mum wouldn't let him move me. Those were the days when he still appeared to consult her about decisions, although she denied him nothing. But maybe he was right: I wasn't a baby who needed her mother. After all, I was almost eleven years old.

Aram was as good as his word. For the protection of my mother's 'journey' to becoming a better person, the sleeping arrangements were changed, and my mother didn't object.

I was distraught. For the first week as I walked away from my parents each night to the opposite end of the house, up a different staircase, knowing they wouldn't be there if I needed them, it felt like the end of the world. In truth it had been a few years since I had crawled into their bed in the middle of the night, but I had known they were there – the other side of the wall – and their presence had always comforted me.

My new room was isolated from everyone. It felt cold whatever the weather, but I think what I was missing was the warmth that comes from feeling loved. I wasn't loved any longer – or at least that's how it seemed to me – and each night I huddled under the duvet, knees pulled to my chest, my head buried in my pillow as I sobbed, wondering what I had done wrong, what was so awful about me that no one loved me. I knew that crying was self-indulgent and Aram would be angry if he knew, so I told no one.

It was weeks before I realised that I wasn't the only one who had moved. Dad was no longer permitted to share Mum's bed. When I asked him about it he tried to smile. 'We still love each other, DeeDee, but if I'm lying next to her, my presence distracts her. Right now she needs space to think, without worrying about me. It won't be for long.'

He was wrong about that, and it wasn't the only change. Aram said that not only did I have to sleep in a different part of the house, he insisted I use my parents' given names – Nicola and Joel – although I secretly continued to think of them as Mum and Dad. Yet despite this – or maybe because of it – we circled Aram like satellites, increasingly worried about causing unrest, ever more eager to win his approval.

I convinced myself I had plenty to look forward to. My eleventh birthday was coming, and I would be going to school in September, so I allowed myself the luxury of being excited. At least until I learned that celebrating birthdays was for the vain and self-obsessed.

Nothing seemed steady or secure, and the ground beneath me kept shifting, but somehow I continued to believe that things would get back to normal once Mum was feeling better and Aram had moved on. He wasn't with us all the time. He had commitments that took him away, but he always returned as if coming home, and was welcomed with open arms by Mum, who was much more subdued in his absence.

Life had settled into a pattern. Apart from the time each of us spent with Aram, Mum cooked our meals and Dad cleared up with my help. Aram ate with us but made no contribution and made little or no comment about the food.

'We eat to sustain our bodies,' he said. 'Food should be nutritious and healthy, that's all.'

I didn't agree, but of course would never have voiced an opinion that was contrary to Aram's. Mum cooked mouth-watering food, and we'd always enjoyed family meals together, but our diet slowly changed, the emphasis moving to bland food that fulfilled its purpose without evoking murmurs of delight. Little did I know then that this was only the start of the ways in which our lives would alter, but I was soon to find out.

Two days before my eleventh birthday, Mum said she would take me into town for new shoes and a school uniform.

Aram stopped us at the door. 'Where are you going?'

As always when she spoke to him, Mum's smile was wide but not entirely steady.

'India starts her new school in a few weeks, and she's grown out of all her shoes,' she said with a slightly tinny laugh.

He glanced from her to me and back again. 'May I have a word, Nicola?'

'Of course,' Mum said to his back as he walked away from us into the sitting room.

He held the door open for her and turned to close it, leaving me in the hall. I could hear the low murmur of his voice, and for a moment Mum's voice was slightly raised, but I couldn't tell what she was saying. I don't know how long they were in there. To me it seemed like hours, but I suspect it was only a few minutes.

When Mum came out, she was pale. She looked at me anxiously. 'Change of plan, India. I've got some exciting news for you. As Aram will be staying with us for a while, he said he's happy to teach you, so you don't have to go to school. Isn't that amazing? He's brilliant! You're so lucky!'

'But I *want* to go to school! I want to make friends with other kids. *Please*, Mum, can I go?'

She sucked her lips into a tight line and shook her head.

'You're forgetting, India. I'm Nicola. How many times do you need to be told? And don't be ungrateful. It's a wonderfully kind offer from Aram. Mixing with other children will unsettle you and pull you from the path to becoming a better person.'

The door to the sitting room was open, and he could hear every word. I didn't want to cry, because I knew there would be consequences, but Mum had gone into that room smiling, looking forward to a day out with me. Whatever he'd said to her, her joy had evaporated.

'Can we go for the shoes, like you promised, even if we're not getting the uniform?'

Mum gave her tinkling laugh, the one I had started to recognise as fake. 'You don't need shoes! That's the joy of not going to school.' She bent down and pulled off her own shoes. 'You see – I won't wear any either!'

I felt a now familiar beat of unease. *What was happening to my family?* But I knew I'd lost. The gates to the world beyond Lakeside were beginning to close. Not just for me, but for all of us.

―――――――

It was more than six years before I had any shoes, apart from a pair I stole from Mum's box in the attic and hid in my room, but I never left the house and its grounds from the week before my eleventh birthday until Aram decided that he needed me to do something for him more than six years later. And because it necessitated straying beyond the locked gates, he bought me one pair of thin slip-on shoes. Good enough for walking, but not for running.

I was allowed to keep them for three months, and then they disappeared.

WEDNESDAY

35

Tom was in the incident room by 7 a.m. the next morning, eager to check any progress on the whereabouts of Martha Porter. He glanced over at the board. Her photo was up there, along with that of Eddie Carlson and, of course, Niall Strachan. The husband wouldn't be ruled out until they were certain his alibi stacked up. They'd confirmed that his car had been driven home at the time he stated, but that wasn't conclusive enough for Tom. There were other possibilities.

He wasn't surprised to see Keith already at his desk, and a few moments later Becky strolled through the door, stifling a yawn.

'Sorry – didn't sleep too well. I thought I'd be out like a light, but I couldn't shut my head up! Rob's on his way in too,' she said. 'He just called. He came back here last night, and I don't think he left until after midnight.'

'He's certainly keen – you have to give him that,' Tom said. 'While we're waiting, any news on Martha Porter?'

Keith nodded. 'Yes, sir. Now she is a confirmed suspect, we've requested her financials, but there's not much chance of anything for a couple of hours until the banks open. The digital team have been going through her computer and have found the payroll files. We hoped it would be a quick route to her bank details. We knew she was paid as a contractor, but her earnings aren't paid into a personal account. She submits invoices to XO-Tech from three companies, each for a different service – bookkeeping, administrative services and human resources. Each invoice is paid to a different account.'

'Complicated. Is her home address the registered office?'

Keith shook his head. 'She uses a virtual office address for each of them. The company that manages the service is required to provide the legal address if we request it, and we're trying to get hold of them.'

'Good God. This woman did her best to keep herself well hidden, which makes me even more suspicious. Good work, Keith. We've got a woman with no passport, no driving licence, no NI number as far as we can tell, who hides her earnings as best she can. I have to wonder if she has another identity.'

At that moment the door swung open, and Rob strode in. 'Sorry, boss, am I late?'

'Hardly, and I gather you were here until midnight.'

Rob grinned. 'I think the adrenaline must have been pumping. I thought I'd check on a few things – see what I could find out about the knife, for one thing. But before we get to that, on my way in I got a call on my mobile. Elise Chapman, no less.'

Becky raised her eyebrows. 'You gave her your number?'

Rob grinned. 'Only in the interests of the job, I can assure you. She took the Facebook post down, as we asked, but not before it had gone viral locally. Someone recognised Martha, but before she had the chance to respond the post disappeared from her newsfeed – presumably when Elise deleted it. She asked all her friends if they knew who posted the picture of the murderer and by some magical crossover between friends of friends of friends, she discovered it was Elise, and sent her a message.' Rob pulled out his phone and read from the screen. '"I don't want to go making trouble for this woman, but I know who she is. Do you know who I should talk to about it?" Elise called me. Smug as hell, she was. She said the woman wouldn't give any details about how she knows Martha, but she's called Naomi Simpson, and it says on her Facebook page that she's a childminder.'

'Martha Porter doesn't have children, does she?' Becky said.

'Not that we know of, but it seems there's a lot we don't know about Ms Porter,' Tom replied. 'Okay, Rob, it should be easy to get hold of her. Make it a priority, but first what about the knife?'

'Not as conclusive as I would have liked. It's a long-bladed paring knife, used by chefs to cut fruit and vegetables. I had a photo of it, so I stuck it in Google Images, and the closest match was one available on Amazon. It had 170 reviews, so finding out who's bought one recently could be a needle-in-a-haystack job. Not sure if it's relevant at all, but along with the blood, forensics said there were traces of lemon juice on the blade.'

Tom shut out the sounds around him. Someone had mentioned lemons in the last few days. Who was it? He ran through the conversations he'd had about the murder of Genevieve Strachan, and suddenly it hit him.

He looked at Becky. 'Niall Strachan mentioned lemons. Do you remember?'

Becky frowned as she concentrated. 'I do. He said something about ice and lemon for drinks when he had visitors.' Her eyes opened wide. 'And he said Martha always prepared them, didn't he?'

Tom felt a beat of excitement. There must be hundreds of knives with traces of lemon on them, but somehow he was sure that this was *the* knife.

'Becky, the search team must have gone through the nook off Martha's office where the knife was kept. Can you call them to see if they saw a knife? If it's still there, that's the end of it. If it's not, get on to Spencer Johansson and ask him if he can describe it.'

Tom sat back in his chair. They were closing in on Martha

Porter as their number-one suspect. All they had to do now was find her.

36

Tom should have been getting back to his office – there was a stack of paperwork waiting for him, and Philippa would want an update on progress – but he wasn't shifting from the incident room. There was too much happening, and he was staying put until they had some results.

Rob was on the phone to Naomi Simpson, who had been every bit as easy to track down as they had thought.

'Can you tell me how you know Martha Porter?' Tom heard him ask.

He could hear a voice at the other end of the line, slightly raised as if anxious at speaking to the police.

'How old is Alfie?' Rob asked.

Desperate as he was to hear everything being said, Tom moved away before he was tempted to reach for the phone and take it from the detective. Alfie must be Martha's son – a child about whom her work colleagues knew nothing. That was strange. Everyone liked to talk about their children – to show photos, to boast about the things they'd achieved or the funny things they'd done to make their parents laugh.

And speaking of parents, where was Alfie's dad?

Tom was pacing, waiting for the nugget that would get them all moving in the right direction, but his team knew what they were doing without him hanging over their shoulders, so he steered himself towards the board.

What was the evidence against Martha Porter? She appeared to have been obsessed with Niall. She'd been seen arguing with Genevieve, although they still didn't know what about. The phone issued to her had been used to call Genevieve and lure her from the house. It seemed possible that the knife used as the murder weapon came from the kitchen area off Martha's office.

It all added up, but it was also circumstantial, and he doubted it would stand up in court. But if Martha wasn't implicated in Genevieve's death, why had she run? They needed more. Whoever killed Genevieve must have been covered in her blood, so what had happened to their clothes? If they could find them, they would have a solid case.

Tom stared at the photos.

Did they have any reason to believe Niall had killed his wife? It would be a mistake to rule out the husband, but although there had been a couple of suggestions that things were not perfect, there was no evidence of domestic violence, or that either of them was having an affair. Indeed, it seemed Martha had offered herself to Niall, and he had turned her down. If he was telling the truth.

Becky had been sceptical and said he didn't seem the kind of guy who would turn a woman down, although Tom had no idea on what she based that assertion.

'I can't explain it, Tom,' she'd said. 'There's something about certain men that women often pick up on. It's not that they specifically *want* an affair, but they're thrill-seekers, and usually they like themselves a bit too much. An offer of free sex is something they wouldn't be able to resist.'

'And you don't think that's a bit of a generalisation?' he'd asked. 'Apart from anything else, it doesn't just apply to men, in my experience.'

'Don't get all defensive. I didn't say *all* men are like that. To some self-indulgent types it seems that casual sex is just a bit of excitement. It means nothing, so why not? He struck me as a guy who was a bit full of himself. When he talked about his business it was as if he'd totally forgotten that his wife had just been murdered.'

Their conversation was interrupted as Rob hung up the phone and spun round in his seat, passing a Post-it note to Cass, the latest recruit to the team.

'Boss, we might be getting somewhere.'

Tom walked over to join him. 'What have you got?'

'Martha Porter has a five-year-old son, Alfie. The contact number that Naomi has for Martha is *not* the number of the company mobile. I've given it to Cass and she's trying it now. Naomi doesn't have an address for Martha – she always pays for Alfie's childcare in cash – and she only looks after him in the school holidays. The thing is, Martha was very strict about there being no pictures of her son, but Naomi says he's so gorgeous she wasn't able to resist. She's sending me photos right now.'

As if on cue, Rob's phone pinged and up on the screen came the first of the images – a profile of a little boy with wild black curly hair. The next photo was full face, the child looking serious.

'That's not all,' Rob said. 'Alfie apparently said they live over a place where "a man does feet". Naomi didn't know what he meant, and he wasn't able to explain further, but she thought it might be useful. Martha doesn't have a car, and Naomi is certain they walk to her house every day.'

'A man who does feet. What do we think? Podiatrist? Chiropodist?'

'Possibly someone who does pedicures,' Rob said with a shrug.

'Does anyone *only* do pedicures, though? Not manicures too?' Tom asked, then shrugged. 'How the hell would I know the answer to that? We can't rule it out, but let's rule in the most obvious first. Google Maps, Rob. Find anywhere relevant that's walking distance from the childminder. And did she say which school he goes to? There may be someone there, even though it's the holidays. They'll definitely have an address.'

Cass, the young detective who had been asked to check out the mobile phone number provided by Naomi, had reported back that there was no answer, and Tom had the feeling that even if they put a trace on the phone, they would find nothing. This woman seemed expert at hiding.

'If we can't find an address for her in the next hour, I'm going to issue a Child Rescue Alert. We have a small child missing in the company of a suspected murderer, so it's justified. If we find out where Porter lives and she's not there, we'll get a picture of Alfie out to the media, plus the one of Martha from the XO-Tech files.'

He walked over to where Becky was still on the phone to the search team and mimed that he wanted to say something.

'Hang on,' she said. 'The boss wants a word.' She lowered the phone and looked at Tom.

'Tell them I want to see if we can get Martha Porter's DNA from the stuff in her office. There has to be some reason why this woman is going to such enormous lengths to hide her whereabouts. Let's run it through the database and see if we get any hits.'

Becky raised her eyebrows and nodded. 'Good idea.'

Tom moved away. Finally, they were making progress. Within the next hour he was confident they would have Martha's address, and the picture of Alfie would make all the difference when it was released to the media.

The scales were always tipped when a child was at risk.

37

MARTHA

Condensation fogs the windscreen, and it feels sticky in the small, stationary car, so I nudge open a window to let out some of the hot, damp air and rub the glass with the back of my hand, wondering why it isn't as light outside as it should be. The reason becomes clear when I lean forward and look up. The sky is black, and there is a distant rumble of thunder. At least a storm will freshen the dead air.

I turn to look at Alfie, who is lying on the back seat under my jacket, his curls sticking to his forehead. I've been watching him all night, my neck stiff with turning to gaze at his face, storing every cell of his skin in my memory. I can't believe what I'm about to do, but how can I do anything else? It's taken me a long time to realise it, but I have to accept that loving my son isn't enough.

He stirs and mumbles and I reach over a hand to rest on him so he will settle again. Sleeping in the car isn't ideal, but the money on the prepaid debit card will run out if I'm not careful, and I can't risk using any cards in the name of Martha Porter. Not yet. Although it will take the police a while to unravel the complexities of my banking, I know they'll succeed. Eventually.

The debit card has been my lifeline, and I remember Dad giving it to me all those years ago. I haven't spoken to him since that day, but I've worried about him ever since.

And now, nearly six years later, I'm back, close to the place in which my life changed beyond recognition when I was only a few years older than Alfie is now.

LAKESIDE

It's surprising how adaptable children are. After my eleventh birthday, the bitter disappointment of not going to school slowly faded. Lessons with Aram became the new norm. He was an excellent teacher, and our study periods were the one time he didn't default to his usual obsession of building me into a better person – just a smarter one. The only exception was during the obligatory religious education lessons. It was then that I began to understand Aram's ideology and how he was influencing my mother.

'As humans, we've been taught to believe some actions we take are right and others wrong. We're expected to acknowledge that these rules have been communicated to us by some supreme being, whoever that might be – Jehovah, Allah, Krishna. But the rules were actually set by men in the *name* of their god: rich, influential men who wanted to control the lives of those around them, to protect what they had – what they *owned*.'

He dragged the final word out, creating a perfect circle with his lips. I didn't understand who these men were who had set the rules, but his voice was compelling.

'We're taught that what we have is ours. That no one should take it from us. Whether it's our homes, our possessions, our wives, we're made to believe that we should hold tight to whatever we think belongs to us. Let me ask you: why do people steal?' He paused for only a few seconds before answering the question himself. 'Because some people have everything, and others have nothing. Do you think that's right, India?'

I didn't know. Questions like that were too complex for me, but I shook my head because I knew it was what he expected.

'We arrive on this earth with nothing, and we leave with nothing. Everything we have in between is borrowed and should be shared.'

This reminded me of something Mum had said months ago after one of her sessions with Aram: about how everyone wanted to own things; how our lottery win had turned friends into enemies; how jealousy was rife because people believed they owned their family, their friends, their lovers. I didn't know what to think. I thought of my mum and dad as mine. Was that wrong? This house was ours, wasn't it?

'Why do people kill, India?' he asked, and those ice-grey eyes bored into mine.

'Because they're angry?' I ventured. Something else I didn't know. I only knew what I'd seen on the television, when we had one. We didn't any more.

'Angry about what? Because someone has taken something from them – their wife, their child, their money? Or do they hate each other because their religions are at war with each other? If we share what we have, loosen the ropes tying us to our possessions and throw away the books that define our beliefs, our souls will be free.'

I stared at him, not knowing whether I was listening to words of great wisdom or total nonsense. Mum would say he was right about everything. Dad would be more sceptical, but would he go so far as to say Aram was wrong?

Aram pushed his face right up to mine, less than an inch away, nose to nose.

'Even killing someone can be the right thing to do, and some religions accept this. If a person threatens to disrupt lives for no reason other than their own glorification, there is clear justification for their elimination. We should plunge in the blade and twist.' He thrust his hand forward and flicked his wrist as if he were holding a knife. Then he pulled back. 'Not for greed, jealousy or anger, but for truth and justice.'

He stopped talking, but didn't move back. I wanted to turn my head away, but his eyes were staring straight into mine, and I felt myself sag in my chair. For a moment I didn't know where I was and whether the last few minutes had been part of a dream. The edges of my vision blurred. I could hear, but I couldn't react.

When my eyes cleared, I was sitting in exactly the same position, but Aram was standing behind me, his thumb gently rubbing the back of my neck. I hadn't seen him move.

I sat frozen in my seat. He had never touched me before, and I didn't know how to react. He must have felt my body stiffen because he removed his hand, but I could still feel the burn of his fingers.

'It's time for mathematics, India. Please take out your exercise book.'

He said it as if nothing had happened, but I knew time had passed. Before, the sun had been shining through the window. Now it had moved to one side, and the room felt cold.

I didn't know what had happened, where I had been in my mind for the last few minutes or maybe hours. It wasn't the last occasion that I would experience that same loss of time and reality.

I had been having lessons for about two months when Aram announced that he was leaving us.

Mum spun round from the Aga, where she was stirring sauce for our pasta, and dropped her spoon with a clatter. 'But why, Aram? Have we done something to upset you?' Her gaze flickered from me to Dad and back again.

I instantly felt guilty. Had I done something wrong? If I had, I didn't know what it was.

'I need to spread the word further than these four walls, Nicola. There are others who need me.'

'But how long will you be gone?' she asked, her voice little more than a squeak. The pasta water was boiling over and sizzling on the hob. Dad stood up and reached behind her to remove it from the heat.

'I've no idea, I'm afraid. As long as it takes for me to help those who are looking for a way forward. It takes time to bring people to their own personal fulfilment.'

I could read the horror on Mum's face. He had been with us for months, and she still didn't believe she had found what she was looking for.

Did this mean he would be gone for a long time? I felt slightly sick. My emotions had shifted: no more did I long for him to be gone; now I lived in fear of what we would be without him. All I wanted was to please Aram. When he was displeased with me, I felt desolate, aching to get his approval again, and I would do anything for one of his rare smiles. I had the impression that without him we would all be lost.

'Was it me?' I blurted out.

Aram turned to me, his mouth a straight line. 'Why would it be anything to do with you, India? Do you think you're so important that I would desert Nicola, who needs me, because of something a mere *child* had done?'

I dropped my head. He was angry and I burned with shame. 'I'm sorry,' I whispered.

Mum ignored me. 'You've just said that I need you, Aram. So how can you leave?'

'I have to help others, and unless they're with me – in my presence – for a prolonged period, I can do little.'

Mum's face lit up. 'Bring them here!' She beamed at Dad. 'We've got loads of room, haven't we, Joel?' Her head swivelled back towards Aram. 'I mean it. We'd make them very welcome. They could all muck in with taking care of the place, and it would be good for everyone. We could learn from each other.'

I was holding my breath. More people, maybe other kids; Aram still here; Mum happy. I looked at Dad. He seemed smaller to me than he used to, and I wondered if that was because I was growing up and getting bigger. He was staring at Aram, and as their eyes touched, I saw Dad's pupils dilate and a strange look came over his face, as if he was no longer with us in the kitchen.

'Joel would be delighted with that arrangement. Wouldn't you, Joel?' Aram said.

Dad nodded slowly and, as Aram stood to leave the room, flopped back in his chair, his eyes closed.

And that was the start of it. They came, two or three at a time – a few couples, although mainly they came alone, but there were no children. I knew Aram's views on how disruptive children could be, and I swallowed my disappointment. Soon the house was bursting at the seams.

I understand now that they were all searching for something that was missing from their lives, and with Aram to guide them, they believed they would find themselves. And I watched as he picked each of them apart – both publicly and privately – until they were mere shells of the people who had arrived. Then gradually he showed them his love, so that – like me – all they wanted to do was please him.

38

There was only one chiropodist within walking distance of the childminder's house, and despite the early hour he was already in his surgery when Rob called.

'Martha Porter? Yes. She rents the flat upstairs with her son, Alfie. I don't know much about her. She keeps herself to herself. I'm not sure if she's in. I haven't heard anything, but she's always quiet. Do you want me to check?'

'No, sir. We'll send an officer, so please leave it to us.'

Rob immediately dispatched a car. If Martha was at home, he asked that she be kept there until he arrived.

'Okay, you know what to do, Rob,' Tom said. 'You should be able to get a magistrate to sign a search warrant in the next hour, and then we need to go over every inch of that place for evidence, and find out anything and everything about this woman: who she is and where she came from. Let me know as soon as you're at the flat, and if she's not there I'll issue the Child Rescue Alert. Let's see if anyone's seen the boy.'

'Boss,' Becky called as Rob picked up his things and headed for the door. 'Just had a call from one of the other lawyers at the offices in Manchester, Deborah Bridges. She heard about our enquiry. She wasn't in the meeting with Niall Strachan, but she was in the offices working on another case and went outside for a cigarette. She disturbed Niall, who was lurking round a corner speaking to someone on the phone. He walked away when he saw her and carried on talking further down the road.'

'She's sure it was him?'

'Yep. She says she's seen him around, and one of the girls who works for her says he's a bit of a lech. She'd been considering making a complaint, but Deborah thought she was being a bit oversensitive. She decided to keep an eye on him, though.'

Becky put her head on one side and opened her eyes wide as if to say 'Told you so', but Tom just smiled at her.

'What time was it?'

'Twelve twenty, so he couldn't have got home and back.'

'Did she hear any of the conversation?'

'Only "Hang on a minute" as he walked away. We've already got his phone records, so I'll take a look to see who he was talking to. Not many people I'd call for a chat after midnight.'

That was true enough, although Niall was in the middle of a big negotiation about the future of his business. Tom had the feeling Becky was hoping there would be another woman on the scene so she would be proved right about Niall Strachan, and he didn't want her to become too hung up on that. He was already worried that they were getting tunnel vision about Martha Porter without his best detective becoming fixated on a philandering husband as the only credible suspect.

'Fancy going to talk to a man who, by all accounts, is equally difficult?' he asked her. 'Eddie Carlson is apparently back home from Spain for the summer. He's got a house in Hale Barns from when he played for United, and despite living most of the year in Cadiz, he still comes back. Let's see what he thinks of Genevieve now, after all these years.'

'Fine. Are you coming?'

'No. I'm going to have another go at the team in XO-Tech. In fact, why don't you come there with me first, and then you can go to see Eddie? We'll take both cars.'

'Okay. I'll get someone to phone and make an appointment with Carlson for me. Shall I aim for late morning?'

Tom looked at his watch. 'Sounds good. I need to wait to hear from Rob, but then we'll head off.'

Tom had spoken too soon. 'Sir! I've got Detective Superintendent Stanley on the line for you. She says she's been trying to reach you.'

Tom held up a hand to acknowledge the shout and turned to Becky. 'She's not been trying very hard; I've got my mobile in my pocket.' He walked over to the desk phone. 'Yes, ma'am,' he said, always respectful in front of junior officers with the possible exception of Becky.

He held the phone away from his ear and stared at it. The line was dead. She'd gone because she didn't 'do' hanging on for a junior officer – Tom, in this case.

He bit back his irritation. 'I'll be in my office, Becky. If Rob calls with any news from Porter's place, put him through. And feel free to interrupt if I'm on a call with a certain female senior officer!'

She grinned, and Tom marched back to his office.

He sat at his desk and picked up the phone. 'I gather you were looking for me, Philippa.'

'I was indeed. It's after eight thirty and I haven't had an update on the Strachan case from you. Did you oversleep? Has the baby been disturbing you?'

She wasn't asking out of concern for either him or the baby. He knew that. She was concerned that his attention wasn't solely on the job. He wasn't going to make excuses or protest that he'd been in since seven.

'None of the above. I was waiting until we've gained access to Martha Porter's home. DS Cumba's on his way there now with a search team – or he will be as soon as the warrant is signed.'

'Are we convinced she's the killer?'

Tom thought about it for a moment. 'Convinced is too strong a word. The only motive we know of is that she seemed to be obsessed with the husband. The mobile evidence is interesting but circumstantial, particularly as we found the phone in her desk drawer. One of her colleagues says she saw her put it there that morning, but she could be wrong; it could just as easily have been there all the time. Anyone in the company could have taken it. Interesting that her prints weren't on the phone – only those of the guy who took it from her drawer. Not sure what to make of that, but I asked the search team to try to grab some DNA, and they just got back to me. Apparently *all* the surfaces in the office were clean – obviously wiped down. That tells me she has to be guilty, however weak I find the motive.'

'Next steps, Tom?'

Tom talked her through everything they were planning, including raising an alert using the photo of the child.

'You've ruled out the husband, then?'

'Unless he can fly a helicopter and has a helipad in his back garden, it seems highly unlikely – he was seen in central Manchester – but we're sending someone over with photos of him together with pictures of three or four men of a similar age, to be sure the witness picks him out correctly.'

Philippa continued with her questions, but then he heard Becky's footsteps hurrying down the hall, and with a single knock she pushed open the door.

'She's not there, Tom. Neither is the child.'

Tom nodded. 'Sorry, Philippa. I need to go. No sign of Martha Porter, so I need to get the photo of Alfie circulated as widely as possible.'

He hung up.

39

MARTHA

Alfie was so excited to see the sea when he woke up, and he showed no signs of suffering from his night on the back seat of the tiny car. He jumped up and down with glee when I told him we had time to get breakfast at a café overlooking the beach.

Now he's sitting eating his scrambled eggs at our table by the window, unable to draw his gaze from the water.

'This is the best breakfast ever, Mummy.'

I smile as I look at him, wanting to drink in his joy. It takes so little to please him, and until now he's seemed happy with our monotonous existence – just him and me, our tiny flat and a few board games. It can't last, though, and however much I want to pick him up and run again, I have to set him free – set us *both* free.

The danger is on all sides now, and much as I try to convince myself that they can't possibly find evidence that I killed Genevieve, there's one fear that has haunted me for years.

They could have proof that I have killed before.

We all make mistakes. No one is infallible, and I can chart my life by my missteps along the way. Each poor decision, whether mine or my parents', has brought us to where we are today.

LAKESIDE

As the months wore on, Aram invited more and more people to join us, and Mum became increasingly exhausted. She and Dad welcomed everyone into our home, but it soon became clear that Mum was expected to cook all the meals as they took their places at our table. She was feeding twenty people three times a day, and the numbers were set to grow as Aram's influence spread.

She looked as if a strong breeze would knock her down, and I could see Dad watching her. There was a distance between them now, but there was no doubt in my mind that he loved her as much as he always had. One day a look of determination settled around his mouth, and he turned from her to the other people around the table.

'Listen, everyone. We need a rota. You all need to help. It's too much for Nicola to do this alone. I do what I can, as does India, but Nicola does all the cooking, and then there's the cleaning and everything else. I'm sorry, but if you're eating at our table every day, we need you to help with food preparation, clearing away afterwards, with laundry and keeping the bathrooms clean.'

His comments were met with total silence. Those around the table either looked down or sneaked a quick peek at Aram before dropping their gaze. No one responded.

The meal was just about over. Knives and forks clattered onto crockery as everyone left whatever was remaining on the plate in front of them, waiting for Aram to speak.

'Leave us, please.'

Without a word, chairs were pushed back and everyone left apart from Mum, Dad, me and Aram. He looked from one of us to the other and smiled. 'The manner in which everyone left should have told you all you need to know,' he said.

'What do you mean, Aram?' Mum asked, her voice shrill. I looked at her white face, the skin around her eyes a violet colour, her hands shaking. I wondered where my mum had gone.

'When I said "Leave us", no one in the room had any doubt that we – the four of us – are "us". They are "them".' He looked from Mum to Dad, his head on one side. 'You don't understand, do you? We're all guests in your house – we're not equal. Joel said so himself when he said "you're eating at our table". We have no right to be here, except by your good grace.'

Mum's mouth dropped open. 'But we've welcomed everyone you asked us to. We haven't turned anyone away.'

'That's true – you haven't. And as you say, you've "welcomed" them, because you are the owners, the beneficent ones. You have set yourselves above them all. No, not only *them*. *Us* – because I am included in that number. We all feel we're on borrowed time.'

'We haven't asked anyone to leave,' Dad said, his voice reflecting his horror at the thought.

'You didn't need to. They can't be here forever, because it's not their home. On top of their insecurities and their need to find a better understanding of life – which only I can give them – they know that at any time you may become bored with your benevolence, and then they'll all have to go. Many have told me they're willing to sell their houses so they can stay here with us permanently. But while they are your guests, and no more than that, they can't risk it.'

Mum and Dad looked at each other, and even as a child I could see they had no idea what to say.

'They're not alone,' Aram continued, his lips a thin straight line, his eyes two fierce dark pools. 'I too have to consider the position in which you place me.'

Mum leaned across the table, clasping her fluttering hands

together. 'Oh Aram, you can't believe for a moment we would ever ask you to leave, surely?'

From his pocket Aram pulled the small glass sphere that he often rolled between his palms, and he held it up.

'You see this? This represents the soul of each person I'm helping. I hold it, warm it, soothe it, until it is at one with the temperature of my skin. This is your soul, Nicola, and I hold it in my hands. If I were to drop it, what would happen to you?'

It wasn't a question that required an answer, but he told us anyway.

'If I dropped it right now onto this stone floor, it would shatter, sharp shards scattering to hide under furniture, in cracks in the floor. Some fragments would never be found. And it would be impossible to put it together again, to rebuild it into a whole.' He lifted it high. 'This is your soul, Nicola.' His eyes moved to Dad. 'And yours.' And then to me. 'And yours.' He paused and his gaze flicked back to each of us in turn. 'And yet, despite all that I do for you, I remain nothing but a guest in your house, relying on your generosity for my food. I have to ask for money if I need to buy something that's essential for me to carry on my work, and I rely on your charity. How do you think it makes me feel? How do you think *any* of us feels?'

Mum was staring at him, her eyes filled with pain and remorse. She glanced quickly at Dad, who was biting his lip, then back at Aram. Suddenly her lips curled in a smile.

'I know,' she said. 'We can fix this. We can give you an allowance. That way you'll never have to ask.'

With that, Aram stood up from the table, raised the ball high above his head and let it fall to the floor to fracture into a thousand pieces.

Mum was inconsolable. As Aram had turned to leave the room, she'd jumped to her feet, begging him to come back, but he'd ignored her. Within seconds, Dad had his arms around her – a rare sight these days – and I grabbed a dustpan and brush and tried my best to get up every tiny shard before one of us cut our feet. No one wore shoes.

'What did I say?' Mum sobbed. 'I thought I was being kind.'

For once, even though by then I was only twelve years old, I thought I understood Aram. I may not have had as many self-awareness sessions with him, but he was my teacher, and his lessons reached far beyond any predictable curriculum. He was, he told me, trying to teach me a new way of thinking in a world that knew only selfishness, greed and vanity.

'Can I say something?' I whispered, not knowing if my mum would appreciate my thoughts. We were so distant these days, with all of her energy spent on either feeding everyone or meditating with Aram to heal her soul.

She ignored me and lifted her head from Dad's shoulder, pushing him away. 'No, Joel. That doesn't help. India, go to your room.'

'But I don't think you understand why he was so upset,' I persisted.

She turned, placed her fists on the table and leaned on them. 'You think you know him better than I do? You don't. Do you understand? I'm closest to him, closer than anyone. And I don't know what upset him, so why do you think you do?'

She was angry. The thought that I might have better insight into his feelings was more than she could bear. I realised she thought Aram was hers. I had noticed that when any of the other women laughed with him, or even touched him, she hated it.

'I know you insulted him,' I said, a note of defiance in my tone.

'What did you just say?' She marched round the table, raised her hand and slapped me hard across the face.

'Nicola!' Dad shouted. 'What are you *doing*? There's no need for that.'

She spun round. 'There's every need. She has no respect. What did Aram say at the last group meeting? He singled India out as the person in the room most likely to put herself before others, to think herself better. She looks people in the eye when she's not been invited to. She's too bold. And everyone agreed with him.'

She said this with glee – as if the public humiliation of her daughter was something to be relished. No one had spoken up for me. No one dared.

I bowed my head, my tears splashing onto the stone flags I had just cleaned. I knew I was proving both Mum and Aram correct by speaking, but what if he left?

'You insulted him by telling him you'd give him an allowance. You were treating him as an inferior. He says none of us should be inferior to others. We shouldn't own things which give us power over others,' I whispered into the now silent room.

No one spoke. I could feel Mum's eyes on me, weighing up my words, wondering if I was right. Finally, she broke the silence: 'What are we going to do, Joel? We need him. We *all* need him.'

The thought – even to me – of life without Aram seemed unbearable. We had learned that the world outside these walls was not to be trusted, that if any of us left, we would be turning our back on our family and security.

'Leave it to me,' Dad said. 'I can fix this.'

And he did. Within weeks, ownership of the house was placed in a trust. I never understood its terms, but I knew that Aram was in control. And our money was placed in a fund that he could draw on whenever he wanted, no questions asked.

The money and the house that had given my parents such high hopes and excitement for the future were no longer theirs.

40

The trip to XO-Tech hadn't been as helpful as Becky and Tom had hoped, and they left the building to go their separate ways feeling a little deflated. Elise Chapman had a lot to say, but little of any significance. She talked again about the raised voices in the argument between Martha and Genevieve but said the only thing she heard that she had since remembered was Martha saying 'It's not my place'. But that wasn't even slightly helpful.

A woman called Caroline had said she felt sorry for Martha.

'None of us disliked her, although it's true she kept her distance. Maybe she had the right idea. Exaggeration is Elise's forte,' she said. 'Best not to tell her anything. And, for what it's worth, I can't imagine Martha throwing herself at Niall in the way they're all saying. Yes, I saw her hurry from the kitchen, and she was looking disturbed but not necessarily upset. I'd drunk less than everyone else because I was driving. And I know Niall avoided being alone with her from then on, but I can't see it. She wouldn't even share her home address, for goodness' sake, so I doubt she'd have been willing to share her body!'

Becky saw Caroline's point. She hadn't met Martha, but she seemed a closed book. Why would someone so private lay themselves open like that? Maybe she'd had one drink too many. God knows, Becky had done some daft things in her time under the influence of alcohol, but she preferred not to dwell on them.

A rather sweaty-looking Spencer Johansson, in an even more garish T-shirt than the day before, had confirmed from the photo Tom showed him that the knife recovered from the culvert matched the one they kept in the kitchen – a knife which, according to the search team, was no longer there. He'd also confirmed that he'd spoken to Niall Strachan after midnight to check on progress with the deal.

Now Becky had the pleasure of meeting Eddie Carlson. Would he have held a grievance against Genevieve for so long? Or maybe since he'd come back to Manchester, he'd started seeing her again.

Becky was driving down a road lined on one side by big, impressive houses, looking all the more beautiful because the sun had temporarily broken through the heavy dark clouds and the trees and shrubs were in full leaf. Where she caught glimpses through open double gates, she could see the gardens were well maintained, and the houses were lucky enough to face open fields on the opposite side of the road.

She turned into the drive leading to Eddie's house and was impressed. It was a relatively new property in red brick, built to a traditional design with double windows either side of a central front door, and while the Italian-style cypress trees may have been a bit too much for Manchester, they looked good. She clamped down on her low expectations of the interior as she pressed the bell. She was predisposed to expect all footballers to have poor taste, but remembered Tom telling her once that just because something wasn't *her* taste, that didn't make it bad.

The man who opened the door looked nothing like the pictures Becky had seen in the press when he was with Genevieve. He was above-average height with auburn hair brushed back from a wide suntanned forehead. His smile showed startlingly white teeth that had obviously been treated at great expense, but he seemed affable and friendly enough.

'Come in, Inspector,' he said, showing Becky into a wide hall with a polished oak floor. A cut-glass vase of mixed roses sat on a central circular table, and Becky had to reassess her opinion of footballers' houses.

He showed her into a comfortable living room, and she sank into the soft cushions of a dark turquoise velvet sofa.

'What can I do to help? I assume this is about Genevieve.'

'That's right. We're investigating her murder and trying to find out as much as we can about her – her friends, her life – so we can piece together a picture.'

Eddie gave her a brief smile. 'I know why you've come to talk to me. Genevieve made a big thing of my jealousy, but it was grossly exaggerated. I sometimes felt I had to protect her from herself, if you know what I mean. She would flirt outrageously with other men – beyond flirting, really. I didn't mind so much, and that wound her up and made her do it even more. Sometimes I intervened to stop her from making a stupid mistake. I know she was trying to test me, to see how much I cared.'

'Did it work?' Becky asked.

'In a way. It made me realise that I didn't care much at all. And I never threatened her when our relationship ended. She got her side of the story out first, and so that was that. I behaved like an idiot, drank too much, was a bit of a coke-head, ruined my career.' He shrugged.

Becky looked around the room. 'You don't seem to have done too badly for yourself.'

'It's a good house – always was, although I can't take credit for the revamp. It was fairly gruesome back then, I have to admit.' He pulled a face at the memory.

'Have you had any contact with Genevieve since then?'

Eddie sat back on the sofa and folded his arms. 'It's interesting you should ask that. I hadn't – not a peep for years – but when I got back here in June, she contacted me through my Instagram account. Said it would be great to catch up. I ignored her. I'm married now – happily – and I don't want her back in my life.'

'So what happened?' Becky asked.

'She tried Facebook instead and sent me a message. She suggested there might be things my wife might like to know about me. Why not meet up and talk about it?'

Becky looked at him and waited.

'I did nothing. I don't know what her game was, but I warned my wife to steer clear. She knows the history. I don't know whether Genevieve was interested in getting together again or in making trouble for me, but I was having none of it. I can promise you that.'

Becky didn't like the sound of this. Was there something wrong with Genevieve and Niall's marriage? As she asked Eddie Carlson more questions, the picture she got of Genevieve became less and less favourable.

'I think that's all, and I appreciate your time, Mr Carlson. We might want to look at your social media accounts to check the communications, if that's okay.'

He pulled a face. 'Sorry. I deleted everything.'

'Right. We'll let you know if there are any more questions.'

As Becky made her way into the hall, a door opened from another part of the house and a bone-thin young woman in a T-shirt and shorts stepped through.

'Oh!' she said, flushing. 'Sorry, Eddie. I didn't know you had company.'

She reversed back through the door before Eddie could say a word, and Becky gave him an enquiring look.

'My wife. Kirsten.'

He opened the door to show Becky out, but the smile had faded from his face. He must have known what Becky had seen.

Kirsten's arms were covered in bruises.

41

MARTHA

'We need to go, Alfie. There's somewhere we need to be.'

'Can we come back later?'

His eyes are round with the thrill of the seaside. He wants to paddle, and I feel cruel for saying no, but we're not working to my timetable any longer. I don't know how to answer his question, and I don't want some of my last words to him to be a lie. After today, I don't know when I might next see him.

'Let's see what happens, shall we, baby?' I pick him up and cuddle him tightly. Just the feel of his skinny body makes me want to cry. He'd been such a chubby baby, but in the last year he had grown taller and thinner. 'Come on. We need to make a move,' I say before it all gets too much for me.

The drive takes about forty minutes – plenty of time for me to decide if what I'm doing is totally insane, but the burden of guilt is strong, and growing ever stronger. As Alfie gets older he'll find it more and more difficult to understand why we always have to leave.

I pull into the supermarket car park, which isn't too busy at this hour on a Wednesday morning. It had always been Dad's job to do the weekly shop – he was the only person ever trusted to leave Lakeside. He went alone with no one to help him, and he told me he had to make three trips into the store, leaving each time with a fully loaded trolley to transfer into the back of the Range Rover.

I can't decide when I should show myself, or what I should say. Maybe it would be best to intercept him before he begins. That will give me the most time.

I chew my nails anxiously. What if it's a different car and I don't recognise it? There's no reason to have changed it – Dad only drives about forty miles a week. The bigger question is, what happens if he says no? What I'm about to ask him to do is immense, and I am far from certain he'll even consider it.

I throw my head back and gaze sightlessly at the roof of the car. The police won't be far behind me. If they know who I am by now, they'll trace the car. I should have driven to Leeds, dumped it and caught a train north. They would never have found me.

The thoughts, doubts, conflicts, bang around inside my head, but it's too late to think.

He's here.

My stomach is in knots as I see the dark green Range Rover turn into the car park, but it's a vast car park, and I'm too far away. I could get out of the car now and shout, but he won't hear me. I hesitate. Maybe this is a sign. Maybe something's trying to tell me I'm doing the wrong thing.

I shake my head, frustrated with my weakness, switch on the ignition and start to move. I'll intercept him before he reaches the supermarket entrance.

The Range Rover door opens, and a figure appears.

It's not Dad.

I stare, wondering if I am seeing things. It was *always* Dad. He was the only one trusted with the money, the shopping and the car. For as long as I can remember, the gates to Lakeside were kept locked, although Aram maintained this was to keep people out rather than in. The chains that bound Aram's followers to him were not forged from steel. Had they been, they would have been far easier to break. Dad was the only person who ever left, for no more than a few hours at a time, because Aram knew he would return like a magnet to my mother's side.

Now, to my horror as I drive across the supermarket car park to where the Range Rover has pulled in, I watch Mum get out of the car and head towards the entrance. A sob catches at the back of my throat as I look at my once pretty, vivacious mother. Her long hair is straggly, her clothes look dirty, and she drags her feet as she walks, as defeated as an old woman for whom every step is an effort.

I swerve the car to the left, away from the front of the store, no longer looking to intercept anyone. She hasn't seen me. Her head is lowered, as if she has to look where to put her feet. I don't know what to do. I was relying on Dad still being in charge of the shopping, and I've no idea how Mum will cope with three full trolleys. She doesn't look as if she has the energy to lift a single carrier bag.

As I swing the car round and head to a space from where I can watch her, I pass close to the Range Rover. Someone is in the passenger seat. Perhaps it's Dad, and he's not feeling well so has brought Mum along to help.

I can't keep driving around the car park – someone will notice – so I continue along the row to the end, turn and head back down, parking a little further away, to the side. If it's Dad, maybe all is not lost. Maybe I can get to him now, while Mum is in the shop, but I need him to be alone.

A sudden burst of sunlight breaks through the clouds and illuminates the interior of the Range Rover. I can only see the back of a head, and it's a man, but definitely not Dad. He turns his face into the sun, and the light catches his eyes.

A cry of alarm bursts from me before I can stifle it, and I twist my head away, terrified that he's seen me. The urge to duck down is immense, but any sudden movement is more likely to catch his eye.

Aram!

I want to watch him, to see what he's doing. But to do that, I have to look. And if I look, he'll see me. He'll feel my eyes on him, as he always did. I have to keep still, not draw attention to myself, not look in his direction, but I'm desperate to know if he's still in the car, or if he's got out and is heading towards me.

I slowly turn to look out of the windscreen, hoping I'll catch him out of the corner of my eye if he's coming my way. Each time someone walks by, I jump. Thank God Alfie is being quiet. He's playing with the fuzzy-felt seaside pack I bought from the café gift shop and singing softly to himself.

I wish I'd parked further back, but I can't move the car now without drawing his attention. So I wait. I just want Mum to come back out, and for them to go. For a moment, I consider going into the supermarket and asking for her help. But I daren't get out of the car for fear of Aram seeing me, and anyway, I'm certain she won't help me. All I can do is wait until they've gone.

For twenty minutes I wait, every second filled with the threat that at any moment there'll be a tap on the window and I'll look up into eyes that will see right through me, into the back of the car. To Alfie. Maybe I should go now – risk him spotting me. He's not in the driving seat, so he couldn't follow. But he will know I am here, close to Lakeside. Within his reach.

Finally, I see Mum. She's pushing a trolley, but it's only half full, and I wonder how many trips she'll have to make if that's all she can manage.

As she approaches the Range Rover, Aram makes no effort to get out to help her. She walks to the back and transfers the contents of the trolley into the boot and heads back towards the supermarket. I can't sit here while she repeats the process. The strain of expecting to see Aram's face staring through my window would be too much, and Alfie won't stay quiet forever. I'm about to risk drawing attention to myself by driving off when I see Mum dump the trolley, retrieve her pound coin and head back to the car.

What's going on? She's only done the equivalent of a weekly family shop. Who's buying the food for the rest of the household? There were about thirty people there when I left. And where's Dad?

I have a sudden empty feeling. What if he's died, and I wasn't there to say goodbye to him? He was young, but it isn't only old people who die. My eyes sting. I may not have seen him for years, but knowing he was out there somewhere has always been a comfort.

The Range Rover starts up and moves away. If they're following Dad's routine, they'll go to the post office to pick up the mail. I decide to follow. I don't know what other choice I have.

I hadn't realised how much I was looking forward to seeing Dad, to introducing him to his grandson, and my throat is thick with unshed tears. I had thought this was my chance – not just to see him, but to begin to put right all that had gone wrong.

42

LAKESIDE

After Aram took over our house, our money – in fact, every aspect of our lives – I was strangely content. As I passed through my early-teenage years, I didn't miss what I'd never had, and I had no concept of the joy, excitement and pain that other girls of my age were experiencing. We were a community, and it was our duty to get along with each other. The only exception was on those days or nights when one person was selected by Aram to be publicly lambasted for their failings. There was never a trace of empathy in anyone's eyes then, just relief.

For a long time I believed Aram had been right to demand what he called equality but which I now recognise as something else entirely. After the changes to the financial ownership of the property, more people came to stay, and many of them remained with us for years. We all knew what our roles were, and as long as we understood the rules and behaved accordingly, life was sweet. I still wasn't permitted to leave the grounds. But nor was anyone else.

We all recognised that Aram's word was law, and there could be no hint of argument, not even any discussion that suggested a trace of dissent. The slightest suspicion on his part that any member of the group was straying from his teaching brought about a public session of humiliation, so we all strived to please him.

He continued to teach me, and I continued to swell with pride at his praise and tear myself to shreds with remorse when he rebuked me for some minor misdemeanour. The best times for me were the maths lessons, and it wasn't long before Aram understood that I had an aptitude for numbers and logic, so he decided to put me to work. I was soon responsible for the household accounts and for ensuring that any private purchases Aram wanted to make were paid for. He was the only one allowed access to the Internet, and boxes arrived from all over the world for him.

We didn't welcome guests unless they were expressly invited by Aram. Those who came were required to break all ties with family and friends and agree to have no further contact with anyone outside the community, and I realised quickly that new members of the group always came with money. It was some time before I found out about the agreements they signed in order to secure their future as part of Aram's world. Ownership of anything was to be abhorred, of course, so they were required to hand over control of their property to Aram on entry. In return they were promised that a weight would be lifted from them, their souls set free. Every penny committed went into an account, although not the trust account into which my parents had put all their money to pay for our daily lives. It was a separate account in Aram's name only.

I never dared to question it. I couldn't bring myself to tell my father, and Aram didn't feel the need to explain. I justified it by telling myself he might need the money in the future to finance his teaching, and I didn't want to upset the rhythm of our lives.

Of those who came, few left. Those who failed to go the extra distance, who were unwilling to be moulded into zealots committed to worshipping at the feet of Aram Forakis, were banished, bowing their heads in shame at their failure as they were escorted to the gates. On the rare occasions that someone chose to leave, denouncing Aram's teaching, they were subjected to his abuse, his scorn, his derision. It was spelled out to them that the rest of the world would fail to understand their shortcomings, and that the corruption of society beyond our walls would lead to their ultimate destruction. He told them they would return to a life far emptier, poorer than before. If they stood strong, determined to go, he forced them to leave at night, humiliated and disgraced, when no one but Aram was there to bid them goodbye.

As the years passed, Aram became more affectionate towards me. He would stand behind me during lessons to look over my shoulder, as if to study my work. Sometimes he would rest a hand on the back of my neck or reach forward and stroke my cheek. I couldn't concentrate when he was behind me, not knowing if I was going to feel his hands on me, longing to know that he was pleased with me. Starved as I was of human touch, he made me feel special.

On one such day when he must have been particularly satisfied with me, he had his hands on both my shoulders and was rubbing them gently with his thumbs. I turned my head to look up at him and I saw my mother standing in the doorway, staring, her eyes narrowed. I shivered at her expression.

I realised then what I had no doubt known subconsciously for a long time: Mum was sleeping with Aram. I had been aware for years that Dad no longer shared her room, but I had no experience of what was normal in a marriage and hadn't given it much thought. But from that day on, I watched her. She wasn't the only one to share Aram's bed, and I could see her struggle when she was usurped by one of the other women. I wanted to tell her that perhaps now she could understand how Dad felt, but jealousy wasn't an acceptable emotion, so they both had to suffer in silence.

On the day after I saw Mum watching us, Aram explained his attitude to sex to me. As he spoke, he held both my hands, his touch warm and dry, his thumbs rhythmically skimming over my skin. It made me shiver.

'It's not wise to allow yourself to be possessed by anyone, India. It's a form of ownership, and you know how wrong that is. We all need freedom to be ourselves without being shackled to another person. You're growing up now, and before long it will be your turn to enjoy men, or maybe women. Perhaps both. Don't be afraid of who you are, but don't let any of them own you. Be free. Be true to yourself. Your mother has yet to learn, but I'm doing my best to make her understand.'

Maybe he was, but whatever he said to convince Mum, it definitely didn't work with Dad, who looked hurt whenever his eyes rested on his wife. Back then I didn't know whether I should feel sorry for him, or disgusted by his possessiveness. I was a true convert to Aram's thinking.

Such was his trust in me that when I reached seventeen he said I should learn to drive. I could be useful to him. He didn't like new converts arriving by taxi – too many people were already asking questions about what happened in the house – so I was tasked with collecting arrivals from the station, and while the weekly supermarket shop and collecting the mail from the post office remained Dad's responsibility, it became my job to go to the courier's office to pick up Aram's parcels.

Only I knew what he ordered and where from. Only I knew that, while Lakeside was supposedly a house free from alcohol, tobacco and substance abuse, Aram ordered the finest whisky and wine for his own consumption, and a variety of pills and potions that I had never heard of. He told me he needed medicine in case anyone in the community became ill. He would treat them with remedies from these ingredients.

I accepted every word he said.

43

'Honestly, Tom, Eddie's wife's arms looked dreadful,' Becky said as she walked with Tom from his office to the incident room. 'She has that thin porcelain-white skin – you know, the type that's almost translucent – so the bruises showed up more than they would on most. They looked to me like someone had grabbed her arms and squeezed really hard.'

'And you think it was the husband?'

'I don't know. She seemed a bit apologetic for barging in on us, and I couldn't decide whether she was being polite, or whether she was frightened of annoying Eddie. Or maybe she was embarrassed by the bruises. Eddie said nothing. I should have asked him what had happened, but there didn't seem much point. He would have made some excuse – lied through his teeth. He was hardly likely to say "I gave her a good shaking", was he?'

Tom had to agree. There was rarely any point in asking a question when the answer was most likely going to be a lie.

'What did you make of him?'

Becky grunted. 'I found myself liking him, which made me feel a bit stupid when I saw Kirsten. I had preconceived ideas when I arrived – prejudices, probably. And he seemed so different from what I'd expected, as did his house. Apart from the fact that I needed sunglasses when he smiled, he seemed quite normal, but if Genevieve was in touch with him, what do you think her game was?'

'Not a clue.' Tom thought for a moment. 'Do you want to have another chat with Sara Osborne, see if she can cast any light on it? If not, Rob can ask Genevieve's friends, and at some stage we need to speak to Niall again. Let's rule Eddie Carlson in or out, if we can.'

'And his wife?' Becky added. 'What if Kirsten got upset at the thought of Genevieve chasing her husband?'

'I always want to say it seems extreme to kill someone for something so trivial. Upsetting, but surely not enough to take someone's life? Unfortunately, as we both know, people have killed for much less.'

Tom was about to head over to talk to Keith Sims, when Becky stopped him with a question: 'How's it going at Martha Porter's place?'

Tom scratched the back of his neck. 'Pretty useless. The place is clean. We didn't find any bloodstained clothes, so nothing that connects her to the murder scene. No laptop either. I presume that the other phone she apparently has – according to the childminder – gives her web access if she needs it, but the number isn't registered, so it's a burner. They've literally pulled the place apart to find it. What I don't get, Becky, is why she's been covering her tracks for so long. This isn't a recent thing. If she murdered Genevieve, I can understand why she'd do it now, but why for so many years?'

Becky bit her top lip. 'You don't suppose she's done this before, do you?'

'It's a thought. We can run the DNA we're collecting from her flat and see if anything jumps out, and we could look for similar cases. But what do we base the search on? Do we believe she killed Genevieve out of jealousy? Should we assume a previous killing was for the same reason, or that she has a short fuse and could have killed anyone for any reason at all – which is not remotely helpful?'

Becky lifted her hands from her sides, palms up, in a gesture of hopelessness. 'There aren't many unsolved murders of women, so if this is a pattern it should be easy to spot. On the other hand, lots of women go missing – circumstances unexplained – and any of them could be dead.'

'Marvellous! Let's start with what we know. If Martha killed Genevieve, the most likely motive is jealousy, so let's look at missing women in the right age range who have disappeared in the last five years. But restrict it to the Greater Manchester region. I doubt she would have strayed far with a small child.'

Becky frowned. 'That's a point, you know. The childminder says she seems devoted to her son. Would she have left him alone in her flat at night while she popped out to kill someone?'

'More to the point,' Tom added, 'we've confirmed that she doesn't have a car. So how the hell did she get to the Tyldesley Loopline? It's about four miles each way, so it's walkable, but she'd have had to leave the child alone for a couple of hours, plus the time she spent with Genevieve. Maybe she has a bike. Let's get hold of Rob and check.'

'Leave it with me,' Becky said. She spun on her heel and headed for her desk.

Tom returned to his office to prepare for a forthcoming CPS conference about a recent case and to make a start on some annual performance reviews that were imminent. He loathed paperwork at the best of times; how was he supposed to concentrate on a staff retention plan when there was a killer out there? He also couldn't help being distracted by the fact that Lucy and Kate would arrive back that night and were booked into a hotel at the airport. He couldn't wait to see his daughter, and even though he'd chatted to her onscreen while she'd been away, he was excited about giving her a hug, eating dinner with her, just spending time with her. He'd loved it when she lived with them and had missed her desperately when she left for Australia, but he had to try to curb his desire to keep her close and think what was best for Lucy. If he suggested that she and Kate live near him, would that be to serve his interests rather than his daughter's? At her age, school and friends were so important.

His musings were interrupted by Becky. He was so wrapped up in his thoughts that he didn't know she was there until he looked up to see her standing in his open doorway, a triumphant look on her face.

'They've found a bike!'

'Where?'

'It wasn't in her flat, but there's a cellar accessible from the outside. The chiropodist told her that if she wanted to store anything in there, she was welcome. Anyway, Rob asked his permission to have a look, and there it was.'

'And did the landlord say it was Martha's?'

'Well, no. It's actually his. But Martha had access to it, and so it hardly matters who it belongs to, does it?'

'Let's see what the evidence says. I guess there may be prints – although I honestly can't see her being so stupid given everything else she's done. What about soil on the tyres – can we match anything to the tracks at the Loopline?'

'I don't know, but it would have been easy for her to get there and back. She could have got onto the Roe Green Loopline at Monton, by the church. Then it's a straight run. It's not impossible that there were people out at that time of night, so shall I put out a request for information?'

'Good idea. And ask the team to get me some photos to show where the bike was, please.' Becky gave him a quizzical look. 'Let's not give any defence lawyer a perfectly plausible reason for Martha's prints being on the bike.'

Becky pulled a face and turned to leave, and Tom rested his chin on his knuckles. Everything pointed to Martha's guilt, from her secrecy to the fact that she had run away. He should be pleased that they had a viable suspect. Now all they had to do was find her. In spite of all that, he wasn't prepared to close his mind to other options. There had to be more to it. Had she been acting alone? Was this the first time she had killed?

Her life was shrouded in secrecy, so what was she hiding?

44

MARTHA

I knew as soon as we left the supermarket that Mum and Aram weren't heading to the post office. They turned the wrong way out of the car park, but I followed them anyway.

They didn't stop anywhere else but headed straight back to Lakeside. As they turned off at the final junction I sailed past the end of the road. I was too close for comfort. I'd tried to keep my distance, but there weren't many cars around on those back roads, so it had been difficult. I don't think Mum would have noticed me, though, and she was the one with the rear-view mirror.

I don't know what to do next. My entire plan rests on talking to Dad first. He might not be prepared to help, but I'm confident he won't give me away to Aram.

I drive back towards town, wondering what my options are. There aren't many. I head past the entrance to the supermarket and on towards the smaller shops. The red and yellow post office sign catches my eye. There's one thing I can do, even if it's only to confirm that Dad is still alive.

Fortunately, there's a parking space right outside, and I pull into it. I don't want to take Alfie into the shop with me. What if someone's there from Lakeside – maybe someone I don't know, but who knows about me? But I can't leave him out here on his own, so I have to stop thinking and just act.

'We're going in here, Alfie. Come on.'

I get out and open the back door of the car, pulling his sun hat on before I lift him out of his seat.

The post office has been redecorated and has a new layout, but the lady behind the counter is the same one who was there all those years ago when, as a child, I was still allowed to come here. She's not seen me since I was ten, so I feel relatively safe speaking to her. It's a gamble, though.

'Can I help you, duck?' she says with a friendly smile.

I cling on to Alfie's hand. There's so much in this shop to fascinate him, and I'm scared he'll wander off.

'I'm not sure. I was wondering if Joel Kalu still comes in to collect the post for Lakeside?'

'Ah, that he does. And it was so good to see him again after all this time. It were years, weren't it, Bill?' She turns to a man I hadn't noticed, sitting behind the counter reading a newspaper. He grunts something, and she continues. 'We thought he must have moved on, didn't we, Bill? Do you know him, then?'

I have no idea how much the local people understand about Lakeside and what happens there, but I take a chance.

'Yes. I stayed at the house for a while about seven years ago, and I remember him coming to collect the mail. I was in the area, so I thought I'd catch up with him, but it's not important.'

The woman signals me to step to one side while she takes the money for some chocolate buttons from a little girl. The child's mother mouths 'Thanks' to me as she ushers her daughter out.

'Sorry about that, duck. But as we're just chatting...'

'It's not a problem. You were saying, about Joel Kalu?'

Alfie is tugging on my hand, but for now I have to ignore him.

'Oh yes. Joel. Such a lovely man, but I think he must have been proper poorly. We didn't see him for years, did we, Bill?'

Bill looks over the top of his spectacles and nods, finally goaded into speaking. 'That's right. Quite a shock when he turned up.'

'When was this?' I twist my head from side to side, from one to the other, while casting a glance through the window, wary that someone might turn up.

'It's hard to say,' the woman says. 'I guess it must have been five years or more since he stopped coming, isn't that right, Bill? Another chap came, but he wasn't friendly. Showed his identification – we can't hand the mail over to just anyone, you know – and went. We asked him about Joel, but he said he knew nothing about him. Very odd, we thought. Anyway, it must be about six months ago that Joel turned up. We were that surprised to see him!'

'Did he say where he'd been?' I ask, not sure if I'm pushing my luck with the questions. But it strikes me that the woman wants to talk, and Bill isn't offering much in the way of conversation.

'Said he'd been poorly. Didn't say what with. But he looks different, you know. That black hair of his is white now, and he's so thin! Such a nice man.' She straightens some magazines and it's time for me to stop asking questions.

'Glad to hear he's okay at least,' I say.

Alfie is still pulling at my hand and I bend down.

'Can I have a drink, please, Mummy?' he asks.

I ruffle his hair, pick up a bottle of water and a few treats.

'Didn't he used to come in on a Wednesday, or have I imagined that?' I ask as I hand over my purchases.

'Goodness,' she says, taking the money from me and giving me a sly look. 'You've got a good memory. Yes, it used to be Wednesday after he'd done what he called "the big shop". But he doesn't do that now, so he comes on a Thursday. Usually first thing – about nine-ish. Shall I tell him you were asking for him?'

'No, not to worry. I don't know how long I'm going to be

around. I thought I might bump into him, that's all. Thanks for your help.'

I can feel the woman watching us as we leave. I asked too many questions. Even if I don't come back tomorrow, she'll tell him. And he'll know it's me.

Five years or more since he stopped coming. My guess is it's closer to six – and I'm certain I know what happened.

They punished him for what he did. I have no idea what form that punishment would have taken, but whatever they had done to him, it must have been enough to turn his hair white. I know only too well how it feels to incur Aram's displeasure.

45

LAKESIDE

'You've disappointed me, India. Tonight you'll face the group and acknowledge your behaviour and the harm you could so thoughtlessly have done to our community.'

I went over and over Aram's words as I lay on my bed, waiting for the moment when I would have to stand in front of my friends, the people I thought of as my family, and let them know how I had let them down.

Tears soaked into my pillow, and my stomach ached from hours of crying. But the time was getting closer, and at any moment there would be a knock on the door. Someone would be sent to get me, to take me down to the room where everyone would be seated, waiting for me to give my testimony; to be tried and found guilty.

I swung my legs over the side of the bed, the last vestiges of self-respect coming to my rescue. I wouldn't let them see me like this. I ran to the bathroom and washed my face, splashing it over and over with cold water. Finally, I forced my head into the bowl and opened my eyes, trying to take the redness from them. Then I washed from head to toe, to remove the grimy sweat that had settled on my body as I had lain curled up on the bed, the dust and grass still on my clothes.

I went back to my bedroom, pulled some clean jeans and a T-shirt from the cupboard, brushed my unruly hair and sat bolt upright, waiting. I would take my punishment and face the disgust of the community.

There was one woman living with us – Alice – who I knew disliked me. I had done nothing to hurt or upset her, but although she hid her loathing well from everyone except me, she took every opportunity to undermine me. She was a current favourite of Aram's, and I could only think her thinly disguised animosity was based on her jealousy of my special status with him. Had he known how she behaved towards me, he would have been furious, but it was my word against hers, so I said nothing.

Maybe her antipathy was rooted in a conversation I'd heard between her and Aram a few weeks previously. I'd decided to start work early in Aram's study because a delivery was expected that day and I needed to go to the courier's to collect it. The door between the study and Aram's private rooms was ajar, and I heard Alice's voice.

'You and me would make beautiful babies, Aram. Why don't you let me stay for the next few nights? Surely you'd love a child?' Her tone was plaintive, and I knew it would irritate him.

'Maybe one day I *will* have a child, but I can assure you that it won't be with you, Alice. Now go and do your work.'

I heard a soft sob, and she ran from the room. I pretended to have heard nothing and carried on working. But she knew, and her hatred of me grew.

On the night when Aram decreed that I was to stand before the community to admit to my mistakes, I wasn't surprised when the door opened without so much as a knock and Alice walked in. Aram must have known, somehow, that sending her would be the worst humiliation, which had to mean that he understood how she felt about me. I should have realised he would know. His eyes saw everything – pierced everyone's minds, so they ceased to be their own.

Alice smiled as she looked at me, but it was a smile of self-satisfaction, and I realised at that moment that she had no future there. Aram would use her while she pleased him, but then she would be gone. He wouldn't tolerate tension between members of his family, and it seemed I didn't need to tell him anything.

She was surprised when I smiled back. I would take whatever was about to be thrown at me, and realising Alice's days were numbered made me feel infinitely better.

When I entered the meditation room, everyone was there, seated on the floor or on cushions. I saw Dad glance at me with a hint of concern. He knew better than to show me any sympathy, so he quickly averted his gaze. Mum gave me a stony stare, as if my disgrace reflected badly on her. It was hard to see how, as she hadn't behaved like my parent for years. I was told to stand at the front of the room, and Aram asked me in a mild voice to tell the group why I had been summoned.

I took a deep breath. 'I went to town on an errand for Aram. I was late arriving back because I met a boy and spent some time with him.'

I said no more than that and waited for the next question. The only one that no one would dare ask – and despite my humiliation, I would never answer – was about the nature of the errand.

'Had you seen this boy before?' Aram asked.

'Yes. He works in the courier's office.'

'You understand how we feel about people outside the community, don't you, India? You know they are not to be trusted. You know their values are misguided, that they'll tempt you into a life of sin. You'll be suffocated by the negative emotions that you've learned to overcome. So why did you do it?'

'I like him.' It was an honest answer, and lies wouldn't help me now.

'How much?' one of the men in the room asked, and I knew what he was saying.

'I like him,' I repeated.

One by one the people in the room bombarded me with questions – how I'd met him, what I'd said to him, what he'd asked about our lives – every question loaded with animosity because I had broken the rules. And each of them designed to please Aram.

'Did you allow him to touch you?' Aram finally asked.

I tried my best to hold my head high, even though I was dying inside with shame. 'Yes,' I whispered.

'Tell us exactly what you allowed him to do to you.'

I twisted my head towards where he was sitting to one side. 'What do you mean?'

'You know what I mean, India. I want you to describe everything he did, from the first touch to the last.'

My legs started to shake. I knew what he was doing. This was ritual humiliation, and it would get worse. I was feeling light-headed with the strain. 'We didn't make love.'

'I don't know why you would use that phrase. You're talking about sex. It's copulation. It's pleasure. Love is an excuse, not a reality. But that's not the question I asked. You must describe, step by step, his assault on your body, and yours on his.'

Many times over the years I had been forced to stand in this room, made to feel demeaned, penitent, guilty, but never had I felt so ashamed of my actions. My voice cracked as I spoke.

'He touched my hand, and I wrapped my fingers round his. He led me into a field. We hadn't kissed when I saw him before, but this time we did. We lay down on the grass.'

I said no more.

'And then?' Aram asked.

'We kissed again.'

'Where were his hands, India? Where were yours? Where was his tongue? I asked you to be specific. You need to see our disgust, and we need to feel your shame.'

I gulped, and the tears began to flow. I was eighteen, a virgin. I'd never even been kissed before, and now I had to recount details of the most exciting thing that had ever happened to me in front of all the people who mattered, and feel their contempt.

'He put his tongue in my mouth. I had my hands on his hips. We lay on our sides facing each other, our bodies aligned against each other. I put my hands behind him to draw him closer. His hand slipped inside my T-shirt.' My voice was barely audible. 'He touched my breast.'

I fell silent, apart from the gulps between sobs.

'And then?'

'Nothing! I promise you, that was all. He stopped. He said we have plenty of time – the whole of the summer before he goes to university. He was kind to me.'

'Would you have liked more?'

My head was spinning, but I shook it vigorously, unable to look at Aram because he would know I was lying.

'Are you going to see him again?'

'No! Of course not. I made a mistake, and I'm so sorry.'

I could feel the tension in the room, everyone wondering what would happen next. But I think I knew before Aram said anything.

'I'm glad you've come to that conclusion yourself, India. Because there will be no further opportunities. Your shoes have already been removed from your room, and the car will no longer be available to you.'

I stared at him in horror.

He turned to the rest of the room. 'Leave us, please. I need to speak with India.'

No one demurred; they all got up and quietly left the room. Dad seemed to hesitate, but only for a second, and I was left standing, head bowed, tears still dripping onto the floor.

'I'm disappointed in you, India.'

'I know,' I whispered.

'But I'm not surprised.'

I lifted my head and looked at him. What did he mean?

'Finally, I think you're ready. Come with me.'

He stood and held out his hand, and I didn't hesitate to grasp it. He led me through the door and up the stairs to his rooms. Only the chosen few ever went in there, and despite being one of those closest to him, I only ever went to the outer room – the one he called his study. This was his private area. His sitting room and his bedroom.

He led me straight through and stood by the bed.

'I've been waiting, India, but now it's time. Your body is telling you that you're ready to be a woman. I'm your teacher, India, and it's my job to show you what being a woman means.'

His eyes held me mesmerised, and as I looked into them a dizziness washed over me. I didn't know if this was what I wanted, but it never occurred to me to refuse.

46

Becky was getting frustrated. All the evidence pointed to Martha Porter, and yet Tom seemed ambivalent. He said it was too neat. She flicked the switch on the kettle, deciding that the routine task of making tea would dull her brain for a moment and give it a chance to rest. She pulled a teabag out of the box, staring sightlessly at the kettle as it slowly came to the boil.

The people they had spoken to about Martha – from her landlord to the childminder and the staff at the office – agreed that while she didn't volunteer information about herself and was evasive if asked personal questions, she was quiet, organised, efficient. Nobody had ever seen her display anger or any form of unpleasantness towards others – except Elise, whom she simply ignored as far as possible. She was, more than anything, *polite*. Predictably, Elise said Martha was just plain weird.

Instead of trying to understand their main suspect, maybe if they knew more about Genevieve it might help them to figure out why someone would have wanted her dead. Becky decided to finish making her tea, then call Sara Osborne.

As she wandered back through the incident room, Rob bounced in. He gave her a grin and scooted over to her.

'Well, the bike was a bit of a turn-up, wasn't it?' he said, obviously delighted with his find.

Becky knew she would have to put a slight dent in his enthusiasm by repeating what Tom had said.

'Despite that,' she said when she saw the disappointment in the sergeant's eyes, 'the bike could yet prove decisive. Let's see what comes back from forensics. It does at least make it all feasible. It always seemed a bit of a long shot that she walked.'

Becky told him about her visit to Eddie Carlson and that it seemed Genevieve had tried to get in touch with him.

'Can you call her friends again, Rob? Maybe try those you thought the least phoney to see if they know of any reason why she might have wanted to see Eddie. I'll call Sara Osborne – see if she can help. And then I think the boss has the lovely job of going to ask Niall Strachan exactly the same question.'

Rob pulled a face. 'I always feel for people who lose a loved one only to find out all the dirty secrets that should have died with them. Someone my mum knows lost her husband of thirty years, only to discover that for twenty of them he'd had a mistress. He actually died in her bed. No bloody idea how someone deals with that sort of crap.'

Rob wandered off a good deal less exuberant than when he'd come in, and Becky picked up the phone.

'Becky!' Tom's voice interrupted her thoughts as she finished her call to Sara Osborne.

'What's up?'

'Come on – you're with me.'

Becky didn't question him, just grabbed her light summer jacket, her keys and her bag and followed him as he hurried from the incident room.

'What's going on?' she asked as they both ran down the stairs, Tom too impatient to wait for the lift.

'I think we're being too soft on Niall Strachan. I've had a call from someone in the XO-Tech office – a man called Danny West. Please don't say "I told you so", but his reading of the situation with Martha is very different to the one we've heard. He's backing up what the other woman in the office – Caroline, I think she was called – told us. He's also convinced that Martha wouldn't have had anything to do with Niall. He didn't want to say so in front of the others, because he said it's hard enough being the only bloke in the sales and marketing office without stirring things up by disagreeing openly with bloody Elise, who would have made his life hell. He says it's like being in a gang with one ultimate leader. Disagree with her, and everyone has to turn against you for their own safety. Metaphorically speaking, I presume.'

'I wouldn't want to work with her, that's for sure. But we saw the emails Martha sent. There was nothing misleading about those, was there?'

'The content suggested that she was obsessed with Niall, but they came from her Gmail account, not her office account. I've asked the tech team to take another look, and they've confirmed what Ted told you – there's nothing in Martha's browser history to suggest that she accessed Gmail from her computer, although the emails were buried deep in her temporary Internet files. As Ted says, "it's a weird one", especially as the IP address shows the email originated in XO-Tech's offices.'

'Are you thinking someone else could have set up this email address?' Becky asked.

By now they had reached Tom's car. He jumped into the driving seat. 'Of course! I could set up a Gmail account in a version of your name, if I wanted to. All they had to do was wait until Martha logged on to her computer and left the room – I don't know, to go to the bathroom or whatever – then send an email, wipe Gmail from the browser history, and that's it! What I'm saying is, we can't assume it was definitely Martha. I'm not saying it wasn't either. I'm just not prepared to close my mind to other possibilities.'

Becky was silent for a moment.

'Bloody Elise!' she said as she spun round to face Tom. 'I wouldn't put it past her, you know – to stir up trouble. I wonder if she's got a bit of a thing about Niall herself? She said she'd been to the house with some papers for him, and according to one of the girls Niall invited her in for a drink as it was late afternoon. She went on and on about the inside of the house, until the one guy in that office – Danny, I presume – risked his life by telling her to shut up.'

'It's an interesting idea. Would she be that devious? I don't know why I'm asking that; people never fail to surprise me with what they're capable of – good and bad.'

'Here's a wild theory. What if Elise has fallen for Niall but thinks he's got a thing about Martha? What better way of getting rid of both of her competitors than to kill off his wife and make her greatest rival the prime suspect?'

'I know they say truth is stranger than fiction, Becky, but can you honestly believe she's clever enough? I guess we'd better see what Mr Strachan has to say.'

47

MARTHA

The police are getting closer. I can feel it. By now they will know everything there is to know about Martha Porter, and that isn't much. Because of Alfie, they will look harder, worried that a child is missing and with someone they suspect of murder.

I would never hurt Alfie, but they don't know that.

I can't make him sleep in the car for another night. I know children are resilient, but so much has changed for him in the past couple of days. He must be confused. Our lives have always been very ordered – Alfie goes to school every day or to the childminder in the holidays, and I go to work. Always at the same time. I pick him up at the same time, and we go home. We watch TV for an hour, have something to eat, read or play a game, and then it's bed. It's not exciting, but it's safe – and one thing I have wanted since the day I knew about Alfie was to keep him safe. There's no way I can rectify all of my mistakes, but there are things I can do to ensure my son has as normal a life as possible. The thought of what that entails makes me shiver.

For now, I'm going to concentrate on giving Alfie the best day I can, so I drive back to the seaside and I check into a small bed and breakfast. The sun has broken through the heavy cloud, and after we've dumped our few clothes in the room, we walk down to the beach, his hand in mine. He's excited about everything he sees, and we find a shop so I can get him a bucket and spade. He's never played in the sand before, not the real sand of a beach. I don't have any swimming trunks for him, but it doesn't matter. He can paddle for now. I have never taught him to swim – the thought of all those sociable mums inviting me to meet for coffee and maybe asking Alfie to their children's parties was more than I could cope with. It's one thing to avoid telling work colleagues the story of my life; it's another to refuse to divulge anything to people who are trying to be friendly.

I don't allow myself to make friends. Not since Leah – the only friend I've ever had. When she came to Lakeside she helped me see the world beyond its walls. I try not to think of her now. When memories hit me of those days spent listening to her as she told me how life could *really* be for someone of my age, I thrust them aside. But her name pops into my head when I'm least expecting it.

Leah. Leah.

Thinking of her is too painful, and I try to shut out the reminders, but they keep coming. Since I lost Leah I have stuck to one aspect of Aram's teaching – never trust anyone; never divulge unnecessary information; never ask questions of others.

With Leah it had been different. She arrived in my life at a time when I needed someone, when I felt isolated from everyone around me. But her friendship with me was her ultimate downfall.

48

LAKESIDE

My mother's relationship with me had been distant for years, but the day after Aram took my virginity I passed her in the corridor and she gave me a look of pure contempt. Over the following weeks I became an almost permanent fixture in his bed, and I realised I had taken the thing she wanted most in the world. The sad part was that I didn't value it.

Alice had been asked to leave, and finally I understood why she despised me. She must have seen this coming, and as she left she accused me of plotting all along to steal Aram. It had never entered my head.

Aram was right about my body, though. It was ready, and it responded as a car responds when a foot is pressed to the accelerator. But my mind and soul remained detached. For months any thoughts I had about what was happening as he touched me were with the boy in the field, the boy who had talked about university life in Sheffield – the bars, the lectures, the cinema. He'd laughed when I told him I had only been to the cinema once, when I was eight. It was a very special treat back then, and now, of course, it wasn't an option. There was nothing scathing about his laughter. He thought I was sweet and innocent, and that's why he never pushed me. He also thought I was beautiful and wanted me to travel to Sheffield to see him when he went back there, so he could show me what life could be like. It was *his* body I yearned to lie next to mine at night, his young, free soul that I wanted to learn from, and I ached to understand how life might be in his world.

Despite those thoughts, the nights Aram chose someone else to join him in his bed were painful. I felt rejected, dismissed, as if I had failed to please him. I think he did it to punish me, but we never talked about it. It made me try all the harder to be everything he wanted me to be, and yet he must have known my heart wasn't with him, even though my body was.

Over the next couple of years life settled into a rhythm that seemed effortless because of its predictability. Gradually my longing for the boy disappeared, but I still had dreams of one day finding someone like him, someone I could love without fear. I still wasn't trusted to go out in the car, and Aram was right to have no confidence in me. There was something growing inside me – a desire to see beyond the river, the lake and the nearby village, to venture into uncharted territories, experiences and emotions – and he could sense it, as he could sense my every thought. But he didn't like it. He couldn't understand how a part of me remained aloof from him, and it tormented him. I did nothing to disturb the status quo, and slowly the feelings of restlessness were carefully filed away in a box labelled IMPOSSIBLE in my mind.

And there they stayed. Until Leah joined us.

Whenever an opening arose for a new recruit, either because Aram had evicted someone he deemed unsuitable, or more rarely when one of the community demanded to leave and was forced to sneak off in disgrace into the night, Aram would use his recently created YouTube channel to whip up an audience for one of his infrequent talks in cities around the country. These sessions gave him the opportunity to ask for donations so he could continue his work, and enabled him to identify those most suited to become part of the inner circle – the chosen few who were invited to live at Lakeside. And, of course, each new convert meant a new injection of cash.

His most recent outing to Liverpool had resulted in only one newcomer.

Leah Medway had travelled to Liverpool from her home in Stoke-on-Trent to listen to Aram speak. She had heard how he helped those who followed his guidance to regain balance and strength, and said he was exactly what she needed. Tall and skinny with glossy dark hair that just touched her shoulders, she made us love her from her first day. She stood at the front of the room where we were all gathered and talked about the pain she had experienced at the death of her mother, how it had left her feeling she had no one to love. Aram, as was his custom, showered her with affection and asked Mum to prepare a special dinner to welcome her.

She befriended me early on, but was sufficiently aware of the rules to know we couldn't be seen to have any kind of exclusive relationship. That would result in one or both of us suffering some form of humiliation to drive us apart, and for the moment Leah was being love-bombed by everyone. It was difficult to find a private space with so many people around, but we managed to meet by the lake, out of sight of the house, as often as we could. When we weren't together, Leah made sure she spent time with others too, but it was my company she enjoyed the most.

One day we sneaked into one of the sheds at the far end of the garden, and she danced with me.

'Come on, India, move those hips!' she called as she sang a song that had been in the top twenty when she'd arrived at Lakeside. I'd never heard it, of course. I remembered Dad dancing with Mum, and tried to copy his moves as Leah swayed and whirled beside me. In the end we both collapsed on the floor in fits of laughter. It felt good, and I realised that I rarely laughed. At least, I hadn't until Leah came.

I knew what was coming, but I didn't know how to tell her. I was certain she was starting to believe there was nowhere in the world as perfect as Lakeside, and I should have warned her that she, like everyone else who came to live with us, would have to suffer at Aram's hands sooner or later. But I didn't. It happened when she had been with us for about four weeks. We were all invited to the meditation room, and I knew someone was about to be commanded to acknowledge their imperfections and weaknesses. That day it was Leah's turn.

There was a sense of relief in everyone else that they weren't in the spotlight, and it changed what might have been sympathy to a kind of gloating, as if everybody was thinking, *I've been there. It's happened to me. Thank God it's someone else's turn today.*

The hum of conversation died as Leah walked to the front of the room to stand before us. All eyes were on her as Aram listed the failings he had identified in the time she had been with us, presenting them as the reason she hadn't been able to find happiness and fulfilment in her life. He accurately identified every insecurity she had. He stuck the knife in and twisted. I didn't want to look at her, but I knew Aram would notice if I didn't and I would be dragged up there too.

She stood straight, not lowering her head with shame, as expected. Only her clenched jaw and her pale skin, flushed pink above her cheekbones, gave away how much he was hurting her. He ended with his usual words: 'We want you with us, Leah. We think we can help you understand the right way, the only path to contentment. But you must recognise that your self-centred, arrogant, evasive nature is disgusting to us. We will gladly give you our love – I believe we've shown you that – but you must earn it. Leave us now.'

With that, the community rose to its feet, and every one of us turned our backs as she left the room.

I didn't see her for three days. I was desperate to go to her, to offer comfort, but that wasn't the way it worked. If I'd done that, shown that she was in any way special to me, Aram would have banished her. He wouldn't accept any friendship that undermined his authority, especially if it involved me, and I was certain I wouldn't be the one to be cast aside. It would be Leah.

Finally she sought me out down by the lake. She looked pale, but there was a fire in her eyes, which I knew she would have to quell if she wanted to stay.

'I'm so sorry, Leah. I should have told you he would do that to you at some point. It's part of the process, you see, and you have to obey him. If you want his love and approval, it's the only way. And then you'll be happy. Really you will.'

She smiled. 'Lovely India. You have no idea how delightful you are, you know. You're so eager to please and I'm scared for you.'

I turned to her, shocked to the core. 'No, Leah, you should be scared for yourself! If you don't follow the rules, he'll force you to leave and he'll shatter you before you go.'

She reached for my hand and gave it a squeeze. 'He won't, you know. India, there are things I want to tell you, but I'm frightened of what that knowledge might do to you. It's too soon, but some day I promise I'll explain to you why I'm here.'

I didn't know what she meant, but I was too scared to ask. I had long since learned that if I had thoughts, Aram could read them. I had seen others leave his room with a dazed expression on their face – an expression I was certain I sometimes shared – and I wondered what tricks Aram used to read our minds. I knew nothing of hypnosis.

'Listen, let's not talk about all of that – not yet,' she said, smiling gently. 'Let me tell you about my life before I came here. About where I lived, how I spent my days, who I've loved. I want you to understand that there's a world beyond here, outside these walls.'

And so she did. For weeks we grabbed whatever moments we could to be together, and it was always the best part of the day. She told me about her life in a series of chapters, each sounding more exciting than the one before, and I couldn't wait to hear more. She said that although she originally came from Stoke, she hadn't lived there for years, but she didn't want Aram to know. She talked about the place she loved most, the city where she had gone to university and had chosen to live after her degree. She painted vivid pictures in words of the clubs, the shops, the friendly people; how she had whiled away hours outside cafés in the sunshine with friends. She made me fall in love with all her favourite places, and I hung on every word.

The images stayed so clear in my mind that when I finally left Lakeside I knew where I wanted to go – to the city Leah loved. I planned to visit the places she had told me about, although I never did. I was too scared to go out, to be seen. But I felt I was there for her, knowing she would never come back herself.

I went to Manchester.

49

As Tom drew the car up outside Niall's home, Becky ended a call on her mobile.

'Rob?' Tom asked.

'Yep. Before we go in, I should fill you in on his chat with Genevieve's friends, and mine with Sara Osborne.'

Tom nodded as Becky shuffled round in the passenger seat to face him.

'Sara is probably the more likely to tell us the unvarnished truth, and she said that Genevieve had mentioned Eddie a couple of times recently – something about how he might prove useful. Sara hadn't understood what she was talking about and had pushed her, but Genevieve just smiled and said, "You'll see." Later she'd said the stupid bugger had got married and the wife would be an inconvenience to the narrative she needed to create, but she thought she could take care of that.'

'What the hell does that mean?'

'Sara didn't know. She'd tried to get an explanation, but Genevieve smirked and changed the subject. Rob got a bit more from one of the friends, though. She said she knew something was going on with Genevieve because she'd stopped droning on about her marvellous marriage. Every time she mentioned Niall, there was a self-satisfied smile on Genevieve's face that could have suggested marital bliss, but the friend was sceptical. She'd seen Genevieve in a café in town with a woman she didn't recognise – she wasn't one of their group, and this made her curious, although God knows why. They were sitting in a window, so she'd taken a photo on her phone to show her other friends.' Becky's eyes were popping. 'Honestly, Tom, what's wrong with these people? What does it matter if she was out having coffee with someone different?' She gave a hopeless shrug and continued. 'Believe it or not – and I find it difficult to – she then went home and used Google Images to see if she could identify the woman. And she did. Kirsten Carlson. There are lots of photos of her online – that's what comes of having a famous, or maybe infamous, husband. So Genevieve met Kirsten. And recently.'

'Before or after her conversation with Sara?'

'I'm not sure. The café and photo pantomime occurred the week before Genevieve was killed. Oh, and they seemed to be arguing.'

Tom pulled his phone out of his pocket and scrolled through some screens.

'Here we go,' he said. 'The message that invited Genevieve outside to her death. "Last week you begged me to tell you what I know, and I refused. But I've changed my mind. I'll give you what you want if you give me what *I* want – and you know what that is. He's mine – not yours." We assumed this was Martha claiming rights over Niall. But what if it was Kirsten? And she was referring to Eddie?'

Becky nodded slowly but then frowned. 'The words fit, but it was Martha's phone.'

'True. But we don't know it was in Martha's possession, do we?'

Becky turned away and slumped back against the seat. 'No, but how the hell would Kirsten have got it? Whatever was going on, however much you think it's all too neat, it *has* to have come from Martha Porter or at least someone at XO-Tech.'

'You know how my mind works. I never accept the most logical answer until every piece slots into place, and some bits don't quite line up for me. Without a doubt Martha is key to our investigation, but let's try to keep an open mind when we talk to Niall Strachan. If we assume he loved his wife – and as yet we've no reason to doubt it – then learning she was trying something on with Eddie Carlson will be a body blow. He'll have no way of ever finding out the truth.' Tom reached for the door handle. 'I'm not looking forward to this.'

Niall Strachan led them through to the back of the house, where wide open bi-fold doors led from the kitchen-cum-dining room into a perfectly manicured back garden. Becky chose a seat with her back to the view because she would have found it difficult to concentrate without staring out at the plants. She was desperate for a garden, and all she had was the balcony of their central Manchester apartment.

'I apologise for disturbing you again, Mr Strachan,' Tom said. 'I know this must be a difficult time for you, but I want to assure you we're doing everything we can to find out what happened, and who your wife met in the lane on Monday night.'

Niall was facing the light, and the sunshine illuminated a face that looked pale, with black circles around bloodshot eyes. There was no doubt this man was suffering, and they were about to make him feel worse.

'I thought you knew the answer to that,' Niall said, his voice slightly croaky as if it hadn't been used for a while.

'We have a suspect, but at the moment the evidence is circumstantial, so while that's the case we have to keep looking.'

Niall's eyes narrowed. 'What do you mean, circumstantial?

How can that be if it was her phone that called Genevieve? And Spencer said the knife looks like the one from our kitchen. She's an oddball. I've always felt there was something weird about her, even though she was bloody good at her job.'

'We'll have to take your word for that, but as I said, sir, the evidence is not conclusive and it allows for more than one interpretation. At least, that's what any defence team will say. For example, her emails. How certain can you be that they came from her?'

Niall scowled. 'You saw them. They were from her account.'

'Come on, Mr Strachan. Even I know that anyone could have set up that account, and you know far more about technology than me. Did you seriously never suspect they could have been from someone else?'

'Why would I, after her behaviour at the party?'

'When we find Martha Porter, and we will, it's one of the questions we'll be asking her. We're getting closer.'

Becky wasn't sure that was the case, but she wasn't about to disagree with Tom.

'I'd like to confirm one piece of information. On Monday night – or rather, the early hours of Tuesday morning – you made a phone call from outside the lawyers' offices in central Manchester. Can you tell me who you spoke to, please?'

'Of course. It was Spencer. He wanted to know whether the deal had gone through. He has a vested interest – his future's on the line too, you know.'

There was no point in him denying it. Strachan knew they could check.

'Thank you for confirming that. Now, if it's not too painful, we'd like to talk to you about your wife. We feel it would help us if we understood more about Genevieve and your relationship with each other,' Tom said.

Niall leaned back and folded his arms. 'All that matters is who killed her. Not what came before. We were happy, okay? We were like every other couple – good days, bad days. But we both got what we needed from the marriage, and that's about as good as it gets, I think.'

'What do you believe your wife got from the marriage, as you put it?' Tom asked.

'The life she wanted. A man who didn't try to control her, who let her do her own thing, took her to the right places, wasn't an embarrassment.'

Jesus! Becky thought. Was that his definition of a good marriage? For a moment she wondered if Genevieve had gone looking for Eddie Carlson for a bit of sheer passion, even if last time it involved lamping someone for getting too close.

'And you, Mr Strachan?'

'I had a very presentable wife who had the same values as I do. We enjoyed the same things – we loved the life we shared. Look around you. This house isn't a mansion, but there were only the two of us and it has everything we need.'

'I'm sorry to have to ask,' Tom continued, 'but did either you or Genevieve – to the best of your knowledge – have an affair during your marriage?'

Niall leaned his forearms heavily on the table. 'What the hell has that got to do with anything?'

'I'm sorry if the notion upsets you, but we have to rule out current or ex-lovers as part of the process. I'm not here to judge and neither is DI Robinson, but it would be helpful to know.'

The most interesting part of that speech as far as Becky was concerned was that Tom had referred to her as DI Robinson, whereas he usually referred to her as Becky when talking to the bereaved. She knew what that meant – Tom didn't like Niall, and he didn't trust him.

'Well, you won't find any skeletons in my cupboard. I didn't have time, to be honest. We had an active social life, and I had a hectic business life. Genevieve had far more time, but I doubt she had the inclination.'

'Can you explain?'

'She loved our life and wouldn't have risked it. That's all I mean. She loved me – not in a gushing, romantic way, but we were a team. We were happy.'

Tom was quiet, and Becky waited for the moment she knew was about to come. She was watching Niall Strachan carefully for his reaction.

'Would it surprise you to know that Genevieve had been in touch with Eddie Carlson recently, and that she had suggested they should get together?'

'*What?* You're joking, surely? She said he was a total tosser – an embarrassment. I think you must have got that wrong, Chief Inspector.' Two spots of colour brightened his otherwise pale cheeks, and Becky was in no doubt at all what he thought of this revelation. He was surprised. But he was angry too. Angry at what she'd done, or angry because he didn't know?

Tom waited, saying nothing, hoping Niall would jump in with some telling statement that would change everything, but he took a few deep breaths and stood up.

'If you have no more questions, I'd like you to go, please. What you've just told me is hurtful, and I need some time. Was there anything else?'

Tom pushed back his chair and stood up. 'No. That's all for now. We'll keep you informed.'

With a last longing look over her shoulder at the garden, Becky followed Tom out of the room.

50

It was the end of another frustrating day for Tom. They had made some progress, but not enough.

'Okay everyone, a last review of where we are, and then home for a well-earned rest for us all. Becky will fill you in on our conversation with Strachan, but where the hell was Charley? I thought she was spending time at the Strachan house to keep him informed – and us, for that matter.'

'He asked her to leave,' Keith answered. 'Apparently he said – and I quote – "It's doing my head in having someone lurking round my house making it look untidy".'

'Bollocks,' Tom muttered. He wasn't surprised, but he'd have much preferred her to be there, picking up on any nuances of Strachan's behaviour. 'I guess there's not much we can do about that. Becky, can you recap on Strachan, Eddie Carlson and his wife Kirsten?'

When Becky had summarised the various conversations, Tom looked around the table. 'Any thoughts?'

'Not really,' Rob said, looking bewildered, 'other than it makes no sense to me that Genevieve would try to entice Eddie into a relationship.'

'I thought Niall was angry,' Becky said. 'Not in a hurt way – in a "what the hell was she playing at?" kind of way. Sara Osborne finds it hard to believe that her sister wanted to get back into a relationship with Eddie, and even if she did, why would she meet up with Kirsten? I think I should call in at the Carlson house on my way home and ask her.' Becky looked at Tom.

'Good idea. Where are we with Martha Porter? Keith, Rob?'

Keith shook his head. Progress was frustratingly slow.

'Nothing at the flat, boss,' Rob said. 'I don't think the bike's much help either. The chiropodist's prints are all over the handlebars, and the only others we found did match some from Martha's flat, but they were on the crossbar. The bike was propped against some children's toys and it looked as if she might have grabbed it so she could get at them.'

It was proof that she had touched the bike, but nothing more. They needed one piece of hard evidence – one single irrefutable fact that would tie Martha to the murder.

'DCI Douglas and I have been pondering the fact that Martha's obviously been trying to live under the radar for years,' Becky said, 'so all this secrecy isn't because she killed Genevieve Strachan – if she did. Does that suggest she's done it before? She's certainly hiding from something. We're waiting for the lab to get back to us on the DNA collected from the flat so we can run it through the system, but in the meantime we've looked at unsolved murders of women in the right age range, but there are very few, to be honest – shows what a splendid job we've been doing!' She gave a cheeky grin, and there was a bubble of laughter from around the table. 'We're widening the search to include missing women, on the assumption that she may have killed a previous rival and we just haven't found the body. I'll ask the night duty team – and Rob, that *doesn't* mean you – to go through the list and come up with the most likely so we can follow them up tomorrow.'

Rob seemed as if he was about to object, but Tom saw Becky give him a fierce look. He might appear to have boundless energy, but fatigue would catch up with him eventually, and everyone needed to be on their A-game.

Tom pushed the key into his front door, glad to be home and looking forward to a long cold drink in the back garden. He was disappointed he wouldn't be seeing Lucy. It would have been the first time in months he'd seen her in the flesh and not on a screen, and ever since he'd heard she was on her way back he'd been looking forward to it. But Kate said jet lag had caught up with them both, so they wouldn't be coming round. He'd offered to drive out to the hotel to see them, or to pay for a taxi for Lucy, but Kate was adamant.

'Our flight got in at four o'clock this afternoon, Tom, and we've been up for nearly forty-eight hours. You can't expect her to stay awake for another four or five hours until you can get here. Anyway, she's fast asleep.'

There was no way he could argue with that, and maybe he wasn't in the best frame of mind tonight anyway. He'd made Kate promise that if Lucy woke any time before midnight, she would FaceTime him.

He closed the front door and made his way into the kitchen. Louisa was sitting in an armchair in the corner, dozing. He didn't want to disturb her, so he quietly opened the fridge to hunt for a bottle of wine. He poured himself a glass and was about to tiptoe into the garden when his phone burst into life. Louisa jumped in her chair, a startled expression on her face.

Tom gave her an apologetic smile and looked at his phone. FaceTime – but from Kate's phone, not Lucy's.

He sat at the table, propping his phone up against a glass candleholder as his ex-wife's face appeared on the screen.

'Kate. I thought you'd be sleeping. Is Lucy okay?'

'Of course she's okay. Better than I am, it has to be said. Long flights don't suit me at all. We should have come back by ship, but there wasn't time before Lucy has to go back to school, and I don't suppose you'd have approved of her having a couple of weeks off.'

Tom decided not to comment. 'Can I speak to her?'

'She's sleeping, and that's not why I'm calling.'

Tom saw Louisa bite her lip, trying not to laugh. She knew how frustrated Tom got with Kate.

'What can I do for you? I know things didn't turn out the way you wanted them to in Australia, and I'm sorry about that. I hope you're feeling okay about it all.'

'Are you relishing my folly, Tom? I hope not, because right now I'm trying to think what's best for our daughter.'

'Not at all. And we both want the best for Lucy.'

'I've come out to reception because I don't want her to overhear, but I think you and I need to get together to discuss where we go from here.'

Tom had no idea how much money Kate had left from the sale of her house. Had it *all* gone? He didn't want to ask because it wasn't his business, but he felt sure she was about to *make* it his business.

'I don't think I can afford to buy in Manchester now. I did a bit of research, and Durham seems affordable, as are parts of Scotland.'

Tom managed with difficulty to keep his voice even and reasonable. 'Lucy left all her friends to move to Australia. Do you think she would be okay with starting again, from scratch, for the second time in six months?'

'She's got no choice, has she?' Kate's voice was rising. '*I've* got no choice. What do you expect me to do?'

Tom took a large swig of his wine. 'I don't know, Kate. I just want to discuss the options.'

'And what *are* the options?'

Here we go, Tom thought. She was waiting for him to make the first move.

'I need to understand what you'd like to see happen, what Lucy wants, and then work out how we can accommodate that. We want to see as much of Lucy as we can, as does her little brother, who hasn't had any contact with her since he was a couple of weeks old.'

'Well, you can hardly blame me for that. You put your daughter in danger!'

Tom looked at Louisa, who could hear every word, and raised his hands, palm upwards, in a hopeless shrug, forgetting that Kate could also see what he was doing. They'd had versions of this argument endless times, but once Kate discovered that Tom's brother, Jack, was alive and still being hunted by his old enemies, she had been adamant that Lucy had to be whisked away to the other side of the world.

He turned back to the screen. 'I'm not blaming anyone. I need to understand how you're thinking, and then I want to speak to Lucy. She'll be leaving home for university in a few years – if that's the route she decides to take – or be heading off to follow whatever ambitions she has. We need to make these years as good as they can be, so she grows up to be a confident and happy young woman.'

'I can tell by your face and your body language that you're irritated with me, Tom. I'm happy to give this some thought, but unless you want to see your daughter brought up in a one-bedroomed bedsit – which is all I can afford in Manchester – you'll need to be creative. I'll be in touch.'

With that, she hung up.

'*Christ*, that woman is irritating!' Tom leaned back in his chair. 'Why can't I deal with her?'

Louisa smiled grimly. 'She's your ex-wife, and when you split, emotions ran high. She knows she made a mistake, and it's irked her ever since – especially when you decided you wouldn't take her back. All you can do is bear in mind she's probably humiliated by it all.'

'So what do I do?' Tom got up and walked back to the fridge. He hadn't been planning on drinking more than a glass before eating, but he hadn't even noticed the first one go down, let alone savoured it.

'You know what she's getting at. She's pleading poverty, and you've already told me you're going to have to sub her in some way.'

'What,' Tom said with mock horror, 'with money sullied by the hands of my reprobate brother? Are you suggesting she would take his money even though he's such a danger to us all?'

Tom had barely touched Jack's considerable wealth since he had 'died', and there was no way to give it back because Jack was still technically dead, and anyway, he was adamant he didn't want it.

'Let's both try to remember that the cancer nearly killed her, and she's living in fear of it returning,' Louisa said. 'It's hard, and I want to throttle her for the way she speaks to you. But we have to keep the peace for Lucy's sake, so all you can do is talk to them both and find a solution that keeps Lucy close and doesn't piss Kate off too much.'

Tom topped up his glass and said nothing for a few moments.

'Fine. But if she wants money to move to bloody Aberdeen or the Outer Hebrides, she can whistle for it. Shall I make a start on dinner?'

THURSDAY

51

MARTHA

I wake up early, my body drenched in sweat once again. I've been dreaming. I saw the blood, smelled it, practically tasted it, and I stared, entranced, at the knife in my hand. The voice whispered in my ear, telling me it was the only thing I could do. It was the *right* thing to do. And yet how could it have been right? I can't remember when I lost control of my own will, but with the benefit of hindsight, I realise that it was eroded over many years.

Now, my thoughts and memories of life at Lakeside are interrupted as Alfie stirs beside me. I reach over and stroke his soft cheek and he shuffles around, makes a purring noise, snuggles closer and settles again.

My chest feels tight and I raise my hand to push the hair from my hot forehead. Until Genevieve's murder, I'd thought I was safe – hidden behind my fake identity. I have no way of knowing if Aram has carried out the threat he has been holding over me for years and has exposed me for my sins. If he has, the police could already be hunting me down. A fear no less acute has always been that one of Aram's army of supporters would find me, and I would be dragged back to Lakeside, where my son would grow up to believe it's normal to strive endlessly to please one person, to dread causing their displeasure, to have no thoughts or desires of his own.

Since gaining my freedom, I've realised that the total domination of one person over another, or a group of others, is not confined to the kind of life I led as I grew up. It can happen within a family, within a place of work, within a group of friends. Anywhere where one person dictates the rules without fear of dissent.

I should have escaped sooner, when I was twenty years old and still had the chance of a normal life. I had a golden opportunity, but I threw it away.

LAKESIDE

My favourite spot at Lakeside was by the huge weeping willow at the edge of the lake. Sometimes I would sit far back, cocooned in the shelter of the trailing branches, invisible from the house, but the final time Leah found me there I was sitting right by the water, enjoying the sunshine. Without a word, she sat down beside me. I glanced at her, and her face was serious. Sad, almost. I knew then that she had come to tell me she was leaving.

We didn't speak for a while. We just watched the moorhens glide silently across the still water.

When she broke the silence, Leah's voice was quiet. 'It's time for me to go, India. I'm sorry, but I've done what I came to do.'

I felt a pressure in my chest. She'd been with us for three months – not long, but for someone as starved of love as I was, long enough for her to mean everything. She was the only friend I'd had in ten years. I couldn't bear the thought of her leaving me.

'Has he asked you to go?'

She gave a soft laugh. 'No. It's my choice, and I haven't told him yet. So please... I understand it's hard for you, but I don't want him to know until I tell him myself.'

I was stunned. When people left, it was usually because Aram had decided they had nothing to offer to our community, and so he sent them on their way, more broken than when they'd arrived.

'You can't leave! You'll lose everything you brought with you.' I held my breath, hoping she would say I was right, but she didn't.

'Don't worry about that. I'll get it back. And if I don't, it doesn't matter. My mother would be proud of me for using her inheritance for this.'

I had no idea what she meant, but I had been conditioned not to ask questions and was already feeling bad about my outburst.

She leaned her shoulder against mine. 'Do you want to come with me?'

Leave Lakeside?

I had often wondered what it would be like to live the life that Leah had described to me, where people broke every rule that had been drilled into me and indulged in those emotions provoked by the desire to possess: jealousy, greed, envy. Did I want to live in a world where possessions meant more than cooperation, sharing and equality? But that same world would allow me the freedom to have my own thoughts, love whoever I wanted to love, go to the cinema, bars, nightclubs, without fear of retribution. I pushed those thoughts away.

'What would I do?' I asked. 'I'm not really good for anything.'

Leah tutted. 'Honestly, India, you underestimate yourself. I've watched how you organise the running of Lakeside. Aram might – theoretically – take care of our souls, but you're the one that makes everything work. You're only twenty years old, and although you don't realise it, when things need fixing everyone comes to you.'

Me? She couldn't be serious. I just did the things I was given to do, as everyone did. Mum took care of the kitchen. A man who had joined us a few years ago had been in the building trade, so he looked after the maintenance. We all fell into the roles that suited us the best. It had never occurred to me that I was *good* at something.

I was quiet for a moment as I wondered if maybe she was right. But no. I was sure she wasn't.

'You know, it's okay for you to ask me questions,' she said. 'I won't think you're prying, being nosey, any of those forbidden traits.' She smiled to take the sting out of her sarcasm.

'Tell me why you're leaving.' The words burst from me before I could stop them.

'I thought you might ask that.' She took a deep breath. 'I think it's time I was honest with you, but for everyone's sake, India, you mustn't repeat any of this. If I tell you, will you keep it to yourself? I'm not asking you to lie. I appreciate that would be too difficult for you. But as no one will know what questions to ask, you need to assure me that you won't volunteer the information. Is that okay?'

Secrets were not part of the framework of my life, although I had kept a few just to spend time with Leah over the past weeks. But I nodded, scared of knowing something I couldn't share, and, keeping her voice low, she told me why she had come to Lakeside.

'There was nothing wrong with me when I came here. At least, nothing more than is wrong with any other person. We all have insecurities, faults, characteristics that are less than perfect. Most of us accept that and do our best, but some – like the people here – are constantly searching for ways to feel better about themselves, to be healed.'

She paused, and we watched the lake for a moment as I waited for her to find the right words.

'I came here for my mother, India. She died just over a year ago, and left me her house, which is how I was able to buy my way in here, but she also asked me to do something for her. She wanted me to expose Aram Forakis for who he is.'

I could hear my own breaths, short and sharp, as if I'd been running.

'I'm sorry,' she said, putting her arm around my shoulders,

waiting for me to settle. 'I know you think he's wonderful, but that's only because you've been conditioned to think that way, as everyone here has. He preys on the weak, controls them by degrading their self-worth. It's disgusting, and he can't be allowed to continue.'

I stared at her in horror. 'Are you saying what he does is against the law?'

'Not his preaching or his ideology – at least, no more than many belief systems. Aram demands obedience, as many religions do. He makes his followers confess their sins, then shames them and forces them to take their punishment, and he promotes an ideology which is at odds with the outside world. Again, he's not alone in any of that. So no – what he does is not illegal. But the damage he causes is immeasurable.'

'He doesn't believe in worshipping any god,' I mumbled. Her words had shocked me, but I couldn't stop myself from wanting to defend him.

'Of course he doesn't. Because then he would only be a messenger and have to adhere to some holy laws that don't match his. That's not his style. His followers would have to believe in a divine being superior to him, and that would never do.'

I heard the sarcasm in her tone again, and I didn't know how to handle it.

'So why come here?'

She squeezed my shoulder. 'I had an older sister. She went to university in Manchester, like I did, but she got involved with a group of people who were essentially a cult.'

She must have seen how puzzled I was, and she grabbed my hand and pulled me gently round to face her.

'It may not be a word that you know, India, but what Aram is running here *is* a cult – a group in which the leader uses psychological coercion to indoctrinate people with his values. There are hundreds of cults in England – far more than anyone would think. People are recruited because they're looking for something in life, something that's missing. Religion used to be the most common way to ensnare people, but now it can be therapy, self-help, even yoga. Some communities are vast, with hundreds of members; others are small, with only a handful of devotees.'

'I don't understand,' I said, panic gripping me. Was my entire life part of some evil plot?

'Aram controls you by intimidation, by shaming you. He's created a dependency, a dominance, by exploiting your fear of rejection. First he makes you feel you're the most important person in the world, and then slowly but surely you're made to question your own judgement. He does everything he can to lower your self-esteem. Look at you, India. You're beautiful, but you don't know it. You're smart, but I've heard him tell you publicly that you're stupid. He's isolated you from your parents, and them from each other. You all have to kneel at the altar of Aram. Exactly as my sister did.'

We were both quiet for a moment. I knew what I had to ask. She'd said, 'I *had* an older sister.' Past tense.

'What happened to her?'

She paused as if she was going to say something, and then gave an almost imperceptible shake of the head. 'He destroyed her. Aram made her feel worthless. She cut herself off from us – from me and Mum. She said we were a bad influence, and she could have no more to do with us. My dad was long gone, and I was young. I didn't understand what was happening. We lost her.'

I dropped my head. I knew how it felt to be destroyed by Aram. But he had always pulled me back from the brink when I was at my lowest ebb by showering me with affection. Until the next time.

'Doesn't he recognise your name?'

She smiled. 'My sister had a different father – a different surname. She was Jordan Callahan; my name's Medway. Aram has no idea who I am. I'm going to leave here, India, but I'm not going empty-handed.'

I spun towards her. 'What do you mean?'

'I've got evidence – not of what Aram did to my sister; no one can prove that. But I can prove he's guilty of extortion, fraud, call it what you like. He convinces people that by handing over their property, they're guaranteed some form of utopian existence, free from all the sins in the world. He's making false promises in return for money.'

I couldn't speak, because at the back of my mind, I had known all of this. I had seen the paperwork.

'Then I'm guilty too,' I said softly.

Leah pushed herself up onto her knees, turning to face me. 'No, India. You are *not* responsible. You've known no other life since you were ten, and you have no way of knowing what's right and wrong. You've been indoctrinated by that man. I would do anything to get you out of here, to persuade you to leave with me.'

I stared at her. '*Leave?*'

I'd said the word out loud for the first time, and it echoed around me as if I'd shouted it. I spun round to check there was no one within earshot.

'Leave?' This time I whispered the word, but it made me shiver – not with horror, but with hope. 'How?'

I couldn't ask permission. Aram would rip me to shreds and convince me that the minute I walked through the gates the world would hurl its worst at me. The only option was to escape in secret, but the gates were always locked.

'You mustn't tell a soul, you understand that, don't you? You can't trust anyone – not even your parents. Especially not your mother.'

She was right. Mum – Nicola – had never forgiven me for being Aram's favourite, a role she'd considered to be hers for years. I had never wanted to attract his attention, and yet the nights when he wanted me in his bed gave me feelings of dread and anticipation in equal measure. My body responded to him, even though my mind wanted to reject him. He was both repulsive to me and thrilling.

'If you're coming with me,' Leah said, breaking into my

thoughts, 'then I won't tell Aram I'm leaving. It will complicate things because he'll want to see me off the premises. I can't do that if you're with me. I'm leaving tomorrow night, so it's up to you. I've worked out a way of getting out, hoping you'd come. If you decide it's what you want, meet me by the river at two in the morning. But, India, he mustn't know any of this. Can you keep it from him?'

I looked at her and nodded slowly, not knowing if I believed it.

'Listen to me,' she said, both my hands in hers. 'Aram gets inside your head. I've seen it a hundred times, and there's only one thing you can do to stop him. Close your eyes. Don't look at him. Then he can't reach you.'

With that, Leah leaned towards me and kissed me on the cheek, stood up and walked away. I watched her go, excitement pulsing through my veins, going over and over her words in my head as they became more jumbled and confused.

As it turned out, she was right about everything. I should have done what she said. I should have closed my eyes.

52

Tom had only been in the incident room for five minutes when he sensed Keith standing by his shoulder, hopping from foot to foot with impatience. He had told the man twenty times that he was allowed to speak, but he said he always assumed Tom was too busy to be interrupted.

'Yes, Keith.'

'News, sir. Good news, I think. A receptionist at a hotel in central Manchester saw the Child Rescue Alert online, with the photos of Martha and Alfie Porter. She says the woman was barely recognisable, but she's sure about the child.'

Tom slapped the desk with the palms of his hands. 'That's excellent news. What else do we know?'

'She paid for two nights, but she'd gone by the first morning. They don't know if she even stayed overnight. She used a debit card, but it was in another name entirely – India Kalu – and she said the child was called Jamie.'

'It's no surprise she's using another name. Let's hope she uses the card again. We'll get her now. Track the card – I presume the hotel has supplied the details?'

'Yes, sir. We'll get the financials as soon as we can.'

Tom looked at his watch. It was still early. Damn it, they were going to have to wait. He gave a grunt of frustration.

'Morning, boss,' Becky said as she flung her bag under her desk and sat down. 'What's up?'

'The good news is we have a new identity for the elusive Ms Porter. Bad news – we've got to wait to track her debit card. She has a lovely name, actually – India Kalu! Keith's on the case. Keith, try to find out everything we can on the assumption this might be her original name, Martha Porter being the assumed one.'

'Fantastic,' Becky said, 'although I do wish it was obligatory for people to register the details if they change their name. It would make our job a lot easier.'

Tom had to agree. Had they known Martha Porter was also India Kalu, they might have caught up with her sooner.

'It is what it is – and finally we're on to her. Keith, as we've got a name now, let's see if she has a driving licence, a passport – the usual checks.'

Becky switched on her computer monitor. 'While we're waiting, I'll take a look at the list of missing women they were working on overnight, but no one's called me, so I can only assume nothing stood out.'

As Becky finished speaking, her eyes flicked to something going on behind Tom, and he turned to follow her gaze.

'Seems we're getting a bit of excitement over there,' she said, and both she and Tom got to their feet and hurried over to where Cass was pointing to something on her screen.

'What have we got?' Tom called as he strode across the office.

'I've found something online,' Cass said. 'I did a search on India Kalu and came across a thread on social media – a group of people from a school in London who are getting together for some form of reunion.'

'What does it say?' Becky asked.

'It seems these women – all late twenties now – went to

primary school together. They've kept in touch. One of them posted a school photo from when they were about nine challenging anyone to name everybody in the picture. India Kalu is one of the names. Someone remembered her mum talking about the Kalus, saying there was something shady going on. India didn't turn up to school one day, and the teacher told the other kids that the family had moved away. But there were all kinds of rumours flying around.'

Tom leaned his hands on the desk beside Cass. 'Where was the school?'

'East London, sir.'

'Cass, can you make a list of every scrap of info that you can glean from this, then we need to run a check on her parents. Good work.' Tom could feel they were getting closer. 'Becky, did you see Eddie Carlson and his wife?'

'I did. It's a sad story, actually. Turns out that Kirsten has leukaemia. Eddie says he meant to say something when I was there, but he knew she'd be uncomfortable about that and he wanted me to leave so he could be with her.'

'And the bruises?'

'She had a dizzy spell, and he caught her. He says she bruises at the slightest touch. I know it could all be lies, but Kirsten wasn't there so I couldn't check. He said she's in a clinic getting treatment and I wasn't about to go and interrogate her. Apparently after I left last time, Kirsten told Eddie she'd met up with Genevieve. She didn't tell him sooner because she knew he'd be mad.'

'And did Genevieve explain what she was up to?'

'Kirsten asked what kind of game she thought she was playing, and although Eddie asked what she'd said, Kirsten told him he really didn't want to know and assured him they wouldn't be bothered again. He said he wasn't interested enough to pursue it, but if it's important he'll ask her as soon as she's feeling up to it.'

Tom raised his eyebrows at Becky. 'And you believed all of this?'

'I believe she's ill – it's easy enough to check – and I'm certain she couldn't attack anyone. She wouldn't have the strength.'

'No, but Eddie would. Have someone check it out, Becky. He may seem like an okay bloke now, but he used to be a troublemaker. Let's not take him at face value.'

53

The incident room was buzzing. Keith had the financial details for India Kalu, and there was one crucial piece of information. The debit card had been registered nearly six years ago and pre-loaded with cash up to its limit. Apparently it had never been used until she paid for the hotel in Manchester. But then she'd used it again – this time to hire a car from Manchester Airport on Tuesday evening.

'Should I inform DCI Douglas?' Keith said to Becky, his voice impassive. He wasn't a man to whoop for joy.

'Let's not disturb him yet. See if we can find her – work out where she's gone. Have you spoken to the car hire company?'

'Yes, to the office at the airport. They've got a system glitch at the moment, but the bloke I spoke to gave me the registration number. They'll be able to track her on GPS once they've sorted out their tech problems.'

'Bloody typical,' Becky muttered. 'In the meantime, let's check for any other cards in her name and use the car's registration number to check CCTV close to the airport, and then ANPR when we get an idea where she's heading. And tell the car hire company we need to know the minute their problem's fixed. While we're at it, how are we doing with the birth records?'

'Her father is Joel Kalu, her mother Nicola. We're getting bank records for them too, and the debit card is registered to an address in Lincolnshire.'

'Okay. We may need to get the local force to pay the parents a visit.'

'Whoa!' The shout came from Rob, who was sitting at the next desk. Becky and Keith swivelled towards him. 'Come and look at this! I put the father's address into Google Maps. The house is called Lakeside, and I expected a modern house on an estate – near a lake, to state the obvious. But this place *is* an estate. It's bloody massive!'

Becky peered over his shoulder. 'The social media stuff that Cass found suggested that when she was a kid India lived in a fairly poor area of London, so what's this? Did he rob a bank?'

'Inheritance?' Rob said. 'It seems the move was fairly sudden.'

'But they might not own the house. Perhaps they're staff and they just live there. Keith,' Becky said, 'you know what to do.'

She returned to her desk, where her email was pinging constantly as fresh information arrived. A driving licence, also in the name of India Kalu, was nine years old and close to expiry. It too was registered to the address in Lincolnshire.

Then came the Land Registry information. Joel and Nicola Kalu had bought Lakeside without a mortgage, and several years later put the property into a trust, the trustees being themselves and Aram Forakis. Who the hell was he?

She didn't have long to wait for an answer. Rob sent her a link, then bounded over to her desk and pulled up a chair.

'Click the link.'

Becky did as he asked, and up came a photo of a man with white skin, a long thin nose and eyes that sloped down at the outer corners. There was something magnetic about his face, but more than anything it was the pale grey eyes that drew Becky's attention.

'I can't decide if he's the best-looking man I've seen in a while, or the most creepy,' she said. 'His features are powerful, but there's something about his expression that terrifies me. It's intense.'

Rob pointed at the text below his name.

Are you lost, feeling that the world has turned against you, that your life holds nothing of value?

Aram Forakis has spent years helping people like you to find their way to a more fulfilled future in a tough world, giving them the strength to understand their emotions together with the tools to deal with negativity. Spend time in his care, and he promises to build up your resilience by giving you insight into the reasons for your unhappiness.

'Selfishness, greed, envy, pride – these are the keys to misery. We should learn to embrace simplicity, accept our vulnerabilities and strengthen our souls. I can show you the way.'

His words are truth.

If you have an opportunity to listen to Aram speak – do it! You won't regret it.

'Bloody hell,' Becky said. 'That's not for me. I don't like people messing with my head – it's messed up enough as it is. And this guy is now a trustee of the Kalus' house?'

'He is indeed,' Rob responded. 'And...' Rob looked away from the screen.

Keith was standing by the desk, his face solemn. 'I know something about Mr Forakis, if it's the same man, and I think maybe DCI Douglas should hear it too.'

54

MARTHA

As I drive along the unfamiliar roads from our bed and breakfast, I cling to the steering wheel as if my life depends on it. I'm excited and terrified in equal measure. I'm eager to see Dad, but the thought of what's ahead, if he agrees to help me, fills me with dread.

I don't want Alfie to realise how unsettled I am so I've switched on the radio, the volume turned high, and it's playing the kind of pop songs that he loves to sing along to, even though he can't possibly understand the words.

Memories of Leah have left me feeling sickened by my own weakness, and I wonder if I'm right to believe that I can withstand the strength of Aram's control over me. I thought I could once before, but I was wrong, and the outcome was catastrophic.

LAKESIDE

After Leah told me of her plans to leave Lakeside, I had a day and a half to get through before it was time to meet her and make our escape. The anticipation was almost unbearable.

What would I do, out in that strange world that I knew so little about? Where would I go? How would I live? I had no money; I didn't even have shoes! Leah had told me not to worry – she had everything in hand and she would take care of me, help me find a job. I could live with her – in Manchester!

With no television and no Internet except in Aram's office – a part of the house banned to most – I didn't know what to expect. I hadn't been off the premises for more than two years, and I couldn't decide whether euphoria or fear of the unknown was the cause of my racing heart.

I kept well away from Aram and prayed he didn't want me that night. I rarely stayed with him until the morning; it wasn't an act of love with a gentle awakening in each other's arms. It was sex – nothing more. I needed Mum's help to avoid Aram on the night before Leah and I were due to escape. I couldn't tell her what I was planning; I had no idea how she would react. We were so far apart that I struggled to understand anything she did. She was distant, hostile almost, and in Aram's thrall. She was still my mother, but she wanted Aram far more than I did, and I thought I might be able to use that to my advantage.

I walked into the kitchen where she was standing, as always, at the Aga. A man and two women were chopping vegetables for the meal, and they turned and nodded a greeting before getting back to the mammoth task of feeding our community.

I dropped my head and let my shoulders hunch, then pulled out a chair and sat down.

Mum glanced over her shoulder. 'Get the plates out for supper, India.'

I rested my elbows on the table and put my head in my hands.

She looked at me again. 'Plates, India.'

With a deep sigh I pushed my chair back and trudged across to stand next to her.

I kept my voice low. There was no sympathy for weakness in this house. 'I don't know what's up with me. I'm weary; aching all over. I hope Aram isn't expecting me tonight. I don't want to give him a bug, if that's what this is.'

Mum's back straightened slightly as if she'd had a thought. And I knew what it would be. With any luck, she would tell Aram that I was ill. He needed to keep his distance or he might catch it. She would offer her own services instead.

'I'll get the plates, but then I'm going to bed. Sorry, Nicola.' I was used to calling her by her name, even though I still thought of her as Mum, and knowing I was about to leave made me long for one last connection with her. I rested a hand on her shoulder.

She froze. We didn't go in for displays of affection, and I pulled away before she did, got the plates, put them on the table and left the room.

I passed the night in peace, and the next morning I didn't go down for breakfast. I wasn't entirely surprised when just before lunch my door was thrust open.

'Aram wants to see you.'

It was Mum, and there was no enquiry about my health. I couldn't refuse, but by then I was genuinely feeling sick. Was I doing the right thing? Living at Lakeside was safe. It was all I had known since I was ten years old, and it wasn't all bad.

It wasn't enough, though. I wanted more, although at that moment what I wanted most was to hide what I was feeling from Aram, because in a little over twelve hours I would be meeting Leah by the river.

I walked into his room, my head lowered.

'Look at me, India,' he commanded. I raised my eyes slowly and looked beyond him, through the window at the gloomy clouds hovering over the house. 'Look at me!' he repeated, and I knew he wanted me to look into his eyes. 'Sit.'

In front of him was a cushion, and as I sank to the floor, my eyes locked on to his. I felt as if my pupils were being pierced by white light, so strong was his stare, but I didn't drop my gaze. I couldn't. I remembered Leah's words. 'Close your eyes,' she'd said. But it was too late.

'I understand you're not well. Is that true?'

'I've been feeling light-headed, weak. I'm sure it will pass if I can stay in my room for a day or two.'

'You know I don't encourage frailty.' He reached towards the table by his side, where a glass was sitting. 'Drink this,' he said. 'When you wake you will feel better.'

I felt a flash of alarm. How long would it make me sleep for? Would I miss Leah? Would she be gone before I woke?

'No, Aram. I'll be fine. I just need to rest.'

He leaned towards me and took my hand. His voice was soft, little more than a whisper. 'You're lying to me, India, and it hurts me deeply. You are so important to me, to our community. You are special, the beauty in our lives, and we need you. We love you. *I* love you! If something is troubling you, you must tell me.'

I was shocked by his words. I was used to the swing of emotions from joy at his approval to the misery of being condemned for any and all weaknesses, but this was extreme, and I found myself basking in his praise. My eyes were still locked on his, and I felt every decision, every hope of life outside those walls, drain from my mind.

He loves me! He thinks I'm special!

I had been conditioned to please him, and it brought me joy. I was overwhelmed, but at the same time I felt as if I was being ripped in two. I had always treasured every crumb of praise, holding it tightly in my heart until it was undermined by at best disapproval, and at worst humiliation. And yet there was now a part of me that wanted to run – to be with Leah.

If I lied to Aram, Leah would leave and accuse him of fraud. It would be the end of my world, of everything I knew and trusted, and I would be letting the whole of our community down. For years Aram had nurtured me, taught me to resist temptation, to fight material cravings. How could I disappoint him now?

And he loved me.

I had to tell him. I really did. And because of me, no one left Lakeside that night.

55

Tom opened the door to the incident room, having been summoned by Becky, and walked over to have a quiet word with Keith. Becky watched as Keith spoke, Tom nodding his head.

'Are you happy to share this with the team?' she heard Tom say.

Keith stood a little straighter. 'If you think it would help, then yes, sir.'

Tom turned to the room. 'Can I have your attention for a moment, please?' The room fell quiet and everyone looked to where Tom and Keith were standing. 'As you know, our suspect, Martha Porter, is using a prepaid debit card in the name of India Kalu. Further research has uncovered the fact that she was brought up for part of her life in Lincolnshire, in a property that is partly owned by a man called Aram Forakis. DI Sims has some information that he would like to share with us.' Tom stood to one side. 'Keith?'

'Thank you, sir. Prior to joining the police force, I attended university for a few months here in Manchester. It turned out it wasn't for me, and in the early days after my arrival I felt – as I imagine many students do – somewhat lost. I was out of my comfort zone.'

Becky felt for Keith. He was a very private man, and he was

having to publicly admit to his insecurities. His back was straight, but his cheeks were slightly flushed.

'A few days after I arrived, I was approached by an attractive young woman, asking if I was feeling lonely. She said there were many people feeling the same as me, and she'd found it a great help to attend meetings held in a nearby hall. She'd love to take me along, if I'd like to go. I was delighted – if somewhat terrified.'

He grimaced, and there was a ripple of friendly laughter.

'The meeting was run by what appeared to be a Christian society of some kind, and the speaker talked to us about his work, about why people felt insecure – the root cause of all our problems. He was compelling. After a few meetings, I was asked to make a commitment – financial – to help with his work. I refused. Not because I didn't want to be part of this group, but because – as I'm sure you'll appreciate – I had my money planned to the nth degree and there was no room for manoeuvre.'

Becky smiled. Many people would have been put off by demands for money, but few because it messed with their cash-flow forecast.

'I was harangued, pestered. The girl waited for me and told me I'd let her down, let them all down, and she was being shunned because of her failure to bring me to the light. It was relentless. In the end, I reported what they were doing to the university.' Keith took a sip of water from a glass on his desk, but no one moved, gripped by what he was saying.

'Some of you may already be aware of this, but it's not unusual for universities to be a target for recruitment into quasi-religious groups. These bright young people may already have wealthy parents, and even if they don't, they have good future earning power. I know many recruits were told to take part-time jobs and had to hand over most of their earnings.'

'So this was a cult, Keith?' Tom asked.

'They didn't call it that, but yes. Some groups refer to themselves as new religious movements. Those which don't worship any god often say they are merely a group of people devoted to a person or an idea. But essentially cults have three features: a charismatic leader who has absolute power; a process of indoctrination which can be described as either coercion or thought control; and an element of economic, sexual or other exploitation by the leader. It sounds brutal, but when we all met together, it was supportive, happy, and I felt everyone genuinely wanted to get to know me. Then there were the small-group sessions in which each of us had to identify our failings, our shortcomings, and the group would join in and add their own criticisms to the list. They still claimed to love me, to be saving me, but the price of belonging was to demean myself. It was monstrous, but I didn't realise what was happening to me until they asked for money.'

Thank God for spreadsheets, Becky thought.

'How do they exert so much control?' Rob asked.

'They isolate you from everyone except the cult members, make you believe anyone who isn't one of them is a danger to you; they humiliate you, then shower you with praise so that you are conditioned to seek their approval. I could go on.'

'Do they use hypnotism?' Cass asked.

Rob tutted. 'I don't believe in hypnotism,' he said, his tone scathing.

'What about Derren Brown?' Cass asked.

'That has to be a con,' Rob answered, clearly sceptical.

'DS Cumba, let me put this to you,' Tom said, his eyes twinkling in a way that told Becky the story he was about to tell amused him. 'Back in the nineteenth century a Scottish surgeon called James Esdaile performed operations on prisoners. In one case he caused such pain in the first part of an operation that he decided he was going to try mesmerism – hypnosis, if you like – for the second part. He was successful, and the patient experienced no signs of pain. No raised pulse, no screams. Pretty impressive, I think you'll agree, as he was actually injecting and draining one side of the patient's scrotum.'

There was general laughter as Rob winced. 'Okay, I take it back!'

Tom turned back to Keith. 'Do you want to explain how you think this relates to Aram Forakis?'

'Of course, sir.' Keith cleared his throat and faced the room. 'When I withdrew from the cult, I saw a counsellor at the university for a while. We got on well, and we stayed in touch when I joined the police. He told me that cults were an ongoing problem on campus, but there had been one particularly sad case of a girl who'd been demeaned repeatedly for not bringing in enough money or new recruits. Finally, she was banished as a total failure, and she was so distraught that she killed herself. Her name was Jordan Callahan. The leader of the cult in question was Aram Forakis.'

The silence was broken by Tom. 'DI Sims, thank you for being honest with us about what must have been a dreadful time in your life. All I can say is that the university's loss is the police force's gain.'

There was a smattering of applause, which brought even more pink to Keith's cheeks, but it was interrupted by a shout from Cass, who had returned her gaze to her computer screen.

'Sir! I think we've got her! She was picked up on ANPR on Tuesday evening – first travelling towards Leeds and then heading down the A1(M). We lost her at Retford.'

Becky knew what that meant. 'If that's where she came off the A1, sounds to me like she was going home. To Lincolnshire.'

'We're getting close,' Tom said with a smile. 'Becky, I think we have a road trip to make. There has to be more to this woman's story than the killing of Genevieve Strachan, and I want to know what it is. It's as if India Kalu knew that at some point she would have to adopt a different persona and run. You don't plan your escape and shroud your life in mystery unless you have something to hide.'

He was right. Becky knew Tom had not been able to reconcile Martha's long-term planning with Genevieve's murder. Maybe she really *had* done this before, although perhaps Manchester had been the wrong place to look. Perhaps something happened while she was living in Lincolnshire.

He walked over and perched on the edge of her desk.

'The local force can locate and arrest her if we're right about where she's heading,' Tom said, 'but we need to take a long hard look at her background – most of which, at least since she was about ten, seems to have been in Lincolnshire. We could drag her back to Manchester on suspicion of murder and interview her here, but she has a child, and that's an added complication. Let's organise an interview team – Rob can lead it – but I want to be there when she's questioned. I want to see her face to face. When we know what we're dealing with, we can decide if we should set up a mini-incident room down there. Can you pull together the preliminary team and get someone to organise a hotel for tonight at least?'

'No problem. I'll need to make arrangements in case we're there for longer than we expect to be.'

Tom groaned.

'What?' Becky asked.

'I've been looking forward to seeing Lucy tonight – for the first time in nearly six months. She'll understand, but she won't be happy.' He pulled a face. 'Not much I can do about it. The only way we'll be back tonight is if they don't find her.'

'Or they *do* find her, and she immediately confesses.'

Tom nodded. 'That would certainly make life simpler. I'll see if I can get hold of Philippa. I have a feeling she won't be too impressed with my decision.'

'Rather you than me,' she muttered with a grin.

'No, Tom. There's absolutely no need for you to go rushing off to Lincolnshire with half of the Greater Manchester Police. Send your interview team. Let them do their jobs, and they can bring her back so you can interview her yourself when she gets here.'

'Philippa, my suggestion of four officers hardly constitutes fifty per cent of our workforce, and I have to tell you I wouldn't be suggesting it if I didn't think it was a necessity. We're not talking about a jolly to the sunny beaches of Cornwall – it's a small town in the middle of nowhere. Come on, Philippa, I don't do things like this often.'

Philippa's eyes opened wide. 'I beg your pardon! You do things that are wildly inappropriate on a fairly regular basis. I won't remind you of them all.'

Tom couldn't deny it, and he tried not to smile at her outrage. 'Okay, I'll concede that I don't always stick rigidly to the rules. But only in the interests of justice, and I'm concerned about this suspect. There's something else going on. There has to be. I can't believe she changed her name over five years ago just in case she happened to kill her boss's wife at some point in the future. There's an assumption of guilt right now, which is entirely justified, but I think it's more complex. I can feel it. She hasn't been hiding for nothing, and I want to know why. What if Genevieve wasn't the first to die?'

Philippa grunted. 'I could tell you to stay here, but I know you. Somehow you'll prove me wrong.' She rested her forearms on the desk and leaned towards him. 'Here's the deal. You don't leave here until she's been located. They may not find her, and then we'll have had you and Becky chasing round the country for hours wasting your time. You can be there in under two hours when you're needed. Then you follow procedure – the official one, not the Tom Douglas version.'

It wasn't perfect, but it was as good as it was going to get.

56

MARTHA

We arrive at the post office before it's even open. The woman said Dad usually gets here about nine, and I can't afford to miss him. It has to be today. I'm more convinced with every passing minute that the police are right on my tail, and there's something I have to do before they reach me.

The sun is already beating down, and my poor little boy is sitting in the back of a hot car. I open the windows as wide as I can and sing to him softly. Not a pop tune, but his favourite song – 'London Bridge Is Falling Down'. He joins in, his piping voice drawing smiles from passers-by. I want to ask him to keep his voice down so people don't stare, but he has enough to deal with today.

I'm so busy gazing at my child, painting his features onto my memory, that I miss the Range Rover pulling into the space two cars away from me. By the time I notice it's there, all I see is the back of a man disappearing into the shop.

I'm frozen to the spot. Is this my dad? So often when I'm playing with Alfie I remember how he used to swing me round in those big powerful arms of his, and how I used to scream with delight. I've told Alfie all about him, hoping that one day they would meet. This man is thin, stooped and looks old – and yet my dad is in his mid-forties. He wasn't much more than a boy when I was born.

I have to get my act together. I can't show any shock when I see him. Who wants anyone to look at them with horror at the changes life has wrought?

I force myself to take some deep breaths, ready to paint on a smile. I push open my door and reach into the back for Alfie. What I'm about to ask my dad to do will seem all the easier with his grandson by my side.

I'm shaking. I don't know if it's fear of rejection or worry that he won't recognise me. Or maybe he won't care what's happened to me. And I am about to let go of my son. The ache in my chest grows stronger.

Suddenly, he's there, standing stock still in the open doorway of the post office, staring at me with his mouth slightly open. His gaze goes from me to the little boy by my side, and even from where I'm standing I can see his eyes fill with tears. And still he hasn't moved. And neither have I.

A woman walks in front of him and looks up. 'Can I get past?' she says in a slightly peevish voice.

It seems to jolt him out of his reverie, and in three long strides he's in front of me, reaching out his arms and pulling me close, squeezing the breath from me.

'DeeDee, oh God, DeeDee,' he mumbles over and over.

Alfie knows something is wrong and starts to cry. Dad lets go of me immediately and crouches down.

'I'm so sorry, little one. I didn't mean to frighten you. I just wanted to say hello to your mum.' He looks up at me as if seeking my permission. I know what he's asking, and I nod. 'Do you want to tell me your name?'

'I'm Alfie, and I'm five and a half – nearly,' he says with a final sniff, stopping crying as quickly as he started in that way small children do.

Dad smiles, and all the strain goes out of his face. 'Are you indeed? Well, my name is Joel, and you might not know this, but I'm your grandad.'

Alfie's eyes widen and he looks at me. I nod again.

I give them a bit of time to explore each other's faces with their eyes, and then Dad stands up.

'DeeDee, I can't tell you how wonderful it is to see you, but you know how things are, and I have to get back.' The pain in his expression nearly tears me in two.

'Is it still like that?'

'It's taken a long time for me to win back the trust I lost. I don't regret it for one moment, especially now, but I can't go back to how things were after you left. I just can't.'

This time it's my turn to cry. 'I'm so sorry. I should never have asked for your help.'

He reaches out and puts his hands on my shoulders. 'You should. Absolutely.'

'What did he do to you?' I'm not sure I want to know, but I have to ask.

Dad shrugs. 'You know how it is.'

I do, but I need him to tell me, so I wait.

'They shunned me. I wasn't allowed to speak to anyone. I had to eat alone. You've seen it happen to others.'

'Yes, for a few days. And I remember it was terrible. How long?'

He drops his head. 'Two years.'

I did this to him. I am the reason my dad looks like an old man. I risked everything to escape, and now I'm planning to risk everything to go back – to win our freedom so Alfie will never suffer the despair and humiliation I was forced to endure. But at what cost? Was I right to do this to my dad?

57

LAKESIDE

The realisation that I was pregnant crept up on me. My periods had always seemed regular, but I'd never specifically checked my dates, and one day was much the same as another. It was only when I opened the bathroom cabinet and saw a packet of tampons that I realised it had been a while.

For a day or two I assumed time must have been passing more slowly than usual. I didn't have any frame of reference, like going out to work each day, to tell me that a week had passed. When I woke feeling nauseous, I thought I must have eaten something that had disagreed with me. I was twenty-one years old, and hadn't seen or spoken to a pregnant woman since I was ten. I didn't know what the signs were and there was no longer anyone I trusted to ask.

Then a memory hit me. I must have been about thirteen and I'd just come into the house from the garden when I heard someone being sick in the laundry room. I was about to open the door when I heard Aram's voice – calm, controlled, with a slight note of distaste.

'I hope you weren't planning to keep this from me, Nicola. How long have you known that you're pregnant?'

I clamped my hand over my mouth, scared I was going to gasp out loud.

Mum was silent for a moment. 'Three weeks,' she whispered.

'You should have told me sooner. I'll give you something to take.'

'Will it make the sickness go away?' she'd asked, a note of relief in her voice.

'I should think so. Go to your room when you've cleaned up, and stay there.'

Mum was pregnant! At long last, I was going to have a little sister or brother.

I heard Aram's footsteps retreating, pulled the door open, peeked around to check he had gone and rushed across to Mum, wrapping my arms around her, hugging her tight.

'What are you *doing*?' she said, shrugging me off.

'Does Dad know yet? He'll be thrilled, and I'm so excited!'

She slowly turned her head towards me and looked into my eyes. Her expression was almost a sneer. 'It's got nothing to do with Joel. Forget what you heard.'

I didn't understand what she meant about Dad. How could it have nothing to do with him? But I could tell she didn't want to talk to me. She ran the tap to clean the sink and turned to walk out of the door.

I didn't see her after that for four days, and was told she was in bed, ill, not to be disturbed. When she returned to her duties in the kitchen, she was pale and even more quiet than usual. I caught Dad looking at her with a puzzled frown and realised she hadn't shared the good news, so I waited, expecting to see more obvious signs of the baby growing inside her. It never happened.

I didn't know why there was no baby and knew better than to ask, but eight years later, at the moment I realised that I might be pregnant, I felt icy trickles down my spine. Why were there never any babies born at Lakeside?

By that time our home was full of people – all invited by Aram – and there were a few young couples who had been with us for years. But there were never any babies.

Aram hadn't stinted on my biology lessons, and I knew about contraception. I also knew that anything that came into the house arrived via the bulk weekly supermarket shop, and the storeroom was open to anyone to help themselves. I was certain there were no contraceptives there.

I lowered myself back onto the bed. In the years since Mum appeared to have lost her baby, there had been other times when other women had been confined to their bedrooms for a few days without explanation, and Aram rarely allowed anyone to plead ill health. He preferred people to battle through any illness, saying we shouldn't give in to weakness. Aram had said from the very first day that children were a distraction to his teaching. They just weren't allowed here, and I was beginning to understand why. He demanded one hundred per cent devotion, and a baby would give its parents different priorities – he would no longer be the sole recipient of their adoration.

As the shocking thoughts of what he might have done ran through my mind, the nausea ratcheted up a notch. What if the 'something' that Aram had given Mum to take away her sickness had taken away far more than that? Would he do that? Would he intentionally abort a baby?

I knew the answer.

Until that moment I hadn't known whether to be delighted or appalled that I was pregnant, but I was now certain that Aram must never know. I was not going to let him harm my baby. I wrapped my arms around my stomach, stroking my skin, and promised my baby that I would keep him or her safe.

But how could I? Aram wouldn't allow me to leave; he believed he had the power to make me stay, evidence of what I'd done that he said would tie me to him forever, and I'd never doubted it. Could I defy him? Could I risk everything?

For my child, I knew I had to, and there was only one person who could help me.

The next couple of days were an agony of waiting, of pretending that everything was normal, even faking period pains, but I could do nothing until Wednesday. I could barely eat. I managed to hide the nausea, which was helped by my lack of appetite and dry mouth, and finally Wednesday morning arrived.

I sneaked out of the house, terrified that someone would see me, but at the last moment I had the wit to pick up a laundry basket as if I was heading to the washing line. I was too early, so I crouched low at the back of the garage, waiting for the sound of footsteps crunching over gravel. I knew he'd be alone, but I didn't want him to call out at seeing me there, so I waited until he was unlocking the car. Wednesday was his day to do the shopping, and my only chance of catching him alone.

'*Dad!*' I whispered.

He jumped and spun round, first in one direction then the other. I hadn't called him Dad for years, but he was still Dad in my head. Then he saw me hiding in the far corner.

'India!' His voice was too loud, and I put my finger to my lips.

'I need your help. Don't ask me any questions, but I need to get away from here.'

He said nothing, just stared.

Finally he spoke, his voice brittle with emotion. 'You're not just talking about a trip into town, are you?'

'No. I need to go.' I swallowed hard. 'And I won't be coming back.'

He shook his head slowly. 'He won't let you go, girl.'

I knew he was right. Aram had become increasingly obsessed

with possessing my soul as well as my body, but something inside me was fractured, and he found my remoteness infuriating. He wanted to own me, and I was certain he would never let me leave.

'I'm not going to ask him. I'm asking *you*.'

He looked towards the open garage door as we heard footsteps heading our way. I scuttled back into the shadows as a figure appeared. It wasn't Aram, but it didn't matter. Anyone who saw us having a private conversation would report back.

I listened to a brief exchange as Dad was asked to pick up some white emulsion paint, and then heard the footsteps retreating.

'He's gone,' Dad called softly, and I stepped back towards him. 'We can't talk now. If the car's not out of here in the next minute or two, there'll be questions. And I need – for your sake as much as anyone's – to keep his trust. But I'll help you, I promise.'

'Why don't you leave too? Please, Dad. We could just get in the car and drive away. Come with me.'

A look of such sadness clouded his big brown eyes, and for a moment my mind flashed back to our little flat: to Mum and Dad swaying, their arms round each other, laughing, his eyes dancing faster than his feet. And in that instant I wanted to commit murder.

'We'll speak soon. I'll find a way to help you, DeeDee,' he said, and tears blurred my eyes at his use of my old pet name. 'But you know why I can't leave.'

I did, although I didn't understand. He was staying for Mum – the wife who barely spoke to him, who worshipped at the feet of another man.

'She gave up everything for me, you know.' He shook himself. 'I must go. Take care, my lovely girl.'

All that had happened since we moved to Lincolnshire meant nothing to him. Mum had given up her comfortable middle-class life to be with him, and she had stuck by Dad, never wavering even when she had to work every hour possible to help feed and clothe us all. As far as he was concerned, it was payback time.

58

MARTHA

I feel so ashamed of what I asked Dad to do for me all those years ago, and I'm appalled by the impact it's had on his life. In spite of that, I'm about to ask him to make another life-changing decision, and I realise it's selfish of me.

Before I can say anything he reaches out a hand and gently clutches my arm.

'Should you be here, DeeDee? Isn't it dangerous? He's had people out looking for you, you know,' he says. 'He sent them all over the country. He posted a picture of you on his YouTube channel, and he has hundreds of thousands of followers now. They searched everywhere but still I wouldn't tell him anything. I'm so relieved they never found you.'

I'd known about Aram's channel but had never dared to look. I wasn't sure if a channel owner could see who was watching and I couldn't risk it. I was petrified his eyes would reach out to me and somehow drag me back into his control, although that wasn't the worst of my worries.

For years I have been driven by two fears: that Aram will find me and claim access rights to Alfie, or he will use the evidence he holds – proof of what happened on the most shameful night of my life – and the police will hunt me down and lock me up for years. In either case, Aram will get his hands on my son, not because he wants his child, but to torment me – to punish me for running away. Whatever his motivation, it is something I cannot bear to think about. Now I have a third fear – that the Manchester police will arrest me for Genevieve's murder, and Alfie will be taken from me by social services. The end result will be the same: Aram will hear that I am in prison, and he'll get custody of Alfie.

I will kill before I allow that to happen.

In spite of my fierce determination to protect my son, when I think of Dad being shunned for two years, it nearly breaks my heart.

'I'm so sorry,' I tell him, knowing the words are inadequate.

'No, DeeDee, *I'm* sorry. Aram tried everything to make me tell him what I knew, but I refused to look him in the eye. He was livid. I've never seen him like that. Nicola told him things would be better now that you'd gone, but he said she understood nothing. That hurt her.'

'Poor Mum,' I say, and I mean it. She was so tightly in his thrall that she no longer knew the difference between right and wrong.

Dad reaches out a hand and rests it gently on Alfie's curls. 'She always wanted more children, you know. We'd planned to have three or four – do you remember us talking about it?' He looks at the floor. 'She's been pregnant twice since he came. Both times she lost the baby.'

I only knew about one occasion, and I'm not convinced it was a natural miscarriage, but I'm not about to tell Dad what I think.

'I'm so sorry,' is all I can think of to say again. 'What happened after they shunned you?'

'I became ill. They kept me alive but otherwise ignored me.' He lifts his eyes to mine. 'I'm better now, and it was worth it to get you away from him. I owed you that. We should never have let things get to the way they were. We failed, me and your mum, and even though she can't bring herself to admit it, she knows, deep down.'

I want to ask how she is, but time is precious.

'I saw her yesterday at the supermarket. Aram was with her, but there was hardly any shopping. What's going on?'

He looks anxiously at his watch. 'Aram said he wanted some quiet time for reflection. Everyone except me and your mum has gone – for now, at least. They're due back next week.'

This sounds strange to me. Aram thrives on the adulation of his followers and the vast sums of money he collects from them along the way. What *is* going on?

I don't have time to worry about that. I've been planning the words I would say to Dad, and now they all come out in a rush.

'Dad, I need to ask you something. I need your help – desperately. I've thought so hard about it, but I don't think I have any choice but to beg you to help me again. This time it's huge – a sacrifice so much greater than last time.'

A look of wariness crosses Dad's face. I know he'll want to help, but he has no idea of the scale of what I'm about to ask.

'I don't have long, DeeDee.'

'If you agree to help me, you'll have all the time in the world. I'm asking you not to go back – ever – to Lakeside.'

He wasn't expecting that. His head jerks back as if I've hit him. He stutters, 'I… I c-can't… What?'

I reach out and grasp his arms. 'This is dreadful of me, I know. But because of how things are, mistakes I've made, I need to ask you to make this huge decision, and I have so little time to persuade you. If you're with me, we have only minutes to discuss it. If you're not, you need to go.'

Finally he seems to get his voice back, but he's looking around as if he's expecting someone to be watching. 'What do you want me to do?'

'I want you to take care of Alfie. I'm going to go back to

Lakeside to face Aram. I need you to look after your grandson in case something happens to me. I may be back in a few hours, but it could be days – or even years.' I don't say never, but I know it's a possibility. 'If I'm not back, I need you to do what I did. Take Alfie and run as far as you can, to somewhere Aram won't find you.'

Dad's eyes go to Alfie, to me and then back to Alfie. A look of despair crosses his face, and I am in no doubt how difficult this is. I don't know why, but I wasn't expecting his next words.

'What about your mum?'

The silence between Dad and me has lasted at least a minute, and it seems longer. Alfie is tugging at my hand, wondering what is going on, but I have to ignore him and keep my eyes on Dad. The longer he is here with me, the more difficult it will be for him to go back.

Finally, he speaks, his voice croaky as if the words are almost too difficult to say. 'Why have you come back, DeeDee?'

'It'll take too long to explain, Dad. We don't have time, and if I tell you, you'll be implicated too. If you can't take your grandson, you need to leave in the next few minutes. A queue in the post office could have delayed you, but not by much.'

He's torn, I can see that, and I have to speak quickly, putting every ounce of urgency into my voice.

'Aram must never take Alfie. You do understand that, don't you? I'm going to make sure of it – as far as I can. But to do that, I really need you.' He nods, and I thank God that he doesn't need me to spell it out. 'I'm in trouble – big trouble – and I can't keep running. I need to deal with Aram and I can't take Alfie to Lakeside with me. You must see that. If you agree to this, I know you can never go back. If you don't help me, I have no idea what will happen to my baby.'

'Why are you in trouble?'

'I can't explain it to you in five minutes. It would take much longer – and just as you don't have time, neither do I. It's enough to say that without you, social services will take Alfie – probably today – and they'll want to know who his father is. I can't let that happen, Dad. You must see that?' I pause, and I can see he's torn. 'I'm booked into a B and B. You can take Alfie there. I've got money, and you'll be able to access it if you need to – if I'm not back.' He's shaking his head slowly from side to side. 'Please, Dad, you're the only chance Alfie has. You may be *all* he has. You could love him like you used to love me.'

My voice cracks as I say the words, and it's Dad's undoing.

'I never stopped loving you, child. It was all so difficult.'

I nod, unable to speak.

'But even if I say I'll help you, what will we do about your mum?'

This is so hard to do, but I force myself to say the words. 'Does she even know you're there any longer, Dad? Did she shun you too?'

I know the answer, and he looks away. 'Yes, but since I've been ill, things have changed. Only a little, but still, it's progress. There's a definite shift in her behaviour. She comes to me now when she's confused, when he's done something to hurt her. I think she needs me. She even told me about the babies.'

That was kind of her.

For a moment I think I've said the words out loud, sarcasm dripping from my tongue, but fortunately I haven't. His love for my mother never wavers, whatever she does. I've been assuming that by now he would have accepted defeat, but he hasn't.

'I don't have time for you to go back and talk to Mum. If I get a chance, I'll talk to her. But I don't know when everything's going to explode. We're talking hours, maybe minutes. Dad, without you Alfie has no happy ending. You're his only chance.'

I want to play on his guilt, tell him he ruined my childhood, and he owes me this. But that's not how I feel. He was a victim as much as anyone. I glance at my watch. Time is running out. I need to get to Aram before the police get to me.

'Take my car. Go to the B and B with Alfie. I'll take the Range Rover and go to Lakeside. I'll try to find a way to talk to Mum. I'll do my best to persuade her to leave – to come to you. But Dad, I can't emphasise this enough. We don't have long.'

Dad looks understandably bemused by everything I'm saying, and Alfie is starting to whimper again. He can sense my stress, and he's so in tune with my feelings that he'll know something is killing me inside. I put my hand on his head and stroke the wiry curls.

Dad looks at him too.

'We stole your childhood, me and your mum. It was never our intention, but everything was so overwhelming. It all seemed right at the time. It felt as if we'd discovered the truth about life, but now I know what it really was, and it destroyed us all. If I do as you ask, I'll be deserting your mother, something I swore I would never do.' He pauses, lips clamped firmly together. 'I don't know if I'm strong enough. It's not a perfect life, but it's the one I know. Everything I have is in that house.'

I want to scream 'Not everything!' but I've been out of his life for six years. I knew this would be difficult, and I've always known I might fail. I should have boarded a train with Alfie and gone to Northumberland. We may never have been found. I push the thought away. We would always have been on the run. Would Aram have ever given up? I either run for the rest of my life, or I stand up and face him.

I have no more words for Dad. I should have planned for his refusal, worked out what I was going to do, and I didn't. I feel my shoulders sag. I feel defeated.

'I understand. It was too much to ask. But you're still a young man with a long life ahead of you. Are you prepared to live the rest of it the way you're living now?' I wait a moment, but he doesn't answer, so I reach up a hand to touch his cheek. 'Bye, Dad. I'm so sorry if I've upset you.'

I give Alfie's hand a squeeze and turn back towards my car. I hadn't realised walking away would be so difficult – every bit as devastating as it had been the first time – and my throat aches with suppressed tears.

59

LAKESIDE

For three weeks after I'd asked Dad to help me escape, I waited. I went out of my way to pass him in the corridor, to say hello, to catch his eye. But we were never alone. I had to be careful how I looked at him during meals, desperate to make sure no one noticed the pleading in my eyes. Was he going to help me? I didn't know.

Every cell in my body, every thought in my mind, was focused on the tiny speck inside me that was growing into a child – someone for me to love, who might even love me back, if I was worthy of anyone's love. The one thing driving me was the compulsion to protect my baby, to keep him or her safe.

How long could I hide my pregnancy? I always wore baggy, ill-fitting clothes, mostly cast-offs from other women, so I was certain that no one would realise for a while – except Aram.

I tried to keep out of his way as much as I could, but it was difficult, and Mum watched, her eyes narrowed, as Aram's gaze followed me when I walked into a room. He seemed to want me with him more than ever at night, and each time he ran his hand over my stomach I froze. I had to leave soon, before the changes to my body became obvious. And before I lost my nerve.

I was beginning to lose hope when I found a note under my bedcovers.

Wednesday. Garage. Bring nothing.

I no longer knew if I was doing the right thing. Maybe I had been wrong about the other babies. Perhaps the whole community would welcome a child and would love him or her. It had to be safer to stay than to go. Then I thought of the life my child would have if I stayed. At what age would he be taken from me, put into another room away from me, because he no longer 'needed' me? Would he be allowed to go to school, to be friends with other children? Would he be shamed for his weaknesses, have his self-esteem shattered?

Aram had always told me what would happen if I left, how the police would hunt me down. I was scared, but I was more scared for my baby. I talked myself into staying and then five minutes later into going.

I couldn't sleep for the next two nights. What did I know of life outside Lakeside? Nothing. I had nowhere to go, no money, no job, no friends outside these four walls. What was I *thinking*? I would be totally on my own.

I put my hand on my belly. I didn't know if I should be able to feel the baby kicking yet, but thought maybe it was too soon. I had no one to ask. But I knew one thing: I *wouldn't* be on my own. I had someone else to think of. Someone else to put first.

Aram knew something was wrong. He could sense it, as if my agitation was vibrating in the air, bouncing off the walls. He'd seen me like this once before. That time he had read me well, and the outcome had been a disaster. This time I had to do a better job of hiding my plans.

'Tomorrow we need a private session, India,' he said. 'You're unsettled, and it's having a negative impact on everyone around you. Go to your room now, and I'll see you at nine tomorrow.'

I lowered my gaze to the floor. The good thing was that my mood made me unappealing to him, and he didn't want my company. Nor did he want my restlessness to affect the others. He always said that moods could spread like a virus, which is why we were conditioned to be calm, thoughtful and introverted. He would prefer me to be alone, to reflect on my behaviour. But if he planned to see me at nine, he would know all too soon that I'd gone. I was hoping no one would notice until at least lunchtime.

'I said I'd help in the laundry.' It wasn't true, but Aram didn't bother himself with mundane details, other than to specify that no one should ever fail to fulfil their obligations.

I could see he was annoyed, but he didn't argue.

'Two p.m. then. Go to your room now. At this moment you are unworthy of us, and if you want our love, you need to clear your mind of whatever is unsettling you.'

It was never clear to me whether he was using the royal 'we, us and our' or if he meant the entire group – who were looking at me with blank stares. I knew no one would speak out in support of me.

I was glad to leave the room, but I got no sleep.

I got up in the half-light just before sunrise and looked around at the walls of my room, the place I'd once hated but that had become my sanctuary over the years. The sickness I was feeling had nothing to do with the baby. My hands were jittery as I dressed and even fastening a button seemed too difficult. It wasn't too late to back out, but it would be soon. What if Aram caught me leaving? What would he do? I knew, better than most, what he was capable of.

I left the house soon after daybreak. Aram wouldn't be up, and if I met anyone, I would say I was going to the laundry early so I had more time to meditate later. They might not believe me, but they were unlikely to report such a minor modification in my schedule.

The stress was making my head pound, and my tongue was sticking to the roof of my mouth as I made my way into the garage to wait for Dad. I crouched at the back, like last time, my arms wrapped tightly round my stomach, and I rocked backwards and forwards, talking to my child.

'We'll be okay, baby. I'll take care of you, I promise.'

Suddenly, Dad was there. I had been so wrapped up in my thoughts that I hadn't heard him approaching. Without a word, he opened the back of the Range Rover and signalled for me to get in. I didn't argue. The back was piled with rubbish for the tip, and I crawled between some bags and dragged an empty bin liner to cover my head, curling myself into a ball.

Still without speaking, Dad shut the tailgate, went round to the driver's side and got in. The car started, and before long he had reversed out, turned and was making for the drive. Then, without warning, he stopped. He didn't speak, and for a moment I wondered if he was going to demand that I get out of the car. I imagined the whole community standing silently on the steps of Lakeside, pre-warned of my treacherous bid for freedom, staring as I climbed out from under the rubbish, hanging my head in shame. *Would he do that to me?*

Then I heard a voice, and I gulped to swallow the cry of fear that almost escaped me.

'Have you seen India this morning, Joel? She told me she was due in the laundry, but apparently not.'

Aram's voice was measured, but I could hear his fury simmering below the surface. I had lied to him, and that was something he would not tolerate.

I held my breath. Was Dad going to give me away? It struck me, rather later than it should have, that eventually Aram would realise that Dad had helped me to escape, and for that he would suffer. I shouldn't have done this to him.

'I've seen no one, Aram. Would you like me to help you look for her?'

'No. Follow your routine. I'll send someone to try down by the river. She's been unsettled for the last few days and I need to calm her.'

With that, Dad put the car in gear and set off down the rutted drive. I held my breath as he stopped again after a few moments. The driver's door opened, and feet hit the gravel. Dad was out of the car. I waited, scared to move, unable to sit up to see what was happening, certain I would hear Aram telling him to open the tailgate. Then I heard the clatter of a chain falling to the ground. Dad was unlocking the gates. I'd forgotten about the padlock. He got back in the car, pulled forward and stopped again, then got out to refit the chain. His door slammed as he climbed in once more. Finally I could breathe again as we started to move. Neither of us spoke, as if we needed some miles between us and Lakeside before we felt safe. It was at least three minutes before I heard his voice.

'Listen to me, DeeDee, and don't ask questions until I've finished. We don't have long. I'm going to drive to the supermarket as usual. When we get there, I'll park as close as possible to a small white car – a Ford. It's yours, and you need to get in and drive away.'

What did he mean? I don't know what I'd expected to happen, but I suppose I had some vague hope that Dad would come with me, set me up somewhere and then come back for Mum. It was a stupid dream because he wouldn't have been allowed back onto the premises.

'In the boot you'll find a suitcase with clothes, shoes, everything I could think of that you might need. It's all supermarket stuff, and I wasn't sure of your size, so I went for elasticated waists.'

He knew!

'Dad?'

'Yes, DeeDee. I know you're pregnant.' He paused. 'I'm just sorry I won't be there to meet my grandchild.'

'How did you guess? Was it obvious?'

'Not to me, no, but I heard Nicola telling Aram.'

I struggled up from under the rubbish. We were far enough from Lakeside for it not to matter.

'*What?* Aram knows?'

'It seems so. Nicola was asking if he was going to give you something to help with the morning sickness.'

I grabbed the back of the seat in front of me and clung on tightly. 'What did he say?'

'He said he didn't think it was necessary. I hope he was right and you're not feeling too bad.'

Did that mean Aram *wanted* this baby? *Why?* I remembered him telling Alice that perhaps one day he would have a child, but the thought of him demanding access to my son or daughter scared me almost as much as his anti-sickness remedy. He must never find us.

Oblivious to the impact of his words, Dad carried on explaining what he'd done for me, and I tried my best to concentrate.

'In the glove compartment are your birth certificate and your driving licence. There's also a prepaid debit card. It's not linked to any bank account, and I've loaded as much money onto it as I could. Once the money is spent, it's no use. It's in the name of India Kalu, so it's for emergencies only.'

He took a deep shuddering breath, and I didn't know whether it was emotion getting to him, or fear.

'There's something else. When we first won the money, before we met Aram, we put a lump sum into a trust fund for you. It'll be paid out on your twenty-seventh birthday, but the trustees will need your bank details in order to transfer the money. Their address is with the other papers.'

I felt a stab of relief. 'Thanks, Dad. I know I can't get the money for nearly six years, but it's reassuring to know it's there.'

'If it were up to me I'd change the terms so you could have it now, but I'd have to tell your mum, and we both know what that would mean.'

My relief changed to concern. 'Will Aram be able to find out where I am when I claim the money?'

'I don't know. Maybe. I know nothing about the law, sweetheart, but when the time is right you should ask a solicitor to contact the trust company. Tell them to keep your address – even the city you live in – a secret. You should be okay.'

Should. I didn't like that word. He must never find me.

'You're right to be concerned about him. He's not going to take this well, and when he knows you're gone, he'll be devastated. He'll want you back, and he'll probably report you missing to the police. He'll say you're vulnerable, that you're mentally disturbed. No one at the house will dispute that, and you need to remember that the police can track you if you use the card or do anything using the name India Kalu.'

What I knew, and Dad didn't, was that Aram might tell the police a whole different story about me – one that would make them far more eager to find me. The sheer horror of what was ahead almost made me beg him to take me back.

Dad must have heard me sniff, because I heard a faint groan.

'India, my darling girl, please don't cry. I hate this as much as you do, but listen carefully. The next bit is so important. There's an envelope with some money in it. Find yourself somewhere to live and offer cash. Say you'll pay two months in advance, until you get a bank account. You'll have to change your name by deed poll. You can no longer be India Kalu – find another name. It's easy – and legal. Now, about a bank account...'

I listened as he went over what I had to do so that the police would find it difficult to track me down, but how was I going to remember all these instructions?

Finally, Dad had finished. 'Are you with me, DeeDee?'

Where was I going to go? It had all seemed so far away back at Lakeside – a day that might never come – but now it was happening.

'How did you get the money for the debit card, Dad?' I knew

that wouldn't have been easy for him, not after everything that had happened.

'I may have been a fool, but some semblance of common sense made me keep some of our money separate. No one knows about this, not even your mum.'

Especially not her, I would have thought.

'What am I going to call myself?'

'I don't want to know, and don't tell me where you're going. You know I would never voluntarily tell anyone, but – well – he has ways of finding things out, doesn't he?'

He did indeed, as I knew only too well. 'I'm scared, Dad.'

'I know, sweetheart. You're being incredibly brave, but for what it's worth I think you're doing the right thing. Just take care of yourself, try to stay under the radar, and you'll be fine.'

The car was slowing down. We were nearly there. I would have to jump out of the Range Rover and into my new car – and I might never see Dad again. I was heading out into a world I didn't know with no one to help me. And I was having a baby.

The car stopped, and I peered over the back seat at Dad's tear-streaked face. He had aged so much in the last eleven years.

'DeeDee, I know it's going to be difficult for you, but you're a clever girl. You can do this. Never forget, though, that Aram doesn't like to lose. You're different from all the other women. I've seen the way he looks at you. He'll use every trick in his extensive book to get you back. He'll even use your mother. If he finds out where you are, he'll tell you she's dying. He may even get her to tell you herself.'

I wanted to tell him about the bigger threat, about Leah, but I couldn't.

'I don't want to leave you, Dad.' I was sobbing, and he was trying his best not to.

'I am so, so sorry, baby. I should have seen what was happening and understood what he was doing to us. But all I could see for years was your mother and how he somehow made her feel that her life had meaning. She was lost, and he made her better. And he worked on me too – humiliating me for my failures until I wanted to strive to be a better person, a better husband. And all the while I forgot to be a better father. I love you, DeeDee, and I'm more sorry than I can say.'

I didn't want him to be sorry, or sad. I wanted to be the child who adored the tall warm-hearted man with laughter in his eyes and once again feel his strong arms pick me up, hug me, dance with me, carry me on his shoulders.

'What's he going to do to you, Dad, when he knows what you've done?'

'I don't know, child, and I don't care. I should have got you out of there long ago.'

Little did he know that had been my plan too. Just over a year earlier Leah would have helped me get away. She could see what was happening and had offered to set me free. I should have listened to her. I should have been stronger.

'You need to go, DeeDee. Stay safe, my darling.'

He walked round the back of the Range Rover, opened the tailgate and handed me a car key. I felt his arms squeeze me until I could barely breathe, and then he was gone. Back to the place I had once thought I would never leave, the home that felt both secure and threatening in equal measure.

60

Tom had decided to bend Philippa's rules slightly and set off for Lincolnshire. She'd said not to leave until the local force had located Martha, but they were bound to find the car once the hire company's system was working again, and the earlier they got there, the greater the chance of getting home that night so he could see Lucy.

'I thought we'd have the location by now. Why's it taking so long for them to sort out their bloody computers?' he grumbled.

'I told you – they've taken part of the system down for "essential maintenance".'

'On a Thursday!'

'Apparently it's a quiet day for them. The weekends – Friday to Monday – are chaos at this time of year, so they can't touch those days. They do it overnight, but there's a bug that's taking longer to fix than they thought.'

Tom grunted. 'I love computers most of the time, but sometimes they make our lives infinitely more complicated. Look at that new app XO-Tech are creating. Imagine your phone predicting everything you're about to do and pre-empting your actions? I think it's bloody creepy. We'll need an app to think for us soon. Do you know, I only realised a few months ago when I was talking to Lucy that most kids think "app" is a word. I suppose it is now. But she had no idea that it was short for "application", as in "software application".'

Becky turned towards him. 'Really? I honestly didn't know that.'

'Erm – eyes on the road, Becky,' Tom said, realising they were approaching a roundabout and Becky didn't seem to have considered slowing down.

She grinned as she hurtled towards the junction.

'Speaking of the brains behind the app, we can't pin anything on Niall. His car's clean, as is the house, and the lawyer in Manchester has confirmed it was definitely him she saw talking on his mobile. Let's hope that when we catch up with Martha Porter we'll get all our answers.'

'Rob's on his way too, isn't he?'

'Yep, he left half an hour before us to set everything up with the local team. He's bringing Jenny Stillwell with him – she's great in interviews.'

Tom's phone chose that moment to interrupt them. He had the feeling it might be Philippa, somehow guessing that he had disobeyed her, but he was delighted to see it was Lucy.

'Hi Lucy! It's good to speak to you, and great to have you back in the country. I can't wait to see you. How's the jet lag?'

'It's okay. I would have been fine last night. Mum was fussing, but to be honest I slept from yesterday afternoon until this morning, so perhaps she was right. I'm dying to see you. And Louisa and Harry. I can't wait to give him a cuddle. He was so tiny when we left, and Louisa says he's laughing now and very funny.'

'He is! We're all looking forward to seeing you.' Tom closed his eyes. 'I have to tell you that I'm on my way to Lincolnshire for a case, but I'm hoping to be back tonight, love. I'll do my best and I'll let you know if there's a problem. It's rubbish timing and I'm really sorry, but I guess you're used to it.'

Tom held his breath, wondering if she would be upset.

'Oh.' He could hear the disappointment in her voice, and it matched his own. 'It's okay, Dad, but can we sort out where I'm going to live quickly, please? The last year's been a bit bonkers, and now Mum's talking about moving to Scotland or something. I'll never see you.'

'I think it's Durham, so not quite as far as Scotland – and nowhere near as far as Australia, sweetheart.' That was true, but to Tom it might as well have been.

He heard a sigh. 'I know, but first I was at home, then Mum got ill and I moved in with you – which was brilliant, by the way – and then Australia, and now I've no idea. I want to make friends, pass my exams and – you know – go to parties and stuff.'

'It's a priority to get it sorted, Luce – I promise. I'll sit down with you and your mum and we'll work it out. You're old enough to have a say in this, and I promise we'll listen.'

'Yeah, but can Louisa be there too?'

Tom was surprised but pleased. 'Of course, as long as your mum doesn't mind.'

'It's just that you and Mum... Well, it's always a bit competitive, and Louisa and Mum don't irritate each other the way you two do.'

Another pang of guilt hit Tom. He always tried to be reasonable with Kate, but she somehow managed to wind him up every time.

'Fair comment. I'll speak to Louisa and get her to set it up. Speak soon, love.'

'Okay. Is Becky with you?' Lucy had known Becky since she was five, and they had always got on well.

'She is – she's driving, though.'

'Oh, God help you, Dad! Say hi from me.'

'Lucy says hi.'

'Hiya, Lucy!' Becky shouted, and Tom heard his daughter's response, loud in his right ear.

He ended the call, feeling deflated by his ongoing battles with

Kate and how they must affect Lucy, but all thoughts of his ex-wife and daughter were rudely interrupted as his phone rang again.

'Keith. You must have news.'

'I do, but not what we were expecting, sir. The hire company finally got their system up and running. We patched them through to the team at Lincolnshire police control so they could convey updates on the car's movements. A squad car was dispatched, but they decided not to stop the hire car or apprehend the driver without further instruction.'

'Because?'

'Because the driver isn't a young woman, sir. It seems to be a middle-aged man.'

61

MARTHA

We were almost at the car when I heard Dad shout.

'Wait, DeeDee!' I turned back, not daring to hope. He hurried towards me. 'I'll do it, but try to persuade your mum to leave too. Please, I'm begging you to do your best. Tell her I love her. I've not been allowed to say that for years, but I've never stopped.'

I had no time left to explain what I was doing, or why. I'd have to take the Range Rover, and I'd have to go immediately. Aram would see the car and assume it was Dad returning with the post. It might not give me much time to do what was needed, but it was the best I could think of.

I crouched down to my son's eye level. 'Alfie, sweetheart, you know that this is your grandad, and I've told you lots of lovely things about him before. You know what a grandad is, don't you?'

He nodded, but his eyes were round with alarm. He didn't know what was happening, but he could feel the tension fizzing around him. 'Is he your daddy?'

'That's right, darling. He's my daddy. Do you remember I said that he lives a long way away, but I was hoping that some day you'd meet him? Well, that's why we're here, and I know you're going to love him. When I was your age, he used to dance with me and sing, and he's really good fun. I've got to go and see someone for a while, so Grandad's going to look after you. That's exciting, isn't it?'

He didn't look excited. He clutched my hand a little tighter and bit his bottom lip.

'Do you remember your first day at school? You were worried about that, but after the first half an hour you had a great time, didn't you? And now you love school. It'll be like that, you'll see, and I'll be back soon.'

I said the words and swallowed hard. I had no idea when I would see him again.

Alfie leaned against me and whispered in my ear, 'Is Grandad nice, Mummy?'

I turned my head so my lips were next to his ear, and I inhaled his sweet scent. 'He's lovely, and he'll look after you really well. I love you, baby.'

It was all I could do not to howl with the agony of it all, but I had to make him feel that going with his grandad was nothing special – a bit like going to the childminder's.

Dad crouched in front of his grandson. 'It's okay, Alfie. We're going to have some fun. Do you like the seaside? I thought we could get some ice cream. I haven't had ice cream for years and years. What do you think? Good idea?'

The twin lures of ice cream and the beach did it, and with a final look at me Alfie couldn't wait to get into his car seat. Once he was fastened in, Dad reached for me. Despite leaving behind everything he knew for a reason he didn't understand, he looked almost happy. I realised then it must have been a long time since he'd had any fun.

'I wish I knew what was happening,' he said, 'but I know you have to go. Please, take care of yourself, and of Nicola. She's still your mum.'

I hugged him as tightly as I could and forced myself to give my son a cheery wave through the window. Then, with tears almost blinding me, I made my way towards the Range Rover.

I fumbled the key into the ignition and, without another backward glance, drove away.

I feel as if my heart has been ripped out, but I don't have time to pull over and give in to the pain. I'm trying hard to concentrate, because I haven't driven on these roads since that fateful day when I met the boy from the courier's office. He was so kind, so gentle with me when he realised how little I knew of the world outside Lakeside, and I'll never forget how I felt when he kissed me. I wonder what he thought when I never went back?

Although I followed Mum yesterday along this same route, the only thing I was looking at was the back of her car. Today, everything seems different, and I don't recognise the new houses, a factory and a roundabout that I'm sure weren't here last time I drove along this road. At least while I'm fretting about finding my way, I don't have the space in my head to worry about what I'll do when I get there.

The last couple of miles are through open countryside with no distractions, and that's when the enormity of what I'm about to do hits me. I'm going back to the house in which my every action was controlled, every thought examined, and I feel as if I am being dragged into a vortex, spinning out of control as I head towards its centre. It's making me dizzy.

I want to pull the car over and catch my breath, but the later I am the more likely it is that Aram will be watching for Dad's return. If he looks out of the window, I need him to believe it's Dad coming back with the car. He'll lose interest then; Dad's whereabouts, once he's safely inside, are of no concern to him. I force my foot to stay on the accelerator. I can pause to think when the car is safely at the back of the house, out of sight.

The gates suddenly loom in front of me. I don't have to get out to open them, though. Dad explained that electric gates have long since replaced the chain and padlock, and they are opened either from inside the house or with the remote inside the car. I click the button, and the gates part in front of me, slowly, laboriously, heavily. I stare down the long drive, and I can almost feel those ice-grey eyes piercing the air. My heart thuds.

There's a clunk as the gates stop moving, and I have to go, to drive over the threshold into the grounds, not knowing how I will ever get out again. But as the gates automatically close behind me, I look at the remote, still clasped in my damp fingers, and I push it into the pocket of my jeans.

I drive straight around the back and into the garage. Dad has left the doors open. I know the sensible thing would be to close them, but I'm struggling to find the strength to get out of the car. Every second I expect to see an ominous shadow blocking the light streaming through the gaping doorway. But Aram doesn't come.

I clamp my lips together to stop them from trembling. If he sees me, I don't know what he'll do, although I know he'll make me suffer. I'll be forced to listen as he tears me to shreds for what I've done, but it isn't Aram's words that I fear. It's his eyes – their strength as they pull me in, their ability to make me forget everything that happened the minute I leave his presence. I know it's a combination of suggestion, obedience and conditioning that causes this trance-like state, and I tell myself he can't do it to me now. I'm too strong, and his will can't break me like it used to. It's what I have to believe.

I lean my head back on the headrest and think of everything I need to do to secure the future for me and Alfie – and now Dad too. I have to destroy the evidence that Aram believes will send me to prison for life.

Much as I try to focus on the future and what has to be done, nothing can change the events that have brought me to this moment, and as the memories flood back, I shiver. In the weeks that followed the night I was due to escape with Leah, Aram kept me by his side day and night. I told no one what had happened, and passed from one day to the next as if in a dream – no longer believing in him but unable to shake myself free. I caught people looking at me from time to time and was convinced they knew what I had done. But perhaps they just wondered why I rarely spoke, not realising that I was scared to open my mouth in case I blurted out the truth.

Now I have to confront what happened and face up to what I have been running from. Try as I might to block it from my mind, it haunts my nights and fills me with a crushing guilt.

LAKESIDE

The dark night settled around me like a thick blanket as I slowly made my way down towards the river. I wanted to stop, to turn back, to run to the house before it was too late, but I knew I couldn't.

Leah was waiting for me exactly where she said she'd be. When she heard the crunch of my feet on the shingle along the water's edge, she must have thought I was alone. 'India! I'm so glad you've come.' She rushed towards me to grab my hands in hers.

Then she saw Aram standing behind me. Her eyes went to my face, and I felt myself flush with shame. I knew I should have said nothing to him, even if I had decided not to leave with her. My only defence was that I was just twenty years old, and she was going to tear apart the only world I knew. It was a poor excuse.

I felt Aram's hands on my shoulders. 'Leave us, India.'

With one last look at Leah, I bowed my head and turned back towards the house. Blinded as I was by my tears and the impenetrable blackness of the night, I could still make out a lighter patch at the side of the path – a figure, standing alone, watching. I knew it was my mother. I stumbled past, ignoring her.

I could hear shouting behind me, and wondered what Aram was saying. He was bound to make Leah suffer – to ensure that she left with her confidence shattered – and I didn't want to witness her degradation. But when a scream pierced the night air, I stopped dead.

Silence.

I tried to fool myself into believing it was the pained cry of a fox, but I had to be sure. I spun on my heel and ran, stumbling, back along the path. Not to the house, but towards Leah.

I shouldn't have turned; I should have carried on, as Aram had demanded. If I had, everything would have been different.

62

'Rob, what have you got?'

Rob had been tasked with accompanying the local force to interview the driver.

'The car's been under surveillance since the hire company gave us the GPS coordinates. It stopped at a B and B, and the driver – IC3 male, middle-aged, tall, white hair – lifted a small boy from the back seat. I checked the photo I've got on my phone of Alfie Porter, and it's definitely him. No sign of Martha. They went into the B and B, but came out five minutes ago, and they're off towards the beach. We've got eyes on him – he's not going to get away. How would you like us to proceed?'

'We've got no choice. You'll have to talk to him, but try to do it without making a song and dance. Ask the locals to stay in the background in case he decides to leg it. Martha Porter's father is black, mid-forties, so it could be him. On the other hand, this guy may have abducted the child for all we know. We can't make any assumptions.'

'I don't think so. The child seems okay with him, at least, he's not kicking off.'

'We need him to tell us where Martha is. And Rob, that child is old enough to know something's wrong. I know you'll handle it sensitively, so make sure you're the one to do the talking.'

'Okay. I'll get back to you.'

Tom ended the call and didn't speak for a couple of minutes, his eyes drawn to the passing countryside. This part of Lincolnshire was a bit too flat for his liking, but pretty nonetheless.

'I think we should stick to the plan and go to Lakeside, unless we learn something different from Rob. How far away are we?'

'Thirty minutes.'

Tom and Becky fell silent again, each lost in their own thoughts. Five minutes later Tom's mobile rang again.

'Yes, Rob. How did it go?'

'You were right. The man is Joel Kalu. He has his driving licence with him. India Kalu – or Martha Porter, as we know her – is his daughter. Until today, he hadn't seen Martha since she left home before Alfie was born, and it was a complete surprise when she turned up. I've no reason to doubt he's telling the truth. He thinks she's in trouble. She's told him there's something she has to do, and she has to do it now, today. It's something to do with Aram Forakis, he thinks.'

'Does he know where she is now?'

'She's taken his Range Rover. He said she was planning to go to Lakeside but her nerves might get the better of her. She might be too scared.'

'Scared of what?'

'He wouldn't say. He said it was too difficult to understand. I said "Try me" but he just shook his head. He doesn't have a mobile phone – never has, apparently – but I think we need to keep an eye on him in case he goes to her, or she turns up here.'

'Okay. I'll sort that. You get yourself and Jenny to the local station so you're ready to interview her. We'll get her now. I'm certain of it.'

Tom hung up. Martha had left her child and was running again, but they were close behind. Her every action spoke of guilt, but what exactly was she guilty of?

63

MARTHA

I can't sit out here in the garage for much longer. I'm wasting time. I think about the layout of the house. Aram has his meditation room at the back with floor-to-ceiling windows facing east into the garden. He may have seen the car heading for the garage, but he wouldn't have been able to make out who was driving. From the garage I can get round the west side of the house without being seen, unless he's at an upstairs window.

Aram's private rooms are at the front, but I don't know where my mother sleeps now. He occupied a whole wing of the house, with his main bedroom and bathroom plus a study, a sitting room, and two other bedrooms for the women who were currently in favour. I occupied one of those rooms on and off for the last three years of my time here, and I'm fervently hoping I don't have to venture there. The memories would overwhelm me.

It's late morning. Mum will be in the kitchen preparing lunch. I don't know if I'll have time to talk to her, to persuade her, before Aram comes through to eat, but for now that will have to wait.

Indecision is not helpful. The police will be getting closer, and they are bound to come here. I don't want it to end like this. I don't want them to find me here.

I push open the car door and climb out. I'll have to go into the house. It's what I came to do, but it's harder than I thought. I close my eyes and think of Alfie's face, laughing, happy, free from the fear that holds me captive. Then I move. I creep out through the back of the garage, past the outhouses and round to the west side of the house. I either have to go in through the kitchen, and risk Mum being there, or through the front door. It seems like the better option.

Keeping close to the wall, I duck beneath the windows in case someone is inside, looking out. Dad told me the house is empty except for Mum and Aram, but maybe he was wrong.

I gently push the door ajar, remembering that when it gets to half open it creaks. I slither through the gap and into the hall. Immediately the memories bombard me as I breathe in the unique smell that is Lakeside – the slight mustiness that we never quite got rid of, overlaid by incense wafting from the meditation room each time the door opens. I expect to hear the sound of people moving between the rooms, speaking quietly to each other, the occasional cough, the gentle closing of a door, but not a sound disturbs the stillness. My senses are alert, drawing me in, almost convincing me that this is home.

I shake my head. *No.* This is not my home, and I have a job to do.

With every bone in my body I want to turn and run away from this place. But I don't. My legs feel weak, as if they can barely support me as I creep across the hall and head for the stairs to begin my search for the evidence that Aram held over me for the last months of my life at Lakeside, and ever since. I tiptoe up the staircase, keeping close to the wall to avoid the groaning of old wood. I don't know where to start looking. Can I face Aram's bedroom, a room that for years I visited all too often? I can't bear the thought.

I should have searched before, when I lived here. But I was too broken, and it had seemed easier to abide by his rules. If I hadn't become pregnant I would still be here, living my life as he demanded, a hostage to the devil that is Aram Forakis.

I start in his sitting room – a room few visited. It seems more likely than his bedroom, which saw more than its fair share of traffic. I have to move quickly, silently, as I pull open drawers and bend low to look beneath furniture. I find nothing.

The study might be a better option, although I am sure there was nothing there in the months before I left. This was my territory, and I would have known. Nevertheless, I have to look. There are papers neatly stacked on a table. They look official, and I can see Aram's signature and my mother's. I don't have time to read them, but I pull out my phone and take a quick photo. Then I open the top drawer of the filing cabinet. It's empty. I pull out the second, the third, the fourth. They are all empty. Where are his papers?

I look back at the table, and underneath, pushed towards the back, there are boxes. I kneel down and pull them forward. Each one is marked alphabetically – A–E, F–J – in neat capital letters. There are five boxes in total, all taped shut.

I hesitate for a moment. If I tear off the tape, he'll know someone has been in here, and neither Mum nor Dad would open his boxes. But it's too late to be timid, and I rip open the first box. Inside are the missing files from the cabinet – the agreements signed by every new member of the community. I open the second, and it's the same. More files. I sit back on my heels.

I doubt it's worth opening the other boxes, but why has Aram emptied his filing cabinet?

I have no time to think, and it's not why I'm here.

I hadn't thought it would be so difficult to find what I am looking for. I had imagined I would instinctively know, but I don't and it's a huge house. It could be anywhere. I sit on the sofa and drop my head into my hands. *What was I thinking?* I'm an idiot, an arrogant fool who thinks she knows better than Aram Forakis. I'm never going to find it.

I waste far too much time sitting there, and finally come to my senses with a groan. A few moments in this house, and he's in my head, telling me I'm stupid. But I'm not. *I* may not know where to look, but I know someone who will. I just have to persuade her to tell me.

I make it back down the stairs and out of the front door without being seen. To avoid any chance of encountering Aram I have to get to the kitchen from the back of the house, so once more keeping close to the wall, I approach the door that leads to the boot room. Not that it was ever used as that given that no one wore shoes, but the name stuck. I gently ease open the door from there into the laundry.

I stand still, not breathing, just listening. I can hear movement in the kitchen and realise the door is ajar. I creep into the laundry. I can't hear talking, but Aram doesn't chatter. He only speaks if he feels there is something to be said, so he could be in there, sitting at the table, drinking one of his herbal brews. Mum used to chatter, but her need to talk gradually deserted her over the years.

On tiptoe, I head to the crack of light seeping into the dark laundry from the brightly lit kitchen with its north-facing windows. I peer through the gap, and there's Mum at the huge black Aga, stirring a pan of soup on the hob. Even from behind, she seems smaller. She's slightly bent, without an ounce of flesh on her body. Despite everything, I want to go to her and put my arms round her. Even now I can remember her as she was, how gentle, thoughtful and considerate to our friends and neighbours when we lived in London. My hatred of Aram ratchets up a notch, and with it my courage.

It's now or never. I ease the door open and slip through the gap.

I'm not making a sound, but even though she has her back to me, Mum's shoulders stiffen. She stops stirring, but she doesn't turn.

I don't need to tiptoe now. She knows someone is here, and she knows it's neither Aram nor Dad. In Aram's case she would have turned. Had it been Dad, she'd have carried on stirring.

'Mum,' I whisper, using the term that had been banned for years.

She turns slowly, wooden spoon raised in her hand, as if to defend herself against an attack from me. She stares, and once again I see the dark circles round her eyes, the look of defeat on her features.

I move closer, and finally she speaks: 'Where's Joel?'

She doesn't seem to care that her daughter, who she hasn't seen for almost six years and had barely spoken to for many years more, has just walked through the door. If I had been expecting her to rush to me and gather me in her arms, I would have been bitterly disappointed. As it is, I feel a twinge of sadness but nothing more.

'Where's Aram?'

'He's meditating. He'll be here for lunch in about an hour. Why are you here?'

I walk across and touch her arm. She flinches and looks scared of me, and I don't understand why. Maybe she thinks I've come back because I want Aram, and I'm about to ruin everything again.

She retreats until her back is flat against the Aga, her hands grasping the chrome bar behind her, and I guess that's where she's going to stay. I remain where I am.

'Dad's not coming back. He's left, Mum, but it's not you he's deserting. It's this place. This... situation. I know where he is, and I can take you to him. He loves you – he's never stopped, in spite of everything.'

Two lines appear briefly between her eyes as if I've struck home, and it hurts. But then her face clears.

'Joel thinks I'm his. But we don't belong to others. We belong only to ourselves, and it's for each of us to choose how we share our souls, our bodies, our minds.'

I groan, but I know there's no point arguing.

'I need your help. I'm still your daughter, and I know you loved me once, so please help me, then we can *both* get away from here. You can be happy again.' She looks at me as if I'm mad, but I plough on, hoping that something will get through to her. 'You must realise that Aram has *consumed* you; sucked out the core of you and left an empty shell. Come with me, Mum. Dad will help you. You're both still young. Please, I beg you, take a good look at yourself and see what's happened to you.'

She swallows, and for a moment I think I may have reached her. She must know that life before Aram had more to offer, but I don't have time to persuade her. For now I just need her help.

'Where would Aram hide something? Something important. You must know. You know this house like the back of your hand – a large plastic bag, maybe a small suitcase. Think, Mum.'

'What do you want it for?'

'Aram can use what's in it to drag me back here. Even if you don't want to leave, you don't want me here, do you? So help me find it.'

She stares at me, weighing up my words, and this time I *know* I've struck home. She doesn't want me to return to Lakeside, and for a moment I believe she might help me.

'What's in the bag, India? Why is it so important?'

I don't know if I'm doing the right thing or not, but I decide it's the only thing I can do.

'A knife, Mum – with my fingerprints on it. And clothes, *my* clothes, covered in Leah Medway's blood. He has proof that I killed Leah.'

64

MARTHA

I don't know how I expected Mum to react to my words, but they are met with silence. Her eyes narrow slightly, as if she is trying to work something out, but neither of us speaks.

A wasp buzzes at the window, trying to get out. The soup bubbles gently on the hob. The air between us feels heavy with unspoken hostility. Will she help me or not?

Before I get the chance to say any more, Mum jerks her hand into the air, palm out, and it's not at my words. I heard it too – a door closing somewhere else in the house. There's only Aram here, and he's on the move. She's telling me to be quiet. Maybe she's going to help me after all.

I scuttle towards the door to the laundry room. 'Don't tell him I'm here,' I whisper frantically. 'Please, whatever you do, don't tell him.'

I disappear into the laundry just as I hear the kitchen door opening.

'Nicola, did I hear you talking to someone?'

There is a moment of silence, and I wonder what excuse she's going to come up with.

'Yes, Aram. I was talking to India. She's hiding in the laundry room.'

In the seconds after Mum speaks, I can hear my own heartbeats, the sound thumping in my ears. I don't know why I'm surprised that she told Aram where I am. I should have realised her loyalty is still to him, and the pain of her betrayal shouldn't still burn, but it does. I'd forgotten how every rejection always stung, each dismissal yet another thrust of the knife.

I want to run, but I feel as if my feet are stuck to the stone flags of the floor. I'm waiting for him to speak. He won't come to find me. He won't chase me if I run. He moves slowly, never rushes, and he will wait for me to come to him. As I always have done. But I don't move.

The seconds tick by, and I know I could get away. I *should* get away.

My whole body jerks as pinpricks of fear skim the surface of my skin.

'Join us, India.' His voice is soft, seductive.

I don't know what's happening to me. It's as if a giant magnet is pulling me towards the kitchen door. I know he's doing it again – drawing me in, controlling me – and yet I can't seem to stop him. The still silence of the laundry room is broken as a sob catches in my throat. I know he's heard.

Almost of their own volition, my feet move. Not towards the back door, to my escape, but towards Aram. He will be angry. I have displeased him. My head tells me he can't control me. My heart and soul tell me I want his forgiveness.

I slowly open the door and step into the kitchen. I gaze at the floor and still he doesn't speak. Inch by inch, my chin lifts. In my head I hear Leah's voice – 'Close your eyes, India!' – but it doesn't work. I have been conditioned to obey him, and my eyes meet his.

Once again I am the ten-year-old child that looked into their depths and wanted to run and hide. But I can't move.

'Where have you been, India?' His voice is calm, measured, but his eyes sparkle like ice.

I can't answer. What can I say? I glance quickly at Mum, but she is looking at the floor, and I've no idea what she's thinking.

'We looked for you. I worried that you were unwell, that perhaps the events of recent years had disturbed your mind. Come with me, India. We'll speak alone, and you will tell me everything.'

He turns towards the door, confident that I will follow as I have done so many times before. It's as if my body remembers what it's supposed to do, and my feet begin to move. I know he's got me – I'm his again. And I don't know how to break free. No one speaks as Aram reaches the door. I'm right behind him, and Mum hasn't shifted an inch.

A loud buzz shatters the thick atmosphere of the room, and I jump as if I've been struck. The ties to Aram fray a little, and I wonder what I'm doing. We all stand perfectly still, as if any movement would break the spell.

The buzzer sounds again.

'Ignore it,' Aram says.

I know who it is. No one comes here uninvited. There's only one explanation.

'It's the police,' I say. 'They're here for me.'

65

Becky pressed the button beside the gates for a third time and waited. Nothing happened. She glanced over her shoulder at Tom and shrugged, then turned back and pressed it again, keeping her finger on the buzzer. Finally, there was a crackle and then a voice.

'Yes?'

'Greater Manchester Police, DI Becky Robinson and DCI Tom Douglas. We'd like to speak to Mrs Kalu, please.'

'I'm sorry. Mrs Kalu is unwell at the moment. Can I help at all? My name is Aram Forakis.'

'We're looking for her daughter, India Kalu, also known as Martha Porter.'

There was silence from the other end of the intercom.

'Mr Forakis?'

'I haven't seen India for nearly six years. Thank you for visiting.'

The line went dead.

Becky swivelled round to face Tom, hands on her hips and a look of indignation on her face. She was about to turn back and press again when Tom put up a hand. 'I'll have a go. Maybe he's the type of guy who objects to females in authority.'

He gave Becky a grin, knowing the mere thought would wind her up, and pressed the buzzer.

'I think I made myself clear,' the disembodied voice said.

'I'm Detective Chief Inspector Tom Douglas of the Greater Manchester Police. Mr Forakis, we have come a long way today in search of Martha Porter, who I believe you know as India Kalu. I'd be grateful if you would let us in so we can talk to you and her mother.'

'I'm sorry, but she's not here, and if you want to come in, you'll need a warrant.'

Before Tom had a chance to respond, Becky stepped forward to the intercom again. 'We *will* apply for a warrant, Mr Forakis, and in the meantime, just so you know, we'll be sitting at your gates. You may as well let us in now, don't you think?'

There was no response, other than a click as they were disconnected.

'Sorry for butting in, Tom, but he riled me.'

'You don't say!'

Becky's phone rang.

'DI Robinson,' Tom heard. There was a pause. 'And you're sure that's what she said?'

Tom turned towards Becky as she hung up. 'What was that about?'

'Eddie Carlson's wife – Kirsten – called. She's feeling okay and wants me to call her about her conversation with Genevieve. She told Kirsten she was planning to leave Niall, and Kirsten wants to tell me exactly what she said.'

'Why doesn't that surprise me? Genevieve definitely seemed to have her own agenda, although Niall gave no hint of that, did he?'

'Maybe he didn't know. I'll call Kirsten later, but this is a little more important. Do you think Martha's in the house? Do you think he's lying?'

'Almost definitely, although why he would isn't at all clear to me. From what we've been told, this is the only way in or out, so the stupid bugger's got nothing to gain.'

'Except perhaps time.'

'For what, though? What's he up to?'

66

MARTHA

Aram's aura of calm seems to have cracked. The police are here, and they are looking for me, as I knew they would be. For once in his life I don't think Aram knows what to do.

Before he has a chance to decide on his next steps, a sound seldom heard in this house fills the room. It's the telephone – used so rarely, and only with Aram's authorisation, that I often forgot we had one. Aram doesn't want to take his eyes off me, so he motions to Mum to answer it.

'Hello,' she mumbles, her voice at first flat and uninterested. 'Joel!'

A sudden cold courses through my body. *Dad! What are you doing?*

Aram swivels towards Mum, and the last of the slender threads binding me to him are broken. I want to dash to the phone, grab it from Mum and tell Dad to stay away, but Aram is right there, blocking my way. I'm about to scream, knowing he would hear me, but as always Aram reads my thoughts and he lunges at me, grabbing me by the throat.

'Not a word, India.'

Both his hands are around my neck now, squeezing – not hard enough to kill me, but enough to let me know that he could, if he wanted to. He always said that killing can be justified, and I don't need to ask myself if he really meant it. I know he did.

I would die for my son, but my death would put him in his father's hands, so I take deep breaths to try to control the panic.

The police are at the gates. If I could get to the intercom, I could summon help. But once again Aram reads my mind and squeezes tighter. By the time they get their search warrant he could have strangled and buried me. He's told the police I'm not here. And Mum would back him up.

Aram turns me round, so my back is against his chest. He has one arm around my shoulders, one hand grasping my throat, his thumb pressed hard on my larynx.

Mum has barely said a word to Dad, but from where I'm standing I can hear his voice, pleading with her. I have no idea what he's saying, but my heart is filled with dread.

'She's not here, Joel,' she says. Then, 'No.' With that, she hangs up.

She turns to face us. 'Joel asked if India was here. He said she was going to try to persuade me to leave with her.' Her voice is a monotone, as if none of this matters to her. 'He says we have a grandson. He's five years old and he's called Alfie. He says I'm not to tell you.'

A choked sob bursts from my lips. *Dad!* I know how much he loves Mum, and he must have hoped that the lure of a grandchild would bring her rushing to his side.

'So the child is a boy,' Aram says.

I sense no warmth in his voice, or curiosity about his son, and for one precious moment I allow myself to believe that he's not interested, that maybe I've been wrong for all these years.

There's been a heavy silence in the room since Dad called, and I am sure Aram is working out his next move. He lets go of me, and I scurry to the other side of the table, out of his reach. But he's watching me. He must realise that with the police at the gates I have a chance to tell them who he is, what he's done. But I have no evidence. He holds all the cards.

'Nicola, get the bag – the one with the clothes,' he says.

I was right. She knew all along where they were.

Without a word, she walks out of the kitchen into the laundry room. I can't believe I never thought to look there, where a bag of dirty clothes wouldn't look out of place. Aram always said he would keep the evidence hidden while I was with him at Lakeside, but there was a clear threat that if I tried to leave or told anyone what had happened to Leah, he would use it against me. My clothes, her blood. A sharp knife, my fingerprints. What more did he need?

I feel as if my legs are about to fold under me, just as I felt in the days after she had gone, when I was too scared to look anyone in the eye in case they could see into my soul, to the black guilt at its core.

Poor Leah. She didn't deserve to die.

Moments later Mum is back, clutching a large clear polythene bag. I can see what looks like a T-shirt and some light-coloured linen trousers inside. Both are covered in blood. At the bottom, weighing heavily against the plastic, is a long thin-bladed knife. Aram's evidence. She throws it on the table.

I lift my eyes to look at her. She's watching me, saying nothing. I wish I knew what she was thinking.

I've no idea what's going to happen next. Is Aram going to hand these clothes over to the police?

To my surprise he walks across to the intercom and presses the button to open the gates. He could have waited until the police had a warrant, but he doesn't want them in the house. If he gives them what they have come for – me – they will have no reason to step over the threshold. He turns to give me a look of such ferocity that it seems to pierce my skin.

'You've brought this on us, India,' he says finally, his voice brittle with anger. 'Why are the police here?'

I debate whether or not to lie to him, but there's little point. He holds all the cards. 'A woman I knew was murdered.'

For a moment he looks shocked, and I realise he thinks I mean Leah. I don't enlighten him. Then he realises he has to be wrong. They said they were from Manchester.

'Did you kill her?' he asks.

I don't answer. It has nothing to do with him.

'Do you think evidence of a previous murder might make your conviction more likely?'

I shiver and glance at the bag on the table. 'If you've hidden them for years, that makes you an accessory.'

He just smiles. 'Oh no, India. This is the first time I've seen them. You came back for them, to destroy them, didn't you? They will see my shock, my horror at what you did. Nicola will back me up – you know she will.'

Any thoughts I had of trying to talk to the police about what happened here all those years ago are now gone.

I have no chance to say any more. There is a knock at the front door. They are here.

'Stay here,' he tells me.

I don't know why he thinks I would obey him. Maybe because I always have, but with a last glance at Mum, who looks as if she's been cast adrift with no idea where she's heading, I follow him through the kitchen door.

There's another knock, this time louder. I keep to the shadows as he opens the front door.

I can hear talking, but I can't make out the words. I know what I must do.

I take a step into the hall. A tall man in shirtsleeves, rolled to just below the elbow, stands in the open doorway, his feet apart. A woman with auburn hair is by his side. They are both looking up at Aram, who stands one step above them, barring their entry.

Without a backward glance, I emerge from the gloom and head for the door, my eyes on the policeman. From the corner of my eye, I see Aram turn and look at me, but I avoid his gaze. I focus on the police.

My heart is pounding, my mouth dry, and my throat aches with constant swallowing. I don't know what evidence they have that I killed Genevieve, but I know, should he wish to produce it, that Aram believes he has indisputable evidence that I killed Leah.

Tom looked at the raised chin, the eyes staring straight ahead. Martha was finding it to hold herself together. He could see the fear lurking behind the determination in her brown eyes.

She walked out through the front door and turned to grasp the huge brass handle. She didn't look at Aram Forakis, but appeared to focus on a spot above his head. Finally, he took a step back, and she pulled the door closed behind her.

'I was planning to come to you voluntarily,' she said, her voice steady. 'But first I had to see my mother. I'm sorry you had to come here for me.'

'Martha Porter,' Tom said, 'I am arresting you on suspicion of the murder of Genevieve Strachan. You do not have to say anything, but it may harm your defence if you do not mention when questioned something which you later rely on in court. Anything you do say may be given in evidence.'

He watched the young woman closely. There was something else going on. Tom could feel it. She hadn't looked at Aram Forakis, and yet he had never taken his eyes from her. Whatever she'd done, Tom could only imagine the childhood Martha must have had growing up with this man, and he felt a flash of sympathy for her.

67

MARTHA

I understand why the police want to question me about Genevieve. By now they will know about our argument. Elise will have told them about the party and how Niall has avoided being alone with me ever since. But is that enough to suspect me of her murder? They must have something more, although I have no idea what that can be. I grasp my hands tightly together in an effort to stop them shaking.

Maybe it's because I ran. I evaded them, using every trick I had. Will they understand that I had no choice, that fear for my son and the need to keep him away from his father is what motivated me? With Genevieve dead I'd had visions of the press gathering at the entrance to XO-Tech, trying to catch the staff unawares, taking photographs for their papers or their online newsfeeds – including, very possibly, a picture of me for the world to see. The world including Aram.

Since my escape from Lakeside I have always assumed I would be listed on the police database as missing and vulnerable, although it seems I was wrong. I was even more terrified that Leah's body had been found in the years since I left and that I was wanted for her murder. It seems I was wrong about that too. Aram must have always had a different ending in mind for me.

As the detectives drive me towards the gates of Lakeside I look to my left, to a small copse of trees by the river, the spot where I was due to meet Leah that night, and from where we would have made our escape, had I not betrayed her. I swallow hard. Is that where she is?

I remember the moment I heard her scream, the second at which the full force of my treachery hit me, and I tore back down the path towards her.

I was too late.

She was lying on the ground in the mud. There was barely any light, but what little there was glinted on the knife sticking out of her body.

I cried out, and Aram grabbed me. I pushed him away and fell to my knees, pulling the knife from her. Thick red blood was pumping from her body. She was still alive, and I tried to stem the flow. But then it stopped, and I knew she was dead.

'*No!* Why, Aram? Why did you have to do this?'

'She was a traitor, India. She would have ruined our lives.' I shivered and heard myself moan quietly. 'You did what you had to,' he said. 'You had no choice.'

I was still holding the knife, and Leah wasn't moving. I should have known he could never let her leave.

Aram spoke again. 'No one will ever know. You need to go, India. Strip off your clothes, put them in a bag and give them to me later. I'll take care of them. Go now.' He paused. '*Now!*'

Still grasping the knife, I ran, pushing through the trees, onto the path. I looked down at my hand, at the knife, and threw it as hard as I could towards the water. I heard it hit stone, but I didn't stop. Aram told me later that he'd found the knife and kept it safe.

Mum was still there, standing silently by the path. I saw her.

Leah's blood is on my hands. I should have screamed out loud to the whole community that Aram had killed my friend, but I was shocked, scared and totally under his control. Had I told anyone, he would have shown compassion and understanding, saying I was fantasising – that I was distraught because Leah had left without telling me, and everyone would have believed him. And the only evidence of her murder – as far as I knew – pointed to me. To my shame, I said nothing. Had I gone to the police after I escaped, Aram still had the evidence, and he wouldn't have hesitated to use it.

This is my chance to tell the truth, but I know I won't take it because the police are unlikely to believe me. They have just arrested me for murder. They think I killed Genevieve.

I clamp my lips together to stop myself from crying out as I try to convince myself that they can't have any proof.

But they wouldn't have arrested me unless they believe I'm guilty.

68

Tom and Becky took their seats to watch the interview through the monitors as Rob and Jenny entered the room. They introduced themselves to Martha, and as they completed the formalities Tom turned to Becky. 'What did you make of Aram Forakis?'

'Bit full of himself, wasn't he?'

Tom smiled but said nothing. Becky had the best nose for bullshit of anyone he knew. He turned back to the monitor as Rob asked once again if Martha was sure she didn't want a solicitor.

'I'm quite sure, thank you.'

'Okay. Maybe you could start by telling us about your movements from when you left work on Monday afternoon until you arrived back there on Tuesday morning,' Rob said.

'I walked to Alfie's childminder, picked up my son, walked home. We were home by five thirty, and I didn't leave the house until eight thirty the next morning. We ate together, I bathed him, put him to bed, read him a story, and then read a book myself until bedtime.'

'At any point during those hours did you leave the house?'

'No. I wouldn't leave my son on his own.'

'Do you know where the Tyldesley Loopline is?' Jenny asked, changing tack completely to see if it threw Martha.

'No.'

'You're not aware that it's a path that runs directly behind Genevieve Strachan's home?'

'I've never been to their home. I know it's in Worsley, and I understand from Elise that it's lovely. I think she used the word "lush".'

Tom glanced at Becky. There was no doubt that Elise's antipathy towards Martha was reciprocated.

'You've never walked along there, or cycled?'

'I don't have a bike, and as I said, I don't know where it is.'

'You mentioned Elise earlier. That would be Elise Chapman, would it?'

'Yes. She works at XO-Tech too.'

'Miss Chapman tells us there was an argument between you and Mrs Strachan a few days before she died. Can you tell us about that, please?'

Rob's manner was calm, but Tom could see that beneath Martha's apparent composure she was agitated. The camera captured her hands in her lap, and she was pulling on her fingers one by one, right hand first and then left.

'She wanted information about the company that I didn't think it was my place to share. I told her to ask her husband.'

'What information?'

'She wanted me to tell her the basis of the deal her husband was negotiating to raise extra funds. She said she had a right to know what the company – and therefore her husband – was worth.'

Rob rested his forearms on the table and leaned forward slightly.

'And you knew?'

'Yes. I prepared the paperwork, but I wouldn't share that information with anyone. She said she was a director and shareholder of the company, so it was my job to tell her. She was neither, and I can't imagine why she would think I didn't know she was lying.'

'You didn't like Genevieve much, did you, Miss Porter?'

'I didn't have any feelings about her one way or the other.'

Jenny leaned forward. 'In spite of the fact that you wanted her husband for yourself?'

Tom watched Martha's response. There was a flash of anger in her eyes, but her voice remained calm.

'I had no interest in Niall. If this is about the party and Elise telling the world that I made a pass at him which he rejected, that's total nonsense. *He* came on to *me*, and I was appalled.'

Jenny didn't give up. 'So why did he avoid being in a room with you alone after that? Everyone noticed.'

Martha sighed. 'I'd turned him down. People knew something had happened, so he had to make it look as if I was doing the chasing and he didn't feel comfortable around me. It was childish nonsense, and I chose to ignore it. I wanted to keep my job, despite his behaviour.'

Jenny pulled a piece of paper from a file and pushed it across the table. 'Can you explain to me why you would send him a message telling him how much you wanted to be with him, and how you would be so much better for him than Genevieve?'

Martha frowned and leaned forward to read the paper without touching it. Finally she flopped back in her chair, looking for a moment as if all the fight had gone out of her. 'I didn't send that. I don't have a Gmail account and I have no interest in Niall Strachan other than as my boss. It's malicious nonsense.'

'Can you think of anyone else who might have sent it, posing as you?'

Martha shook her head slowly. 'Elise, maybe? She's not my greatest fan. I know she'd be thrilled if Niall were interested in her, but I'm not sure she's smart enough to do this. We work for a tech company, though, and those guys can predict every move we make through their app, which I find spooky and uncomfortable but clever nonetheless. Setting up a Gmail account wouldn't exactly tax their skills.'

The more Tom saw of Martha Porter, the more he was inclined to believe her. There was nothing about her demeanour that suggested she would try her luck with a man, uninvited. She was withdrawn, tightly held together, and he couldn't see her exposing her weaknesses to anyone, let alone her boss.

'You mention your phone. Where was your company mobile during the hours of Monday night?'

'It was with me. We're supposed to have our phones on all the time so the app can record our actions and predict our next moves. I refused. I didn't want them to know where I live, let alone give them the ability to switch on some audio device so they can detect what I'm watching on television. I switch it on as I enter the office each morning – it flags up on the system when someone enters or leaves the building – then I switch it off and stick it in my drawer for the rest of the day – then on again when I leave – but only for a few minutes. Then it's off for the rest of the night.'

'And the phone was with you that night, when you were alone apart from Alfie, in your home?'

'Yes.'

'So how do you explain, Miss Porter, that your phone was used to contact Genevieve Strachan on Monday night, to lure her from her home to where she was stabbed to death?'

Martha narrowed her eyes and stared at Rob. When she spoke, her voice was so quiet Tom could barely hear her. 'I can't.'

At that moment Becky's phone vibrated on the table in front of them. She picked it up and left the room.

During the minutes that she was gone Tom watched and listened as Rob and Jenny questioned Martha from every angle about her phone, about the fact that Genevieve's iMessage records showed the number of the phone that called her, and that it was irrefutably Martha's phone. But nothing shook her. She simply denied she had anything to do with it.

Becky quietly let herself back into the room and dropped into her chair as Tom glanced at her. He didn't want to miss anything that was being said in the interview, but Becky was frowning.

'What's up?' he asked.

'Kirsten called – Eddie's wife. She expanded on what she'd told him before. Genevieve was going to leave Niall and was planning on taking him to the cleaners. She told Kirsten she was going to get what was owing to her – half of everything, including the business – and after that she wanted a good time. Niall was boring – always working, obsessed with his new app. She'd contacted Eddie because he was the best at getting into the flashiest parties – or at least he had been – and while she was disappointed that he was married, he'd never been renowned for his faithfulness, so she thought he'd be up for it. Kirsten had given her a mouthful and left. We know Kirsten's telling the truth about where she met Genevieve. We have photo evidence from the so-called friend, and it checks out with the location data that Niall gave us.'

Tom felt strangely unsurprised by any of this. Everything they'd heard about Genevieve suggested she was only interested in one thing – the position of Genevieve Strachan in her own little world. And it also tied in with what Martha had said about the argument in her office. Genevieve was trying to work out how much she was likely to get.

Although he had never run a business himself, Tom knew enough to understand that the paper value of a company was very different to how much money there was in the bank, and if Genevieve had demanded half the perceived value of the business, Niall would have had to sell a further chunk of his shareholding to raise the cash to pay her off.

At that moment Tom's phone buzzed.

Speaking quietly so Becky could continue to listen to the ongoing interview, he answered: 'Yes, Keith.'

'Sir, something has come to light. Something that I think might change everything.'

69

Tom left the room to take Keith's call, leaving Becky to continue observing the interview.

'Tell me, Keith.'

'It's quite technical, and I may not be the best person to explain this. But I can hand you over to someone else if you have questions when I've finished.'

'Just do your best.'

'Do you remember when the telecoms team told us that Martha's company phone had never been used?'

'Yes. No texts, no calls. I remember.'

'Well, it wasn't only that, sir. She hadn't used any mobile data either – you know, 4G or whatever.'

'You mean to log on to the Internet?'

'Not only that, she hadn't used mobile data for anything at all. We know the message to Genevieve asking her to come outside was an iMessage, so it could only have been sent either by mobile data or WiFi. The telecoms team have confirmed that it *definitely* wasn't sent via mobile data.'

Tom was beginning to get a glimmer of where this was going.

'You're saying that if she messaged Genevieve from outside the house it had to have been transmitted via WiFi?'

'Correct. The thing is, the only WiFi signal in the alley is from the Strachan house, if we discount the elderly neighbours who don't even know their own password because their grandson set it up.'

Tom said nothing, but he felt a tingle at the back of his neck. Martha had just said she'd never visited Niall's home, so how would she know his password?

'Bearing this in mind, sir, I took Ms Porter's phone to the passageway myself. The Strachans' WiFi showed up, as I expected, but I was denied access. Ms Porter's phone doesn't have their password stored. The iMessage could not have been sent via WiFi from that mobile phone.'

'So how the hell was it sent, Keith? We know the message came from Martha's number.'

'We do, but the *number* is controlled by the SIM. WiFi *passwords* on this model are stored on the mobile itself – the actual handset. The only conclusion is that the message was sent using Martha's SIM, but it wasn't in Martha's mobile phone at the time.'

Tom's head was buzzing. Someone must have taken her SIM and put it in their own phone. Someone who wasn't Martha Porter. Not only that, whoever that person was, they must already have had the password to the Strachans' WiFi on their phone.

'Martha Porter has told us categorically that she had her mobile with her all night, Keith, and she switched it on in the morning. The SIM must have been in the phone then, and later when Spencer Johansson switched it on again.'

'My thinking exactly, sir, but according to our digital team, a company like XO-Tech would certainly have the know-how to clone a SIM.'

'Christ – it's a tech company! It sounds bloody complicated to me, but it would be a piece of cake for them. Okay – let's see if I've got this: either Martha is lying through her teeth – she *has* been to the Strachan house at some point and logged onto the Internet while there – that should be easy to check; or Martha left her phone in her desk overnight, although she said she didn't, and someone whipped the SIM.' Tom paused, because the last option was the big one, and probably the one most difficult to prove. 'Or this murder was meticulously planned, and her SIM was taken some time prior to the event, cloned, and the original SIM replaced in her phone. Do you agree with those options, Keith?'

'I do, sir. Except if it's the first option, she must have deleted the password after she killed Genevieve, because it's definitely not stored on her device. What do you need me to do?'

'Get on to Niall Strachan and ask him how many members of his staff have visited his home, and how many of them would have been given his WiFi password. We know Elise Chapman has been there, but we don't know who else. Get back to me as soon as you've spoken to him. If we're right, whoever did this was very keen to frame Martha Porter for this murder.'

As the call ended, the door to the interview room opened and Jenny and Rob came out.

'Thought she needed a break, sir,' Jenny said. 'This fella –' she lifted two fingers of both hands as if pointing twin guns at Rob '– is tireless. He could go on all day, but I need a cup of tea, and so does Martha.'

Rob rubbed his hands together. 'She's a tricky customer. She won't crack easily, but I'm waiting to show her the knife. That should be interesting.'

'I'd like you to go back in and ask her a couple more questions, if you could. We need to know if she's certain she had her phone with her on the night of the murder, and also if the phone has been out of her possession for any period of time.'

Rob frowned. 'What's the thinking?'

Tom quickly ran through the conversation with Keith, and Rob's eyes opened wide. 'That's a fascinating twist! And it tells us for sure that our killer has to be someone known to the Strachans – close enough to have been given their WiFi password. Your tea will have to wait, Jenny.' With that, he spun on his heel and headed back for the door.

Becky could sense a new intensity in Tom as he walked back into the room. Something must have happened.

'Why are Rob and Jenny going back in so soon? What's going on?'

Tom explained what Keith had told him.

'Whoa – that's interesting. So someone else could have had Martha's SIM – or a clone – in their phone? God, that's clever.'

'Yes, but not clever enough. Our killer should have realised that their phone would default to a WiFi network if the password was on it. Having said that, I'm not sure I would have considered that if I'd been about to kill someone.'

Becky laughed. 'The idea of you killing someone is slightly beyond the scope of my imagination, so I wouldn't start worrying about how you might get caught just yet.'

Tom smiled vaguely, but Becky could see his mind was firmly on the case. Her eyes returned to the monitor. The two detectives had retaken their seats in the interview room.

'Sorry about the cup of tea,' Rob said. 'We'll sort that in a moment, but we have a couple more questions. Earlier, you told us you had never been to Niall and Genevieve Strachan's home. Are you sure that's the case? They never had a staff party at their house, for example? Summer barbecue, that sort of thing?'

'If they had, I wouldn't have gone. Sergeant, if you've been to the office and met my colleagues, you'll know that I'm no one's favourite person. I don't consider them my friends. They're people I work with, and the less they know about me, the better.'

'You don't like people to know who you really are. Is that it? Is that why you changed your name and lied about where you live?'

Rob was going off script, but on the other hand it was the perfect time to ask the question.

'I didn't want people from my old life to find me. I've become adept at hiding everything about myself, and it made it much easier if I didn't get too close to anyone.'

Becky thought what a sad statement that was. To have no friends, to keep your distance because of something in your past.

'Why would anyone be looking for you, Ms Porter? What is so terrifying that you needed to change your name and hide yourself away from everyone? Your father says he hasn't seen you in nearly six years, and he's never met his grandson before today. And yet you turned up here, asked him to take care of Alfie and then handed yourself in to the police. You have to accept this is difficult for us to understand.'

For the first time Martha looked worried. 'Don't bring my son into this. Please.'

Rob said nothing for a moment. 'We'll leave that for now and come back to it. In the meantime, you told us earlier that your mobile was with you for the whole of Monday night. Did you switch it on at all?'

'As I told you before, only when I left the office, then immediately off again, and back on when I arrived on Tuesday morning.'

'And your phone worked as normal?'

'Yes, of course. I don't know what you're getting at, Sergeant.'

'Has anyone else had access to your phone at any time in the last few weeks?'

Martha's eyes narrowed, and Becky leaned closer to the monitor. She could see that Martha was trying to work something out.

'My phone had to be updated, so I was asked to hand it over for a day.'

'Surely updates are done via WiFi?'

'Usually, but the app isn't live yet. It's a prototype, so I guess it's easier to upload revised versions manually. Not that I ever use it. I find it unnerving.'

'And who asked for your phone?'

'Elise. She said she had to take it to the tech team.'

Becky sat back in her chair and looked at Tom. They both knew that Elise had been to Niall's home. Had she used the WiFi when she was there?

'Do you really think someone cloned the SIM in Martha's phone, Tom? It sounds a bit far-fetched to me.'

'More to the point, Becky, if someone did, and it wasn't Martha who killed Genevieve, then someone went to great lengths to set her up. Who would do that? And why?'

70

Tom, Becky, Rob and Jenny crowded round the computer in the borrowed office. Keith was sitting far too close to the screen back in Manchester, and his face looked wider in the middle and narrower at the top and bottom. It was disconcerting, but Tom didn't have the heart to ask him to sit back a bit.

'I want to go through the evidence against Martha Porter with everyone. Let's see what we've got,' Tom said. 'Start with motive. Our assumption was that Martha had formed a romantic, sexual or obsessive attachment to Niall Strachan, and she needed to get Genevieve out of the way so her path was clear. I've always thought it was a weak motive, but it's not unheard of. It's not that long ago that a woman was stabbed to death by her love rival – and not a million miles from Manchester either.'

'Hang on a minute, boss,' Rob said. 'If I remember rightly, the evidence that solved the case was the ability to place the killer's mobile phone at the scene. It was big news. If someone set Martha up, maybe that's where they got the idea from.'

Tom nodded. 'Good point, but let's decide if we're ruling Martha in or out first. Could there be any other motive?'

'I think we should have the company's finances fully audited,' Keith said. 'Maybe she was stealing from XO-Tech.'

'But why kill Genevieve? Did she have access to any of the financial information that could have implicated Martha in theft or fraud? I doubt it, but it might provide a real motive. Going back to the love angle, do we believe Martha offered herself to Niall and became obsessed with him?'

'I don't,' Becky said. 'She's so self-contained. We could get a forensic linguist to look at the messages to see if she wrote them.'

'Excellent idea. Next, let's consider opportunity. Rob, your thoughts?'

'Chiropodist's bike, maybe? She'd have had to leave Alfie unattended, but he's not much of an alibi. Sadly, people do it all the time.'

'Keith, what did Niall Strachan say about people who might have access to his WiFi password?'

'He wanted to know why it mattered. I didn't tell him, but he's not stupid. I sensed unease, and I wish I'd been talking to him face to face instead of on the phone. He sent me a list of people who have been to the house. I can go through it now, if you like, but we're looking into each of them back here.'

'No need. Is Elise Chapman on the list?'

'She is. But then so is everyone else we've talked to. Spencer Johansson goes round for marketing meetings, and Bao, the techie, regularly goes out to update Niall's home system.'

'It doesn't narrow it down much,' Tom said, his shoulders drooping. He glanced around at the members of his team and then back at the screen, where Keith was even closer to the camera. 'I'll talk to Detective Superintendent Stanley, but personally I think the CPS would throw out the case against Martha based on the evidence we have. For everything we can prove, there's an answer. I'm not ready to release her yet, but we can't charge her. We've got twenty hours left before we have to apply for an extension. Let's use that time to see what else we can discover. Everyone agreed?'

One by one the members of his team nodded slowly, disheartened that the case they believed they had closed with Martha's arrest was now wide open again.

Tom could feel their despondency; he needed to get this case back on track. 'On a positive note, based on what Kirsten Carlson said, it seems Genevieve was planning to leave Niall on the grounds of boredom. She wanted to fleece him, and that gives Niall the perfect motive. Sadly we haven't found a single piece of evidence that puts him in the frame.'

Around him, the team began to theorise. Tom shut their voices out then stood up. 'Rob, you're with me.'

Becky glanced at him with a question in her eyes.

'We're going back in to talk to Martha, and I want you listening and watching, Becky. If we're prepared to accept that maybe she isn't the killer – for now, at least – we also have to accept that whoever killed Genevieve wanted Martha to take the fall for it. The case against her was carefully constructed and only falls apart because of a WiFi password. If we accept that Martha *didn't* offer herself to Niall – and I know you have a strong tendency to believe her – then someone wanted to make it seem she did, through the emails. Those emails demonstrated motive, and that took time to build. I think Rob's right: they got the idea from the recent murder case in Lancashire. The mobile phone had to be the evidence.'

'If Martha didn't try to seduce Niall, why was he keeping his distance?' Rob asked.

'That was for show,' Becky said. 'I bet Niall tried it on, she rejected him and was seen running from the room. He couldn't let the world know someone had turned him down, so he played the part of a man scared of being grabbed by the balls in his own office.'

'Nicely put, Becky!' Tom said. 'And I agree he wouldn't want to be seen as the one who was rejected. So, if anyone knows why Martha would have been set up, I think we know where to get the answer. Martha herself.'

71

MARTHA

Their questioning has unnerved me. How do they have so much evidence that seems to point to me? I think back to the party and that awful moment with Niall in the kitchen.

He'd stood behind me, talking about what a great boss he was and how he thought I should be kind to him, given everything he did for me.

Everything he did for me? I worked for him, kept his financial secrets – and any others as and when appropriate. All I asked in return was to be paid a fair salary and to be left to get on with my job. I was good at it.

Why did he choose me to try to seduce? I'm certain that half the women in the office would have considered it an honour. I was the exception, and I can only think that must have been his motivation. Perhaps I was a challenge.

Unfortunately I was slicing lemons for gin and tonics when it happened, holding the knife that we keep for the purpose. Niall came up behind me, put his hands on my hips and nuzzled my neck as if we were already lovers. When he whispered his suggestion, a smile in his voice as if I was unlikely to refuse, I spun round with the knife in my hand. I had no intention of using it, but he looked at it in horror.

'Jesus, Martha, I thought you'd be flattered!'

Why? Why would I have been flattered? I dropped the knife and ran from the room, passing Spencer on the way. I can see how Niall was able to spin it to suggest I was the guilty one, but at the time I didn't care. He wouldn't sack me – I was too good at my job – but he had to make me look stupid in front of everyone else, which was fine by me.

Then there was the argument with Genevieve. It was clear she had no idea how much XO-Tech might be worth, and she was the sort of woman who'd want facts and figures before showing her hand. She was a schemer, and there was little point filing for a divorce if Niall's shareholding in the company was worthless. Timing was everything. It irked her that I wouldn't give her the information she needed and told her to ask her husband, and she hated me for knowing she couldn't. She'd turned nasty, saying she'd tell Niall to sack me.

I don't believe Niall had ever concerned himself with how much I knew until then. I'm fully aware of where he hides the money he's been siphoning out of the business, and I know how he does it. He's a clever man. If Genevieve was planning to fleece him – which was the only interpretation that made sense to me – then there was only one person who knew where the bodies were buried.

Me.

The tall, good-looking chief inspector and his energetic young colleague have come back into the room with yet more questions. I just want this over, because all I want to think about is Alfie – where he is, what he's doing. I wanted to speak to Dad when I was arrested, but I only had the number for the B & B, and the woman who answered told me he'd gone out. I hope that means they have just gone to the beach.

'Ms Porter,' the chief inspector says, dragging my mind back into the room. 'Detective Sergeant Cumba and his colleague have been interviewing you about the murder of Genevieve Strachan, and there is considerable evidence against you. I'd like to put it to you that if you're telling the truth, someone has gone to a great deal of trouble to set you up. Why would they do that?'

I stare at him, unable to answer. My thoughts go first to Aram, as they always do. If he already knew about Alfie, what better way would there be to get me out of the way? But he couldn't have done this. The questions have all been about emails I'm supposed to have sent to Niall and my argument with Genevieve. Aram couldn't have set that up.

'I don't know,' I tell him finally. 'I can't think of any motive. It can't be jealousy. Everyone believes Niall rejected me. Maybe I was an easy person to set up because I have no social life, friends, partner – anyone to provide me with an alibi.'

'You went to significant lengths to eradicate any trace that you'd ever been at XO-Tech, including wiping details of your mobile from the system. Why would you do that?'

I shrug. 'Habit. I remove all traces of myself from anywhere I've ever been.'

The chief inspector leans forward. He doesn't seem aggressive; he seems genuinely interested.

'Why?' he asks.

'Do you know anything about Aram Forakis?' I ask.

I think I see a hint of compassion in his eyes as he answers. 'We do.'

'Since I escaped from Lakeside, Aram Forakis has been looking for me. If he'd found me, he would have forced me to return, and he'd have done everything in his power to take my son away from me.'

'He's the father?'

'He is, but please don't preach to me about a father's rights. Alfie is not being brought up by that man. I won't see him forced, as I was, to stand in front of everyone he knows and listen as his faults are exposed, as he's told that he's a burden on the community, that he is nothing but a hindrance to the happiness of his parents – who are no longer to be called Mum and Dad…' I hear my voice rise. 'You don't know the half of it. And now he knows Alfie is close by. And I'm stuck here, unable to keep him safe.'

My eyes flood with tears. I take deep breaths. I just need to get this over with.

'Do you think Mr Forakis will harm your son?' the chief inspector asks, and I hear the concern in his voice.

'Define "harm",' I say with a bitter laugh. 'Will he physically hurt or abuse him? No. I doubt it. Will he damage his mind, his soul, his spirit? Oh yes. Beyond a shadow of a doubt. That's why I need to get out of here. I'll answer any questions you want to ask me. Anything to speed this up.'

I see genuine sympathy in the eyes of both men as they wait for me to continue. I try to calm myself and take a sip of water.

'You asked why I remove all traces of myself. It sounds like paranoia, but Aram's followers come from all sorts of professions, and they're often intelligent, successful individuals, but they're also lost souls dominated by him. I'm sure he's spread the word far and wide via his YouTube channel. If any one of his devotees discovered where I was, they would tell him immediately. They would do it because Aram asked them to.'

'I can understand why you felt you had to hide,' the chief inspector says, 'but the question is, what do you know that is potentially so damaging that someone set you up as a murderer? There must be some reason why they chose you.'

I think about the gossip in the office, and there's nothing of consequence. I think of everything I know about the company, about Niall and Genevieve, and maybe there is something.

'I can't tie it all together. I know bits and pieces, but nothing that forms a coherent pattern.'

He smiles at me. 'That's our job. You give us the pieces, and we'll try to match them up.'

'Okay.' I try to concentrate, to put things in a logical order, but the ideas come to me in flashes, images, like a collage that makes no sense. 'Niall used to leave the office via the back stairs a couple of times a week. I don't know where he was going, and I never asked. No one was allowed to know – not even Spencer. If anyone came looking for him, I was to say he was on a conference call.'

I don't add that I think he was having an affair because I don't know for certain.

'Genevieve was interested in the money – how much the company was worth and the value of Niall's shares. I got the distinct impression she was thinking about a potential divorce settlement.'

'Do you know the answers to her questions?' DS Cumba asks.

'It's complicated. Niall has been bleeding money from the company for a while, but the new investors were bound to examine the books as part of their due diligence, so he needed to cover the shortfall. I'm certain Spencer Johansson put in money to repay what Niall had taken. None of it would be documented, because then it could be exposed and used against Niall and XO-Tech. I wasn't supposed to know, but they're not particularly good at hiding their tracks. So Niall's net worth appears much higher on paper than it is in reality.'

I can see a light in the chief inspector's eyes. He likes the sound of this.

'Why would Spencer Johansson hand over a chunk of his money without anything in writing?' the younger detective asks.

That almost makes me laugh. People have been handing over money to Aram Forakis for years on the promise of something as nebulous as eternal happiness. Spencer only had to believe in the boasts of his own marketing materials, and to him Niall is a hero, a demigod, the man who is ultimately going to make him rich beyond his wildest dreams.

'Niall's great at promises,' I tell them. 'People believe him, and believe *in* him. Spencer trusted him to transfer some shares. Not that it's happened. I heard them talking about it, and Niall always had an excuse.'

'And if Genevieve had taken Niall for fifty per cent of the assets shown in the books, where would that have left things?' He's looking at me intently, but I have a feeling he already knows the answer.

'Niall would have had to sell his remaining shareholding, as a minimum. He'd have ended up with nothing.'

72

Tom could feel the buzz he always got when he knew the answers were so close he could almost touch them. If Niall didn't have a cast-iron alibi, Tom would right now be getting someone to drag him down to the police station. But unfortunately, he did.

He strode down the corridor, Becky at his side. She was saying nothing, he was certain her mind would be whirring just as his was.

He pushed open the door to the office and found a number on his phone. His call was answered after two rings.

'Keith, I've got several things I need you to follow up on. I want you to go in person to see Elise Chapman and look her in the eye as she gives you an answer. Ask her why she took Martha's phone to be updated, who asked her, and who did she give the phone to.'

'Got that,' Keith said.

'Then I want you to get someone to go through the company's finances carefully. Check exactly where a recent cash injection came from – not the millions from the venture capital. We think some money came from Spencer Johansson, so look at his finances too.'

'Okay,' Keith murmured, and Tom knew he would be getting all this down in his meticulous handwriting.

'Finally, do some more digging on Strachan. He regularly left the office in the afternoon, but he used the back stairs and no one knew he'd gone out. If he was having an affair, we need to know who with.'

'Anything else?'

'No. I think that's plenty to be going on with. My gut is telling me it's Niall Strachan, and I wish to God we could break his bloody alibi. But unless inspiration strikes, it's not looking likely.'

Tom ended the call and looked at Becky. 'Thoughts?'

She didn't have time to reply before they were interrupted by Tom's phone.

'Jumbo! What news?'

'All good, Tom. All good. We've found a branch we believe was used to attack our victim. You might remember that opposite the bottom of the steps from the murder scene to the Loopline there's another flight. They lead through a rickety gate to a field. We'd already searched the path, but I extended the search beyond that, and my guy spotted it straight away. It wasn't just a broken branch. It had been cut, and even with the naked eye we can see some hairs stuck to it. My betting is that they belong to Genevieve Strachan. We may find prints, but only if our killer is really stupid, which I suspect he or she isn't.'

'Let's hope they've made another mistake, because we think they've made one with the phone.' Tom quickly explained what they had discovered.

'Excellent! I love it when a carefully constructed plan fails through a tiny mistake. And I haven't finished with the good news. At the far end of that field there's a rough piece of land that we thought was a likely parking spot.'

'I know where you mean.'

'Here's the thing. It rained on Monday night, but it stopped at about ten p.m. There are tyre tracks in the dried mud. Looks like an SUV, but we're having them checked to be sure.'

A thought struck Tom. 'If they went that way, why did we find the knife under the culvert? That's in the opposite direction.'

Jumbo chuckled. 'I'm wondering if the plan was to leave the knife where we would find it, especially if they were setting someone up. It's always worried me because it could have been hurled into the undergrowth anywhere, but instead it was just inside the culvert – easy to spot. I'm guessing our killer jogged down, dropped the knife where we would find it, then ran back, hoping we'd check parking spots further on along the Loopline beyond the culvert.'

'Smart, but not smart enough. Thanks, Jumbo.' Tom ended the call.

Their killer might not be that clever, but Tom had to admit they still didn't know who it was.

FRIDAY

73

By the time they had finished interviewing Martha Porter the previous evening, Tom and Becky had both admitted to feeling weary. They'd been working long hours, and despite wanting to get home, they'd decided the sensible thing to do was to take advantage of the hotel that had been booked. If they had driven back it would have been far too late for Tom to see Lucy, and when he spoke to Louisa she'd told him to make the most of an uninterrupted night's sleep.

They were on the road shortly after 7 a.m., and Becky had been driving for a little over half an hour before Tom voiced his thoughts.

'Enough shilly-shallying with Niall Strachan. If we believe Martha, and he's the one that made the pass at her – and I know you do, Becky – then he lied to us. What else has he lied about, and why the hell was he sneaking out of the office a couple of times a week?'

They were back on the A1(M) heading towards the M62 and home. The sooner they could tell Rob to let Martha Porter go, the happier he would be. He no longer trusted the evidence against her, but she was still their chief suspect – and a flight risk, as well they knew.

'You're getting grumpy, Tom,' Becky said. 'You always do at this point in an investigation.'

He turned to look at her, and she quickly glanced his way and laughed.

'Don't look so surprised! You genuinely believe you should know from day one exactly what happened, and who did what. And when you follow a lead that turns out – despite evidence to the contrary – to be wrong, you blame yourself. And then you get grumpy.'

Tom turned back and stared out of the window. She was probably right. He'd said all along that he didn't want to become blind to other possibilities just because Martha seemed so obvious a suspect, and here he was, trailing around the east of England when he should have been back in the office.

'I'm going to call Strachan,' he said. 'See what he's got to say for himself.'

'You sure about that?'

'Absolutely. And if he stalls, I'll say we're sending someone to bring him in for questioning.'

He pulled out his mobile, put it on speaker and called the number he'd stored.

'Mr Strachan. DCI Douglas here. I need to ask you a question, and I would be grateful if you would give me a straight answer. I don't want to have to ask you to come in for an interview unless it's necessary.'

'Of course. Ask whatever you like.'

There's a confident man, Tom thought. Something about Niall Strachan rankled, or maybe it was just the way he was feeling at that moment. The man seemed too smooth – as smooth as Brylcreem, as his dad used to say. He wouldn't repeat that to Becky. She'd have no idea what he was talking about.

'Were you having an affair?'

Out of the corner of his eye he saw Becky look at him. He knew he was being blunt, but there was no point beating around the bush.

Niall Strachan was quiet, and Tom waited.

'Not exactly. I was seeing someone occasionally, but I wouldn't call it an affair.'

Tom struggled to keep the irritation out of his voice. 'I guess that's just semantics, Mr Strachan.'

Strachan sighed. 'Come on, Mr Douglas. You know how it is.' Tom turned towards Becky, who had heard every word, and raised his eyebrows. She flashed him a cheeky grin. 'There was someone, but it wasn't serious.'

'To you, maybe not. But what about the woman – sorry, that's an inappropriate assumption – the person you were seeing.'

'*She*... is no more interested in a relationship than I am. If you're thinking she had something to do with Genevieve, then you're wrong.'

'Did your wife know about her?'

'No. I'm not sure it would have mattered to her, though. She wasn't the jealous sort.'

Tom didn't comment. He found it strange not to care if one's partner was having sex with someone else, but each to their own.

'Does she work at XO-Tech?' He was tempted to ask if her name was, by any chance, Elise Chapman. But he resisted.

'Of course not. I'm not that stupid.'

There was no suitable response to that, much as Tom wanted to make one.

'We need her details, please. Maybe you could text me her name and phone number. And Mr Strachan? You should have told us this at the start.'

With that, Tom hung up and slouched back in his seat.

'You only said that because you don't like him,' Becky said.

'Possibly, but it's true. He should have told us. Anyway, he's an insolent bugger, suggesting that because I'm a man I would understand his cheating ways. And it was a bit rich saying he wasn't stupid enough to have an affair with someone in the office when he'd tried it on with Martha.' Tom glanced at Becky, who was clearly amused by his antagonism towards Niall Strachan. 'Anyway, irritation aside, let's get back to motive. We know – or at least we *believe* – that Genevieve was planning to leave Niall and take half his assets, and adultery would have provided handy grounds for claiming irretrievable breakdown of the marriage.'

'You think this is all to do with money, don't you?'

'I think it's the most likely reason, yes. But that still points to Niall, and we know it couldn't have been him.'

'Contract killer?' Becky said.

'He'd certainly know how to get on to the dark web to recruit one.'

It was a startling fact that contract killings were becoming more common, and not only by hitmen who charged six-figure sums. If you knew what you were doing you could head to the right pub, in the right part of town, and find someone down on their luck who would do just about anything for the price of a good meal.

Tom's phone interrupted them, and once again he put it on speaker.

'Yes, Keith. What have you got?'

'How long until you're back, sir?'

Tom looked at Becky. 'About an hour and a half,' she shouted.

'Excellent, because I think we may have got him.'

Tom shuffled upright in his seat. '*What?*'

'I followed up on everything on your list. Elise Chapman says Spencer Johansson asked her to get Martha's phone. We also checked the finances. I'm assuming you already know part of this, which is why you asked us to look, but money was put into the company to replace withdrawals by Mr Strachan. The money *appears* to have come directly from Strachan himself, as far as the company accounts go. But I don't think it's that simple.'

Keith paused, and Tom shook his head. Why did he have to drag everything out?

'Tell me, Keith. What do you think it is?'

'We looked into Mr Johansson's finances. He owns an apartment in Ancoats, in one of those converted mills, you know? He paid cash – money that he made in the last company he worked for. He recently remortgaged it and raised half a million, which it appears he gave to Strachan to put into XO-Tech – to cover the shortfall.'

'Christ, that's a risky thing to do. The powers of persuasion and the promise of a better life!'

'He didn't put quite all of his money into XO-Tech, though. He used over forty thousand of it to buy a top-of-the-range Jeep Wrangler. An SUV.'

Tom knew what a Jeep Wrangler was, and it certainly suited the image that Johansson liked to portray. He seriously hoped this meant what he thought it did. All they needed was for Jumbo to compare tyre tracks.

Tom tried to curb his growing excitement. 'There's more, isn't there?'

Keith was smiling; Tom could hear it in his voice. 'Yes, sir. If you remember, Mr Johansson made a call to Mr Strachan after midnight. It appears Johansson switched his phone off at eleven p.m., but at twelve eighteen a.m. the signal was re-established. He was travelling at that time, and he spoke to Mr Strachan at twelve twenty. He was driving along Regent Road towards his home in Ancoats.'

Tom thought of the geography in his head. The best route from Worsley to Ancoats included Regent Road – the end of the M602. The timing worked too. Time to run partway along the Loopline, dispose of the knife and run back to where his car was parked.

'You are a superstar, DI Sims!' There was silence from the other end of the phone. Keith wasn't a man who knew how to accept praise. 'Go get him, Keith. Seize his car, check the tyres, blood in the car, you know the drill. Bring him in, and he can wait for us. Let him stew a while. And well done.' He hung up and turned to Becky. 'I think I might kiss Keith when we get back.'

'*Please* make sure I'm there when you do. Anyway, great as all of this is, why kill Genevieve? Why set up Martha?'

'I can guess, but let's hear what he has to say.'

74

MARTHA

Last night, they brought me to this cell. I stood in the doorway for too long, but the officer was kind. I don't know why he would be. They must be used to locking people up, but he seemed to realise that the thought of being shut in terrified me. Despite everything that happened during my life at Lakeside – the ritual humiliation, the shunning – I was never locked in. I was ignored, stared at with disdain, saw faces turn away at the sight of me, but never shut behind a locked door.

I didn't think I would suffer from claustrophobia, but since the moment the bolt slid into place, I have shivered despite the humid heat, which barely eased during the night. Every time I stand up, I have to sit down quickly as dizziness overtakes me, and I feel as if the previous inhabitants of the cell are laughing at me for being so pathetic.

I will be interviewed again this morning, apparently. I'm still their main suspect – their only suspect at the moment as far as I know – and they have twenty-four hours to charge me, ask for an extension or let me go. It's all been explained to me.

I lay awake all night, missing Alfie with every bone in my body. I have never been apart from him overnight before, and he's going to wonder why I have deserted him. Is he still safe with Dad?

I've made such a mess of this. When I turned right on the motorway towards Lincolnshire instead of left to Northumberland I was thinking only of putting an end to it all – of freeing myself finally from Aram's control by destroying the evidence he holds. But he shouldn't be allowed to get away with what he did. A wonderful young woman died, and I have said nothing.

Right now I have to focus on getting out of here, getting Alfie to safety. I close my eyes and picture my son giggling at a silly face I drew on his boiled egg; his look of concentration, tongue sticking out, as he decorated a pizza; his eyes filling with tears when he saw a neglected puppy on the television. If I confess that I have hidden knowledge of Leah's murder for years, there is no happy ending for him, and I'd still have to convince the police that I am the one telling the truth; that Aram's evidence proves only that I touched Leah and pulled out the knife. There's nothing that points to Aram being her killer, so it would be my word against his.

I can't do it. I need to save my son from his father.

I have no more time to think. I hear the lock on my door clunk. Someone is coming.

It's the kind officer from last night – either at the end of his shift or starting a new one.

'Come on, Ms Porter. The policeman from Manchester, DS Cumba, wants to talk to you.'

I stand up too quickly and have to reach out for the wall.

'Steady on,' the officer says. 'I'll get someone to bring you some tea. You had your breakfast, didn't you?'

I shake my head and nod towards the tray, where I left it.

'Sorry,' I whisper.

'I'll get you a sandwich, then. Can't have you passing out on us. Come on.'

He extends an arm – not to touch me, but to let me know he's there if I need help.

When I walk into the interview room, DS Cumba is there with another policeman that I don't recognise.

'Martha, I have some news,' DS Cumba says. 'My colleagues in Manchester are about to arrest someone else for Genevieve's murder. We'll be checking your story against theirs and hopefully we'll have more information soon. I'm afraid they've not been charged yet, so I can't tell you who it is.'

He doesn't need to. I'm sure I know. My head spins again and I hold on to the desk. I know they still have to check my story, but I'm telling the truth. Maybe it won't be long before I can go and get Alfie.

'But that's not the only reason we want to talk to you. While we have you here, this officer would like to pick your brains about someone who we think may have stayed at Lakeside a few years ago.' DS Cumba nods at his colleague.

'Ms Porter, I'm DI Oldbury from the Lincolnshire Police. A few years ago, someone came looking for her friend, a young woman who she believed had visited Lakeside, perhaps even stayed there for a month or so. No one had heard from her for quite a long time, which was apparently unusual, so the friend became concerned and wasn't sure if she should report her missing. The woman had no close family, so we decided to make some routine enquiries and went along to speak to Mr Forakis. He confirmed that she had indeed been a visitor, but she'd left to go travelling. It's now an open missing person's case, so any light you can throw on it would be helpful. I thought as the two of you are close in age, she might have mentioned to you where she was planning on going.'

I know what's coming, and I don't know if the horror I'm feeling is showing on my face.

'Her name's Leah Medway. Do you remember her?'

The room turns black. I feel hands grabbing me as I slide to the floor.

75

'What the hell happened?' were Tom's first words as he marched into the incident room. 'How did he get away?'

Keith stood up straight. 'I'm sorry, sir. I got the search warrant, and Cass went with some uniformed officers to arrest Johansson and seize his car about thirty minutes ago. When the officers buzzed his apartment from the entrance to the building, he answered and told them to come to the fourth floor. While they waited for the lift, he must have run down the fire escape to the underground garage. They reached his door, but he didn't open up. It took a while for them to realise he'd gone.'

'Bollocks!' Tom looked at Keith's crestfallen face. 'No one's fault. At least he has a distinctive car. We're on it, I assume?'

'We are. Every officer on the streets is looking for him, and the area's well covered with CCTV. I'm amazed we've not spotted him yet, but if I were a betting man, which I'm not, I would say he'll ditch the car as soon as he can.'

Keith was probably right. But what had made Spencer think they were about to arrest him? They could have been going to ask him some more questions. Tom was fairly sure the officers hadn't rolled up with sirens and flashing lights, so how had he known he was under suspicion?

'If you ditched the car, what would you do? Anybody?'

'Head for the nearest train station,' Becky said. 'And I wouldn't worry about where I left my car. I'd just dump it as close as I could get.'

'Closest to Ancoats is Piccadilly. Agreed?'

Becky nodded. 'There's not much in it by car, but if I was on foot and trying to stick to the back roads to avoid being spotted, I'd definitely head for Piccadilly – get the other side of the ring road first, and then abandon the car.'

'Get on to British Transport Police. Send them Johansson's photo. We need them to scour CCTV at both stations and be ready to arrest him the minute he's spotted.'

'I'm on it,' Becky said. As her partner, Mark, was an officer in the BTP, she knew many of his colleagues.

'Keith, did we find out who Niall Strachan was seeing – this other woman of his?'

'We did,' Keith said. 'I asked her to come in this morning. She arrived about ten minutes before you did, but I thought I should check with you before we talk to her, in case there's anything specific.'

'No, only the obvious. Come on. You're with me. Let's see if Strachan let slip any thoughts about his wife.'

Keith looked a little puzzled, as well he might since the man had a cast-iron alibi and they had the perfect suspect in Spencer Johansson.

'For Johansson to run, he must have had a reason,' Tom said. 'No one other than us knew about the tyre tracks, or that we'd traced the location of his phone when he called Strachan. But one piece of information crucial to the investigation is the fact that the call was made from a phone which had the Strachans' WiFi password on it. The only person who knew we were interested in that list was Strachan himself. I'd put money on him telling Johansson. He may have let it drop in conversation, but equally he may have had a specific and rather more urgent reason.'

Keith's eyes opened wide for a second as he realised what Tom was suggesting.

Half an hour later, Tom was back in the incident room. He pulled out a chair next to Becky's desk and flopped into it.

'That was thirty minutes of my life that I'll never get back.'

'No use, then?'

'Bloody waste of time. Do you know, she told me off for using possessive pronouns? "I'm not *his* mistress or *his* lover. In fact, I'm not *his* anything!" Apparently, Strachan was a convenient, if rather uninspired, occasional shag.'

'Do you believe her?'

'I do, actually. She says she's writing an article on sex with older men.' Tom rolled his eyes. 'Niall Strachan is thirty-four!'

Becky laughed, and Tom pulled himself upright.

'It doesn't matter what she said, to be honest; I don't think this is anything to do with Strachan's sex life. Here's what I'd like you to do…'

They were interrupted by Becky's phone. She picked it up, listened, grinned at Tom and punched the air.

'Thanks, mate – just what we wanted to hear.' She hung up. 'They've got him, Tom. Johansson. Piccadilly, trying to board a train to London. He's being brought here as we speak.'

Tom breathed out. Progress at last.

'What was it you were going to ask me to do?'

Tom gave a slow, satisfied smile. 'I want you to take someone and go and arrest Niall Strachan.'

Her eyebrows nearly shot through the roof, but she nodded. 'I presume the grounds are conspiracy to commit murder?'

'Correct. If I'm wrong, we can let him go without charging him. But I'm not.'

76

As Tom took his seat opposite Spencer Johansson, he could see a thin film of sweat on the man's skin and his pupils were dilated. Tom had absolutely no doubt that he was looking at Genevieve's murderer.

He had decided to leave Becky out of these interviews. Both she and Tom had already formed opinions – not at all favourable – of Johansson and Strachan, and it would be good to get someone else's assessment of both characters.

'Mr Johansson, you and I have met before, but this is Detective Inspector Sims. We'd like to ask you a few questions. I understand they read you your rights when you were arrested.'

'*Arrested!* Isn't that a bit extreme? I'm perfectly happy to answer your questions, but you didn't need to *arrest* me. What motive could I possibly have to kill Genevieve?' He tried to smile, but it was a poor attempt.

'That's what we're hoping to find out. You can start by telling us why you ran when our officers came to your apartment.'

'I didn't *run*, exactly. I was planning a trip to London for the weekend and I suddenly thought that if you had a lot of questions, it would delay me. It made sense to leave. I was planning on phoning you from the train to say I'd pop in on Monday to answer anything outstanding.'

'You'd *pop in*! How very considerate of you. This, if I might remind you, is a murder enquiry. It doesn't wait for three days while you go off on a jolly.' Tom could feel his temper rising. It had been a tough week but it wouldn't help the case if he lost it with a suspect.

Spencer had dropped his head and was fiddling with a signet ring, spinning it round and round.

'Tell me about your investment in XO-Tech,' Tom asked, trying to take the heat out of the interview a little.

Spencer lifted his head. 'I wanted in. It's a brilliant concept, and I'm a good marketeer. I had access to some money, so I bought my way in.'

'Except you didn't, did you?'

Spencer flushed slightly and shuffled in his seat. 'The shares haven't been transferred yet, but Niall's on it. It will happen soon.'

'And if Genevieve had divorced him?' Tom asked.

Spencer tried to chuckle, but it didn't quite work. 'She wouldn't have done that. She loved him.'

'She *was* going to do that, and I think you knew it. According to my financial wizards, of which we have a fair number in the police, if she took him for half the perceived value of his shareholding and half the house – although that's mortgaged to the hilt – he would have precious little left, having given away a massive chunk to a second lot of investors. Have I got that right?'

'That's not my problem, though, is it? That's Niall's problem.'

'It is, but he used the cash from you to pay back money he took from the business. If he'd converted your so-called investment into shares for you, it would have diluted his own shareholding even further. Genevieve knew, didn't she – what he'd done? She tried to get Martha Porter to give her information. Martha refused, but somehow Genevieve found out. She would have demanded half of the book value of his shares, and my guess is that by the time

Genevieve had finished with him, he'd have ended up with next to nothing.'

'As I said, his problem.'

Spencer's jaw was clenched, but he kept twitching. Tom knew his theory was spot on.

'Not if there weren't enough shares left to go round. When you gave him the money, did you have an agreement in writing?'

'Not in writing, no.' The words were mumbled, as if Spencer didn't want to admit to his own gullibility. 'You don't need contracts if you trust someone, do you?'

'Maybe not, although I'll be interested to know if you still think that by the end of the day.'

Spencer didn't respond, but he clearly knew the game was up. Not only would Niall have told him they were checking up on the WiFi password, the Strachans' bedroom window had a good view of the field where the CSIs had been searching. Tom watched his face carefully as he spoke.

'We've got your car, Mr Johansson, and we're checking the tyres for mud that matches a field close to the Loopline.' There was no reaction. Tom was right – he already knew. 'We're also checking the interior for any trace of blood – and no matter what you did, there will *be* a trace. We have your phone. Even if you've deleted the password to the Strachans' WiFi, we'll be able to prove that you did have it. Don't doubt that for one second. I just need the answer to one question. Was it your idea to kill Genevieve, or Niall Strachan's?'

77

MARTHA

I must have only lost consciousness briefly, but when I came round there was a glass of water in front of me, and the kind officer from the custody suite was offering me a banana.

'Might be easier to eat than a sandwich right now,' he said, peeling the top of the skin back and passing it to me. I didn't want to eat it, but I needed some strength. 'We're going to leave you in peace for a while until you feel a bit better. Would you prefer to stay here or go back to your cell?'

Not the cell – please, not the cell.

'Can I stay here, please?'

'Of course. There's an officer outside the door, if you need anything, and DI Oldbury will be back to talk to you in a while.'

Since he left, I've been sitting here alone. They know Leah is missing. They're looking for her. I've never been asked about her before, and I don't know if I can lie – she deserves so much more. She was kind to me, the only friend I ever had. Should I say she left to go travelling, or is this my opportunity to tell them the truth? If I do, will that change their view on the murder of Genevieve

Strachan? They may have arrested someone else, but it will inevitably make them wonder if I'm more involved than they think right now. *I don't know what to do!*

I drop my head into my hands. Since I was ten my life has been confusing. It's impossible for me to forget all the times I was told I was selfish, thoughtless, inconsiderate. For years my only goal in life was to please one man and make him proud of me. I find it so hard to identify who the real me is, as opposed to the demoralised, oppressed version, and making decisions for myself is so difficult.

I have no more time to think, because the door opens and DS Cumba and DI Oldbury are back in the room.

'How are you feeling?' DS Cumba asks.

I grasp my hands tightly together so they can't see how much they're shaking. 'A little better. I've been worried about my son all night. I'm sorry if I've been a bit pathetic.'

He shakes his head. 'Not at all. And before we go any further, I have more news. DCI Douglas has called and asked me to tell you that you are now free to leave.'

He gives me a wide smile, and I just stare at him.

The words take a minute to sink in, but while I'm absorbing them, DI Oldbury speaks: 'I'm sorry. I shouldn't have asked you about Leah Medway when you'd just spent a night in a police cell for something that it now seems clear you didn't do. You must have been feeling very unsettled. If you do think of anything, though – anything that might help us track Leah down – can you let me know? Here's my card.'

I reach out to take it and it's obvious to everyone how much my hand is shaking. 'Sorry. I should have eaten my breakfast.'

'And last night's dinner, I'm told,' DI Oldbury adds with a sympathetic look.

'Are you up to leaving now?' DS Cumba asks. 'You need to pick up your things from the desk, and then we can arrange a car to take you back to Lakeside, or to the B and B, if you prefer.'

'I need to find my father. Alfie's with him. Can I call the B and B, please?'

'Of course,' DS Cumba says. 'I've got the number stored, in case we needed to get in touch with him.' He scrolls up his screen and passes the phone to me.

'Victoria House,' a woman says in a sing-song voice.

'It's Martha Porter. Is my father there, please?'

'Oh, hello, Ms Porter. Your dad's such a nice man, and what a cute little boy you have.'

I know she's being pleasant, but I just want to speak to Dad.

'Thank you. Is he there, or have they gone to the beach?'

'No, he had a call last night. The woman who asked to speak to him said she was his wife. I wasn't listening, of course, but I did hear him say "I'll be there first thing in the morning". I don't know where he meant, I'm afraid.'

She might not know, but I do.

He's gone to Lakeside, and he's taken my son.

78

A faint cheer went up when Tom and Keith returned to the incident room. While they were in with Johansson, Jumbo's team had confirmed they had found traces of blood in the car. They didn't yet have an analysis proving that it was Genevieve Strachan's, but there was little doubt in anyone's mind – including, it seemed, Spencer Johansson's – that they soon would. The tyre tread marks matched, and they could pinpoint where Spencer was when he called Niall Strachan shortly after the murder. The digital team were also confident they would be able to find evidence of the message to Genevieve on Spencer's phone, even if they couldn't locate the cloned SIM. He knew the game was up, and he was keen to put the blame squarely on Niall Strachan, who was by then sitting in another interview room.

'I'd have given that man anything and everything I owned,' he said. 'But he told me I was an incompetent wanker – just because I didn't know about WiFi passwords. That's not my job – that should have been his.'

It was no wonder Strachan had seemed so distraught since his wife's body had been found. It wasn't grief at all. He must have known something hadn't gone quite to plan and was horrified his perfect plot was falling around his ears.

Tom had decided that Becky and Keith could conduct Strachan's interview. He couldn't tolerate another moment in the company of either of the two men.

Setting Martha up had apparently been Niall's idea. He hated the fact that she'd turned him down, but it was her argument with Genevieve that made him realise how exposed he was. Martha may have refused to tell his wife anything, but she knew how much money he was bleeding from the company, and that made her dangerous. Martha's remoteness from everyone had played into his hands.

'She had victim written all over her,' Spencer said. 'From what we could discover, she had no one in her life – no friends or family. We didn't know about her son. I was pretty sure she'd changed her name too, so she was already running from something. She seemed like a woman no one cared about.'

Tom had held himself firmly in check. There was nothing he could say or do that was appropriate or that would come close to demonstrating the disgust he felt with Johansson.

'I understand why Strachan wanted his wife out of the way, and he would obviously have been the prime suspect if she was murdered, so how did he persuade you to do it?'

Spencer looked Tom in the eye. 'Half a million quid is a pretty big incentive, don't you think? That's what I stood to lose, but more to the point, XO-Tech was going to make me a fortune. Half a million would look like small change. Besides, Genevieve was a leech – always demanding, never giving. She'd have held us back and made Niall's life hell for giving me shares. She told me *she* should have been on the board, not me. Snotty bitch.'

Tom gazed at the man opposite him. Was that the trace of a self-satisfied smile on his face? Tom had a horrible feeling that Johansson was strangely proud of what he had done.

79

MARTHA

The police car pulls up at the gates. I jump out and bang my fist on the intercom buzzer over and over again. No one answers, but the gates start to open. I don't get back into the police car; I squeeze through the gap and run down the drive towards the door.

Where's Alfie? Where's Dad?

I don't see any sign of my rental car, and I have a wild hope that maybe I'm wrong. Maybe Mum has gone somewhere to meet Dad, and he hasn't brought Alfie here.

The police car catches up with me as I get to the steps.

'Are you okay, Ms Porter?' the officer asks. He doesn't know anything about me – he's just been asked to drive me home – but he can see I'm panicking.

I spin towards him. 'Yes, I'm fine. I'm sorry, but I've never spent a night away from my son before, so I just want to get to him.' The officer shrugs, and I turn back to race up the steps.

I hear the tyres crunching on the gravel as he drives away and I wonder if I've made a mistake, but I can't think of any way I could have kept him here.

I push open the front door. 'Alfie!'

There's no answer. The house is quiet, and I hurry towards the back, to the kitchen.

Mum is there, slicing vegetables at the worktop. She has her back to me, but she's alone.

'Where's Dad? Where's Alfie?'

Before she can answer, I hear footsteps behind me.

'DeeDee!' Dad says, then drops his chin as if he can't bring himself to look at me.

'Why did you come here, Dad? I told you to keep Alfie away from here!'

He still doesn't look up. 'I'm sorry. I thought Nicola would leave with me. She said Aram wasn't around, so I thought I could make everything okay again.'

I want to scream at him for falling for Aram's tricks, but he looks so hurt, and I was asking a lot of a man who was beaten into submission years ago. But I haven't got time to worry about him now.

The edges of my vision blur; only Mum is in sharp focus.

My voice is surprisingly calm. 'Where's Alfie, Mum?'

She turns slightly, her head on one side. 'He's with his father, of course.'

'*Where?* Where is he?'

She doesn't reply, and with nothing more than a scornful smile, she turns back to preparing the food.

I race to the door. I know where they'll be.

I can see them in the distance as I tear round the side of the house. Aram is holding Alfie's hand, as he used to hold mine, and I pray that this is the nice version of Aram – the one who told me about the plants and the creatures that live in the water. I want to run, to tear Alfie's hand from Aram's and pick him up so we can escape to safety, but I know that would only frighten him.

Instead I get close, then call his name softly. I expect him to run to me, but he doesn't.

He looks up at his father as if asking permission before he turns. Aram has had hours to influence him, and I don't know what he's done. I know that children respond more readily to hypnosis than adults, but although it has always been one of the weapons in his armoury, Aram only uses it when his usual forms of mental torture fail. In Alfie's case, though, speed would have been important; Aram had no idea when I would be back and he will have done whatever he thought necessary.

I try to appear casual as I walk towards Alfie and crouch down. 'Hi, baby. Are you okay?'

He nods, seeming a little unsure, so I reach out to pull him close. His limbs feel taut, but then it's as if his body remembers how good it feels to be hugged and he sags against me.

'Is it true that he's my daddy?' he whispers.

I don't know what to say, but before I have the chance to speak I feel a damp patch on my neck and Alfie's body shudders slightly. He's crying and trying to hide it.

'He says crying's bad, and I've got to live here with him. You're not Mummy; you're India. He made me say it lots of times.'

I lift my eyes to Aram's and a white-hot fury sears through me. I know I shouldn't look at him, but no power on earth is as strong as the love for my child.

'Come on, Alfie. Let's go back to the house. Do you want me to carry you?'

His head nods against my shoulder, and without another word I pick him up and turn away from Aram.

I walk back into the kitchen, clutching Alfie tightly, and Dad pushes himself unsteadily from a chair.

'Is he okay?' he asks.

Mum doesn't bother to turn round, the rhythmic thwack of the knife hitting the chopping board demonstrating her indifference.

'Barely,' I say, my mouth tight. 'Where are the car keys, Dad? We're leaving.'

Dad glances at Mum. 'What did he do with them?' I know he means Aram.

She doesn't have time to answer before Aram strides through the door.

'You're being melodramatic, India. The child is fine, and he needs to get to know me. He'll be living with me from now on. You both will.'

No one speaks, and it feels as if the air has been sucked from the room. The corners of Aram's mouth curve up in a self-satisfied smile. Mum turns, and her body hunches over as if she's fighting back a sob. Dad is biting his lip. I can't breathe.

It's Mum who breaks the silence, her voice tentative. 'Are they coming with us, Aram?'

He glances her way for a moment and then back at me.

'No. That's not how it's going to work.'

Dad and Mum both speak at the same time.

'What do you mean?' she asks.

'Where are you going?' Dad says.

Alfie starts to whimper. He shouldn't be here to witness this.

'Dad, I know I'm asking a lot of you again, but will you take Alfie outside, please? Play with him, keep him occupied until this is sorted.'

'There's nothing to sort,' Aram says.

But there is, and with a last imploring look at Mum, Dad takes Alfie from my arms.

'Go with Grandad, poppet. He's going to teach you to play tig. It'll be fun.'

As soon as the door closes behind them, I turn to Aram. I look at the point of his chin rather than his eyes, even though I think my rage will protect me against his tricks.

'Where do you think we're going, and why do you think I'll agree?'

'I'm leaving Lakeside,' he answers, folding his arms. 'I've sold it.'

I think back to the boxes of files, to the papers upstairs, to the signatures on what looked like legal documents. I forgot all about them after I was arrested. That's why he has sent everyone away. They are never coming back, and they don't know.

'Can you do that? What about Dad?'

'Two trustees are all it takes, India.' I know Mum has signed.

'I'm going with him,' Mum whispers. She glances at him uncertainly. 'Aren't I?'

'I'm sure Joel will take care of you, Nicola. India and the child will be coming with me.'

I hear a soft moan from Mum, but I ignore it.

'What makes you think I'm going anywhere with you?' I spit out the words, wanting to shout but scared my voice will carry to the garden.

'You have no choice. You either come with me, or I hand over the clothes and knife, and you go to prison. I can take care of Alfie.'

He's enjoying this, knowing that leaving Alfie with him has to be my worst fear.

'Why are you doing this? What do you want with us?'

Mum's face is flushed, her breathing fast. 'He doesn't want you, India,' she hisses, each syllable laden with years of resentment. 'I know you always thought you were special to him, but it was all part of his game. It's never been about you. It's the money – it's *always* been the money.'

'Shut your mouth, woman.' His tone drips with contempt, but he doesn't look at Mum; he's watching me.

For a moment I wonder what she's talking about. I don't *have* any money! Then it dawns on me. She means the trust fund that will pay out when I'm twenty-seven. She must have told Aram about it.

'What makes you think I'll give you a penny of it?' I ask.

'I think you'll find I hold all the cards, India.' He throws me a self-satisfied smirk, then, barely turning his head, speaks to Mum over his shoulder. 'Get the bag, Nicola. I see your daughter needs persuading.'

Mum doesn't move.

'The bag,' he repeats, his voice edged with irritation.

'I can't,' Mum whispers.

He spins to face her. 'Get the bag! The clothes!'

Mum has backed up against the Aga. Her hands grip the chrome bar. I can barely hear her words. 'We don't have them any more, Aram. I burned them.'

80

MARTHA

Through the open window I can hear my son giggling, and not for the first time I am astounded by the resilience of children. And even though it must be killing Dad to pretend that everything is fine, I hear him call, 'I can catch you, Alfie! I'm coming!'

Inside the kitchen Aram is staring at Mum, the first sign of uncertainty in his eyes. 'Say that again.'

Mum bites her lip and leans towards him, her hands reaching for him. He doesn't move, and her arms drop back to her sides. It's as if I'm no longer in the room, and I realise that all this – me, Alfie, Dad, Aram's rejection – is too much for her. I can hear a raw desperation in every word as she starts to speak.

'I'm sorry, Aram. Please forgive me. Don't you see, I had to destroy the evidence. It was the only thing tying her to you – to *us*. I wanted to do it years ago when I realised she was pregnant. Do you have any idea how it felt, knowing you wanted her to have your baby? Knowing you planned to keep her close until she got the money? But she was only twenty-one. She'd have been here, with you, with *us*, for another six years. *Six years!* I couldn't bear the thought. Thank God she left when she did. But now she's back, and you were going to use the clothes to force her to stay with you. I had to burn them. It was the only way to get rid of her again.'

For one wild moment I wonder if perhaps she destroyed the clothes to save me. But I know that's not true. She did it so she could have Aram to herself. I can see it in her face. She wants me gone.

She turns to me, her arms clasped around her hunched body. 'There's nothing keeping you here now. He can't make you go anywhere with him. Aram and I can be alone, together.' She picks up the knife she was using to chop the vegetables. 'I even bleached the knife.'

I wonder for a moment if it's the *same* knife. The thought sickens me.

She turns back to Aram. 'It doesn't matter that I burned them. You'd never have used them.' She makes a sound that's somewhere between a high-pitched giggle and a sob. 'I knew that.'

Aram is watching her, his face expressionless. He doesn't move. He barely blinks, but I can feel the searing heat of his anger.

I don't know what Mum means, and I don't care. All that matters now is Alfie.

'Why did he want me to have my baby, Mum? Aram doesn't like children. What does he want with my child?'

'Don't you know? Haven't you worked it out? The baby is his route to the money! He wants to keep you close until the trust fund pays out and the money's in your bank. Then you're expendable. When you're dead the money will belong to the child – and as his father Aram will have control of it.' She jabs the knife towards me, and although I'm beyond her reach, I take a step back. 'He can't let you die *before* your birthday, though. If that were to happen, the money would remain in trust for the boy until *he's* of age. Another twenty years or so.'

I know she's telling the truth. It was never me he wanted. His plan must always have been to keep me by his side, then kill me as soon as the money becomes mine. Alfie will inherit it all. That's what she's saying. Maybe he plans to kill his son too, once the money is his. I know what he is capable of.

I feel the rage building in me. I won't let him win. I have to do something – put an end to the constant running, hiding. Even if Mum has destroyed the evidence he held over me, he might still demand access to his child – not because he has any interest in Alfie, but because it ties the two of us to him.

The money means nothing to me. If it sets me and Alfie free, Aram can have every penny. I'm about to tell him when Mum speaks.

'Go, India,' she says. 'Leave, and take the child. There's nothing to hold you here now. He won't kill you until the money's yours. You should never have come back. You've made everything so much worse.'

Before I can move, Aram steps towards her and rests his hands on her shoulders.

His voice is so low I can barely hear it. 'Look at me, Nicola.' He shakes her. 'I said *look at me*!' I watch as Mum's eyes lock on to his. 'Jealousy is not a trait to be proud of. Have I taught you nothing? Look what it's done to you.' He gives a grunt of disgust. 'I was never taking you with me. I have no further use for you.'

His words are harsh, but his voice is strangely seductive. His hands draw closer together on either side of her slender neck and his thumbs press lightly against her throat.

I watch as Mum leans towards him and raises her face to his, trying her best to give him a shaky smile. 'You don't need her, Aram. Let her go. We've got the money from the house. It's enough. We can be happy. And you can trust me. You know you can.'

She gasps on the last word as he begins to squeeze.

'India is coming with me. She'll do exactly as I tell her, as she always has. But you have nothing left to give. You were a means to an end. Nothing more.'

I hear her start to choke, and I break free of the paralysis that's been gripping me. I lunge towards them, dragging on his arms, trying to free Mum from his grasp. He's too strong, and I'm having no impact. I'm about to scream for Dad, when suddenly Aram sighs and his hands fall to his sides.

He turns slightly and lurches towards me, dragging me to the floor with him.

Aram's arm is lying over my body. He's on his side, facing away from me, but I know he's dead. Blood is pooling on the floor. His blood, not mine.

'DeeDee?' Mum's voice is soft, shaky, as if she can't believe what she's seeing.

I groan and wriggle out from under Aram's arm. My body is bruised from the fall, but nothing is broken, and slowly I sit up, gradually regaining the breath that was knocked out of me.

Mum lifts her hands to her face. 'I killed him,' she whispers, as she falls to her knees by his side, reaching out a hand to stroke the back of his head.

A shriek of childish laughter comes through the window, and I push myself to my feet to hurry towards the door and lock it. Alfie can't see this.

Mum grasps Aram's shoulder and shakes it gently, as if to wake him. Tears are running down her cheeks, dripping from her chin.

'I *killed* him,' she wails.

He had pushed her too far, broken what little was left of her, and I realise that the knife she was holding is no longer in her hand. It's in Aram's neck.

I walk towards the phone.

'What are you doing?' she cries.

'I'm calling the police. It'll be okay, Mum. It was self-defence.

And we can tell them about Leah – say he admitted to it before he tried to kill you.'

'No!'

'Mum, we have to call the police. They can search the grounds. They'll find Leah. She deserves a decent burial.'

'No, DeeDee, you can't!'

I don't know what to say, but I know what I have to do, so I pick up the phone. She leaps to her feet, rushes over, yanks it out of my hand and slams it down.

'We'll bury him,' she says, gasping for breath as if she's been running.

I stare at her in horror. What is she thinking?

'We'll put him with the others.'

81

As Tom pushed open the front door to his home, he could hear laughter coming from the kitchen and recognised his daughter's giggle.

He threw his keys into the bowl on the hall table and was heading towards the kitchen when the door flew open and Lucy came charging through, throwing herself at him.

'Dad!'

She didn't say any more and hugged him as tightly as he was hugging her. He'd missed her so much.

Eventually her hold slackened, and she grabbed his hand and dragged him towards the kitchen.

'Sorry, Dad, I can't bear to be away from Harry for another moment. He's so cute! He laughs every time he looks at me!'

'Well, who can blame him,' Tom said, and Lucy punched him lightly on the arm.

Harry was indeed laughing, and so were Kate and Louisa.

'I think you'll find you're no longer the top man in our daughter's life, Tom,' Kate said by way of greeting. But she was smiling, and that was something.

'Good to see you, Kate,' he said. He hadn't been sure if she would be suffering from the pain of a broken relationship, but she seemed fine.

'It's actually, and surprisingly, good to be back. Australia was an experience, an episode, and entertaining in its own way,' she said with a shrug.

Tom resisted the temptation to say that not only had Kate's 'experience' cost her a small fortune, she had also dragged Lucy to the other side of the world for six months, disrupting her life and education, although she didn't look as if she'd come to any harm.

'What's the plan for this evening?' he asked, not knowing if his ex-wife and daughter were about to get up and leave.

'Kate and Lucy are staying to eat with us, Tom, and after Harry's in bed we thought we could have a chat about what they're going to do next.'

Tom smiled. He knew a fait accompli when he saw one, and as he looked at his family – his *extended* family, if he included Kate – he had the feeling it was going to be an expensive evening.

'I'll tell you all now, before you ask, that I'm not going to Scotland,' Lucy said, turning briefly away from her baby brother. 'I'm not leaving this little one – are you listening, Mum?'

Tom waited, expecting fireworks. But to his surprise there weren't any.

'We'll talk later, Lucy. But noted.'

Tom risked a look at Louisa, who winked. He guessed she'd been talking to Kate about how great it would be for Harry to see more of Lucy, and Kate would think she was doing everyone a favour. At a cost, of course.

He had never had much regard for money, and it was without doubt the least important factor in this equation. If it meant spending more time with Lucy, whatever the price was, it would be worth it.

As he had witnessed this week, the pursuit of wealth could tear families apart, and Tom had to grudgingly admit that, despite the moments of friction he and Kate shared, she was a good mother.

As far as Tom was concerned, he had his daughter back. That was all that mattered.

MONDAY

82

MARTHA

I stand by the gates of Lakeside, looking at my old home, my prison for so many years. I can't go in – the house and grounds are now a crime scene as the police search for remains. Dad and I have spent two days being interviewed, and the police seem to have accepted our version of events, but I still feel knocked sideways by what happened. If it wasn't for the bruises on my back, I would think I had dreamed the whole thing.

When Mum had said we could put Aram's body with 'the others' I didn't speak. I couldn't find any words.

'We'll bury him with the others,' she repeated. 'The ones who had to die. The ones like Leah, who threatened our wonderful life. They were disloyal. They were going to betray Aram and ruin all the amazing work he was doing. The loss of a few for the benefit of many. You understand, DeeDee, don't you?'

I didn't, and I still don't.

'Why do you think everyone had to leave at night? You must have known,' she said.

Had I known what really happened to those who supposedly

left Lakeside? No, I hadn't. Aram told me more than once that sometimes people deserve to die, but I had never thought – until Leah – that he would kill. Did Dad know? The shock on his face when he learned what had happened could never have been faked.

Moments after Mum told me about the others, buried in the soft boggy soil near the river, she had fallen on the floor next to Aram and cradled his head in her lap, rocking to and fro, pleading for his forgiveness.

I had turned away, picked up the phone and called the police.

Dad is distraught, but I asked him to take care of Alfie today in the hope that entertaining his grandson will take his mind off the horror of the last sixteen years, and they've gone to the seaside. It's going to take a long time for him to heal, but Alfie and I will do our best. And tomorrow we're going to see a solicitor, to make sure that my money is kept safe for Alfie, should anything happen to me.

Now, though, I have to be here – as close as I can get – to say goodbye to Leah and, I suppose, to Mum. Whether she will go to prison or end up in psychiatric care, we don't know. There's a long way to go. I try to pretend to myself that she killed Aram to save me, but I know that's not true. He shattered her into a thousand pieces, just like the glass orb he used to roll between his fingers. But she called me DeeDee, and I cling to that memory, desperate to believe that for one last moment, she was my mother.

I had to admit to the police that I knew about Leah's death all those years ago. The threat that Aram held over me, added to his plan to murder me as soon as the trust paid out, will apparently go a long way towards a lenient sentence. I understand now why Mum said he would never have used his fake evidence against me. He couldn't expose me to the police; they would have dug up the grounds to search for Leah and found so much more. They know that I've been hiding myself away for years, and now they understand why. That's another point in my favour.

From my position by the gates I can't see much. I hear the

occasional bark of a dog, and I can see figures in white coveralls milling around in the distance. They've erected individual tents along the river bank – I count six already. I don't know how many more there will be.

It's time to go, and I turn my back and walk towards the hire car. I'll never come here again. I climb into the driver's seat and close my eyes. I'm suddenly transported back in time. I'm in a car that smells of new leather. Mum and Dad are in the front seats, excited about our new life.

'Everything will be different now, DeeDee. You'll see,' Mum said.

She wasn't wrong.

AUTHOR'S NOTE

A Note about Cults

Before writing this book, I read endless articles on cult activities, and was truly shocked by some of the practices.

It's hard to believe that a mother will turn against her own child, as Nicola does, but I have read reports of a mother of twins – not yet one year old – being instructed to kick the children away from her when they were clinging tightly to her skirt. She resisted, but ultimately obeyed, even though she said it violated her sense of being a mother or even a human being. She did it because it was expected, and the punishment would have been harder to bear.

In other cases, children under five have been removed from their mother's care – sometimes for months, sometimes for years – for fear that their bond is stronger than that with the leader.

Some readers may struggle to understand how people become so weakened by the control that is exerted over them, but one ex-cult member describes giving in to pressure as a relief, because it resolves the conflict and may result in being loved, if only briefly, by the leader.

It's easy to think, 'it would never happen to me,' but few people make a conscious decision to join a cult. As one journalist says, "Cults are beautifully packaged to look like something quite different from the outside[1]." You might also assume that all cult members are weak, or perhaps lacking the intelligence to see what is happening to them. That is a myth. The majority of people recruited into cults are normal and healthy, with average or above average intelligence, from economically stable backgrounds. Nevertheless, they become "unwitting victims of deception and subtle techniques of psychological manipulation.[2]" These techniques include humiliation, food and sleep deprivation, repudiation of values, rejection of previous relationships. The list goes on.

It's not unusual for one partner in a relationship to become more committed to the cult than another, as reported by an ex-cult member: "My dad didn't really fit the mould... but eventually his 'ego' was broken." Unconverted partners are often left behind if they don't buy into the ideology. The leader always has to come first.

There are many cults throughout the world. Some are large, with thousands of members who go about their daily lives as normal, but whose allegiance – and often money – belongs to the cult. Others are small – maybe just one household in which the leader's word is law and no one can question their thoughts, decisions or behaviour.

Most people think of cults as organisations with their roots in religion, but therapy cults, often based on self-improvement programmes, are becoming a major threat. Recruitment might take place at a management training seminar or a yoga retreat, but however a person is recruited, once in, escape can be painful.

If you, a friend, or a family member have been affected in any way by cult activity, help is available. There is a plethora of advice online, but one article that I found particularly interesting in identifying cult behaviour, can be found here: https://www.oprahmag.com/life/relationships-love/a33648485/signs-of-a-cult/

If you feel that you need support, there is an organisation in the UK that has been set up by a former cult member. This article is particularly revealing - https://cultinformation.org.uk/article_caring-for-cult-victims.html and they do take calls, if people need more direct help. They also have a useful list of links to international organisations in their HELP section.

---

1. www.insider.com
2. Cult Information Centre

A LETTER TO MY READERS

Dear Reader

Thank you so much for taking the time to read *Close Your Eyes*. I thoroughly enjoyed researching and writing this book and do hope you enjoyed reading it.

The inspiration for the book started with two separate ideas: how would it feel to be suspected of murder, and what would it be like to be brought up in a cult? From the start I could feel the threads twisting around each other as Martha's past defined her behaviour after Genevieve is murdered.

As you will see if you have read my note about cults, I found it disturbing to consider how many people have had their lives destroyed in this way. It was a difficult balance to ensure that Aram's teaching made sense, while at the same time creating a chilling character. He condemns jealousy, envy and greed, which as an ethos is difficult to fault, so the focus had to be on the practices he employs to control those in his community. I hope I managed to convey this effectively.

I do love to hear from readers, and one of the best ways of keeping in touch is via my special Facebook group – **Rachel**

Abbott's Partners in Crime. It's a place where readers can chat about everything thriller related and discuss books they have enjoyed from a wide range of authors. If you haven't joined in yet, you can find it by searching Facebook Groups for PartnersInCrimeRA.

I send regular newsletters, so that I can share some of my own favourite reads and let you know when I'm going to be out and about, although of course the horror of Covid made 2020 a very different year, with all appearances being online. Whatever the means, it's always great to 'meet' people who have read my books and to have an opportunity to answer any questions. I also use the newsletter to let people know when any of my books are on special offer, so if you've not already signed up and would like to do so, here's where to go: www.rachel-abbott.com/contact

And of course there is always social media – currently I'm on Facebook and Twitter. I am trying harder with Instagram, but there are only so many hours in a day!

I'm now settling down to write the next in my Stephanie King series – the books that I have set in beautiful Cornwall. *And So It Begins* was the first in the series, and the second book – *The Murder Game* (called *The Invitation* in the US) – was published in April 2020. I'm hoping to announce the next in the series very soon.

Of course, I always love to hear from readers, and I would be delighted to hear if you enjoyed *Close Your Eyes*, so feel free to tweet me, leave me a message on Facebook. And one very special request – if you have enjoyed this book, I would be thrilled if you would leave a review on Amazon. Every author loves getting reviews, and I'm no exception. And of course, it helps other readers to find my books.

Thanks again for taking the time to read *Close Your Eyes*.

Best wishes,
Rachel

ACKNOWLEDGMENTS

2020 has been a difficult and challenging year for everyone, and I will be forever in awe of the thousands of people who have worked hard to keep us all as safe as possible, struggling through these testing times to take care of those who have suffered illness or loneliness.

As a writer, I am used to working alone, so the last twelve months have probably impacted on me far less than most. But I do recognise that I need help from others to produce the best book I can, and I'm lucky to have found so many people who are prepared to offer their help, advice and support during the writing process. The early stages of a new novel are always fraught with concerns about accuracy, and as always, I have to thank my police adviser, Mark Gray, for his input. Any mistakes with regard to the workings of the police are entirely my own.

During lockdown it was of course impossible for me to go and recce the scene of the crime that opens the book. I could see pictures online, and I had a map – but it's not the same as being there. Once again, my sister and brother-in-law, Judith and Dave Hall, were my eyes and ears. They took their daily one hour of exercise by visiting the Tyldesley Loopline, which is fortunately close to where they live, taking endless photographs and describing to me everything from the species of trees to the birdsong.

Other help came from Ian Stacey, Lesley Chapman and Virtual UK Office Services, each of whom gave advice on their own specialities – everything from WiFi password storage to property trusts!

Writing and publishing books is much more of a team effort than people often realise, and I have the best team there is! My good friend and PA, Tish McPhilemy, not only deals with many of the day-to-day tasks of running an office, she also brings her own brand of joy with her, and the days in my old gunpowder shelter – yes, that's my office – wouldn't be the same without her. She was sorely missed during the early period of isolation, but thankfully is back with me now.

I am forever grateful for the fact that Lizzy Kremer of David Higham Associates became my agent nearly nine years ago. She's the best, as is the entire team at DHA. Maddalena Cavaciuti deserves a special mention for both her wide-ranging abilities and her efficiency. Thanks also to Alice Howe and the foreign rights team for doing such an amazing job of finding publishers for my books all over the world.

Editing is a crucial factor in making any book as good as it can be, and I must again thank both Lizzy and Maddalena for their incredible insight into the structure and pace of this novel, and Hugh Davis and Jessica Read for their parts in polishing the final manuscript.

I'm lucky to have some wonderfully loyal readers, and I am overwhelmed by their fantastic support. Thank you all for not only reading my books, but for reviewing them, talking about them to your friends, and for joining me online whenever the opportunity arises. You are the best!

A shout out to all the book bloggers too. I honestly don't know where writers would be without you. So many of you work hard to get the word out about new books, and it's impossible to over-estimate the help you offer to the writing community.

Finally, as always a huge thanks to my husband John. Anyone who lives with a writer will understand that we spend huge swathes of time locked into another world – and sometimes it's the only thing we want to talk about. It requires a special kind of person to keep smiling throughout!

CPSIA information can be obtained
at www.ICGtesting.com
Printed in the USA
BVHW030859110321
602114BV00013B/275